Grace
Livingston
Hill

Phoebe Deane

BARBOUR
PUBLISHING

© 2000 by R. L. Munce Publishing Co., Inc.

Edited and updated for today's reader by Deborah Cole.

ISBN 1-59310-679-3

Published by Barbour Publishing, Inc., P.O. Box 719, Uhrichsville, Ohio 44683, www.barbourbooks.com

Our mission is to publish and distribute inspirational products offering exceptional value and biblical encouragement to the masses.

ecpa Member of the
Evangelical Christian
Publishers Association

Printed in the United States of America.
5 4 3 2 1

Chapter 1

$\mathcal{T}$he night was hot and dark, for the moon rose late. The perfume of the petunia bed hung heavy in the air, and the katydids and crickets kept up a symphony in the orchard close to the house. Its music floated in at the open window and called to the girl as she sat in the darkened upper room rocking Emmeline's baby to sleep in the wooden cradle.

She had washed the supper dishes. The tea towels hung smoothly on the line in the woodshed, the milk pans stood in a shining row ready for the early milking, and the kitchen, swept and dark, had settled into its nightly repose. The day had been long and full of hard work, but now as soon as the baby slept Phoebe would be free for a while before bedtime.

Unconsciously her foot tapped faster on the rocker in her impatience to be out, and the baby stirred and opened his eyes, murmuring sleepily, "Pee-bee, up-e-knee! Pee-bee, up-e-knee!" Interpreted, it was a demand to be taken up on Phoebe's knee.

But Phoebe toned her rocking into a sleepy motion, and the long lashes drooped again on the little cheeks. At last the baby was asleep.

Phoebe slowed the rocking until she could hear the soft regular breathing. Then she rose from her chair and tiptoed from the room.

As she reached the door the baby heaved a long, deep sigh, and Phoebe paused, her heart standing still for an instant lest the baby would waken and demand to be taken up. How many times had she just reached the door, on other hot summer nights, and been greeted by a loud cry which immediately brought Emmeline to the foot of the stairs, with "I declare, Phoebe Deane! Can't you keep that poor child from crying all night?" And Phoebe would be in for an hour or two of singing and rocking and amusing the fretful baby.

But the baby slept on, and Phoebe stepped over the creaking floorboards and down the stairs lightly, scarcely daring to breathe. She slipped past the sitting room door.

Albert, her half brother, was in the sitting room. She could see his outline through the window—his long, thin, kindly face bent over the village paper he'd brought home before supper. Emmeline sat over by the table close to the candle, her sharp features intent on the hole in Johnny's stocking.

Hiram Green, the neighbor whose farm adjoined Albert Deane's on the side next to the village, sat opposite the hall door, his lank form in a splint-bottomed chair tilted back against the wall. His slouch hat was drawn down over his eyes, and his hands were in his pockets. He often sat with Albert in the evening. Sometimes Emmeline called Phoebe in and gave her some darning or mending, and then Phoebe had to listen to Hiram Green's dull talk. To escape it, she'd slip out to the orchard after her work was done. But she couldn't always elude Emmeline's vigilance, for she seemed determined that Phoebe not have a moment to herself.

Phoebe wore a thin white dress. Those thin white dresses she insisted on wearing in the afternoons were one of Emmeline's grievances—so uneconomical and foolish; they'd wear out sometime. Emmeline felt Phoebe should keep her mother's dresses till she married and so save Albert from spending so much on her. Emmeline had a very poor opinion of Phoebe's dead mother; her dress was too fine to belong to a sensible woman, Emmeline thought.

Like some winged creature Phoebe flashed across the path of light that fell from the door and into the orchard. She loved the night with its sounds, scents, and velvet darkness, with depths for hiding. Soon the summer would be gone, the branches would be bare against the snow's whiteness, and her solitude and dreaming would be over until the spring again. She cherished every moment of the summer like rich gold.

She loved to sit on the fence separating the orchard from the meadow and wonder what the crickets were saying to each other—whether they talked about their fellows the way people were picked to pieces at the sewing bees. That was how they used to talk about young Mrs. Spafford. Nobody was safe from gossip—for they said Mrs. Spafford belonged to the old Schuyler family. When she came as a bride to the town, how cruel and babbling tongues were!

The girl seated herself in her usual place, leaning against the high crotch of the two upright rails supporting that section of fence. The sky was powdered with stars, the fragrance of the pasture fanned her cheek, and the tree toads joined in the nightly chorus. She heard a crackle of the apple branches, and Hiram Green stepped heavily out from the shadows and stood beside her.

Phoebe had never liked Hiram Green since the day she saw him shove his wife out of his way and say to her, "Aw, shut up, can't you? Women are forever talking about what they don't understand!"

She'd watched the faint color flicker into the wife's pale face and then flicker out again as she tried to laugh his roughness off in front of Phoebe, but the girl had never forgotten it. She was only a little girl then, almost a stranger in town, for her mother had just died and she'd come to live with the half brother who'd been married so long she scarcely knew him. Hiram Green hadn't noticed the young girl then and treated his wife as if no one were present. But Phoebe remembered. She grew to know and love the sad wife, to watch her gentle, patient ways with her boisterous children. And her heart always filled with indignation over the coarse man's rude ways with his wife.

Hiram Green's wife had been dead a year. Phoebe was with her for a week before she died. She had watched the stolid husband without a shadow of anxiety in his eyes tell the neighbors Annie would "be all right in a few days. It was her own fault, anyway, that she got sick. She *would* drive over to see her mother when she wasn't able." He neglected to state she was making preserves and jelly especially for him and prepared dinner for twelve men who were harvesting for a week. He also failed to state she only went to see her mother once in six months, and it was her only holiday.

When Annie died he blamed her as always and hinted that he guessed now she was sorry she hadn't listened to him and been content at home. As if any kind of heaven wouldn't be better than Hiram Green's house.

But Phoebe had stood beside the dying woman as her life flickered out and heard her say, "I ain't sorry to go, Phoebe, for I'm tired. I'd rather rest through eternity than do anything else. I don't think Hiram'll miss me much, and the children ain't like me. They never took after me—only the baby that died. Maybe the baby that died'll want me."

Hiram's only expression of regret was, "It's going to be mighty unhandy, her dying just now. Harvesting ain't over yet, and the meadow lot should be cut before it rains, or the hull thing'll be lost."

Phoebe felt a fierce delight in the fact that everything had to stop for Annie. Whether Hiram would or not, for decency's sake, the work must stop, and the forms of respect must be gone through even though his heart wasn't in it. The rain came, too, to honor Annie—and before the meadow lot was cut.

The funeral over, the farmwork went on with doubled vigor, and Phoebe overheard Hiram tell Albert that "burying Annie had been mighty expensive on account of that thunderstorm coming so soon—it spoiled the whole south meadow; and it was just like Annie to upset everything. If she had only been a little more careful and not gone off to her mother's on pleasure, she might have kept up a little longer till harvest was over."

Phoebe had just come into the sitting room with her sewing when Hiram said that, and she looked indignantly at her brother to see if he wouldn't give Hiram a rebuke. But he only leaned back against the wall and said, "Such things are to be expected in the natural course of life."

Phoebe turned her chair so she wouldn't have to look at Hiram. She despised him. She wished she knew how to show him what a despicable creature he was, but as she was only a young girl she could do nothing but turn her back. She never knew that all that evening Hiram Green watched the back of her shining head, its waves of bright hair bound about with a ribbon and conforming to the beautiful shape of her head. He studied the shapely shoulders and graceful movements of the girl as she patiently mended with her slender fingers.

He remembered that Annie had been "pretty" when he married her, and he could see the good points in the girl Phoebe, even though she sat with her indignant shoulders toward him. In fact, the very sauciness of those shoulders, as the winter went by, attracted him more and more. Annie had never dared be saucy or indifferent. Annie had loved him from the first and had let him know it too soon and too often. It was a new experience to have someone indifferent to him. He rather liked it, knowing as he did that he always got his own way when he was ready for it.

As the winter went by, Hiram spent more and more evenings with the Deanes, and Phoebe spent more and more of her evenings with Johnny, or the cradle, or in her own room—anything to get away from the unwelcome companionship.

Then Emmeline had objected to the extravagance of an extra candle. Emmeline was "thrifty" and could see no sense in a girl wasting a candle when one light would do for all, so the days went by for Phoebe full of hard work and constant companionship, and the evenings with no leisure and no seclusion. Phoebe had longed for the spring to come, when she might get out into the night alone and take long deep breaths that were all her own, for it seemed that even her breathing was ordered and supervised.

But through it all it never once entered Phoebe's head that Hiram was turning his thoughts toward her. So when he came and stood beside her in the darkness he startled her merely because he was something she disliked, and she shrank from him as one would shrink from a snake in the grass.

"Phoebe," he said, putting out his hand to where he supposed her hands would be in the darkness, "ain't it about time you and me was comin' to an understandin'?"

Phoebe slid off the fence and backed away in the darkness. Her heart froze for fear of what might be coming, and she felt she mustn't run away but stay and face whatever it was.

"Whatever do you mean?" said Phoebe, her voice full of antagonism.

"Mean?" said Hiram, sidling after her. "I mean it's time we set up a partnership. I've waited long enough. I need somebody to look after the children. You suit me pretty well, and I guess you'd be well enough fixed with me."

Hiram's air of assurance made Phoebe speechless with horror and indignation.

Taking her silence as a favorable indication, Hiram drew near her and once more tried to find her hands in the darkness.

"I've always liked you, Phoebe," he said. "Don't you like me?"

"No no no!" Phoebe almost screamed, snatching her hands away. "Don't ever dare to think such a thing again!"

Then she turned and vanished in the dark like a wraith of

mist, leaving the crestfallen Hiram alone, feeling very foolish and not a little astonished. He hadn't expected his suit to be met quite this way.

"Phoebe, is that you?" called Emmeline as she lifted her sharp eyes to peer into the darkness of the entry. "Albert, I wonder if Hiram went the wrong way and missed her?"

But Phoebe was up in her room before Emmeline decided whether she heard anything or not, and Albert went on reading his paper.

Phoebe sat alone in her little kitchen chamber, with the button on the door fastened. She kept very still so Emmeline might not know she was there. Every time she thought of the hateful sound of his voice as he made his cold-blooded proposition, the fierce anger boiled within her. Great waves of hate surged through her soul for the man who had treated one woman so that she was glad to die and now wanted to take her life and crush it out.

Finally she heard Albert and Emmeline shutting up the house for the night. Hiram didn't come back, as she feared he might.

He started to come, then thought better of it and felt his way through the orchard to the other fence and climbed over it into the road. He felt a little dazed and wanted to think things over and adjust himself to Phoebe's point of view. He felt a half resentment toward the Deanes for Phoebe's action, as if the rebuff had been their fault somehow. They should have prepared her better. They understood the situation fully.

They'd often had an interchange of remarks on the subject, and Albert had responded by a nod and a wink. It was tacitly understood that it would be a good thing to have the farms join and keep them "all in the family." Emmeline, too, had often given some practical hints about Phoebe's capabilities as a housewife and mother to his wild little children.

Then he began to wonder if perhaps after all Phoebe wasn't

just flirting with him. Surely she couldn't refuse him in earnest. His farm was as pretty as any in the county, and everyone knew he had money in the bank. Surely Phoebe was only being coy for a time. Perhaps it was natural for a girl to be a little shy. It was a way they had, and if it pleased them to hold off a little, why, it showed they'd be all the more sensible afterward. Maybe it was a good thing Phoebe wasn't ready to fall into his arms the minute he asked her. Then she wouldn't always be clinging to him and sobbing in that maddening way Annie had.

By the time he reached home he was pretty well satisfied with himself. As he closed the kitchen door he reflected that perhaps he might fix things up a bit in the house in view of a new mistress. That would probably please Phoebe, and he certainly did need a wife. Then Hiram went to bed and slept soundly.

Emmeline came to Phoebe's door before she went to bed, calling softly, "Phoebe, are you in there?" and tapping on the door two or three times. When no answer came, Emmeline lifted the latch and tried to open the door, but when she found it resisted her, she turned away.

"I s'pose she's sound asleep," she said to Albert in a fretful tone, "but I don't see what call she has to fasten her door every night. It looks so unsociable, as if she was afraid we weren't to be trusted. I wonder you don't speak to her about it."

But Albert only yawned good-naturedly and said, "I don't see how it hurts you any."

"It hurts my self-respect," Emmeline said in an injured tone, as she shut her own door with a *click*.

Far into the night Phoebe sat looking out the window on the world she loved but couldn't enjoy anymore. The storm of rage and shame and hatred had passed, leaving her weak and miserable and lonely. She put her head down on the windowsill and cried out softly, "Oh, Mother! If only you were here tonight! You'd take me away where I'd never see his hateful face again."

The symphony of the night wailed on about her, as if echoing her cry in throbbing chords, growing fainter as the moon rose, until a sudden hush fell. Then, softly, the music changed into the night's lullaby. All the world slept, and Phoebe slept, too.

Chapter 2

Phoebe was late coming downstairs the next morning. Emmeline was already in the kitchen rattling the pots and pans significantly. Emmeline always did that when Phoebe was late, and the degree of her displeasure could be plainly heard.

She looked up sharply as Phoebe entered the room. Dark circles showed under Phoebe's eyes, but otherwise her spirits had arisen with the morning light. She felt only scorn now for Hiram Green and was ready to protect herself. She went straight to her work without a word. Emmeline had long ago expressed herself with regard to the "Good morning" with which the child Phoebe used to greet her when she came down in the morning. Emmeline said it was "a foolish waste of time, and only stuck-up folks use it. It was right along with dressing up at home with no one to see you and curling your hair." And she looked at Phoebe's waves, while her own stood straight as a die.

They worked in silence. The bacon was spluttering to the eggs, and Phoebe was taking up the mush when Emmeline asked, "Didn't Hiram find you last night?" She cast one of her sidelong gazes at the girl as if she'd look through her.

Phoebe started and dropped the spoon back into the mush. She sensed something in Emmeline's tone, then understood at once. The family had been aware of Hiram's intention! Her eyes flashed, and she turned abruptly back to the kettle and went on with her work.

"Yes," she answered inscrutably, which only irritated Emmeline more.

"Well, I didn't hear you come in," she complained. "You must have been out a long time."

"I wasn't out five minutes in all."

"You don't say!" said Emmeline. "I thought you said Hiram found you."

Phoebe put the cover on the dish of mush and set it on the table before she deigned any reply. Then she came over and stood beside Emmeline calmly and spoke in a cool, clear voice.

"Emmeline, did Hiram Green tell you what he was coming out to the orchard for last night?"

"For mercy's sake, Phoebe, don't put on heroics! I'm not blind. One couldn't very well help seeing what Hiram Green wants. Did you think you were the only member of the family with eyes?"

When Emmeline looked up at Phoebe's face, she saw it was white as marble, and her beautiful eyes shone like two stars.

"Emmeline, did you and Albert know what Hiram Green wanted of me, and did you let him come out there to find me after you knew that?"

Her voice was calm and low. Emmeline was awed by it for a moment. She laid down the bread knife and stood and stared. Small and dainty, Phoebe had features cut like a cameo, with a childlike expression when her face was in repose. Emmeline thought her too frail-looking and pale. But for the moment the delicate girl was transformed. Her face shone with a light of righteous anger, and her eyes blazed dark with feeling.

"Phoebe! Now don't!" said Emmeline in a conciliatory tone. "What if I did know? Was that any sin? You must remember your brother and I are looking to your best interests, and Hiram is considered a real fine ketch."

Slowly the fire went out of Phoebe's eyes, and in its place came ice that seemed to pierce Emmeline till she felt like shrinking away.

"You're the strangest girl I ever saw," said Emmeline.

"What's the matter with you? Didn't you ever expect to have any beaux?"

Phoebe shivered as if a north blast had struck her at that last word.

"Did you mean, then," she said coldly, "that you thought I'd ever be willing to marry Hiram Green? Did you and Albert talk it over and think that?"

Emmeline found it hard to answer the question, put in a tone which seemed to imply a great offense.

"Well, I'd like to know why you shouldn't marry him!" declared Emmeline. "There's plenty of girls would be glad to get him."

Emmeline glanced out the window and saw Albert and the hired man coming to breakfast. It was time the children were down. Alma came lagging into the kitchen, asking to have her dress buttoned, and Johnny and Bertie scuffled in the rooms overhead. Emmeline was about to dismiss the subject, but Phoebe stepped between her and the little girl and placed her hands on Emmeline's stout, rounding shoulders, looking her straight in the eyes.

"Emmeline, how can you possibly be so unkind as to think such a thing for me when you know how Annie suffered?"

"Oh, fiddlesticks!" said Emmeline, shoving the girl away roughly. "Annie was a milk-and-water baby who wanted to be coddled. The right woman could wind Hiram Green around her finger. You're a little fool if you think about that. Annie's dead and gone, and you've no need to trouble with her. Come, put the things on the table while I button Alma. I'm sure there never was as silly a girl as you are. Anybody'd think you were a princess in disguise instead of a poor orphan dependent on her brother, and he only a *half* at that!" Emmeline slammed the kitchen door and called to the two little boys in a loud, harsh tone.

The crimson rose in Phoebe's cheeks till it covered her face and threatened to bring tears to her eyes. Her soul seemed wrenched from its moorings at the cruel reminder of her dependence upon this coarse woman and her husband. She felt as if she must leave the house at once and never return; only she had no place to go.

Albert appeared at the kitchen door with the hired man behind him, and the sense of duty made her turn to her work, that blessed refuge for those who are turned out of their Eden for a time. She hurried to take up the breakfast while the two men washed their faces at the pump.

"Hello, Phoebe," called Albert as he turned to surrender his place at the comb and mirror. "I say, Phoebe, you're looking like a rose this morning. What makes your cheeks so red? Anybody been kissing you this early?"

This pleasantry was intended as a joke. Albert had never said anything like that to her before. Phoebe guessed that Emmeline had been putting ideas about her and Hiram into his head. It almost brought tears to hear Albert speak like this; he was always so kind to her and treated her as if she were still almost a child. She hated jokes of this sort, and it was all the worse because of Alma and the hired man standing there. Alma grinned knowingly. Henry Williams, the son of a neighboring farmer who had hired himself out for the season, turned and stared admiringly at Phoebe.

"Say, Phoebe," put in Henry, "you do look real pretty this morning. I never noticed before how handsome your eyes were. What's that you said about kissing, Albert? I wouldn't mind taking the job, if it's going. How about it, Phoebe?"

Jesting of this sort was common in the neighborhood, but Phoebe had never joined in it, and she always looked upon it as unrefined. Now that it was directed toward her, and she realized it trifled with the most sacred and personal relations of life, it filled her with horror.

"Please don't, Albert!" she said in a low voice. "Don't!

I don't like it."

Alma saw with wonder that there were tears in Aunt Phoebe's eyes and gloated over it. That would be something to remember and tell. Aunt Phoebe usually kept her emotions to herself with the door shut too tight for anyone to peep in.

"No?" said Albert, perplexed. "Well, 'course I won't if you don't like it. I was only telling you how bright and pretty you looked and making you know how nice it was to have you around. Sit down, child, and let's have breakfast. Where's your mother, Alma?"

Emmeline entered with a flushed face and a couple of small boys held firmly by the shoulders.

Somewhat comforted by Albert's assurance, Phoebe finished her work and sat down at the table. But every time she raised her eyes, she found a battalion of other eyes staring at her.

Emmeline glanced at her in puzzled annoyance that her well-planned matchmaking wasn't running as smoothly as expected. Albert studied her in the astonishing discovery that the thin, sad little half sister he'd brought into his home, who had seemed so lifeless and colorless and unlike the other girls of the neighborhood, had suddenly become beautiful and was almost a woman.

The worst pair of eyes belonged to Henry Williams, bold and intimate, who sat directly opposite her. He seemed to feel that the way had been opened for him by Albert's words and only awaited his opportunity to enter in. He'd admired Phoebe ever since he came there early in the spring, and he wondered that no one seemed to think her of much account. But somehow her quiet dignity always kept him at a distance. But now he felt he was justified in being more free with her.

"Did you hear that singing school was going to open early this fall, Phoebe?" he asked, after clearing his throat.

"No," Phoebe said without looking up.

That rather disappointed him, for it had taken him a long

time to think up that subject, and it was too much to have it disposed of so quickly, without even a glimpse of her eyes.

"Do you usually 'tend?" he asked again after a pause.

"No," Phoebe said again, her eyes still down.

"Phoebe didn't go because there wasn't anyone for her to come home with before, Hank, but I guess there'll be plenty now," said Emmeline with a meaningful laugh.

"Yes," Phoebe said, looking up calmly. "Hester McVane and Polly said they were going this winter. If I decide to go I'm going with them. Emmeline, if you're going to dry those apples today, I'd better begin them. Excuse me, please."

"You haven't eaten any breakfast, Aunt Phoebe! Ma, Aunt Phoebe never touched a bite!" announced Alma.

"I'm not hungry this morning," Phoebe said as she escaped from the room, having baffled the gaze of the man and the child and wrested the dart from her sister-in-law's arrow.

It was hard on the man, for he'd decided to ask Phoebe if she'd go to singing school with him. He sought her out in the woodshed where she sat, and he gave his invitation, but she only made her fingers fly faster around the apple she was peeling.

"Thank you, but it won't be necessary for you to go with me if I decide to go." Then she arose hastily, exclaiming, "Emmeline, did you call me? I'm coming," and vanished into the kitchen.

The hired man looked after her wistfully.

Phoebe was not a weeping girl. Ever since her mother died she'd lived a life of self-repression, hiding her inmost feelings from the world, for her world since then hadn't proved to be a sympathetic one. She quickly perceived that no one in this new atmosphere would understand her sensitive nature.

Refinements and culture had been hers that these new relatives didn't know or understand. She looked at Albert wistfully sometimes, for she felt if it weren't for Emmeline she might in time make him understand and change a little in some ways. But Emmeline resented any suggestions she made to Albert. Emmeline resented almost everything about Phoebe. She had resented her coming in the first place. Albert was grown up and living away from home when his father married Phoebe's mother, a delicate, refined woman, far different from him. Emmeline felt that Albert had no call to take the child in at all when she wasn't a "real relation." Besides, Emmeline had an older sister of her own who would have been glad to come and live with them and help with the work. But of course there was no room or excuse for her with Phoebe there, and they couldn't afford to have them both, although Albert was ready to take in any stray chick or child that came along.

But in spite of her nature this morning Phoebe had much to do to keep from crying. If not for her work she would have felt desperate. As it was she kept steadily at it. The apples fairly flew out of their skins into the pan, and Emmeline, glancing into the back shed and noting the set of the forbidding young shoulders and the fast-diminishing pile of apples on the floor, decided it best not to disturb her. She was anxious to have those apples off her mind. And with Phoebe in that mood she knew it would be done before she could possibly get around to help. There was time enough for remarks later.

The old stone sundial by the side door shadowed the hour of eleven when Emmeline came into the shed with a knife and sat down to help. She looked at Phoebe sharply as she seated herself. She intended to have it out with the girl.

Phoebe didn't help her begin. Her fingers flew faster than ever, though they ached with the motion. With set lips she went on with her work, though she longed to fling the apple away and run out to the fields for a long deep breath.

Emmeline pared two whole apples before she began. She eyed Phoebe furtively several times, but the girl might have been a sphinx. This was what Emmeline couldn't stand, this distant, proud silence that wouldn't mix with other folk. She longed to break through it by force and reduce the pride to dust. It would do her heart good to see Phoebe humbled for once, she often told herself.

"Phoebe, I don't see what you find to dislike so in Hiram Green," she began. "He's a good man. He always attends church on Sunday."

"I would respect him more if he was a good man in his home on weekdays. Anybody can be good once a week before people. A man needs to be good at home in his family."

"Well, now, he pervides well for his family. Look at his comfortable home and his farm. There isn't a finer in this county. He has his name up all around this region for the fine stock he raises. You can't find a barn like his anywhere. It's the biggest and most expensive in this town."

"He certainly has a fine barn," said Phoebe, "but I don't suppose he expects his family to live in it. He takes better care of his stock than he does of his family. Look at the house—"

Emmeline marveled at the scorn in Phoebe's voice. She was brought up to think a barn one of the most important features of one's possessions.

"It's a miserable affair. Low and ugly and with two steps between the kitchen and the shed, enough to kill one who does the work. He should have built Annie a pleasant home up on that lovely little knoll of maples, where she could have seen out and down the road and had a little company now and then. She might be alive today if she had one-half the care and attention Hiram gave the stock!" Phoebe's words were bitter and vehement.

"It sounds dreadful silly for a girl your age to be talking like that. You don't know anything about Annie, and if I was you I wouldn't think about her. As for the barn, I'd think a wife would be proud to have her husband's barn the nicest one in the county. I declare you do have the strangest notions!"

Nevertheless, she determined she'd give Hiram a hint about the house.

Phoebe didn't reply. She was peeling the last apple, and as soon as it lay with the rest, she shoved back her chair and left the shed. Emmeline felt she'd failed again to make any impression on her sister-in-law. It maddened her to have a girl like that around, who thought everything beneath her and criticized the customs of the entire neighborhood. She was an annoyance and a reproach. Emmeline felt she'd like to get rid of her if it could be done in a legitimate way.

At dinner, Henry Williams looked at Phoebe and asked if she'd made the pie. Phoebe said she had.

"It tastes like you, nice and sweet," he declared gallantly.

At this remark, Albert laughed, and Alma leaned forward to look into her aunt's flaming face.

"Betsy Green says she thinks her pa is going to get her a new ma," Alma said when the laughter subsided. "And Betsy says she bets she knows who 'tis, too!"

"You shut up!" Emmeline hissed, giving Alma a dig under the table.

But Phoebe hastily pushed back her chair and fled from the table.

A moment of uncomfortable silence ensued after Phoebe left the room. Emmeline felt that things had gone too far. Albert asked what was the matter with Phoebe, but instead of answering him, Emmeline yanked Alma from the table and out into the woodshed, where a whispered scolding was administered, followed by a switching.

Alma returned to the table chastened outwardly but inwardly vowing vengeance on her aunt. She determined to get even with Aunt Phoebe even if another switching happened.

Phoebe didn't come downstairs again that afternoon. Emmeline hesitated about sending for her and finally decided to wait until she came. The unwilling Alma was pressed into service to dry the dishes, and the long, sunny afternoon dragged drowsily on, while Phoebe lay on her bed up in her kitchen chamber and wondered why so many tortures were coming to her all at once.

Chapter 3

Hiram Green kept his word to himself and didn't go to see Phoebe for two evenings. Emmeline wondered what in the world Phoebe had said to him to keep him away when he seemed so anxious to get her. But the third evening he arrived promptly, attired with unusual care, and asked Emmeline if he might see Phoebe alone.

Phoebe had finished her work in the kitchen and gone up to rock the baby to sleep. Emmeline swept the younger children out of the sitting room and called Albert sharply to help her with something in the kitchen, sending Alma up with a carefully worded message to Phoebe. Emmeline was relieved to see Hiram again. She knew by his face that he meant business this time, and she hoped to see Phoebe conquered at once.

When Phoebe came down to the sitting room, she explained quietly as she entered, "I couldn't come sooner. Alma woke the baby again."

Hiram, mollified by the gentle tone of explanation, arose, answering, "Oh, that's all right. I'm glad to see you now you're here," and reached out with the evident intention of taking both her hands in his.

Phoebe looked up in horror, knowing Alma stood behind the crack of the door and watched it all with wicked joy.

"I beg your pardon, Mr. Green. I thought Emmeline was in here. She sent for me. Excuse me—I must find her."

"Oh, that's all right!" said Hiram, putting out his hand and shutting the door sharply in Alma's impudent face. "She don't expect you—Emmeline don't. She sent for you to see me. I asked her could I see you alone. She understands all about us—Emmeline does. She won't come in here for a while. She knows I want to talk to you."

Cold chills crept down Phoebe's back and froze her heart. Had the horror returned with redoubled vigor and with her family behind it? Where was Albert? Wouldn't he help her? Then she realized she must help herself and at once, for it was evident Hiram Green meant to press his suit energetically. He was coming toward her with his hateful, confident smile. He stood between her and the door. Besides, what good would it do to run away? She had tried that once, and it didn't work. She must speak to him and end the matter. She summoned all her dignity and courage and backed over to the other side of the room, where a single chair stood.

"Won't you sit down, Mr. Green?" she said.

"Why, yes, I will. Let's sit right here together," he said, sitting down at one end of the couch and making room for her. "Come, you sit here beside me, Phoebe, and then we can talk better. It's more sociable."

Phoebe sat down on the chair opposite him.

"I would rather sit here, Mr. Green," she said.

"Well, of course, if you'd rather," he said. "But it seems to be kind of unsociable. And I wish you wouldn't 'mister' me anymore. Can't you call me Hiram?"

"I would rather not."

"That sounds real unfriendly," Hiram said in a tone that suggested he wouldn't be trifled with much longer.

"Did you wish to speak to me, Mr. Green?" said Phoebe, her clear eyes looking at him steadily over the candlelight.

"Well, yes," he said, straightening up and hitching a chair around to the side nearer to her. "I thought we better talk that matter over a little that I mentioned to you several nights ago."

"I don't think that's necessary, Mr. Green," answered Phoebe.

"I thought I made you understand that was impossible."

"Oh, I didn't take account of what you said that night," said Hiram. "I saw you was sort of upset, not expecting me out there in the dark, so I thought I better come round again after you had plenty chance to think over what I said."

"I couldn't say anything different if I thought it over for a thousand years," declared Phoebe. Hiram Green was not thin-skinned; it was just as well to tell the truth and be done with it.

But the fellow wasn't daunted. He admired Phoebe all the more for her vehemence, for here was a prize worth winning.

"Aw, git out!" said Hiram pleasantly. "That ain't the way to talk. 'Course you're young yet and ain't had much experience, but you certainly had time enough to consider the matter all this year I been comin' to see you."

Phoebe rose to her feet.

"Coming to see me!" she gasped. "You don't come to see me!"

"Now, Phoebe. You needn't pertend you didn't know I was comin' to see you. Who did you s'pose I was comin' to see then?"

"I supposed you were coming to see Albert," said Phoebe.

"Albert! You s'posed I was comin' to see Albert every night! Aw, yes, you did a whole lot! Phoebe, you're a sly one. You must of thought I was gettin' fond of Albert!"

"I didn't think anything about it," said Phoebe haughtily, "and you may be sure, Mr. Green, if I had dreamed of such a thing I would have told you it was useless."

Something in her tone and matter ruffled Hiram Green's self-assurance. Up to this minute he'd persuaded himself that Phoebe was only acting coy. Was it possible she didn't care for his attentions and really wished to dismiss him? Hiram couldn't credit such a thought. Yet the firm set of her lips bewildered him.

"What on earth makes you keep sayin' that?" he asked in

an irritated tone. "What's your reason for not wantin' to marry me?"

"There are so many reasons I wouldn't know where to begin," said the girl.

Had he heard her right?

"What reasons?" he growled, frowning. He began to feel that Phoebe was trifling with him. He'd make her understand he wouldn't endure much of that.

Phoebe looked troubled. She wished he wouldn't insist on further talk, but she was too honest—too angry—not to tell the exact truth.

"The first and greatest reason is that I do not love you and never could," she said, looking him straight in the eyes.

"Shucks!" said Hiram, laughing. "I don't mind that a mite. In fact, I think it's an advantage. Folks mostly get over it when they do feel that sentimental kind of way. It don't last but a few weeks, anyhow, and it's better to begin on a practical basis, I think. That was the trouble with Annie. She was so blamed sentimental she hadn't time to get dinner. I think you an' I'd get along much better. You're practical and a good worker. We could manage things real prosperous over to the farm—"

Phoebe arose quickly and interrupted him.

"Mr. Green, you must please stop talking this way. It is horrible! I don't want to listen to any more of it."

"You set down, Phoebe," commanded Hiram. "I've got some things to tell you. It ain't worth yer while to act foolish. I mean business. I want to get married. It's high time there was somebody to see to things at home, but I can wait a little while if you're wantin' to get ready more. Only don't be long about it. As I said, I don't mind about the love part. That'll come all right. And you remember, Phoebe, there's plenty of girls around here that would be glad to marry me if they got the chance."

"Then, by all means, let them marry you!" said Phoebe,

steadying her trembling limbs for flight. "I shall never, never marry you! Good night, Mr. Green."

She swept out the door and was gone before he fully took it in. The latch clicked behind her, and he could hear the soft stir of her garments on the stairs. He heard the button on her door creak and turn. He went after her as far as the door, but the stairway was quiet and dark. He could hear Albert and Emmeline in the kitchen. He stood a moment, puzzled, going over the conversation and trying to make it all out.

What mistake had he made? He had failed, that was certain. It was a new experience and one that angered him, but somehow the anger was blunted by the memory of the look in the girl's eyes, the dainty movement of her hands, the set of her shapely head. He didn't know he was fascinated by her beauty; he only knew that a dogged determination to have her for his own was settling down upon him.

Albert and Emmeline were talking in low tones in the kitchen when the door was flung open and Hiram Green stepped in, his brow dark.

"I can't make her out!" he muttered as he flung himself into a kitchen chair. "She's for all the world like a wild colt. When you think you have her, she gives you the slip and is off further away than when you begun.

"What's the matter with her anyway?" Hiram growled, turning to Emmeline, as though she were responsible for all of womankind. "Is there anybody else? She ain't got in with Hank Williams, has she?"

"She won't look at him," Emmeline said. "He tried to get her to go to singin' school with him today, but she shut him off short. What reason did she give you?"

"She spoke about not havin' proper affection," he said, "but if I was dead sure that was the hull trouble I think I could fix her up. I'd like to get things settled 'fore winter comes on. I can't afford to waste time like this."

"I think I know what's the matter with her," said Emmeline. "She isn't such a fool as to give up a good chance in life for reasons of affection, though it is mighty high-soundin' to say so. But there's somethin' back of it all. I shouldn't wonder, Hiram, if she's tryin' you to see if you want her enough to fix things handy the way she'd like 'em."

"What do you mean?" Hiram asked gruffly, showing sudden interest. "Has she spoke of anything to you?"

"Well, she did let on that your house was a bit unpleasant, and she seemed to think the barn had the best location. She spoke about the knoll being a good place for a house."

Hiram brightened.

"You don't say! When did she say that?"

"Just today," Emmeline answered.

"Well, if that's the hitch, why didn't she say so? She didn't seem shy."

"Mebbe she was waitin' for you to ask her what she wanted."

"Well, she didn't wait long. She lit out before I had a chance to half talk things over."

"She's young yet, you know," said Emmeline in a soothing tone. "Young folks take odd notions. I shouldn't wonder but she hates to go to that house and live way back from the road that way. She ain't much more than a child in some things—though she's first-class when it comes to work."

"Well," said Hiram, "I been thinkin' the house needed fixin' up some. I don't know as I should object to buildin' all new. The old house would come in handy fer the men. Bill would like to have his ma and keep house right well. It would help me out in one way, fer Bill is gettin' uneasy, and I'd rather spare any man I've got than Bill—he works so steady and good. You might mention to Phoebe, if you like, that I'm thinkin' of buildin' a new house. Say I'd thought of the knoll for a location. Think that might ease her up a little?"

"I'll see what can be done," said Emmeline matter-of-factly.

The atmosphere in the kitchen brightened as if extra candles had been brought in. Satisfied, Hiram lit his pipe, tilted his chair back in his accustomed way, and entered into a brisk discussion of politics while Emmeline busied herself with kitchen work.

Emmeline mentally rehearsed the line of argument with which she intended to ply Phoebe the next day. She felt triumphant. Not every matchmaker would have had the grit to tell Hiram just what was wanted. Surely Phoebe would listen now.

Up in her kitchen chamber, Phoebe sat with burning cheeks, looking wildly into the darkness. She didn't hear the nightly symphony outside. She was thinking of what she had been through and wondered if she'd finally freed herself from the hateful attentions of Hiram Green. Would he take her answer as final or not? She thought not, judging from his nature. He was one of those men who never gave up what they'd set themselves to get, be it sunny pasture, young heifer, or pretty wife. She shuddered at the thought of many more encounters such as the one she'd passed through tonight. It was all dreadful to her.

She wondered what her life would be like if her mother were alive—a quiet little home, of course, plain and sweet and cozy, with plenty of hard work, but always someone to sympathize. Her frail mother hadn't been able to stand the rough world and hard work, but she had left behind her a memory of gentleness and refinement that couldn't be crushed out of her young daughter's heart, no matter how much she came in contact with the coarse, rude world.

Often, in her silent meditations, the girl would take her mother into her thoughts and tell her all that had happened that day. But tonight she felt that were her mother here, she couldn't bear to tell her of the horrid experience she'd endured. She knew instinctively that her mother, if alive, would shrink with horror from the thought of her child being united to a man like Hiram Green.

Tonight she needed some close, tangible help, someone all-wise and powerful; someone who could tell what God meant her life to be and make her sure she was right in her fierce recoil from what life seemed to be offering. She felt sure she was right, yet she wanted another to say so also, to take her part against the world that was troubling her.

Her young pride rose and bore her up. She must tell nobody but God. And so she knelt timidly down and poured out her wounded spirit in a prayer. She had always prayed but never felt it meant anything to her until tonight. When she arose, not knowing what she'd asked, or if indeed she'd asked anything for herself, she yet felt stronger to face her life, which somehow stretched out ahead in monotonous torture.

Meanwhile, the man who desired to have her, and the woman who desired to have him have her, formed their plans for a campaign against her.

Chapter 4

It was the first day of October and Phoebe's birthday. The sun shone clear and high, and the sky overhead was a dazzling blue. Off in the distance a blue haze lay softly over the horizon, mingling the crimsons and golds of the autumn foliage with the fading greens. It was a perfect day, and Phoebe was out enjoying it.

She walked with a purpose, as though it did her good to push the road back under her impatient feet. She wasn't walking toward the village but out into the open country, past the farm, where presently the road turned and skirted a maple grove. But she didn't pause here, though she loved the crimson maple leaves that carpeted the ground. On she went, as though her only object was to get away.

A farm wagon approached. She strained her eyes ahead to see who was driving. What if it happened to be Hank and he stopped to talk! She wished she'd worn her sunbonnet so she might hide in its depths, but her departure had been too sudden for that. She'd simply untied her apron and flung it from her as she started. Even now she didn't know whether it hung on the chair where she'd been sitting shelling dried beans or whether it adorned the rosebush by the kitchen door. She hadn't looked back to see.

No one knew it was her birthday, or, if they knew, they hadn't remembered. Perhaps that made it harder to stay and shell beans and bear Emmeline's talk.

Matters had been going on in much the way they'd gone all summer—at least outwardly. Hiram Green still spent the evenings talking with Albert while Emmeline darned stockings, and Phoebe escaped upstairs when she could and sewed with her back to the guest when she couldn't. Phoebe had taken diligent care that Hiram should have no more tête-à-têtes with her, even at the expense of having to spend many evenings in her dark room when all outdoors beckoned her with the lovely sounds of the dying summer. Grimly and silently she went through the days of work.

Emmeline, since the morning she attempted to discuss Hiram's proposed new house and found Phoebe unresponsive, had held her peace. Not that she was by any means vanquished, but, having made so little headway in talking to the girl, she concluded it would be well to let her alone awhile. In fact, Albert had advised that line of action in his kind way, and Emmeline shut her lips and went around with an air of offended dignity. She spoke disagreeably whenever it was necessary to speak at all to Phoebe, and whenever the girl came downstairs in anything other than her working garments, Emmeline showed her disapproval in unspeakable volumes.

Phoebe went about her daily routine without noticing, much as a bird might whose plumage was being criticized. She couldn't help putting herself in dainty array, even though the materials at hand might be only a hairbrush and a bit of ribbon. Her hair was always waving about her lovely face, and a tiny rim of white collar outlined the throat, even in her homespun morning gown. It was all hateful to Emmeline— "impudent," she called it, in speaking to herself. She had tried the phrase once in a confidence to Albert, but somehow he hadn't understood. He almost resented it. He said he thought Phoebe always looked "real neat and pretty," and he "liked to see her around." This had fired Emmeline's jealousy, although she wouldn't have owned it. Albert made so many remarks of this sort that Emmeline felt they'd spoil his sister and make her unbearable to live with.

But Emmeline continued to meditate upon Phoebe's "impudent" attire until the afternoon of her birthday, when the thoughts culminated in words.

Phoebe had gone upstairs after the dinner work was finished and come down arrayed in a gown Emmeline had never seen. It was of soft buff merino, trimmed with narrow lines of brown velvet ribbon, and a bit of the same velvet around the throat held a small gold locket that nestled in the white hollow of Phoebe's neck as if it loved to be there. The brown hair was dressed in its usual way except for a knot of brown velvet. It was a simple girlish costume, and Phoebe wore it with the same easy grace she wore her homespun, which made it doubly annoying for Emmeline.

Years ago when Phoebe had come to live with them, she brought with her some boxes and trunks and a few pieces of furniture for her own room. They were things of her mother's which she wished to keep. Emmeline had gone over the collection with ruthless hand and critical tongue, casting out what she considered useless, laying aside what she considered unfit for present use and freely commenting upon all she saw. Phoebe, fresh from her mother's grave, had stood by in stony silence, holding back the angry tears that tried to get their way. But when Emmeline had reached the large trunk and demanded the key, Phoebe had quietly cropped the string that held it round her neck inside her dress, where it lay cold against her heart.

"You needn't open that, Emmeline. It holds my mother's dresses that she put away for me when I grow up."

"Nonsense!" Emmeline answered sharply. "I think I'm the best judge of whether it needs to be opened or not. Give me the key at once. I'm not going to have things in my house that I don't know anything about. I've got to see they're packed away from moths."

Phoebe's lips had trembled, but she continued to talk

steadily. "It's not necessary, Emmeline. My mother packed them all away carefully in lavender and rosemary for me. She didn't wish them opened till I got ready to open them myself. I don't want them opened."

Emmeline had been very angry at that and told the little girl she wouldn't have any such talk around her. She demanded the key at once.

But Phoebe said, "I've told you it's not necessary. These are my things, and I will not have any more of them opened, and I will not give you the key."

That was open rebellion, and Emmeline carried her to Albert. Albert had looked at the pitiful little face with its pleading eyes—and sided with Phoebe. He said Phoebe was right, the things were hers, and he didn't see why Emmeline wanted to open them. From that hour Emmeline barely tolerated her little half sister-in-law, and the enmity between them had never grown less. Little did Phoebe know, whenever she wore one of the dresses from that unopened trunk, how she roused her sister-in-law's wrath.

The trunk had been stored in the closet in Phoebe's room, and the key had never left its resting place against her heart, night or day. Sometimes Phoebe unlocked it in the still hours of the early summer mornings when no one else was stirring, and she looked lovingly at the garments folded within. It was there she kept the daguerreotype of her beloved mother. Her father she couldn't remember, since he died when she was only a year old. In the depths of the trunk lay several large packages labeled: *"For my dear daughter Phoebe Deane on her eighteenth birthday."*

For several days before her birthday Phoebe had felt an undertone of excitement. It was almost time to open the box which had been packed more than eight years ago by her mother's hand. Phoebe didn't know what was in the box, but she knew it was something her mother put there for her. It contained her mother's thought for her grown-up daughter. It was like a voice from the grave. It thrilled her to think of it.

On her birthday morning she awakened with the light and applied the little black key to the keyhole. Her fingers trembled as she turned the lock and opened the lid. She wanted this sacred gift all to herself now, this moment when her soul would touch again the soul of the lost mother.

Carefully she lifted out the treasures in the trunk until she reached the box, then drew it forth. She placed the other things back, closed the trunk, and locked it. She took the box to her bed and untied it. Her heart beat so fast she felt as if she'd been running. She lifted the cover. There lay the buff merino in all its beauty, complete with the brown knot for the hair and the locket which had been her mother's at eighteen. And there on the top lay a letter in her mother's handwriting. Ah! This was what she had hoped for—a real word from her mother that could guide her in this grown-up life that was so lonely and different from the life she had lived with her mother.

She hugged the letter to her heart and cried over it.

But the house was beginning to stir, and Phoebe knew she would be expected in the kitchen before long, so she dried her tears and read her letter.

Before she was half done, the clatter in the kitchen had begun, and Emmeline's strident voice called up the stairway: "Phoebe! Phoebe! Are you going to stay up there all day?"

Phoebe cast a wistful look at the rest of her letter, patted the soft folds of her merino tenderly, swept it out of sight into her closet and answered Emmeline, "Yes, I'm coming!" Not even the interruption could dim her pleasure on this day.

It didn't take long to dress, and with the letter tucked in with the key against her heart she hurried down, only to meet Emmeline's frowning words and be ordered around like a child.

The morning passed away happily in spite of Emmeline and hard work. Words from her mother's hastily read letter floated back to her. She longed to pull it out and read it once more. But there was no time.

After dinner, however, as soon as she finished the dishes and while Emmeline was looking after something in the woodshed, she slipped away upstairs. She'd decided she would put on her new dress, for it had been her mother's wish in the letter, and go down to the village and call on Mrs. Spafford. She felt she had a right to a little time to herself on her birthday, and she meant to slip away without Emmeline seeing, if she could. With the letter safely hidden she hurried down.

But her conscience wouldn't let her go out the front door as she'd planned. It seemed a mean, sneaking thing to do on her birthday. She would be open and frank. She would step into the kitchen and tell Emmeline she was going out for the afternoon. So, though much against her own desire, she went.

And there sat Emmeline with a large basket of dried beans to be shelled and put away for the winter. Phoebe stood aghast and hesitated.

"Well, really!" said Emmeline, looking up severely at the apparition in buff that stood in the doorway. "Are you going to play the fine lady while I shell beans? It seems to me that's rather taking a high hand for one who's dependent on her relatives for every mouthful she eats. That's gratitude, that is. But I take notice you eat the beans—oh, yes! The beans Albert provides and I shell, while you gallivant round in party clothes."

The hateful speech brought a flush to Phoebe's cheeks.

"Emmeline," she broke in, "you know I didn't know you wanted those beans shelled today. I would have done them this morning if you'd said so."

"You didn't know," sniffed Emmeline. "You knew the beans was to shell, and you knew this was the first chance to do it.

Now you wash your white hands and dress up, no matter what the folks that keeps you have to do. That wasn't the way *I* was brought up. I didn't have a fine lady mother like yours. My mother taught me *gratitude*."

Phoebe reflected on the long hard days of work she'd done for Emmeline without a word of praise or thanks, work as hard or harder than any wage earner in the same position would have been expected to do. She had earned her board and more, and she knew it. She made her clothes from the material her mother had left for her. She hadn't cost Albert a cent in that way. Nevertheless, her conscience hurt her because of the late hour of her coming down that morning. With one desperate glance at the size of the bean basket and a rapid calculation of how long it would take her to finish them, she seized her clean apron that hung behind the door and enveloped herself in it.

"I've wanted to go for a long time, but if those beans have to be done this afternoon, I can do them first."

She spoke calmly and went at the beans with determined fingers.

Emmeline sniffed.

"You're a pretty figure shellin' beans in that rig. I s'pose that's one of your ma's outfits, but if she had any sense at all, she wouldn't want you to put it on. It ain't fit for ordinary life. It might do to have your picture took in or go to a weddin', but you do look like a fool in it now. Besides, if it's worth anything, an' it looks like there was good stuff in it, you'll spoil it shellin' beans."

Phoebe shelled away feverishly and said not a word. Emmeline surveyed her angrily. Her wrath verged on the boiling point, and she felt the time had come to let it boil.

"I think the time has come to have an understandin'," said Emmeline, raising her voice harshly. "If you won't talk to me, Albert'll have to tend to you, but I'm the proper one to speak, and I'm goin' to do it. I won't have this sort of thing goin' on in my house. It's a disgrace. I'd like to know what you mean, treatin' Hiram Green this way? He's a respectable man, and you've no call to keep him danglin' after you forever. People'll talk about you, and I won't have it!"

Phoebe raised astonished eyes to her sister-in-law's agitated face.

"I don't know what you mean, Emmeline. I have nothing whatever to do with Hiram Green. I can't prevent him from coming to my brother's house. I wish I could, for it's most unpleasant to have him around continually."

The cool words angered Emmeline even more.

"You don't know what I mean!" mocked Emmeline. "No, of course not. You don't know who he comes here to see. You think, I suppose, he comes to see Albert and me. Well, you're not so much of a little fool as you want to pretend. You know well enough Hiram Green is just waitin' round on your whims, and I say it's high time you stopped this nonsense, keepin' a respectable man danglin' after you forever just to show off your power over him, and when all the time he needs a housekeeper and his children are runnin' wild. You'll get your pay, miss, when you do marry him. Those young ones will be so wild you'll never get 'em tamed. I think it's time for you to speak, for I tell you plainly it ain't likely another such chance'll come your way ever, and I don't suppose you want to be a hanger-on all your life on people that can't afford to keep you."

Phoebe's fingers still shelled beans rapidly, but her eyes were on Emmeline's angry face.

"I thought I told you," she said, her voice steady, "that I would never marry Hiram Green. Nothing and nobody on earth could make me marry him. I despise him. You know perfectly well that the things you're saying are wrong. It isn't my fault he comes here. I don't want him to come, and he knows it. I have told him I will never marry him. Nothing he could do would make any difference."

"You're a little fool to let such a chance go!" screamed Emmeline. "If he wasn't entirely daft about you he'd give you up at once. Well, what are you intendin' to do then? Answer me that! Are you layin' out to live on Albert the rest of your life? It's best to know what to expect and be prepared. Answer me!"

Phoebe dropped her eyes to hide the sudden tears that threatened to overwhelm her calm.

"I don't know." The girl tried to say it quietly, but the angry woman snatched the words from her lips and tossed them back.

"You don't know! You don't know! Well, you better know! I can tell you right now that there's goin' to be a new order of things. If you stay here any longer you've got to do as I say. You're not goin' on your high-and-mighty way doin' as you please an hour longer. And to begin with you can march upstairs and take off that ridiculous rig of your foolish mother's—"

Phoebe shoved the kitchen chair back with a sharp noise on the bare floor and stood up, her face white with anger.

"Emmeline," she said, and her voice was low and controlled, but it reminded Emmeline of the first low rumbling of a storm. "Emmeline, don't you dare to speak my mother's name in that way! I will not listen to you!"

Phoebe cast her apron from her and went out through the kitchen door, into the golden October afternoon, away from the cruel tongue, the endless beans—and the sorrow of her life.

The sunlight lingered on the buff merino, as though it had come out to meet it, and she flitted breathlessly down the way, she didn't know where, only to get out and away. All the air was filled with golden haze, and Phoebe, in her golden, sunlit garments, seemed a part of it.

Chapter 5

Phoebe felt desperate as she fled along the road, pursued by the thought of her sister-in-law's angry words.

To have such awful words spoken to her and on her birthday! To feel so cornered and badgered, and to have no home where one was welcome, save that hateful alternative of going to Hiram Green's house! Oh, why did one have to live when life had become a torture?

She had gone a long distance before her mind cleared enough to think where she was going. The sight of a distant red farmhouse made her pause in her wild walk. If she went on she'd be seen from the well-watched windows of that red house, and the two women who lived there were noted for their curiosity and their ability to impart news.

In sudden panic Phoebe climbed a fence and struck out across the field toward Chestnut Ridge, a small hill rising to the left of the village. There she might hope to be alone a little while and think it out and perhaps creep close to her mother once more through the letter. She hurried over the rough stubble of the field, gathering her buff garments in her hand to hold them from any detaining briars.

Breathless, at last she reached the hill and found a log where she sat down to read her letter.

> *My dear little grown-up girl,*
> *This is your eighteenth birthday, and I've thought so much about you and how you will be when you're a young woman, that I want to be with you a little while*

on your birthday and let you know how very much I love you. I can't look forward into your life and see how it will be with you. I don't know whether you'll have had sad years or bright ones between the time when I said good-bye to you and now when you are reading this. I had to leave you in God's care, and I know you'll be taken care of, whatever comes.

If there have been trials, somehow, Phoebe, they must have been good for you. Someday you will learn why, and sometime there will be a way out. Never forget that. God has His brightness ready somewhere for you if you are true to Him and brave. I'm afraid there will have been trials, perhaps very heavy ones, for you were always such a sensitive little soul, and you're going among people who may not understand.

In thinking about your life I've been afraid you would be tempted because of unhappiness to take some rash, impulsive step before God is ready to show you His plan for your life. I would like to give you a little warning through the years and tell you to be careful.

You have entered young womanhood and will perhaps be asked to give your life into the keeping of some man. If I were going to live, I would try to train you through the years for this great crisis in your life. But when it comes, remember that I've thought about you and longed for you to find another soul who will love you better than himself, and whom you can love better than you love anything else in the world, and who will be noble in every way.

Dear child, hear your mother's voice, and don't take anything less. It won't matter so much if he is poor, if only he loves you better than himself and is worthy of your love. Never marry anyone for a home or a chance to have your own way or freedom from good, honest work. There will be no happiness in it. Trust your mother, for she knows.

Do not marry anyone to whom you cannot look up and give honor next to God. Unless you can marry such a man it is better not to marry at all, believe me. I say it lovingly, for I've seen much sorrow and want to protect you.

And now, my sweet child, if when you read this anything has come into your life to make you unhappy, just try to lay it all down for a little while and feel your mother's love about you. See, I have made this bright sunny dress for you, every stitch set with love, and I want you to wear it on your birthday to remind you of me. It is yellow, because that's the glory color, the color of the sunshine I've always loved so much. I want you to think of me in a bright, happy way, as in a glory of happiness waiting for you; not as dead and lying in the grave. Think of my love for you as a joy, and not a lost one either, for I'm sure that where I'm going I shall love you just the same, and more.

I'm very tired and must not write anymore, for there's much to do before I can feel ready to go and leave you. But as I write this birthday letter for you I am praying that God will bring some brightness into your life, the beginning of some great joy, on this your eighteenth birthday, that shall be His blessing and my birthday gift to you. I put a kiss here where I write my name and give you with it more love than you can ever understand.

Your Mother

Tears ran down onto her hands as she held the letter, and when it was finished, she put her head on her lap and cried as she hadn't cried since her mother died.

The sunlight sifted down between the yellowed chestnut leaves, sprinkling gold on the golden hem of her gown and glinting on her shining hair. The brown nuts dropped now and then about her, reverently, as if they wouldn't disturb her if they could help it, and the fat gray squirrels silently regarded her, pausing in their work of gathering the winter's store, then whisked noiselessly away.

Phoebe didn't sob aloud. Her grief was deeper than that. Her soul cried out to one who was far away and yet who seemed so near to her that nothing else mattered for the time.

Would her mother have been just as sure her life would all come out right if she had known the real facts? Would she have given the same advice? She thought it over, washing the anger away in her tears. Yes, she felt sure her mother could not have written more truly than she had done. She would have had her say no to Hiram, just as she had done, and exhorted her to be patient with Emmeline and to trust that brightness would come sometime.

She thought of her mother's prayer for her and almost smiled through her tears to think how impossible that would be. But the day wasn't done—perhaps there might be some little pleasant thing yet that she might consider a blessing and her mother's gift. She would look and wait for it, and perhaps it would come.

Then, quite suddenly, she knew she was not alone.

A young man stood in the shadow of the tallest chestnut tree, regarding her with troubled gaze, his hat in his hand.

He was tall, well-formed, and his face was fine and handsome. His dark brown eyes looked like the shadowed depths of a quiet woodland stream. His heavy dark hair was tossed back from a white forehead that hadn't been exposed to the summer sun of the hayfield, and the hand that held the hat was white and smooth also. His graceful aspect reminded Phoebe of David Spafford, who seemed to her the ideal of a gentleman. If it hadn't been for his eyes and the hint of a smile on his lips, Phoebe would have been afraid of him as she lifted shy eyes to the intruder's face.

"I beg your pardon," he said. "I didn't mean to intrude, but some young people are coming up the hill. They'll be here in a moment, and I thought perhaps you wouldn't care to meet them. You seem to be in trouble."

"Oh, thank you!" said Phoebe, rising in sudden panic and dropping her mother's letter at her feet. She stooped to pick it up, but the young man reached it first, and their fingers met for one brief instant over the letter. In her confusion Phoebe didn't know what to say but "thank you" and then felt like a parrot repeating the same phrase.

Voices floated up the hill now, and the girl turned to flee, but there seemed nowhere to go for hiding except a dense growth of mountain laurel that still stood green and shining amid the autumn brown. She looked for a way around it, but the young man caught her thought and, reaching forward with a quick motion, parted the strong branches and made a way for her.

"Here, jump right in there! Nobody will see you. Hurry— they're almost here!" he whispered.

The girl sprang quickly on the log, pausing an instant to gather her golden garments about her, and then fluttered into the green hiding place and settled down like a drift of yellow leaves.

The laurel swung back into place, nodding as if it understood the secret. The young man stooped, and she saw him take a letter from his pocket and put it down behind the log that lay across her hiding place.

Up the hillside came a troop of young people. Phoebe couldn't see them, for the growth of laurel was very dense, but she could hear their voices.

"Oh, Janet Bristol, how fast you go! I'm all out of breath. Why do you hurry so? The nuts will keep till we get there, and we have all afternoon before us."

"Go as slow as you like, Caroline," said a sweet, imperious voice. "When I start anywhere I like to get there. I wonder where Nathaniel can be. It's been five minutes since he went out of sight, and he promised to hail us at once and tell us the best way to go."

"Oh, Nathaniel isn't lost," said another girl's voice crossly. "He'll take care of himself likely. Don't hurry so, Janet. Maria is all out of breath."

"Hello! Nathaniel! Nathaniel Graham, where are you!" called a chorus of male voices.

Then from a few paces in front of the laurel hiding place came the voice Phoebe had heard but a moment before.

"Aye, aye, sir! That way!" it called. "There are plenty of nuts up there!"

He stood with his back toward her hiding place and pointed farther up the hill. Then, laughing, scrambling over slippery leaves, the company of young people frolicked past, and Phoebe was left, undiscovered.

She stooped a little to look at the letter the young man had left and read the address, *"Nathaniel Graham, Esq.,"* written in a fine hand.

The girl studied the name till every turn of the pen was engraved on her mind, the fine clearness of the small letters, the bold downward stroke in the capitals. It was unusual writing of an unusual name, and Phoebe felt it belonged to an unusual man.

As she waited and listened to the happy jingle of voices, the barren loneliness of her own life came over her and brought a rush of tears. Why was she here in hiding from those girls and boys who should have been her companions? Why did she shrink from meeting Janet Bristol, the sweetly haughty beauty of the village? Why was she never invited to their teas and their berry and nut gatherings? She saw them in church, and that was all. They never seemed to see her. True, she hadn't been brought up from childhood among them, but she'd lived there long enough to have known them intimately if her life hadn't always been so full of care.

Janet Bristol had gone away to school for several years and was only at home in summer, when Phoebe's life was full of farm work—cooking for the field hands and the harvesters. But Maria Finch and Caroline Penfield had gone to school with Phoebe. She felt a bitterness that they were enjoying such good times and she was not. They weren't to blame, perhaps, for she'd always avoided them, keeping to herself and her studies in school and hurrying home at Emmeline's strict command. They'd never attracted her as had the tall, fair Janet. Yet she would never likely know Janet Bristol or come any nearer to her than she was now, hidden behind God's screen of laurel on the hillside.

The young man with the beautiful face and kind ways would forget her and leave her to scramble out of her hiding place as best she could while he helped Janet Bristol over the stile and carried her basket of nuts home for her. He wouldn't cross her path again. Nevertheless, she was glad he'd met her this once, and she could know there was one so kind and noble in the world.

She would stay here till they were all out of hearing, then creep out and steal away as she'd come. Her sad life and its annoyances, forgotten for the moment, settled down upon her, but with this change. They now seemed possible to bear. She could go back to Albert's house and work her way twice over. She could doff the golden garments and take up her daily toil and bear Emmeline's hateful insinuations. She could even bear Hank's disagreeable attentions and Hiram Green's hateful presence. But never again would she be troubled with the thought that perhaps she ought to accept the home Hiram Green offered her. Never! For now she had seen a man who looked at her as she felt sure God meant a man to look at a woman, with honor and respect and deference.

All at once she knew her mother's prayer had been answered

and that something beautiful had come into her life. It wouldn't stay and grow as her mother had hoped. This stranger could be nothing to her, but the memory of his helpfulness and the smile of sympathy that lighted his eyes would remain with her always.

Meanwhile, under the chestnut trees but a few yards away, the baskets were being filled rapidly. Nathaniel Graham helped each girl impartially. The laughing and joking went on, but Nathaniel said little. Phoebe watched them and felt that the young man would soon pilot them farther away. She could hear bits of their talk.

"What's the matter with Nathaniel?" said Caroline Penfield. "He's hardly said a word since we started. What deep subject is your massive mind engaged upon, young man?"

"Oh, Nate is thinking about Texas," said Daniel Westgate flippantly. "He has no thoughts or words for anything but setting Texas free. We'll hear of him joining the volunteers to help them fight Mexico the next thing. I wouldn't be one bit surprised."

"Don't, Daniel," said Janet Bristol. "Nathaniel has far more sense than that."

"I should hope so!" echoed Maria Finch. "Nathaniel isn't a hotheaded fanatic."

"Don't you be too sure!" Daniel called back. "If you'd heard the fine heroics he was getting off to David Spafford yesterday, you wouldn't be surprised at anything. Speak up, Nate, and tell them whether you're going or not."

"Perhaps," said Nathaniel, lifting pleasant eyes of amusement toward the group.

"Nonsense!" said Janet sharply. "As if he'd think of such a thing! Daniel, you should be ashamed to spoil the lovely afternoon with talk of politics. Come, let's move on to that next clump of trees. See, it's just loaded, and the nuts are falling with every breath of wind."

The company picked up their baskets and began to move out of sight, but Nathaniel stood still thoughtfully and felt in his pockets, until Phoebe could see none of the others. Then she heard him call in a pleasant voice, "Janet, I've dropped a letter. It can't be far away. Go on without me for a moment. I'll be with you right away."

"Oh, Nathaniel!" came Janet's vexed tones. "Can't you let it go? Was it important? Shall we come and help you find it?"

"No, Janet, thank you. I know just where I dropped it, and I'll be with you again before you've missed me. Keep right on."

Then he turned swiftly and came back to the laurel before the startled Phoebe could realize he was coming.

She sprang up with the instinct of fleeing from him, but the laurel caught her hair. Down came the soft, shining brown waves in lovely disorder about the flushed face and rippling far below the waist of the buff dress. A strand here and there clung to the laurel and made a fine veil of spun gold before her face. Thus she stood abashed, with her hair unbound before the stranger and her face in beautiful confusion.

The young man had gazed on many maidens' hair with entire indifference. In his boyhood he'd even dared to attach a paper kite to the yellow braids of a girl who sat in front of him in school, and he laughed with the rest at recess as the kite lifted the astonished victim's yellow plaits high in the air and she cried out angrily. He'd watched his cousin Janet brush and plait and curl her abundant locks into the various changing fashions—and criticized the effect freely. He had once untied a hard knot in a bonnet string in a mass of golden curls without a thrill. Why then did he feel such awe as he approached in deep embarrassment to offer his assistance? Why did his fingers tremble as he laid them upon a strand of hair that had tangled itself in the laurel? Why did it bring a fine ecstasy into his being as the wind blew it across his face? Did all hair have that delicate, indescribable perfume about it?

When he had set her free from the entangling bushes, he marveled at the dexterity with which she reduced the flying hair to order and imprisoned it meekly. It seemed like magic.

Then, before she had time to spring out of her covert, he took her hands and helped her to the top of the log and then to the ground. She liked him for the way he did it, so different from the way the other men she knew would have done it. She shuddered to think if it had been Hank or Hiram Green.

"Come this way. It's nearer to the road," he said, parting the branches at his right to let her pass.

When she had gone a few steps, she saw that the crossroad lay not far below them.

"But you've forgotten your letter," she turned to say as they came out of the woods and began to descend the hill. "And I can get out quite well now. You've been very kind—"

"I'll get the letter presently," he said with a smile. "Just let me help you over the fence. I want to ask your pardon for my intrusion. I didn't see you at first—the woods were so quiet—and you looked so much like the yellow leaves that lay all about—" His eyes cast an admiring glance at the buff merino.

"Oh, it wasn't an intrusion," she exclaimed, her cheeks growing warm, "and I'm so grateful to you for telling me they were coming. I wouldn't have liked to be found there." She looked up shyly. "Thank you very much."

He saw that her eyes were beautiful, with ripples of laughter and shadows of sorrow in their glance. He experienced a deep satisfaction that his first impression of her face was verified, and he stood looking down upon her as if she were something he was proud to have discovered and rescued from an unpleasant fate.

Phoebe felt a warm glow breaking over her in the kindness of his look.

"Don't thank me," he said. "I felt like a criminal, intruding upon your trouble."

"But you mustn't feel that way. It was only that I'd been reading a letter from my mother, and it made me feel so lonely that I cried."

"That's trouble enough," he said with quick sympathy. "Is your mother away from home, or are you?"

"My mother is dead. She's been gone a good many years," she said. "She wrote this letter long ago for me to read today, and I came away here by myself to read it."

He helped her over the rail fence that separated the field from the road, and they stood, she on the road side and he on the field side of the fence, as they talked. Neither of them saw a farm wagon coming down the road over the brow of the hill, a mere speck against the autumn sky when they came out of the woods.

The young man's face kindled as he answered. "Thank you for telling me. Now I understand. My mother has been gone a long time, too. I wish she'd written me a letter to read today."

Then, as if he knew he mustn't stay longer, he lifted his hat, smiled, and walked quickly up the hill. Phoebe sped down the road, not noticing the glories of the day, not thinking so much of her own troubles, but marveling at what had happened and living it all over once more in her imagination. She knew without thinking that a wagon rumbled nearer and nearer, but she gave it no heed.

When he reached the edge of the wood, Nathaniel Graham turned and looked back down the road, saw the girl in her yellow garments, and watched her intently. The driver of the farm wagon, now almost opposite him, watched glumly from behind his bags of wheat, sneered under his breath at the young man's fine attire, and half guessed who he was. He wondered who the girl was who kept tryst so far from any houses, and with a last glance at the man vanishing into the woods, he whipped up his team, resolved to find out.

Chapter 6

$\mathcal{N}$athaniel Graham went to pick up the letter he'd left behind the log, but as he did so his eye caught something brown lying on the ground among the laurel. He reached out and took it. It was a small bow of brown velvet and seemed strangely a part of the girl who had been there but a few moments before. His fingers closed about the soft little thing. For a moment he pondered whether to go after her and give it to her. Then farther up the hill he heard voices calling him, so he tucked it into his inner pocket. He liked to think he had that bit of velvet himself, and perhaps it wasn't of much value to the owner. It might at least make another opportunity of seeing her. And so he passed on up the hill with something besides the freedom of Texas to think about.

Meanwhile, the load of wheat chased down the road after Phoebe, and its driver, in no pleasant mood because he'd been all the way to Albany with his wheat and was unable to sell it, studied the graceful figure ahead of him and wondered what was so strangely familiar about it.

Phoebe had just reached the high road and paused to think which way she would go when the wagon overtook her. Turning a face bright with pleasure and momentary forgetfulness, she met the countenance of Hiram Green! She caught at the fence to steady herself. One hand flew to her heart, and with frightened eyes she sought the way by which she'd come, hoping to catch sight of her newfound protector. But the hillside lay unresponsive in the late sunshine, and not a soul was to be seen. Nathaniel Graham had just picked up his cousin Janet's basket.

"Well, I swow!" said Hiram Green, pulling his horse up sharply. "If it ain't *you* tricked out that way, away off here!" Then slowly his little pig eyes traveled to the lonely hillside, gathered up an idea, came back to the girl's guilty face, and narrowed to slits. He brought his thin lips together with satisfaction. He felt that at last he had a hold upon the girl, but he could wait and use it to his best advantage.

She never dreamed he'd seen the young man with her and was only frightened of being alone in an unfrequented spot with him. In an instant her courage came to her aid, and she steadied her voice to reply.

"Oh, is that you, Mr. Green? You almost frightened me. I was taking a walk and didn't expect to see anyone I knew. This is the Albany road, isn't it? Have you been to Albany?"

Her unusually friendly tone threw the man off his guard for a moment. He couldn't resist the charm of having her speak so pleasantly to him.

"Yes, been to Albany on business," he responded. "Won't you get up and ride? 'Tain't a very pretty seat, but I guess it's clean and comfortable. Sorry I ain't got the carryall. You're a long piece from home."

"Oh, thank you, Mr. Green," she said. "I'm sure the seat would be very comfortable, but I'm out taking a walk this beautiful afternoon, and I'm enjoying every minute of it. I'd much rather walk. Besides, I'm not going directly home. I may stop at Granny McVane's and perhaps another place before I get home. Thank you for the invitation."

Without waiting for a reply she flew lightly in front of the horses and sped up the road toward the old red farmhouse. It wasn't the direction she would have chosen, but there was no time to do anything else. She dared not look behind lest she was being pursued.

Hiram Green, left alone after his attempt at gallantry, looked after the flying maiden with venom in his eyes. His mouth hardened once more into its cruel lines, and he took up the reins again and said to his horses, "G' long there," pointing his remark with a stinging cut of the whip.

When Phoebe neared the old red house, she noted with relief that the shades were drawn down and a general air of not-at-home-ness pervaded the place. She went on by the house and turned down another crossroad that led to a second road going into the village. On this road, just on the border of the town, lived Granny McVane with her silent old husband. She was a sweet old lady whom care and disappointment hadn't hardened, but only made more humble and patient.

Phoebe had come there on occasional errands, and her kindness had won the girl's heart. From Granny McVane's it would be only a short run home across the fields, and she'd escape meeting any more prying eyes. She wasn't accustomed to calling on the neighbors without an errand, but the idea came to her now to stop and ask how Granny's rheumatism was and wish her a good day. If she seemed glad to see her, she might tell her it was her birthday and this was the dress her mother had made. She longed to confide in someone.

As she walked along the country road, she began to think of home and the black looks she would get from Emmeline. But the day was good yet, though a chill had crept into the air that made her cheeks tingle. The sun was dropping low now, and the rays glowed deeper.

She reached the door of Granny McVane's cottage and knocked. The old lady, in her white ruffled cap with its black band and a soft kerchief folded across her bosom, opened the upper half of the door. Seeing Phoebe, she opened the lower door, too, and invited her in most warmly. She made her sit down and looked her over with delight, the old eyes glowing with pleasure at sight of the visitor.

Phoebe told her about the dress, her birthday, her mother's letter, and her walk. Then Granny McVane urged her to take tea with her, for her husband was off to Albany on business and wouldn't be back that night.

The cat winked cordially from the hearth, the pot of mush sputtered sleepily over the fire, and the old lady's face was so wistful that Phoebe put off her thought of home and the supper she should be getting this minute. She decided to stay just this once, as it was her birthday. Yes, for one short hour more she'd have what her day offered her of joy. Then she'd go back to her duty and cherish the memory of her pleasure.

Precisely at five o'clock the little round table was drawn out from the wall and its leaves put up. The old woman laid a snow-white homespun cloth upon it, followed by lovely blue dishes of quaint designs.

It was a delicious meal, and Phoebe ate it with the appetite gained in her long walk. After it was over she bade Granny McVane good-bye, kissed her for the beautiful ending to her birthday, and hurried guiltily across the fields to the farmhouse she called home.

The family had just sat down to supper when Phoebe opened the door and came in. She had hoped this ceremony would be over, for the usual hour for supper was half past five, but Emmeline had waited longer than usual, thinking Phoebe would surely come back to help. Emmeline had been angry, astonished, and bewildered all afternoon. She hadn't decided what to do about the way her young sister-in-law acted. But now that she was home, after staying away till the work was done, Emmeline's wrath kindled anew. She stood at the hearth taking up the second pan of johnnycake when the girl came in. And when she saw Phoebe looking cheerful, Emmeline set her lips in haughty disapproval.

Alma, with her mouth full of fried potatoes, stopped her fork midway with another supply and stared. The little boys chorused in unison: "Hullo, Aunt Phoebe! Where'd ye get the clo'es!" Hank, who was helping himself to a slice of bread, turned around and gazed in awed embarrassment. Only Albert looked pleased, his chair tipped back and a look of real welcome on his face.

"Well, now, Phoebe, I'm real glad you've got back. I was getting uneasy about you, off so long. It isn't like you to stay away from your meals. My, but you do look pretty in that rig! What took you, anyway? Where've you been?"

She wouldn't have told the others for the world, but somehow Albert's pleasant tones and kind eyes unsealed her lips.

"I've just been for a walk in the woods this afternoon, and I stopped a few minutes to see Granny McVane. She made me stay to tea with her. I didn't mean to stay so late."

"That sounds very sweet, I'm sure," broke in Emmeline's sharp voice, "but she forgets she left me with all her work to do on top of my own."

Phoebe's cheeks flushed.

"I'm sorry I didn't get back in time to help get supper," she said, looking straight at Albert as if explaining to him alone. "But it was my birthday, and I thought I might take a little time to myself."

"Your birthday! To be sure you can. You don't go out half enough. Emmeline, you wouldn't want her to work all day on her birthday, of course. Sit down, child, and have some more supper. This is real good johnnycake. You should have told us before that you had a birthday comin', and then we might have celebrated. Eh, Hank? What do you say?"

"I say yes," said Hank, endeavoring to regain his usual composure.

"Other people have birthdays, too, and I don't see much fuss made over them," sniffed Emmeline, flinging the tea towel up to its nail with an impatient movement.

"Thank you, Albert," said Phoebe. "I don't care for any more supper. I'll go up and change my dress and be ready to wash the dishes."

She headed toward the door, but Albert detained her.

"Wait, Phoebe! You come here and sit down. I've got something to tell you. I'd clean forgot about the birthday myself, but now I remember all right. Let's see—you're eighteen today, aren't you? I thought so."

Hank lifted bold, admiring eyes to her face, and the girl, standing patiently behind her chair at the table waiting for her brother to finish, felt as if she'd like to extinguish him for a little while till the conference was over.

"Well, now, child, I've got a surprise for you. You're eighteen and of age, so you've got a right to know it."

"Wouldn't it be better for you to tell me by and by when the work is done?" pleaded Phoebe, casting a glance about on the wide-eyed audience.

"No," said Albert. "It isn't a secret, leastways not from any that's here. You needn't look so scared, child. It's only that there's a little money coming to you, about five or six hundred dollars. It's a nice tidy little sum for a girl of eighteen with good prospects. You certainly deserve it, for you've been a good girl ever since you came to live with us. Your mother wanted me to keep the money for you till you was eighteen, and then she said you would know how to use it and be more likely to need it."

"Say, Aunt Phoebe," broke in Alma, tilting her nose to its most inquisitive point, "does Hiram Green know you got a birthday?"

"Shut up!" said Emmeline, applying the palm of her hand in a stinging slap to her daughter's cheek.

"Now, Emmeline, don't be so severe with the child! She doesn't realize how impertinent she is. Alma, you mustn't talk like that to Aunt Phoebe." Then, with a wink, he said in an aside to Hank, "It does beat all how keen children will be sometimes."

Phoebe, with scarlet cheeks, felt as if she could bear no more. "Thank you, Albert," she said in a trembling voice. "Now if you'll excuse me I'll change my dress."

"Wait a minute, child. That's a mighty pretty dress you've got on. Look pretty as a peach in it. Let's have a look at you. Where'd you get it? Make it yourself?"

"Mother made it for me to wear today," said Phoebe in a low voice.

Then she vanished into the hall, leaving an impression of victory behind her and a sense of embarrassment among the family.

"There'll be no livin' with her now," snapped Emmeline over the teacups. "I'm sure I thought you had better sense. You never told me there was any money left for her, or I'd've advised you about it. I'm sure we've spent for her, and if there's anything left her it belongs to you. Here she's had a good home and paid not a cent for it. If she had any spirit of right she wouldn't touch a cent of that money!"

"Now look here, Emmeline," said Albert in his conciliatory tone. "You don't quite understand this matter. Not having known about it before, of course, you couldn't judge rightly. And it was her ma's request that I not tell anybody. Besides, I don't see why it should affect you any. The money was hers, and we'd nothing to do with it. As for her home here, she's been very welcome, and I'm sure she's earned her way. She's a good worker, Phoebe is."

"That's so, she is," said Hank. "I don't know a girl in the county can beat her workin'."

"I don't know as anybody asked your opinion, Hank Williams. I'm able to judge work a little myself, and if she works well, who taught her? She'd never done a stroke when she came here, and nobody thinks of the hard time I've had breakin' her in and puttin' up with her mistakes when she was young."

"Now, Emmeline, don't go and get excited," said Albert. "You know we ain't letting go a mite of what you've done. Only it's fair to the girl to say she's earned her way."

"Hmm!" said Emmeline. "That depends on who's the judge!"

"Won't Aunt Phoebe do any more work now she's got some money, Ma?" broke in Alma, panicked about what might be in store for her.

"Haven't I told you to keep still, Alma?" reproved her mother. "If you say another word I'll send you to bed without any cake."

At this dire threat Alma withdrew from the conversation till the cake should be passed, and a gloom settled over the room. Hank felt the constraint and made haste to bolt the last of his supper and escape.

Phoebe came down shortly afterward, attired in her everyday garb and looking meekly sensible. Albert protested weakly.

"Say, Phoebe, it's too bad for you to wash dishes on your birthday night. You go back and put on your pretty things, and Alma'll help her ma wash up this time."

"No, she won't, either," broke in Emmeline. "Alma ain't a bit well, and she's not goin' to be made to work at her age unless she likes. Here, honey, you may have this piece of Ma's cake; she don't want it all. It seems to me you're kind of an unnatural father, Albert Deane. I guess it won't hurt Phoebe to wash a few dishes when she's been lyin' around havin' a good time all day, while I've worked my fingers half off doin' her work. We've all had to work on our birthdays, and I guess if Phoebe's goin' to stay here she'll have to put up with what the rest of us gets, unless she's got money to pay for better."

With that Albert looked helplessly about the room and retired to his newspaper in the sitting room, while Phoebe went swiftly about the usual evening work. Emmeline yanked

the boys away from the cake plate and marched them and
Alma out of the kitchen with her head held high and her chin
in the air. She didn't even put away the cake and bread and
pickles and jelly but left it all for Phoebe, who was glad for this.

Before the dishes were done, the front door opened, and
Hiram Green sauntered into the sitting room. Phoebe heard
him and hurried to hang up her dish towels and flee to her
own room.

And thus ended the birthday, though the girl lay awake far
into the night thinking over all its wonderful happenings—
and not allowing her mind to dwell upon the possibilities of
trouble in the future.

Chapter 7

When little Rose Spafford was born, her young mother—who had been Marcia Schuyler—found no one so reliable and helpful in the whole town as Miranda Griscom, granddaughter and household drudge of her next-door neighbor, Mrs. Heath. David Spafford "borrowed" her for the first three or four weeks, and Mrs. Heath gave reluctant consent, because the Heaths and the Spaffords had always been intimate friends. But Grandma Heath realized during that time just how many steps the eccentric Miranda saved her, and she began to look forward to her return with more eagerness than she cared to show.

Miranda reveled in doing as she pleased in the large, well-furnished kitchen of the Spafford house, using the best china to send a tray upstairs to Mrs. Spafford. She often looked triumphantly over toward her grandmother's house and wondered if she was missed. One little gleam of appreciation would have started a flame of abounding love in the girl's lonely heart. But the grim grandmother never appreciated anything her unloved grandchild, the daughter of an undesired son-in-law, tried to do.

As the days sped by Miranda began to dread the time when she must go back to her grandmother's house again, and Marcia and David dreaded it also. They set about planning how they might keep her, and presently they had it all arranged.

David suggested it first.

It was while they both hung over little Rose's cradle, watching her wake up, like the opening of the little bud she was.

Miranda had come to the door for a direction and stood there a moment. "I thought I'd find you two a-hoverin'. Just keep right on. I'll see to supper. Don't you give it a thought."

And then a moment later they heard her high, nasal tones voicing something about a "sweet, sweet rose on a garden wall," and they smiled at the quaint loving soul. Then David spoke.

"Marcia, we must contrive to keep Miranda here," he said. "She's blossomed out in the last month. It would be cruel to send her back to that dismal house again. They don't need her in the least with Hannah's cousin there all the time. I mean to offer her wages to stay with us. You're not strong enough to care for the baby and do the housework, anyway, and I'd feel safer about you if Miranda were here. Wouldn't you like her?"

Marcia's sweet laugh rang out. "Oh, David, you spoil me! I'm sure I'm perfectly able to do the work and look after this tiny child. But of course I'd like to have Miranda here. I think it would be a good thing if she could get away from her surroundings, and she's a comfort to me in many ways."

"Then it's settled, dear," said David with his most loving smile.

"Oh, but David, what will Aunt Amelia say? And Aunt Hortense! They'll tell me I'm weak—or proud, which would be worse yet."

"What does it matter what my aunts think? We're certainly free to do as we please in our own home, and I'm sure of one thing—Aunt Clarinda will think it's all right. She'll be quite pleased. Besides, I'll explain to Aunt Hortense that I want to have you more to myself and take you with me often, and therefore it's my own selfishness, not yours, that makes me do this. She'll listen to that argument, I'm sure."

Marcia smiled, half doubtfully.

"And then there's Mrs. Heath. She'll never consent."

"Leave that to me, my little wife, and don't worry about it.

First, let's settle it with Miranda."

Just then Miranda presented herself at the door.

"Your supper's spoilin' on the table. Will you two just walk down and eat it while I have my try at that baby? I haven't seen scarcely a wink of her all this blessed day."

"Miranda," said David, not looking at his wife's warning eyes, "would you be willing to stay with us altogether?"

"Hmm!" said Miranda. "Jes' gimme the try and see!" And she stooped over the cradle with such a wistful gaze that the young mother's heart went out to her.

"Very well, Miranda, then we'll consider it a bargain. I'll pay you wages so we'll feel quite comfortable about asking you to do anything, and you shall call this your home from now on."

"What!" gasped the girl, straightening up. "Did you mean what you said? I never knew you to do a mean thing like tease anyone, David Spafford, but you can't mean what you say. It couldn't come around so nice as that fer me. Don't go to talk about wages. I'd work from mornin' to night fer one chance at that blessed baby there in the cradle. But I know it can't be."

The supper grew cold while they persuaded her it was all true and they really wanted her and then talked over the possible trouble with her grandmother. At last, with her sandy eyelashes wet with tears of joy, Miranda went downstairs and heated the supper all over again for them. And the two upstairs, beside the little bud that had bloomed for them, rejoiced that a heart so faithful and true would be watching over her through babyhood.

Perhaps it was a desire to burn his bridges behind him before his maiden aunts heard of the new arrangement that sent David over to see old Mrs. Heath that very evening. Perhaps it was to relieve the excitement of Miranda, who felt heaven had opened before her but counted on being thrust out of her Eden at once.

No one but Marcia ever heard what passed between David and old Mrs. Heath, and no one else quite knew what arguments he used to bring the determined old woman finally to terms. Miranda, with her nose flattened against the windowpane of the dark kitchen chamber, watching the two blurred figures in the candlelight of Grandmother Heath's sitting room, wondered and prayed and hoped and feared—and prayed again.

It was a good thing David went over to see Mrs. Heath that night, if he cared to escape criticism from his relatives. The next afternoon Miss Amelia, on her daily visit to the exalted place of her new grandniece, remarked, "Well, Marcia, has Miranda gone home yet? I'd think her grandmother would need her after all this time, poor old lady. And you're perfectly strong and able now to attend to your own work again."

Marcia's face flushed, and she gathered her baby closer as if to protect her from the chill that would follow.

"Why, Aunt Amelia," she said brightly, "what do you think! Miranda isn't going home at all. David has a foolish idea he wants her to stay with me and help look after the baby. Besides, he wants me to go with him as I've been doing. I told him it wasn't necessary, but he wanted it. So he's arranged it all, and Mrs. Heath has given her consent."

"Miranda stay here!" The words fell like icicles. Then followed more.

"I am *surprised* at you, Marcia. I thought you had more self-respect than that! It's a disgrace to a young, strong woman to let her husband hire a girl to do her work while she gads about the country and leaves her house and her young child. If your own mother had lived she'd have taught you better than that. And then, *Miranda, of all people to select!* The child of a renegade! A waif dependent, utterly thankless and irresponsible! She's scatterbrained and untrustworthy. If you needed anyone at any time to sit with the child while you were out for a legitimate cause to call or visit occasionally, either Hortense or I'd be glad to come and relieve you. Indeed, you mustn't think of leaving this wild, good-for-nothing Miranda Griscom with my nephew's child!

"I'll speak to Hortense, and we'll make it our business to come down every day, one or the other of us, and do anything you find your strength is unequal to doing. We're still strong enough, I hope, to do anything for the family honor. I'd be ashamed to have it known that David Spafford's wife was such a weakling she had to hire help. The young wives of our family have always been proud of their housekeeping."

Now Miranda Griscom, whatever might be said of her other virtues, had no convictions against eavesdropping. And with this particular caller she felt it especially necessary to serve her mistress in any way she could. She was sharp enough to know Miss Amelia wouldn't be in favor of her being in David Spafford's household, and she felt her mistress would have to bear some persecution on her account. She therefore resolved to be on hand to protect her. Soon after the aunt was seated with Marcia in the large front bedroom where the cradle was established, Miranda approached the door and applied her ear to the generous crack. She could feel the subject turning to her and had already devised a plan.

As Marcia lifted her face, trying to remove the angry flash from her eyes and think of how to reply to the old woman, Miranda burst into the room.

"Oh, Miss Amelia, 'scuse me fer interruptin', but did your nice old gray cat mebbe foller you down here, and could it 'a' ben her out on our front porch fightin' with Bob Sykes's yellow dog? 'Cause ef 'tis, sumpin' ought to be done right off, 'r he'll bake hash outa her. S'pose you come down an' look. I wouldn't like to make a mistake 'bout it."

Miss Amelia placed her hand on her heart and looked helplessly at Marcia for an instant. "Oh, my dear, you don't suppose——" she began in a trembling voice.

Then she gathered up her shawl and hurried down the stairs after the sympathetic Miranda.

"Come right out here softly," Miranda said, opening the front door cautiously. "Why, they must 'a' gone around the house!"

The old woman followed the girl out on the porch, and together they looked on both sides of the house. But they saw no trace of dog or cat.

"Where could they 'a' gone?" inquired Miranda excitedly. "Mebbe I ought 'a' jus' called you and stayed here an' watched, but I was afraid to wake the baby. You don't suppose that cat would 'a' run home, an' he after her? Is that them up the street? Don't you see a whirl o' dust in the road? Would you like me to go an' see? 'Cause I'm most afraid ef she's tried to run home, fer Bob Sykes hes trained thet dog to run races, an' he's a turrible fast runner, an' your cat is gettin' on in years. It might go hard with her."

Miranda's sympathetic tone quite excited the old woman, whose old gray cat was very dear to her, being the last descendant of an ancient line of cats traditional in the family.

"No, Miranda, you just stay right here. Mrs. Spafford might need you after all this excitement. Tell her not to worry until I know the worst. I'll go right home and see if anything has happened to Matthew. It would be very distressing to me and my sister. If he's escaped from that dog he'll need attention. Just tell Mrs. Spafford I'll come down or send Hortense tomorrow as I promised." And the dignified old lady hurried off up the village street, for once unmindful of her dignity.

"Miranda!" called Marcia, when she'd waited a reasonable time for the aunt's return and not even the girl presented herself.

Miranda appeared in a minute, with a meek yet triumphant mien.

Marcia's eyes were laughing, but she tried to look serious.

"Miranda," she began, trying to suppress the merriment in her voice, "did you really see that cat out there?"

Miranda hesitated for a reply. "Well, I heard a dog bark—"

"Miranda, was that quite honest?" protested Marcia. She felt she should try to improve the moral standard of the girl thus under her charge and influence.

"I don't see anythin' wrong with that," asserted Miranda. "I didn't say a word that wasn't true. I'm always careful 'bout that sence I see how much you think of such things. I asked her ef it might 'a' ben her cat, an' how do I know but 'twas? And it would be easy to 'a' ben Bob Sykes's dog, ef it *was* round, fer that dog never lets a cat come on his block. Anyway I heard a dog bark, and I thought it sounded like Bob's dog. I'm pretty good on sounds."

"But you shouldn't frighten Aunt Amelia. She's an old lady, and it isn't good for old people to get frightened. You know she thinks a great deal of her cat."

"Well, it ain't good fer you to be badgered, and Mr. David told me to look after you, an' I'm doin' it the best way I know how. If I don't do it right I s'pose you'll send me back to Grandma's, an' then who'll take care of that blessed baby!"

When Marcia told it all to David he laughed until tears came.

"Good for Miranda! She'll do, and Aunt Amelia'll never know what happened to poor old Matthew, who was probably napping quietly by the hearth. Well, little girl, I'm glad you didn't have to answer Aunt Amelia's questions. Leave her to me. I'll shoulder all the blame and exonerate you. Don't worry."

"But, David," began Marcia, "Miranda shouldn't tell things that aren't exactly true. How can I teach her?"

"Well, Miranda's standards aren't exactly right, and we must try little by little to raise them higher. But I'll miss my guess if she doesn't manage some way to protect you, even if she does have to tell the truth."

And thus it was that Miranda Griscom became a fixture in the Spafford household and did about as she pleased with her master and mistress and the baby, because she usually pleased to do well.

The years went by, and little Rose Spafford grew into a laughing, dimpled child with charming ways that reminded one of her mother, and Miranda was her devoted slave.

On the Sunday after Phoebe Deane's birthday, David, Marcia, Rose, and Miranda all sat in church together. Rose, in dainty pantalets and dress, sat between her mother and Miranda and waited for the sugared caraway seeds she knew would be dropped occasionally into her lap if she were good. David sat at the end of his pew, happy and devout, with Marcia beside him, and Miranda alert, one eye on her worship, the other on what might happen about her.

Across the aisle the sweet face of Phoebe Deane attracted her attention. It was clouded with trouble. Miranda's keen eyes saw that at once. Miranda had often noticed that about Phoebe Deane and wondered, but there were so many other people Miranda had to look after. So Phoebe Deane had never before received her undivided attention.

But this particular morning Phoebe looked so pretty in her buff merino that Miranda was all attention at once. Miranda, homely and red-haired and freckled, whose clothes had been made from Hannah Heath's cast-off wardrobe, yet loved beautiful things and beautiful people. Phoebe, with her brown hair and starry eyes, seemed like a lovely picture to her in the buff merino, with her face framed in its neat straw bonnet.

As her eyes traveled over Phoebe's dress they came finally to the face, so grave and sweet and troubled, as if life was too filled with perplexities to have much joy left in it. Then she looked at the sharp lines of Emmeline's sour face with its thin, pursed lips and decided Emmeline was not a pleasant woman to live with. Alma, preening herself in her Sunday clothes, wasn't a pleasant child either, and she wondered if Phoebe could possibly take any pleasure in putting on her little garments for her and planning surprises and plays, the way she did for Rose. It seemed impossible. Miranda looked down tenderly at Rose, then gratefully toward David and Marcia at the end of the pew, and pitied Phoebe, wishing for her the happiness that had come into her own barren life.

The service was about to commence when Judge Bristol, with his daughter Janet and her cousin Nathaniel Graham, walked up the aisle to their pew, just in front of Albert Deane's.

Now Phoebe had debated hard about coming to church that morning, for she couldn't keep her mind off the stranger who had been so kind to her a few days before. It was impossible not to wonder if he'd be there and whether he would see her and speak to her.

And Phoebe would gladly have stayed at home if she wouldn't have had to explain her reasons to Albert.

She rode to church that morning half ashamed of herself for the undeniable wish to see the stranger once more. When she got out of the carryall at church, she didn't look around or even lift her eyes to see who was standing by the door. She resolved not to think about him. If he came up the aisle, she wouldn't know it, and her eyes would be otherwise occupied. No one would dare say she was watching for him.

Nevertheless, as Janet and her cousin came up the aisle, Phoebe knew by the wild beating of her heart that he was coming, and she commanded her eyes not to lift from the hymnbook in her lap. Yet, in spite of her resolve, when the occupants of the Bristol pew had entered it and were about to sit down, and Nathaniel Graham stood so that his head and shoulders were just above the top of the high-back pew, her eyes fluttered up for one glance—and in that instant they were caught and held by the eyes of the young man in pleased recognition.

In a flash Phoebe's eyes were back on her book, and the young man was seated in the pew with only the top of his fine dark head showing. Yet color rushed into the girl's cheeks, and the young man's eyes held a light of satisfaction that lasted through the service. The glance had been too brief for any act of recognition, like a bow or a smile, and neither would have been in place, for the whole audience could have seen them as he was faced about. Moreover the service had begun. Not a soul witnessed the glance, save the keen-eyed Miranda, and instantly she recognized a certain something that put her on the watch. So Miranda, through the whole long service, studied their faces and wove a romance for herself out of the golden fabric of a glance.

Chapter 8

*W*hen the service ended, Phoebe made sure her eyes didn't look toward the stranger. Nathaniel Graham was kept busy for the first few moments shaking hands with old friends and talking with the minister, who came down from the pulpit on purpose to greet him. When he turned around at his first opportunity, the pew behind him was empty, and the eyes that had met his when he came in were nowhere to be seen.

He looked over the receding audience toward the open door and caught the glimmer of the buff merino. Hastily excusing himself to Janet, Nathaniel made his way down the aisle, disappointing some kind old ladies who had been friends of his mother and who lay in wait for him at various pew doors.

Miranda saw it all, and her eager eyes watched to see if he would catch Phoebe. The way being open just then, she pressed out into the aisle and, for once leaving Rose to follow after her mother, hurried to the door.

Nathaniel didn't overtake Phoebe until she'd gone down the church steps and was on the path in front of the church-yard. He stepped up beside her, taking off his hat with a cheery "Good morning," and Phoebe's pink cheeks and smiling eyes welcomed him happily.

"I wanted to be quite sure you were all right after your adventure the other day," he said, looking down into the lovely face with real pleasure.

Before she could answer, Hiram Green stepped up airily as

if he belonged and looked at Nathaniel questioningly, saying, "Well, here you are, Phoebe. I lost track of you at the church door. We better step along. The carryall is waitin'."

Nathaniel looked up, annoyed, then puzzled, recognized Hiram with astonishment and said, "I beg your pardon. I didn't know I was keeping you from your friends," to Phoebe. Lifting his hat with a courteous "Good morning, Mr. Green," to Hiram, he stepped back among the little throng coming out the church door.

Now Miranda had been close behind, for she was determined to read every chapter of her romance that appeared in sight. She saw the whole maneuver on Hiram Green's part and the color that flamed angrily into Phoebe's cheek when she recognized Hiram's interference. She also saw the dismay in the girl's face as Nathaniel left her and Hiram Green made as if to walk beside her. Phoebe looked wildly about. There seemed no escape from him as a companion without making a deliberate scene, yet her whole soul revolted at having Nathaniel Graham see her walk off with Hiram.

Quick as a flash, Miranda caught the meaning of Phoebe's look and flew to her assistance.

"Phoebe! Phoebe Deane!" she called. "Wait a minute. I want to tell you something!"

She had raised her voice on purpose, for she stood directly behind Nathaniel. As she'd hoped, he turned to see Phoebe respond. She noted the sudden light in his eyes as he saw the girl to whom he'd just been talking respond to the name, but she didn't know it was a light of satisfaction because he'd found out her name without asking anyone.

He stood a moment and looked after them. He saw Phoebe dismiss the sulky Hiram with a word and go off with Miranda. He saw that Hiram didn't even raise his hat on leaving Phoebe but slouched off angrily without a word.

"Say, Phoebe," said Miranda, "my Mrs. Spafford"—this was

her common way of speaking of Marcia in the possessive—
"she's ben talkin' a long time 'bout you and wishin' you'd come
to see her, an' she's ben layin' out to ask you to tea, but things
hes prevented. So could you come Tuesday? You better come
early and stay all afternoon, so you can play with Rose. She's
the sweetest thing!"

"Oh, I'd love to come," said Phoebe, her face aglow with
pleasure. "I've always admired Mrs. Spafford so much, and little Rose is beautiful. Yes, tell her I'll come."

Just then came the strident voice of Emmeline.

"Phoebe! Phoebe Deane! Was you intendin' to go home
with us, or had you calculated to ride with Hiram Green? If
you're comin' with us, we can't wait all day."

With angry heart and trembling limbs Phoebe bade
Miranda good-bye and climbed into the carriage, not daring
to look behind her to see who had heard her sister-in-law's
hateful words. Oh, had the stranger heard them? How
dreadful if he had! How contemptible, how unforgivable of
Emmeline! She didn't even dare lift her eyes as they drove
by the church but sat with drooping lashes and burning
cheeks—missing Nathaniel Graham's glance as he stood on
the sidewalk with his cousin, waiting for another opportunity to lift his hat.

Miranda watched the Deanes drive away and turned with a
vindictive look of triumph to see Hiram Green getting into
his chaise alone. Then she began to reflect upon what she'd
done.

About four o'clock that afternoon, the dinner dishes being
well out of the way and the Sunday quiet resting upon the
house, Miranda went to Marcia with the guiltiest look on her
face that Marcia had ever seen her wear.

"Well, I've up an' done it now, Mrs. Marcia, an' no mistake.
I expect I'll have to leave you, an' the thought of it jes' breaks
my heart."

"Why, Miranda!" said Marcia, sitting up very suddenly from the couch. "You're not—you're surely not going to get married!"

"Not by a jugful I ain't. Do you s'pose I'd hev enny man that would take up with freckles an' a turn-up nose in a wife? I've gone and done sumpin' you'll think is a heap worse'n gittin' married. But I didn't tell no lie. I was keerful enough 'bout that. I only told her you'd been talkin' 'long back 'bout askin' her, an' you hed all right 'nough, only I oughtn't to 'a' ast her, an' set the day an' all 'thout you knowin'. I knowed it at the time well 'nough, but I hed to do it, 'cause the circumstances wuz sech. You see thet squint-eyed Hiram Green was makin' it out that she was somewhat great to him, a-paradin' down the walk there from the church an' a-driven' off that nice city cousin of Janet Bristol's with his nice, genteel manners an' his tippin' of his hat, an' her a-lookin' like she'd drop from shame, so I called her to wait, an' I runs up an' talks to her, an' course then she tells Hiram Green he needn't trouble to wait fer her, an' we goes off together in full sight of all. My, I was glad I beat that skinflint Hiram Green, but I was that excited I jes' couldn't think of 'nother thing to do 'cept invite her."

"Who in the world are you talking about, Miranda? And what terrible thing have you done?"

Marcia's laughing eyes reassured Miranda, and she went on with her story.

"Why, that pretty little Phoebe Deane," she explained. "I've invited her to tea Tuesday night. I thought that would suit you better than any other time. Monday night things ain't straight from washday yet, and I didn't want to put it off too long, an' I can make everything myself. But if you don't like it I'll go an' tell her the hull truth on't; only she did look so mortal pleased I hate to spoil her fun."

By degrees Marcia drew the whole story from Miranda,

even to a lavish description of the buff merino and its owner's drooping expression.

"Well, I don't see why you thought I'd be displeased," said Marcia. "It's only right you should invite company once in a while. I'm glad you invited her, and as you do most of the work and know our plans pretty well, you knew it would likely be convenient. I'm glad you invited her."

And she gave Miranda one of the smiles that had so endeared her to the lonely girl's heart. Then Miranda went back to her kitchen comforted.

The prospect of another tea party made Phoebe forget the annoyances of her home all through the dull Sabbath afternoon and the trials of Monday with its heavy work. After supper Emmeline produced a great basket of mending which she announced was "all to be finished and put away that evening." Phoebe sat beside the candle and sewed with weary fingers, longing to be away from them all where she might think over quietly the pleasant things that had come into her life.

Hiram Green came in, too, and with a purpose, for he was hardly seated in his usual chair when he began: "Say, Albert, did you see the nincompoop of a nephew of Judge Bristol in the church? Does beat all how he takes on airs jest because he's been off to college. I ken remember him fishin' in his bare feet, and here he was bowin' round among the ladies like he'd always been a fine gentleman and never done a stroke of work in his life. His hands are ez white and soft ez a woman's. He strikes me very ladylike, indeed he does. Smirkin' round and takin' off his hat ez if he'd nothin' better to do. Fine feathers don't make fine birds, I say. I don't believe he could cut a swath o' hay now to save his precious little life. He makes me sick with his airs. Seems like Miss Janet better look after him ef she expects to marry him, er he'll lose his head to every girl he meets."

Something uncontrollable seemed to steal the blood out of

Phoebe's heart for a moment, and all her strength was slipping from her. Then a mighty anger rolled through her being and surged to her very fingertips; yet she held those fingers steadily as her needle pierced back and forth through the stocking she was darning. She knew these remarks were entirely for her benefit, and she resolved not to let Hiram see she understood or cared.

"Is he going to marry his cousin Janet?" asked Albert. "I never heard that."

"You didn't? Well, where've you ben all these years? It's ben common talk sence they was little tads. Their mothers 'lowed that was the way it was to be, and they was sent away to separate schools on that account. I s'pose they was afraid they'd take a dislike to each other ef they saw each other constant. 'Pon my word, I think Janet could look higher, an' ef I was her I wouldn't be held by no promise of no dead mothers. But they do say she worships the very ground he walks on, an' she'll hold him to all right enough, so it's no sort o' use fer any other girls to go anglin' after him."

"I heard he's real bright," said Albert genially. "They say he's taken honors, a good many of 'em. He was president of the Philomathean Society in Union College, you know, and that's a great honor."

Albert read a good deal and knew more about the world's affairs than Hiram.

"Oh, bah! That's child's play!" sneered Hiram. "Who couldn't be president of a literary society? It don't take much spunk to preside. I ran the town meeting last year 'bout's well 's ef I'd ben a college president. My opinion is Nate Graham would'v' 'mounted to more ef he'd stayed t' home an' learned farmin' er studied law with his uncle an' worked fer his board. A feller thet's all give over to lyin' around makin' nuthin' of himself don't amount to a row o' pins."

"But they say Dr. Nott thinks he's got brains," persisted

Albert. "I'm sure I'd like to see him come out on top. I heard he was studying law in New York now. He was always a pleasant-spoken boy when he was here."

"What's pleasant speakin'!" growled Hiram. "It can't sell a load o' wheat." His unsold wheat was bitterly in his thoughts.

"Well, I don't know 'bout that, Hiram." Albert felt pleasantly argumentative. "I don't know but if I was going to buy wheat I'd a little sooner buy off the man that was pleasant-spoken than the man that wasn't."

Hiram sat glumly and pondered this saying for a few minutes.

Phoebe took advantage of the pause in conversation to lay down her workbasket and say determinedly to Emmeline, "I'll finish these stockings tomorrow, Emmeline. I feel tired, and I'm going upstairs."

It was the first time Phoebe had ever dared take a stand against Emmeline's orders. Emmeline was too astonished to speak for a minute, but just as Phoebe reached the door she said, "Well, really! Tired! I was down half an hour before you this mornin', and I'm not tired to speak of, but I suppose ef I was I'd have to keep right on. And who's to do your work tomorrow mornin' while you do this, I'd like to know?"

But Phoebe had escaped out of hearing, and Emmeline relapsed into vexed silence. Hiram, however, narrowed his cruel little eyes and thought he understood why she had gone.

Chapter 9

*P*hoebe had pondered much on how she should announce her intended absence that afternoon, almost deciding at one time to slip away without saying a word, but her heart wouldn't allow that.

So while the family ate breakfast she said to Emmeline, "I wish you'd tell me what work you want done besides the rest of the ironing. I'm invited out to tea this afternoon, and I want to get everything done this morning."

"Where to?" exploded Alma.

"Indeed!" said Emmeline disdainfully. "Invited out to tea! What airs we're takin' on with our money! Pretty soon you won't have any time to give at home at all. If I was you I'd go and board somewhere; you have so many social engagements. I'm sure I don't feel like askin' a young lady like you to soil her hands washin' my dishes. I'll wash 'em myself after this. Alma, you go get your apern on and help Ma this mornin'. Aunt Phoebe hasn't got time. She'll have to take all mornin' to curl her hair."

"Now, Emmeline!" said Albert, gently reproachful. "Don't tease the child. It's real nice for her to get invited out. She don't get much chance, that's sure."

"Oh, no, two tea parties inside of a week's nothin'. I've heard of New York ladies goin' out as often as every other day," said Emmeline sarcastically.

Albert never could quite understand his wife's sarcasm, so he turned to Phoebe and voiced the question everyone was bursting with curiosity to have answered.

"Who invited you, Phoebe?"

"Mrs. Spafford," said Phoebe, trying not to show how near she was to crying over Emmeline's hateful speeches.

"Well, now, that's real nice," said Albert. "There isn't a finer man in town than David Spafford. His paper's the best-edited in the whole state of New York, and he's got a fine little wife. I don't believe she's many days older than you are, Phoebe. She looked real young when he brought her here, and she hasn't grown a day older that I can see."

"Good reason why," sniffed Emmeline. "She's nothin' to do but lie around and be waited on. I'm sure Phoebe's welcome to such friends if they suit her. Fer my part I'd rather go to see good self-respectin' women that did a woman's work in the world and not let their husbands make babies of them and go ridin' round in a carriage forever lookin' like a June mornin'. I call it lazy, I do. It's nothin' more n' less—and she keepin' that poor good-fer-nothin' Miranda Griscom slavin' from mornin' to night fer her. If Phoebe was my sister I shouldn't choose such friends fer her. Besides, she hasn't got very good manners not to invite your wife, too, Albert Deane. But I suppose you never thought o' that. I shouldn't think Phoebe would care to accept an invitation that was an insult to her relations, even if they wasn't just blood relations—they're all she's got, that's sure."

"Say, look here, Emmeline. Your speech don't hang to-gether. You just said you didn't care to make friends of Mrs. Spafford, and now you're fussing because she didn't invite you, too. It looks like a case of sour grapes, eh, Phoebe?"

Hank caught the joke and laughed loudly, though Phoebe looked grave, knowing how bitter it would be to Emmeline to be laughed at. Two red spots flamed out on Emmeline's cheeks, and her eyes snapped.

"Seems to me things has gone pretty far, Albert Deane," she said in a high, excited voice, "when you can insult your wife in public and then laugh! I shan't forget this, Albert Deane!" And with her head well up she shoved her chair back from the table and left the room, slamming the door shut behind her.

Albert's merry laugh came to an abrupt end. He looked after his wife with startled surprise. Never in all their wedded life had Emmeline taken offense like that around others. He looked helplessly, inquiringly, from one to another.

"Well, now," he began, "you don't suppose she thought I meant that."

" 'Course!" said Alma. "You've made her dreadful mad, Pa. My! But you're goin' to get it!"

"Looks mighty like it," snickered Hank.

Albert looked at Phoebe for a reply.

"I'm afraid she thought you were in earnest, Albert. You better go and explain," said Phoebe.

"You better not go fer a while, Pa," called out Johnny. "Wait till she gets over it a little. Go hide in the barn. That's the way I do!"

But Albert was going heavily up the stairs after his offended wife and didn't hear his young son's hopeful voice. He wished if possible to explain away the offense before it struck in too deep for healing and had to be lived down.

This state of things was more helpful to Phoebe than otherwise. Hank took himself off, embarrassed by Phoebe's dignified silence. The children slipped away. Phoebe went at her work unhindered and accomplished it quickly while her thoughts dwelled on the afternoon before her. Upstairs the conference was long and uncertain. Phoebe could hear the low rumbling of Albert's conciliatory tones and the angry rasp of Emmeline's tearful charges. He came downstairs looking sad and tired about an hour before dinnertime and hurried out to the barn to his neglected duties.

He paused in the kitchen to say to Phoebe, "You mustn't

mind what Emmeline says, child. Her bark's a great deal worse than her bite always. And, after all, she's had it pretty hard with all the children staying in so much. I'm sure she appreciates what you do. I'm sure she does, but it isn't her way to say much about it. You just go out to tea and have a good time and don't think anymore about this. It'll blow over, you know. Most things do."

Phoebe tried to smile and felt a throb of gratitude toward the brother who really wasn't her brother at all.

"You're a good girl, Phoebe," he went on. "You're like your mother. She was little and pretty and liked things nice and had a quiet voice. I sometimes think maybe it isn't as pleasant here for you as it might be. You're made of different kind of stuff. Your mother was, too. I've often wondered whether Father understood her. Men don't understand women very well, I guess. Now I don't really always understand Emmeline, and I guess it's pretty hard for her. Father could be rough and blunt, and maybe that was hard for your mother at times. I remember she used to look sad, though I never saw her much, come to think of it. I was off working for myself when they were married, you know.

"Say, Phoebe," he continued, "you didn't for a minute think I meant what I said about sour grapes and Emmeline, did you? I told her you didn't, but I promised her I'd make sure about it. I knew you didn't. Well, I must go out and see if Hank's done everything."

He went out drawing a long breath as if he'd accomplished an unpleasant task and left Phoebe wondering about her own mother from the words Albert had spoken. Those sentences in her birthday letter came back to her: *Unless you can marry a man to whom you can look up and honor next to God, it's better not to marry at all, believe me. I say it lovingly, for I've seen much sorrow and would protect you.*

Had her father been hard to live with? Phoebe put the

thought from her and was almost glad she couldn't answer it. But it made her heart throb with a sense of a fuller understanding of her mother's life and warnings.

Emmeline didn't come downstairs until dinnertime, and her manner was freezing. She poured the coffee, drank a cup of it herself, and ate a bit of bread but wouldn't touch anything else on the table—food Phoebe had prepared. She wouldn't respond to the solicitations of her anxious husband, who urged this and that upon her. Hank even suggested the hot biscuits were nicer than usual. But that remark had to be lived down by Hank, for Emmeline usually made the biscuits, and Phoebe had made these. She didn't even look at him in response.

Phoebe was glad when the last bit of pumpkin pie and cheese had disappeared and she could rise from her chair and go about the after-dinner work. Glad, too, that Emmeline went away again and left her to herself, for that way she could more quickly finish up.

She was just hanging up her wiping towels when Emmeline came downstairs with the look of a martyr on her face and the quilting frames in her hand. Over her shoulder was thrown her latest achievement in patchwork, a brilliant combination of reds and yellows and white known as the "rising sun" pattern. It was a large quilt and would be quite a job for one person to put on the frames without an assistant.

Phoebe stopped with an exclamation of dismay.

"You're not going to put that on the frames today, Emmeline? I thought you were saving that for next month!"

Emmeline's grim mouth remained shut for several seconds. At last she snapped out, "I don't know that it makes any difference what you thought. This is a free country, and I've surely a right to do what I please in my own house."

"But, Emmeline, I can't help you this afternoon!"

"I don't know that I've asked you!"

"But you can't do it alone!"

"Indeed! What makes you think I can't! Go right along to your tea party. I was brought up to work, thank fortune, and a few burdens more or less can't make much difference. I'm not a lady of leisure and means like you."

Phoebe stood a minute watching Emmeline's stubby, determined fingers as they fitted a wooden peg into its socket like a period to the conversation. It seemed dreadful to go away and leave Emmeline to put up that quilt alone, but what was she to do? No law in the universe would compel her to give up her first invitation to tea so Emmeline might finish that quilt this particular week.

It was plain she brought it down on purpose to hold her at home. Indignation boiled within Phoebe. If she'd slipped stealthily away this wouldn't have happened, but she'd done her duty in telling Emmeline, and she felt perfectly justified in going. It wasn't as if she'd invited herself. It wouldn't be polite, now that she'd accepted the invitation, not to go. So with sudden determination Phoebe left the kitchen and went up to dress.

She fastened on the buff merino, put her hair in order and tied on her locket, but nowhere could she find the little brown velvet bow that belonged to her hair. She hadn't missed it before, for on Sunday she'd worn her bonnet and dressed in a hurry. In perplexity she looked over her neat boxes of scant finery but couldn't find it. She had to hurry away without it.

She went out the other door, for she couldn't bear to see Emmeline putting up that sunrise quilt alone. The thought of it seemed to cloud the sun and spoil anticipation of her precious afternoon.

Once out in the crisp autumn air, she drew a long breath of relief. It was so good to get away from the gloomy atmosphere that had cramped her life for so many years. In a lonely place in the road between farmhouses, she uttered a soft little scream under her breath. She felt as if she must do something to let out the agony of wrath and longing and hurt and indignity that threatened to burst her soul. Then she walked on to the town with demure dignity, and the people in the passing carryalls and farm wagons never suspected she was anything but a happy maiden filled with life's joys.

The autumn days lingered in sunny deep-blue haze, though the reds were changing into brown and in the fields there gathered huddled groups of corn shocks like old crones, waving skeleton arms in the breeze and whispering weird gossip. A rusty-throated cricket in the thicket piped out his monotonous dirge to the summer now deceased. A flight of birds sprang into sight across the sky, calling and chattering to one another of a warmer climate. An old red cow stood in her well-grazed meadow, snuffed the short grass and, looking at Phoebe as she passed, mooed a gentle protest at the decline of fresh vegetables. Everything spoke of autumn and the winter that was to come. But Phoebe, with every step she took from home, grew lighter and lighter-hearted.

She wasn't thinking of the stranger, for there was no possibility of meeting him. The Bristol place, a fine old Colonial house behind a tall white fence and high hedge, was over near the Presbyterian church. It wasn't near the Spaffords' house. She felt the freer and happier because there was no question of him to trouble her careful conscience.

Miranda had gone to the window that looked up the road toward the Deanes' at least twenty times since the dinner dishes were washed. She was more nervous over the success of this, her first tea party, than over anything she'd ever done. She was beginning to be afraid her guest wouldn't arrive.

Fidgeting from window to door and back again to the kitchen, Miranda came at last to the library where Marcia sat with her work, watching a frolic between Rose and her kitten outside the window.

"Say, Mrs. Marcia," she began, "you'll find out what troubles that poor little thing and see ef you can't help her, won't you? She's your size an' kind, more'n she is mine, an' you ought to be able to give her some help. You needn't think you've got to tell me everything you find out. I shan't ask. I can find out enough fer my own use when I'm needed, but I think she needs you this time. When there's any use fer me, I seem always to kind o' feel it in the air."

"Bless your heart, Miranda. I don't believe you care for anyone unless. they need helping!" exclaimed Marcia. "What makes you so sure Phoebe Deane needs helping?"

"Oh, I know," said Miranda mysteriously, "an' so will you when you look at her real hard. There she comes now. Don't you go an' tell I said nothin' 'bout her. You jes' make her tell you. She's that sweet an' so are you that you two can't help pourin' out your perfume to each other like two flowers."

"But trouble isn't perfume, Miranda."

"Hmm! Flowers smells all the sweeter when you crush 'em a little, don't they? There, you set right still where you be. I'll go to the door. Don't you stir. I want her to see you lookin' that way with the sun across the top o' your pretty hair. She'll like it—I know she will."

Marcia sat quite still as she was bidden with the peaceful smile on her lips that David loved so well, smiling over Miranda's strange fancies, yet never thinking of herself as a picture against the windowpanes. In a moment more, Phoebe Deane stood in the doorway, with Miranda beside her, looking from one to the other of the two sweet girl-faces in deep admiration and noting with delight that Phoebe fully appreciated the loveliness of her "Mrs. Marcia."

Chapter 10

The afternoon was one of bliss to Phoebe. She laid aside her troubles with her bonnet and basked in the sunlight of Marcia's smile. Here was something she had never known, the friendship of another girl not much older than she was. Marcia, though she'd grown in heart and intellect during her five years of beautiful companionship with David Spafford, hadn't lost the years she skipped by her early marriage but kept their memory fresh in her heart. Perhaps it was the girl in her that attracted her to Phoebe Deane.

They fell into conversation at once. They talked about their mothers, these two who had known so little of real mothering. And Marcia, because she'd felt it herself, understood the wistfulness in Phoebe's tone when she spoke of her loneliness and her longing for her mother. Phoebe told of her mother's birthday letter and the buff merino, and Marcia smoothed down the soft folds of the skirt reverently and told Phoebe it was beautiful, like a present from heaven. She made Phoebe come out where little Rose was, and they played until the child was Phoebe's devoted slave. Then they all went back to the big stately parlor, where Miranda had a great fire of logs blazing. There in a deep easy chair Phoebe was ensconced with Rose cuddled in her lap.

Marcia played exquisite music on her pianoforte, which to the ear of the girl, who seldom heard any music in her life save the singing in church or singing school, seemed entrancing. She almost forgot the child in her lap, forgot to look about on the beautiful room so full of interesting things, forgot even to think as she listened. Her very soul responded to the music.

Then suddenly the music ceased, and Marcia sprang up, saying, "Oh, there's David!" and went to the door to let him in.

Phoebe exclaimed in dismay that it was so late and the beautiful afternoon was at an end. But she forgot her disappointment in wonder over Marcia's joy at her husband's arrival. It brought back the subject that had been in her thoughts ever since the night Hiram Green followed her into the orchard.

Somehow she'd grown up with very little halo about the institution of marriage. It had seemed to her a kind of necessary arrangement but never anything that gave great joy. The married people she knew didn't seem to rejoice in one another's presence. Indeed, they often seemed to be a hindrance to each other. She had never cherished bright dreams of marriage for herself, as most girls do. Life had been too dully tinted since her childhood for her to indulge fancies.

Therefore it was a revelation to her to see how much these two souls cared for one another. She saw it in their glance, in a sudden lighting of the eye, the involuntary cadence of the voice, the evident pleasure of yielding each to the other, the constant presence of joy as a guest in that house, because of the presence of each other. One could never feel that way about Hiram Green—it would be impossible! But hadn't that been the very thing his poor crushed little wife possessed? Yet how could she feel it when it wasn't returned?

She began to think over the married households she knew, but she knew so few of them intimately. There was Granny McVane. Did her husband feel that way about her? And did she spring to meet him at the door after all these years of hard life? Something about the sweet face in its ruffled cap made Phoebe think it possible. And there was Albert. Of course Emmeline didn't feel so, for Emmeline wasn't that kind of woman. But mightn't a different woman have felt that for Albert? He was kind and gentle to women. Too slow and easy to gain real respect, yet—yes, she felt that some women might feel real joy in his presence. There lurked a possibility that he felt that way toward Emmeline, to some degree. But Hiram Green, with his hat pulled down over the narrow eyes, above his cruel mouth—never! He was utterly incapable of so beautiful a feeling. If only he might leave her world forever, it would be a great relief.

When he entered the parlor, David Spafford not only filled it with pleasure for his wife and little girl but brought an added cheer for the guest as well. Phoebe found herself talking with this man of literature and politics and science as easily as if she'd known him well all her life. Afterward she wondered at herself. Somehow he took it for granted that she knew as much as he did, and he made her feel at ease at once.

He asked after Albert Deane as though he were an old friend and seemed to know more about him than Phoebe dreamed. "He has a good head," he added in response to Phoebe's timid answer about the farm and some improvements Albert had introduced. "I had a long talk with him the other day and enjoyed it." Somehow that little remark made Phoebe more at home. She knew Albert's shortcomings keenly, and she wasn't deeply attached to him, but he was all she had, and he'd been kind to her.

Miranda had just called them to supper, and they had reached the table and settled on the right places when the knocker sounded through the hall.

Phoebe looked up, startled. Living as she did in the country, a guest who wasn't intimate enough to walk in without knocking was rare, so an occasion for the knocker to sound would bring forth startled exclamations in the Deane family. But Marcia gave the sign to be seated, and Miranda hastened to the door.

"It's just one of the boys from the office, I think, Marcia," said David. "I told him to bring up the mail if anything important came. The coach wasn't in when I left."

But a man's voice was heard conversing with Miranda.

"I won't keep him but a minute! I'm sorry to disturb him," the voice said. A moment more and Miranda appeared with a guileless face.

"A man to see you, Mr. Spafford. I think it's the nevview of Jedge Bristol's. Shall I tell him you're eatin' supper?"

"What! Nathaniel Graham? No, indeed, Miranda. Just put on another plate and bring him in. Come in, Nathaniel, and take tea with us while you tell us your errand. You're just the one we need to complete our company."

Miranda, innocent and cheerful, hurried away to obey orders, while David helped the willing guest off with his overcoat and brought him to the table. She felt there was no need to say anything about a conversation she'd had with Judge Bristol's "nevview" that afternoon. It was while Marcia was playing the pianoforte in the parlor. Miranda had gone into the garden to pick a bunch of parsley for her chicken gravy—and, as was her custom, to keep a good watch upon all outlying territory. She'd sauntered up to the fence for a glance about and saw Nathaniel Graham coming down the road, wistfully. Yet she dared not add another guest to her tea party, though the very one she would have chosen had wandered her way.

He'd tipped his hat to her and smiled. Miranda liked to have hats tipped to her, even though she was freckled and red-haired. This young man had been in the highest grade of village school when she entered the lowest class, yet he remembered her enough to bow. Her heart swelled with pride in him, and she decided he'd do for the part she wished him to play in life.

"Ah, Miss Miranda," he had paused when almost past, "do you happen to know if Mr. Spafford will be at home this evening? I want to see him very much for a few minutes."

Now, though Miranda had dared not invite another guest, she saw no reason why she shouldn't put him in the way of an invitation. So she'd said thoughtfully, "Let me see! Yes, I think he's at home tonight. Thur's one night this week I heerd him say he was goin' out, but I'm pretty sure it ain't this night. But I'll tell you what you better do ef you're real anxious to see him. You better jest stop 'long about six o'clock. He's always home then, 'n' he'll tell you ef he ain't goin' to be in."

The young man's face had lighted gratefully.

"Thank you. That will suit me very well. I don't need to keep him long, and he can tell me if he'll be in later in the evening. I'll be passing here about that time."

Then Miranda had hustled in with satisfaction to see if her biscuits were beginning to brown. If this plan worked well, nothing further was to be desired.

She spent the remainder of the afternoon in stealthy watch between the kitchen and the parlor door, where, unseen, she could inspect the conversation from time to time and keep advised as to any possible developments. She'd set out to see if Phoebe Deane needed any help, and she meant to have no stone unturned to get at the facts.

So it all happened just as Miranda would have planned. Things were mostly happening her way these days, she told herself with a chuckle and a triumphant glance toward the lights in her grandmother's kitchen, as she went to get another sprigged plate for Nathaniel Graham.

Meanwhile Phoebe's heart was in a great flutter over the introduction. The color came into her cheeks, and her eyes shone like stars in the candlelight as David said, "Nathaniel, let me make you acquainted with our friend, Miss Phoebe Deane. I think she's a newcomer since you left us. Miss Deane, this is our friend Mr. Graham."

And then she found herself murmuring an acknowledgment as the young man took her hand and bowed low over it, saying, "Thank you, David, but I'm not so far behind the times as you think. I've met Miss Deane before."

That flustered her quite a bit, so she could hardly manage to seat herself with her chair properly drawn up to the table. She wondered if they all noticed how her cheeks burned. Ah! If they did they were keeping it to themselves, especially Miranda, who was meekly dishing up the chicken. Wily Miranda! She'd called them to supper without serving it, making due allowance for the digression of another guest she'd planned.

The meal moved along smoothly, with the conversation flowing until Phoebe regained her balance and could take her small, shy part in it. She found pleasure in listening to the talk of David and Nathaniel, so different from that of Albert and Hiram. It was all about the great outside world—politics and the possibilities of war; money and banks and failures; the probabilities of the future; the coming election; the trouble with the Indians; the rumblings of trouble about slavery; the annexation of Texas; the extension of the steam railway.

All of it was new and interesting to Phoebe, who'd heard only a stray word now and then of all these wonderful happenings. Who, for instance, was this "Santa Anna" whose name was spoken of so familiarly? Neither a saint nor a woman, apparently. And what had he or she to do with affairs so serious?

And who was this brave Indian chief Osceola, languishing in prison because he and his people couldn't bear to give up their fathers' home? Why had she never heard of it all before? She'd never thought of the Indians before as anything but terrible, bloodthirsty savages, and, lo, they had feelings and loves and homes like others.

Her cheeks glowed, and her eyes were alight with feeling, and when Nathaniel turned to her now and again, he thought how beautiful she was and marveled that he hadn't heard her praises sung from every mouth as soon as he reached the town. He'd been home very little during his college life and years of law study.

Then the conversation came nearer home, and David and Nathaniel talked of their college days. Nathaniel spoke a great deal of Eliphalet Nott, the honored president of his college, and told many a little anecdote of his wisdom and wit.

"This chicken," he began laughingly, as he held up a wishbone toward Phoebe, "reminds me of a story that's told of Dr. Nott. It seems a number of students planned a raid on his chicken house. Dr. Nott's family consists of him, his wife, and his daughter, Sally. Well, the rumor of this plot against his chicken house reached the good president's ears, and he prepared to circumvent it.

"The students had planned to go to a tree where several favorite fowls roosted, and one was to climb up while the others stood below and took the booty. They waited until it was late and the lights in the doctor's study went out. Then they stole silently into the yard and made for the hen roost. One man climbed carefully into the tree so as not to disturb the sleeping birds, and the others waited in the dark below.

"The first hen made a good deal of cackling and fuss when she was caught, and while this was going on the students below the tree saw someone approaching them from the house. They scattered into the dark and fled, leaving the poor man in the tree alone. Dr. Nott, well muffled about his face, came quietly up and took his stand below the tree, and in a moment the man in the tree handed down a big white rooster.

" 'This is Daddy Nott,' he said in a whisper, and the man below received the bird without a word.

"In a moment more a second fowl was handed down. 'This is Mommy Nott,' whispered the irreverent student. Again the bird was received without comment.

"Then a third hen was handed down with the comment,

'This is Sally Nott.' The doctor received the third bird and disappeared into the darkness, and the student in the tree came down to find his partners fled, with no knowledge of who had taken the fowls.

"They were much troubled about the circumstance but hoped it was only a joke some fellow student had played on them. But the next day they became extremely anxious when each one received an invitation to dine with Dr. Nott that evening. Not daring to refuse, they presented themselves at Dr. Nott's house at the appointed hour and were received courteously as usual. They began to breathe more freely when they were ushered out to dinner, and there, before the doctor's place, lay three large platters, each containing a fine fowl cooked to a turn.

"They dared not look at one another, but their embarrassment came to a climax when Dr. Nott looked up pleasantly at the student on his right, who had been the man to climb the tree, and asked, 'Hastings, will you have a piece of Daddy Nott or Mommy Nott or Sally Nott?' pointing in order to each platter.

"I think if it hadn't been for the twinkle in the doctor's eye those boys would have taken their hats and left without a word, for they say Hastings looked as if you could knock him over with a feather. But that twinkle broke the horror of it, and they all broke down and laughed until they were heartily ashamed of themselves. And every man there was cured forever of robbing chicken roosts. But, do you know, the doctor never said another word to those fellows about it, and they were his most loyal students from that time on."

Amid the laughter over this story, they rose from the table. Little Rose, who had fallen asleep at the table, was whisked off to bed by Miranda, and the others went into the parlor where Marcia played the pianoforte. Phoebe, entranced, listened until suddenly she realized it was half past eight o'clock, and she was some distance from home.

Now, for a young woman to be out after nine o'clock in those days was little short of a crime. It would be deemed highly improper by every good person. Therefore, as Phoebe noted the time, she started to her feet in a panic and made her adieus with haste. Marcia went after her bonnet and tied it lovingly beneath her chin, saying she hoped to have her come again soon. David made as if he'd take her home, but Nathaniel waved him back and begged for that privilege himself. So with happy good nights the young man and the girl went out into the quiet village street together and hastened along the way, where already many of the lights were out in the houses.

Chapter 11

*A*s she stepped out into the moonlight with the young man, Phoebe's heart fluttered so she could scarcely speak without letting her voice shake. It seemed so wonderful that she, of all the girls in the village, should be going home with this bright, handsome, noble man. There was nothing foolish or vain in her thought about it. He would never be anything more to her than he was on this walk, for his life was set otherwise, and he belonged to others—in all likelihood, to his cousin Janet. Nevertheless, she felt honored he'd take the trouble to see her home, and she knew the memory of this walk, her first alone with a young man, would remain with her for life.

He seemed to enjoy her company as much as he had David's, for he talked on about the things that had interested them in the evening. He told more college stories and even spoke of his literary society. Remembering Albert's words, Phoebe asked if it was true he'd once been president of the Philomatheans. He modestly acknowledged it, as though the office gave him honor, not he the office. She asked him shyly of the meetings and what they did, and he gave her reminiscences of his college days. Their voices rang out now and then in a laugh.

Out in the quiet country road he suddenly asked her, "Tell me, Miss Deane. Suppose I knew of some people who were oppressed, suffering, and wanting their freedom; suppose they needed help to set them free. What do you think I should do? Think of myself and my career, or go and help set them free?"

Phoebe raised her eyes to his earnest face in the moonlight and tried to understand.

"I'm not wise," she said, "and perhaps I wouldn't know what you ought to do, but I think I know what you would do. I think you would forget all about yourself and go to set them free."

He looked down into her face and thought what it meant to a man to have a girl like this one believe in him.

"Thank you!" he said gravely. "I'm honored by your opinion of me. You've told me where duty lies. I'll remember your words when the time comes."

In the quiet of her chamber a few minutes later Phoebe remembered the words of the young people that day upon the hillside and wondered if it was the people of Texas he thought needed to be set free.

He had bid her good night with a pleasant ring in his voice, saying he was glad to know her and hoped to see her again before he left for New York in a few days. Then the door closed behind her, and he walked briskly down the frosty way. The night was cold, even for October, and each startled blade of grass was furred with a tiny frost-spike.

Suddenly, out from behind a cluster of tall elder bushes that bordered the roadside stepped a man, and without warning, he dealt Nathaniel a blow between the eyes that made him stagger and almost fall.

"Thet's to teach you to let my girl alone!" snarled Hiram Green like an angry dog, the moonlight illuminating his livid face. "Hev yeh learned yer lesson, er d'yeh need another? 'Cause there's plenty more where that come from!"

Nathaniel's senses were stunned for an instant, but he was a master at self-defense, and before the bully had finished his threat with a curse he found himself lying in the ditch with Nathaniel towering over him in a righteous wrath.

"Coward!" he said, looking down on him contemptuously. "You've made a mistake, of course, and struck the wrong man, but that makes no difference. A brave man doesn't strike in the dark."

"No, I haven't made no mistake either," snarled Hiram as he got up from the ground. "I seen you myself with my own eyes, Nate Graham. I seen you trail down the hill out o' the woods after her, 'n' I seen you try to get a kiss from her, an' she run away. I was an eyewitness. I seen yeh. Then you tried to get 'longside her after meetin' was out Sunday, tippin' yer hat so polite, as ef that was everythin' a girl want'd. An' I seen yeh takin' her home tonight after decent folks was a-bed, walkin' 'long a country road talkin' so sweet an' low butter would've melt in yer mouth. No, sir! I ain't made no mistake. An' I jest want you to understand after this you're not to meddle with Phoebe Deane, for she belongs to me!"

By this time Nathaniel had recognized Hiram Green, and his astonishment and dismay knew no bounds. Could a girl like that have anything to do with this coarse, ignorant man? Indignation filled him. He longed to pound the insolent wretch and make him take back all he'd said, but he realized this might be a serious matter for the girl, and it was necessary to proceed cautiously.

So he drew himself up and replied, "There has never been anything between me and Miss Deane to which anyone, no matter how close their relationship to her might be, could object. I met her in the woods while nutting with a party of friends and had the good fortune to help her out of a tangle of laurel and show her the shortcut to the road. I merely spoke to her on Sunday as I spoke to my other acquaintances, and this evening I escorted her home from the house of a friend where we both have been taking tea."

"You lie!" snarled Hiram.

"What did you say, Mr. Green?"

"I said *you lie*, an' I'll say it again, too, ef I like. You needn't git off any more o' your fine words, fer they don't go down with me, even ef you have been to college. All I've got to say is *you let my girl alone from now on*! Ef yeh don't I'll take means to make ye!" And Hiram raised his big fist again.

But the next instant Hiram was sprawling in the dust, and this time Nathaniel held something gleaming in his hand as he stood above him.

"I always go armed," said Nathaniel in a cool voice. "You'll oblige me by lying still where you are until I'm out of sight down the road. Then it will be quite safe for you to rise and go home and wash your face. If I see you get up before that, I'll shoot. Another thing. If I hear another word of this ridiculous nonsense from you I'll have you arrested and brought before my uncle on charges of assault and blackmail and several other things perhaps. As for speaking to the young lady or showing her any courtesy that is ordinarily shown between men and women in good society, that shall be as Miss Deane says, and not in any way as you say. You are not fit to speak her name."

Nathaniel stepped back slowly a few paces, and Hiram attempted to rise, pouring forth a stream of vile language. Nathaniel halted and raised the pistol, flashing in the moonlight.

"You will keep entirely still, Mr. Green. Remember that this is loaded."

Hiram subsided, and Nathaniel walked deliberately backward till the man on the ground could see only a dim speck in the gray of the distance, and a nighthawk in the trees mocked him in a clamorous tone.

All this happened not a stone's throw away from Albert Deane's front gate and might have been discerned from Phoebe's window if her room hadn't been set on the other side of the house.

After a little while Hiram crawled stiffly up from the ground, looked furtively about, shook his fist at the distance where Nathaniel had disappeared, and slunk like a shadow close to the fence till he reached his house. Only a bit of white paper ground down with a great heel mark and a few footprints in the frosty dust told where the encounter had been.

The moon spread her white light over all, and Phoebe slept, smiling in her dreams of the happy afternoon and evening. But Nathaniel sat up far into the night till his candle burned low and sputtered out. He was thinking, and his thoughts weren't all of the oppressed Texans. It occurred to him that other people in the world might be harder to set free than the Texans.

If Hiram Green didn't sleep it was because his heart was busy with evil plans for revenge. He was by no means done with Nathaniel Graham. He might submit under necessity, but he was a man in whom a sense of injury dwelt long and smoldered into a great fire that grew far beyond all proportion of the original offense.

But Phoebe slept on and never dreamed that more evil was brewing.

The lights had been out when she came home, all except a candle in Emmeline's room, but the door was left on the latch for her. She knew Emmeline would reprove her for the late hour of her return, and she was fully prepared for the greeting next morning, spoken frigidly.

"Oh, so you did come home last night, after all! Or was it this morning? I'm surprised. I thought you had gone for good."

At breakfast, things were uncomfortable. Albert persisted in asking Phoebe questions about her tea party, in spite of Emmeline's sarcasms. When Emmeline complained that Phoebe had "sneaked" away without giving her a chance to send for anything to the village and that she needed thread for her quilting that very morning, Phoebe rose from her almost untasted breakfast and offered to go for it at once.

She stepped into the crisp morning with a sigh of relief and walked briskly down the road, happy she had escaped her prison for an hour of the early freshness. Then she stopped suddenly, for there before her lay a letter ground into the dust. There was something strangely familiar about the writing, as if she'd seen it before, yet it wasn't anyone's she knew. It wasn't folded so the address could be seen but lay open and rumpled, with the communication uppermost. The words that stood out clearly to her as she stooped to pick it up were these:

> *It is most important that you present this letter, or it will do no good to go. BUT BE SURE NO ONE ELSE SEES IT, OR GREAT HARM MAY COME TO YOU!*

She turned the paper over, and there on the other side lay the name that had gleamed at her pleasantly just a few days before through the laurel bushes: *Nathaniel Graham, Esq.*

Was this letter an old one, useless now and of no value to its owner? Surely it must be, and he'd dropped it on his way home with her last night. The wind had blown it open, and a passerby had trodden upon it. That must be the explanation, for surely if it were important he wouldn't have laid it down behind the log so carelessly. Yet the words in the letter read, *It is most important that you present this letter, or it will do no good to go.* Well, perhaps he had already "gone," wherever that was, and the letter had seen its usefulness. But then it further stated that great harm might come to the owner if anyone saw it. She could make sure no one saw it by destroying it, but how would she know she wasn't really destroying an important document? And she might not read further because of that caution, *Be sure no one else sees it.* It was a secret communication to which she had no right, and she must respect it.

She saw there was only one thing to do, and that was to go at once to the owner and give it to him, telling him she hadn't read another word than those she saw at first.

Her troubled gaze saw nothing of the morning's beauties, the bejeweled fringes of grass along the road or the silver-coated red and brown leaves lingering on branches. She passed by Hiram Green's farm just as he was coming down to his barn near the road. He was in full view and near enough for recognition. He quickened his pace as he saw her coming, but her eyes looked straight ahead, and she didn't turn her head toward him. He thought she did it to escape speaking. It angered him anew to have her pass him by unseeing, as if he weren't good enough to treat with ordinary politeness as between neighbors at least. If he needed anything more to justify his heart in its evil plot he had it now.

With lowering brow, he raised his voice and called, "Where you goin' this early, Phoebe?"

But with her face set straight ahead and her mind busy with perplexing questions, she went on her way and never even heard him. Hiram Green's blood boiled.

He waited until she'd passed beyond the red schoolhouse that marked the boundary line between the village and the country and then slouched out from the shelter of the barn and followed her. He wouldn't let her see him, but he meant to know where she was going. She held a letter in her hand as she passed—at least it looked like a letter. Was she writing his rival a letter already? The thought brought a throb of hate toward the man who was better than he, toward the girl who had scorned him and toward the whole world.

Phoebe, unsuspecting and thinking only of her duty, not all a pleasant one for her, went on her way. She felt she must get the letter out of her hands before she did anything else, so she turned down the street past the church to the stately house with its white fence and high hedge, and her heart beat fast against her blue print dress. Seeing the great house, she suddenly felt she wasn't dressed for such a call, yet she wouldn't turn back or even hesitate, for it was something that must be done at once. She gave herself no time for thought of what would be said but entered the tall gate, which to her relief stood open. She held the letter tight in her trembling hand.

Hiram arrived at the church corner just in time to see her disappear within the white gates, and his jaw dropped down in astonishment. He hadn't dreamed she'd go to his house. Yet after a moment's thought his eyes narrowed and gleamed with the satisfaction they always showed when he'd seen through some possibility. The situation was awkward for the girl, and his being an eyewitness might someday give him power over her. He took his stand behind the trunk of a weeping willow tree in the churchyard to see what might happen.

Phoebe raised the brass knocker held in the mouth of a lion. How hollow it sounded as it reverberated through the great hall, not at all the cheerful thing it had been when Nathaniel knocked at Marcia Spafford's door. A black woman in a large yellow turban and white apron opened the door. Phoebe managed to ask if Mr. Graham were in.

"Missis Gra'm! Dere ain't no Missis Gra'm," said the old woman, looking her over carefully and rather scornfully. The young ladies who came to that house to visit didn't dress as Phoebe was dressed, in working garb. "Dere's only jes' Mis' Brist'l. Mis' Janet, we calls her."

"Mr. Graham. Mr. Nathaniel Graham," corrected Phoebe, her voice trembling. She thought she felt a rebuke in the woman's words that she should call to see a young man. "I have a message for him. I will wait here, please. No, I'd rather not come in."

"I'll call Miss Janet," said the servant and swept away, closing the door with a *bang* in Phoebe's face.

She waited several minutes before it was opened again, this time by Janet Bristol.

Chapter 12

"You wished to see me?" questioned the tall, handsome girl in the doorway, scrutinizing Phoebe haughtily.

"I wished to see Mr. Graham," said Phoebe, trying to look as if it were quite natural for a young woman to call on a young man in the morning.

"I thought you had a message for him," said Janet sharply, wondering what business this very pretty girl could have with her cousin.

"Yes, I have a message for him, but I must give it to him, if you please," Phoebe said with gentle emphasis. She lifted her eyes, and Janet couldn't help noticing the lovely face and smile.

"Well, that will not be possible, for he is not here," Janet said stiffly.

"Oh! He isn't here? What shall I do? He ought to have it at once. When will he come? I could wait for him."

"He will not be at home until evening," said Janet. "You'll have to leave your message."

"I'm sorry," Phoebe said in a troubled tone. "I can't leave it. The one who sends it said it was private."

"That would not mean you could not tell it to his family," said Janet. She was bristling with curiosity.

"I don't know," said Phoebe, turning to go.

"I can't understand how it is that you, a young girl, should be trusted with a message if it's so private that his own people are not to know," Janet said in a vexed tone.

"I know," said Phoebe. "It is strange, and I'm sorry it happened so. But there's nothing wrong about it, really." She looked up wistfully with her clear eyes so that Janet could scarcely think evil of her. "Perhaps Mr. Graham may be able to explain it to you. I would have no right." She turned and went down the steps. "I will come back this evening."

"Wait," said Janet sharply. "Who are you? I've seen you in church, haven't I?"

"Oh, yes," said Phoebe. "I sit just behind you. I'm Phoebe Deane."

"And who sends this message to my cousin?"

Phoebe's face clouded over. "I don't know."

"Well, that is very strange, indeed. If I were you I wouldn't carry messages for strange people. It doesn't look well. Girls can't be too careful what they do."

Phoebe's face was pained.

"I hope Mr. Graham will be able to explain," she said. "I don't like you to think ill of me." Then she went away, while Janet stood perplexed and annoyed.

She tucked the letter safely in the bosom of her gown and held her hand over it as she hurried along, not looking up or noticing any more than when she had come. She passed Miranda on the other side of the street and never saw her, and Miranda wondered where she was going and why she looked so troubled. If she hadn't been hurrying to the store for something that was needed at once, Miranda would have followed her to find out—perhaps even asked her point-blank.

Phoebe made her way through the village and out onto the country road, and in a short time she arrived at the kitchen of her home, where Emmeline had just finished the breakfast dishes.

"Well," she said grimly, looking up as Phoebe entered and noticing her empty hands. "Where's the thread? Didn't they have any?"

"Oh!" said Phoebe. "I forgot it! I'll go right back!" And

without waiting for a word from the amazed Emmeline she turned and sped down the road again toward the village.

"Of all things!" muttered Emmeline as she went to close the door that had blown open. "She needs a nurse! I didn't suppose going out to tea and havin' a little money in the bank could make a girl lose her head like that! She has turned into a regular scatterbrain. The idea of her forgetting to get that thread when she hadn't another earthly thing to do! I'd like to know who 'twas brung her home last night. I don't know how I could hev missed him till he was way out in the road. It didn't look egzactly like David Spafford, an' yet who could it 'a' ben ef 't wasn't? She must 'a' went to Mis' Spafford's again this mornin' 'stead o' goin' to the store, er she never would 'a' forgot. I have to find out when she gits back. It's my duty!"

Emmeline snapped her lips together over the words as if she anticipated that the duty would be a pleasant one.

In her hasty flight down the road Phoebe almost ran into Hiram Green, who was plodding back from his fruitless errand to his belated chores.

"Boy howdy!" he said as she started back, blurting, "Excuse me, Mr. Green! I'm in such a hurry I didn't see you." She was gone before her sentence was quite finished, and the breeze wafted it back to him from her retreating figure.

"Boy howdy!" he said again, looking after her. "I wonder what's up now?" And he turned doggedly and followed her again. If this kept up, detective business was going to be lively work. Two trips to the village on foot in one morning were wearisome. Yet he was determined to know what all this meant.

Phoebe did her errand swiftly and was so quick in returning with her purchase that she met Hiram face-to-face outside the store before he had time to conceal himself.

Thrown off his guard, he rallied and tried to play the gallant.

"Thought I'd come 'long and see ef I couldn't carry yer bundle fer yeh."

"Oh, thank you, Mr. Green," said Phoebe. "But I can't wait, for Emmeline is in a great hurry for this. I shall have to run most of the way home. Besides, it's very light. I couldn't think of troubling you." She backed away as she spoke, and with the closing words she turned and flew up the street.

"My!" said Hiram under his breath, almost dazed at the rebuff. "My, but she's a slippery one! But I'll catch her yet where she can't squirm out so easy. See ef I don't!" And with scowling brows he started slowly after her again. He didn't intend to allow any move on her part to go unwatched. He hated her for disliking him.

Miranda, from her watchtower in the Spafford kitchen window, saw Phoebe's flying figure and wondered. She didn't know what it meant, but she was sure it meant something. She felt "stirrings" in her soul that usually called for some action on her part. She was ready when the time should arrive, and she felt it arriving fast and sniffed the air like a trained warhorse. In truth she sniffed nothing more than the aroma of mince pies just out of the great brick oven, standing in a row on the shelf to cool.

The remainder of the morning was not pleasant for Phoebe. Her mind was too busy with her perplexity about the letter to spend much time in planning how to excuse her forgetfulness. She merely said, "I was thinking of something else, Emmeline, so I came back without going to the store at all."

Emmeline scolded and sniffed and scoffed to no purpose. Phoebe silently worked on, her eyes faraway, her whole manner showing that she was paying little heed to what her sister-in-law said. This made Emmeline even more angry. But Phoebe's lips were sealed. She answered questions when it was necessary and quietly worked away. When everything else was done she seated herself at the quilt and began to set tiny stitches in a brilliant corner.

"Don't trouble yourself," said Emmeline. "You might ferget to fasten yer thread er tie a knot in it. I wouldn't be s'prised." But Phoebe worked mechanically on and soon was a whole block ahead of Emmeline.

At dinner she was unusually silent, excusing herself to go back to the quilt as soon as she had eaten a few mouthfuls. Emmeline scrutinized her and became silent. It seemed to her there was something strange about Phoebe. She would have given a good deal to know all about her afternoon at the Spaffords', but Phoebe's monosyllabic answers brought forth little information.

Albert looked at her in a troubled way, then glanced at Emmeline's forbidding face and said nothing.

The afternoon wore away in silence. Several times Emmeline opened her lips to ask a question and snapped them shut again. She made up her mind that Phoebe must be thinking about Hiram Green, and if that was so she'd better keep still and let her think. Nevertheless, there was something serene and lofty about Phoebe's look that was hardly in keeping with a thought of Hiram Green, and her sphinxlike manner made Emmeline feel it was useless to ask questions, though of course Emmeline had never heard of the Sphinx.

At five o'clock Phoebe arose from the quilting frame and without a word got the supper. Then, eating little or nothing herself, she cleared it away and went up to her room. Albert took his newspaper, and Emmeline went grimly at her basket of stockings. She wondered whether the girl intended to come down to help her with them. After all, it was rather profitable to have Phoebe work like this—things got done quickly.

"Is Phoebe sick?" Albert asked suddenly, looking up from his paper.

Emmeline started and pricked her finger with the needle.

"I should like to know what makes you think that," she

snapped, frowning at the prick. "You seem to think she's made of some kind of perishable stuff that needs more'n ordinary care. You never seem to think I'm sick as I've noticed."

"Now, Emmeline!" he began pleasantly. "You know you aren't ever sick, and this is your home, and you like to stay in it, and you've got your own folks and all. But Phoebe's kind of different. She doesn't seem to quite belong, and I wouldn't want her to miss anything out of her life because she's living with us."

"Bosh!" said Emmeline. "Phoebe's made of no better stuff 'n I am. She ken do more work when the fit's on her than a yoke of oxen. The fit's ben on her today. She's got her spunk up. That's all the matter. She's tryin' to make up fer losin' yesterday afternoon, jes' to spite me fer what I said about her goin' out. I know her. She's done a hull lot on that there quilt this afternoon. At this rate we'll hev it off the frames before the week's out. She ain't et much 'cause she's mad, but she'll come out of it all right. You make me sick the way you fret about her doldrums."

Albert subsided, and the darning needle clicked in and out with the rapid movement of Emmeline's fingers. They could hear Phoebe moving about her chamber quietly, though it wasn't directly over the sitting room, and presently the sounds ceased altogether, and they thought she had gone to bed. A few minutes later Hiram opened the sitting room door and walked in.

"Where's Phoebe?" he asked, looking at the silent group around the candle. "She ain't out to another tea party, is she?"

"She's gone to bed," said Emmeline. "Is it cold out?"

Phoebe, upstairs by her window, arrayed in her plain brown delaine, brown shirred bonnet, and brown cape, waited until the accustomed sounds downstairs told her Hiram had come and was seated. Then she softly climbed out of her window to the roof of a shed a few feet below her window, crept out to the back edge of this and dropped like a cat to the ground. She had performed this feat many times as a child, but never since she wore long dresses. She was glad the moon wasn't up yet and hurried around the back of the house and across the side yard to the fence.

Her feet had scarcely left the last rail when she heard the door latch *click*, and a broad beam of light flashed across the path not far from her. To her horror she saw Hiram Green's tall form coming out, and then the door slammed shut, and she knew he was out in the night with her.

But she was in the road now with nothing to hinder her, and her light feet flew over the ground, treading on the grassy spots at the edge so she would not make a sound. Somehow she felt he was coming nearer with every step she took. Her heart beat wildly, and great tears started to her eyes. She tried to pray as she fled along. Added to her fear of Hiram was her dread of what he would think if he found her out there in the dark alone. She also feared for the secret of the letter she carried, for instinctively she knew that of all people to find out a secret, Hiram Green would be among the most dangerous. She put her hand over the letter, hidden under her cape, and clenched it fast.

When she passed the silent schoolhouse, she turned her head as she hurried along and felt sure she heard him coming. The sky was growing luminous. The moon would soon be up, and then she could be seen. Quite distinctly she heard a man's heavy tread running behind her.

Her heart nearly stopped for an instant, and then, bounding up, she leaped ahead, her lips set, her head down. A few more steps. She could not hold out to run like this much farther. But at last she reached the village pavement and could see the friendly lights of the houses all about her.

She hurried on, not daring to run so fast here, for people were coming ahead. She tried to think and to still the wild fluttering of her heart. If Hiram Green were really following her it would not do for her to go to Judge Bristol's at once. She could hardly hope to reach there and hide from him now, for her strength was almost spent, and not for anything must he know where she was going.

She fled past the houses, oblivious to where she was. She could hear the man's steps on the brick pavement now, and his heavy boots rang out distinctly on the frosty air. She felt as if she had been running for years with an evil fate pursuing her. Her limbs grew heavy, and her feet seemed to drag behind. She half closed her eyes to stop the surging of her blood. Her ears rang, her cheeks burned, and perspiration stood on her lips and brow. Her breath came hard and hurt her.

And then, quite naturally, as if it had been planned, Miranda stepped out from behind the lilacs in the Spafford garden by the gate and walked alongside her, fitting her large, easy gait to Phoebe's weary steps.

"I heard yeh comin' an' thought I'd go a piece with yeh!" she explained, as if this were a common occurrence. "D'ye hev to hurry like this, 'r was yeh doin' it fer exercise?"

"Oh, Miranda!" gasped Phoebe, slowing down and putting a plaintive hand out to reach the strong, friendly one in the dark. "I am so glad you're here!"

"So'm I," said Miranda, "but you jest wait till you git your breath. Can't you come in and set a spell 'fore you go on?"

"No, Miranda, I must hurry. I had an errand and must get right back—but I'm almost sure someone is following me. I don't dare look behind, but I heard footsteps and—I'm. . .so. . . frightened. . . ." Her voice trailed off, trembling into another gasp for breath.

"Well, all right, we'll fix 'em. You jest keep your breath fer walkin', an' I'll boss this pilgrimage a spell. We'll go down to the village store fer a spool o' cotton Mis' Spafford ast me t' get the fust thing in the mornin' to sew some sprigged calico curtains she's been gettin' up to the spare bed, an' while we're down to the store we'll jest natcherally lose sight o' that man till he don't know where he's at, an' then we'll meander on our happy way. Don't talk 'r he'll hear you. You jest foller me."

Chapter 13

*P*hoebe, too exhausted to demur, walked silently beside Miranda, and in a moment more they were safely in the store.

"Say, Mr. Peebles, is Mis' Peebles t' home? 'Cause Phoebe Deane wants t' git a drink o' water powerful bad. Ken she jest go right in and get it whilst I get a spool o' cotton?"

"Why, certainly, young ladies, walk right in," said the affable storekeeper, arising from a nail keg.

Miranda had Phoebe into the back room in no time, and she was calmly debating the virtues of different spools of thread when Hiram Green entered, puffing and snorting like a porpoise. He glanced around, then a blank look spread over his face. The one he sought wasn't there? Could he have been mistaken?

Miranda, paying for her thread, eyed him furtively and put two and two together, figuring out her problem with a relish. She said good evening to Mr. Peebles and deliberately went out the door into the street. Hiram watched her suspiciously, but she held her head high as if she were going straight home. Instead she slipped through the dark around to the side door where she walked in on Mrs. Peebles and the astonished Phoebe without ceremony.

"Did yeh get yer drink, Phoebe? Ev'nin', Mis' Peebles. Thank yeh, no, I can't set down. Mis' Spafford needs this thread t' oncet. She jest ast me wouldn't I run down and git it so's she could finish up some pillar slips she's makin'. Come on, Phoebe, ef yer ready. Ken we go right out this door, Mis'

Peebles? There's so many men in the store, an' I can't bear 'em to stare at my pretty red hair, you know." And in a moment more she had whisked Phoebe out the side door into the dark yard, where they could slip through the fence to the side street.

"Now which way?" asked Miranda in a low tone as they emerged from the shadow of the store to the sidewalk.

"Oh, Miranda, you're so kind," said Phoebe, hardly knowing what to do, for she dared not tell her errand to her. "I think I can go quite well by myself now. I'm not much afraid, and I'll soon be done and go home."

"See here, Phoebe Deane. D'yeh think I'm going t' leave a little white-faced thing like you with them two star eyes t' go buffetin' round alone in the dark where there's liable to be lop-sided nimshies follerin' round? Yeh can say what yeh like, but I'm goin' to foller yeh till I see yeh safe inside yer own door."

"Oh, you dear, good Miranda!" said Phoebe with a teary smile, clasping her arm tight. "If you only knew how glad I was to see you."

"I knowed all right. I cud see you was scared. But come 'long quick er that hound in there'll be trackin' us again. Which way?"

"To Judge Bristol's," said Phoebe in a low whisper.

"That's a good place to go," said Miranda. "I guess you won't need me inside with you. I'm not much on fancy things, an' I'll fit better outside with the fence posts, but I'll be thar to take yeh home. My! But you'd orter 'a' seen Hiram Green's blank look when he got in the store an' seen you wa'n't there. I'm calculatin' he'll search quite a spell 'fore he makes out which way we disappeared."

Phoebe's heart beat wildly at the thought of her escape. She felt as if an evil fate were dogging her every step.

"Oh, Miranda!" she shivered. "What if you hadn't come along just then!"

"Well, there ain't no use cipherin' on that proposition. I was thar, an' I generally calculate to be thar when I'm needed. Jest you rest easy. There ain't no long-legged, good-fer-nothin' bully like Hiram Green goin' to gather you in, not while I'm able to bob round. Here we be. Now I'll wait in the shadder behind this bush while you go in."

Phoebe timidly approached the house while Miranda, as usual, selected her post with discernment and a view of the lighted window of the front room, where the family was assembled.

Janet didn't keep Phoebe waiting long this time but swept into the doorway in a dress of ruby red with a little gold locket hung from a bit of black velvet ribbon about her neck. Her dark hair was arranged in clusters of curls on each side of her face, and the glow on her cheeks seemed reflected from the color of her garments.

"I'm afraid my cousin is too busy to see you," she said in a kind but condescending tone. "He's busy preparing to leave on the early stage in the morning. He found out he must go to New York sooner than he expected."

"I will not keep him long," said Phoebe earnestly, "but I must see him for just a minute. Will you kindly tell him it is Phoebe Deane and that she says she must see him for just a moment?"

"He will want you to send the message by me," said Janet. "It does not do to say 'must' to my cousin Nathaniel."

But contrary to Janet's expectation Nathaniel came down at once, with welcome in his face. Phoebe stood with her hand on the letter over her heart waiting for him. The watching Miranda eyed him through the front windowpane to see if his countenance would light up properly when he saw his visitor— and was fully satisfied. He hastened to meet her and take her hand in greeting, but she only held out the letter to him.

"I found this, Mr. Graham, spread out in the road and read the one sentence which showed it was private. I haven't read any more, and I shall never breathe even that one, of course. After I had read that sentence I didn't dare give it into any hands but yours. I may have been wrong, but I tried to do right. I hope you can explain it to your cousin, for I can see she thinks it very strange."

He tried to detain her to thank her and introduce her to his cousin, who had by this time entered and watched them coolly. But Phoebe was in haste to leave, and Janet was haughtily irresponsive.

He followed her to the door and said in a low tone, "Miss Deane, you have done me a greater service than I can possibly repay. I've been hunting frantically for this letter all day. It is most important. I know I can trust you not to speak of it to a soul. I'm deeply grateful. You may not know it, but not only my life and safety but that of others as well has been in your hands today with the keeping of that letter."

"Then I'm glad I've brought it safely to you. I've been frightened all day lest something would happen and I couldn't get it to you without its being found out. And if it has been of service I'm more than glad, because then I have repaid your kindness to me in the woods that day."

Now that she was away from Janet's scrutinizing eyes Phoebe could venture a smile.

"What I did that day was a little thing beside your service," he said.

"A kindness is never a little thing," answered Phoebe gently. "Good night, Mr. Graham. Miranda is waiting for me." And she sped down the path without giving him opportunity for a reply.

Miranda had wandered into the shaft of light down by the gate that streamed from the candle Nathaniel held, and Phoebe flew to her. They turned and looked back as they reached the gate. Nathaniel was still standing on the top step with the candle held above his head to give them light, and through the window they could dimly see Janet's slim figure standing by the mantelpiece toying with some ornaments.

Phoebe gave a sigh of relief that the errand was accomplished and grasped Miranda's arm, and so the two walked softly through the village streets and out the country way into the road that was now white with the new risen moon. Meanwhile Hiram Green, baffled, searched vainly through the village for a clue to Phoebe's whereabouts and finally gave up and dragged his weary limbs home.

Nathaniel turned back into the house again, his vision filled with the face of the girl who had just brought his letter back to him. His relief at finding it was almost lost in the thought of Phoebe Deane and a sudden pang of remembrance of Hiram Green. Could it be? Could it possibly be that she was bound in any way to that man?

Janet roused him from his thought by demanding to know what on earth the message was that made the girl so absurdly secretive.

Nathaniel smiled. "It was just a letter of mine she had found. A letter that I have searched everywhere for."

"How did she know it was your letter?" There was something offensive in Janet's tone.

Nathaniel felt his color rising. He wondered why Janet should be so curious.

"Why, it was addressed to me, of course."

"Then why in the world couldn't she give it to me? She was here in the morning, and we had a long argument about it. She said it was a private message and the person who sent it did not wish anyone but you to see it, and yet she professed not to know who the person was who sent it. I told her that was ridiculous, that of course you had no secrets from your family, but she was quite stubborn and went away. Who is she, anyway, and how does she happen to know you?"

Nathaniel could be haughty, too, when he liked, and he

drew himself up to his full height.

"Miss Deane is quite a charming girl, Janet, and you would do well to make her acquaintance. She is a friend of Mrs. Spafford and was visiting her last evening when I happened in on business, and they made me stay to tea."

"That's no sign of where she belongs socially," said Janet. "Mrs. Spafford may have had to invite her just because she didn't know enough to go home before supper. Besides, Mrs. Spafford's choice in friends might not be mine at all."

"Janet, Mr. and Mrs. Spafford are unimpeachable socially and every other way. And I happen to know that Miss Deane was there by invitation. I heard her speaking of it as she bid her good night."

"Oh, indeed!" sneered Janet, beside herself with jealousy. "I suppose you were waiting to take her home!"

"Why, certainly," said Nathaniel, looking surprised. "What has come over you, Janet? You're not talking like your usual kind self."

His tone brought angry tears to Janet's eyes.

"I should think it was enough," she said, trying to hide the tears in her lace handkerchief, "having you go off suddenly like this when we've scarcely had you a week, and you busy and absentminded all the time. And then to have this upstart of a girl coming here with secrets you won't tell me about. I want to know who wrote that letter, Nathaniel, and what it is about. I can't stand it to have that girl smirking behind me in church knowing things about my cousin that I don't know. I must know."

"Janet!" said Nathaniel. "You must be ill. I never saw you act this way before. You know very well I'm just as sorry as can be to have to rush off sooner than I had planned, but it can't be helped. I'm sorry if I've been absentminded. I've been trying to decide some matters of my future, and I suppose that has made me somewhat abstracted. As for the letter, I would gladly tell you about it, but it is another's secret, and I could not do so honorably. You need fear no such feeling on Miss Deane's part, I'm sure. Just meet her with your own pleasant, winning way and tell her I've explained to you it was all right. That ought to satisfy both you and her. She asked me to explain it to you."

"Well, you haven't done so at all. I'm sure I can't see what possible harm it could do for you to tell me about it, since that other girl knows all about it, too. I should think you would want me to watch and be sure she doesn't tell—unless the secret is between you two."

Something about Janet's tone hinted at an insinuation. Nathaniel grew stern.

"The secret is not between Miss Deane and me," he said, "and she does not know it any more than you do. She found it open and read only one line, which told her it was absolutely private. She tells me she did not read another word."

"Very likely!" sneered Janet. "Do you think any woman would find it possible to read only one line of a secret? Your absolute faith in this stranger is quite childlike."

"Janet, would you have read further if it had fallen into your hands?"

"Well, I—why, of course, that would be different," she said, coloring and looking disconcerted. "But you needn't compare me—"

"Janet, you have no right to think she has a lower sense of honor than you do. I feel sure she has not read it."

But Janet, with flashing eyes, swept up the stairs and took refuge in her room, where a storm of tears and mortification followed.

Nathaniel, dismayed, after vainly tapping at her door and begging her to come out and explain her strange conduct, went back to his packing, puzzling over the strange ways of girls with one another. Here, for instance, were two well suited to friendship, and yet he could plainly see they would have nothing to do with each other. He loved his cousin. She had been his playmate and companion from childhood, and he couldn't understand why she had suddenly grown so inconsiderate of his wishes. He tried to put it away, deciding he would say another little word about the charming Miss Deane to Janet in the morning before he left. But the next morning Janet forestalled any such attempt by sending down word that she had a headache and would try to sleep a little longer. She called out a cool good-bye to her cousin through the closed door as he hurried down to the stage waiting for him at the door.

Meanwhile, Miranda and Phoebe hurried out past the old red schoolhouse into the country road, white with frosty moonlight. Phoebe kept protesting that Miranda mustn't go with her.

"Why not, in conscience!" said Miranda. "I'll jest enjoy the walk. I was thinkin' of goin' on a lark this very evenin'; only I hadn't picked out a companion."

"But you'll have to come all the way back alone, Miranda."

"Well, what's that? You don't s'pose anybody's goin' to chase *me*, do yeh? If they want to, they're welcome. I'd jest turn round an' say, 'Boo! I'm red-haired an' freckled, an' I don't want nothin' of you nor you of me. Git 'long with yeh!' "

Miranda's manner brought a laugh to Phoebe's lips and helped relieve the tension she had been under. She felt like laughing and crying all at once. Miranda seemed to understand and kept her in ripples of laughter till they neared her home. Not until she saw her charge safe inside her own door would the faithful Miranda turn back.

When they were close to the house, Phoebe suddenly turned and said confidentially, "Well, Miranda, I'll have to tell you how I got out. There was a caller—someone I didn't care to see—so I went upstairs, and they thought I'd gone to bed. I just slipped out my window to the low shed roof and dropped down. I'll have to be very still, for I wouldn't care to have them know I slipped away like that. It might make them ask me questions. You see, I found a letter Mr. Graham had dropped, and it needed to go to him at once. If I had asked Albert to take it, there would have been a big fuss, and Emmeline would have wanted to know all about it, and maybe read it, and I didn't think it would be best—"

"I see," said Miranda, "so you tuk it yourself. O' course. Who wouldn't, I'd like to know? All right, we'll jest slip in through the pasture and round to your shed, an' I'll give yeh a boost up. Two's better'n one fer a job like that. I take it yer caller ain't present any longer. Reckon he made out to foller yeh a piece, but we run him into a hole, an' he didn't make much. Hush, now. Don't go to thankin'. 'Taint worthwhile till I git through, fer I've jest begun this job, an' I intend to see it through. Here, put yer hand on my shoulder. Now let me hold this foot. Don't you be 'fraid. I'm good an' strong. There yeh go! Now yer up! Is that your winder up there? Wal, hope to see yeh again soon. Happy dreams!" And she slid around the corner to watch Phoebe till she disappeared into the dark window above.

Miranda made for the road, looking in at the side window of the Deanes' sitting room on the way to make sure she was right about the caller being gone and to see if they had heard Phoebe, for she thought it might be necessary to invent a diversion of some sort. But she only saw Albert asleep in his chair and Emmeline working grimly at her sewing.

About halfway to the red schoolhouse Miranda met Hiram Green. He looked up, frowning. He thought it was Phoebe and wondered if it were possible she was making another trip to the village that night.

"Ev'nin', Mr. Green," said Miranda nonchalantly. "Seen anythin' of a little white kitten with one blue eye and one green one, an' a black tip to her tail an' a pink nose? I've been up to see if she follered Phoebe Deane home from our house las' night, but she's gone to bed with the toothache, an' I wouldn't disturb her fer the world. I thought I'd mebbe find her round this way. You ain't seen her, have yeh?"

"No," growled Hiram. "I'd 'a' wrung her neck ef I had."

"Oh, thank you, Mr. Green. You're very kind," said Miranda sweetly. "I'll remember that, next little kitten I lose. I'll know jest who t' apply to fer it. Lovely night, ain't it? Don't trouble yerself 'bout the kitten. I reckon it's safe somewheres. 'Taint everyone ez bloodthirsty's you be. Good night." And Miranda ran down the road before Hiram could decide whether she was poking fun at him or not.

At last he roused himself from his weary pondering and went home to bed. He hadn't been able all day to fathom the mystery of Phoebe's vanishings when he had started out with her in plain view. And this new unknown quantity was more perplexing than all the rest. What, for instance, had Miranda Griscom to do with Phoebe Deane? His slow brain remembered she had been in the store where Phoebe disappeared. Had Miranda spirited her away somewhere? Ah! And it was Miranda who had come up to Phoebe after church and interrupted their walk together! Hang Miranda! He'd like to wring her neck, too. With such charming meditations he fell asleep.

Chapter 14

Nathaniel sat inside the coach as it rolled through the village streets and out into the country road toward Albany and tried to think. All remembrance of Janet and her foolishness had left his mind. He had a problem to decide, and it was all the more difficult because the advice of his dearest friends was so at variance.

He took out two letters which represented the two sides of the question and began to reread. The first was the letter Phoebe had brought, disfigured by the dust but still legible. It bore a Texas postmark and was brief and businesslike.

Dear Nephew,

If you are as keen as you used to be you have been keeping yourself informed about Texas and know the whole state of the case better than I can put it. Ever since Austin went to ask the admission of Texas as a separate state into the Mexican Republic and was denied and thrown into prison, our people have been gathering together; and now things are coming to a crisis. Something will be done and that right soon, perhaps in a few days. The troops are gathering near Gonzales. Resistance will be made. But we need help. We want young blood and strong arms and hearts with a conviction for right. No one on earth has a right to deprive us of our property and say we shall not own slaves which we have come by honestly. We will fight and win, as the United States has fought and won its right to govern itself.

Now I call upon you, Nathaniel, to rise up and bring honor to your father's name by raising a company of young men to come down here and set Texas free. I know you are busy with your law studies, but they will keep, and Texas will not. Texas must be set free now or never. When you were a little chap you had strong convictions about what was right, and I feel pretty sure my appeal will not come to deaf ears. Your father loved Texas and came down here to make his fortune. If he had lived he would have been here fighting. He would have been a slave owner and asserted his right as a free man in a free country to protect his property. He would have taught his son to do the same. I call upon you for your father's sake to come down here—for it is the place where you were born—and help Texas. Use your utmost influence to get other young men to come with you.

Your uncle the judge will perhaps help you financially. He owns a couple of slaves himself, I remember, house servants, doesn't he? Ask him how he would like the government of the United States to order him to set them free. I feel sure he will sympathize with Texas in her hour of need and help you do this thing I've asked.

I am a man of few words, but I trust you, Nathaniel, and I feel sure I am not pleading in vain. I shall expect something from you at once. We need the help now, or the cause may be lost. If you feel as I think you do, go to the New York address given below. This letter will be sufficient identification for you as I have written to them about you, but it is most important that you present this letter, or it will do no good to go. BUT BE SURE NO ONE ELSE SEES IT, OR GREAT HARM MAY COME TO YOU! There is grave danger in being found

> *out, but if I didn't know your brave spirit, I would not*
> *be writing you. Come as soon as possible!*
>
> *Your uncle,*
> *Royal Graham*

The other letter was kept waiting a long time while the young man read and reread this one. Then he let his eyes wander to the brown fields and dim hills in the distance. He was going over all he could remember of his boyhood in that faraway Southern home. He could dimly remember his father, who had been to him a great hero and had taken him with him on horseback wherever he went and never been too weary or too busy for his little son. A blur of sadness came over the picture—the death of his beloved father and an interval of emptiness when the gentle mother was too full of sorrow to comprehend how her young son suffered.

Then one day his uncle Royal, so like yet not like his father, had lifted him in his arms and said, "Good-bye, little chap. Someday you'll come back to us and do your father's work and take his place." And he and his mother had ridden away in an endless succession of coaches until one day they arrived at Judge Bristol's great white house set among the green hedges, and there Nathaniel had found a new home. There, first his mother and then Janet's mother had slipped through the mysterious door of death, and he grew up in the home of his mother's brother, with Janet as a sister.

From time to time he received letters from this shadowy uncle in Texas, and once, when he was about twelve, there had been a brief visit from him which cleared the memory and kept him fresh in Nathaniel's mind. Always there was some hint that when Nathaniel was grown and educated he would come back to Texas and help make it great. This had been a hazy undertone in his life, in spite of the fact that his other uncle, Judge Bristol, constantly talked of his future career as a lawyer in New York City, with a possibility of a political career also.

Nathaniel had gone on with his life, working out the daily plan as it came, all the time feeling that these two plans were contending for supremacy. Sometimes during leisure moments lately he had wondered if the two could ever be combined and, if not, how they were both to work out. Gradually it dawned upon him that a day was coming when he would have to choose. And now, since these two letters had reached him, he knew the time had come. Yet how was he to know how to choose?

His uncle Royal's letter had reached him the afternoon of the nutting party on the hill. Pompey, his uncle's house servant, had brought it to him just as they were starting out. He had glanced at the familiar writing and put it in his pocket for later reading. He always enjoyed his uncle's letters, but they were not of deep importance to him. He had been too long separated from him to have many interests in common with him. And so he hadn't read the letter until after his return from the hillside, which explains how he had carelessly left it behind the log by Phoebe, as an excuse to return and help her out of the laurel.

In the quiet of his own room, after Janet and the others were sleeping, he had remembered the letter and, relighting his candle, read it. He was startled to discover its contents. The talk of the afternoon floated back to him, idle talk about his going down to set Texas free. Talk that grew out of his own keen interest in the questions of the day and his readiness to argue them out. But he'd never had a definite idea of going to Texas to take part in the struggle until the letter brought him face-to-face with a possible duty.

Perhaps he would have had no question about his decision if the very next day he hadn't received another letter which put an entirely different spin on the issue—and made duty seem an uncertain creature with more faces than one.

The coach was halfway to Albany before Nathaniel finally folded away his uncle's letter and put it in his inner pocket. Then he took up the other letter with a perplexed sigh and read:

Dear Nate,

I'm sitting on a high point of white sand, where I can look off at the blue sea. At my right is a great hairy, prickly cactus with a few yellow blossoms in delicate petals and fringed stamens that look as out of place amid the sand as a diamond on a plank. The sun is very warm and bright, and everything around seems to be basking in it.

As I look off to sea, the Gulf Stream is distinct today, a brilliant green ribbon in the brilliant blue of the sea. It winds along so independently in the great ocean, keeping its own individuality in spite of storm and wind and tide. I went out in a small boat across it the other day and could look down and see it as distinctly as if there were a glass wall between it and the other water. I can only think that God took pleasure in making this old earth.

I'm having a holiday, for my pupils are gone away on a visit. This is a delightful land to which I've come and a charming family with whom my lot is cast. I'm having an opportunity to study the South in a most ideal manner, and many of my former ideas of it are becoming much modified. For example, there's slavery. I am by no means so sure as I used to be that it was ordained by God. I wish you were here to talk it over with me and study it, too. Certain possibilities in the institution make one shudder. Perhaps, after all, Texas is in the wrong. As you have opportunity, drop into an abolition meeting now and then and see what you think. I've been reading the Liberator *lately. I find much in it that is strong and*

appeals to my sense of right. You know what a distur-
bance it has made in the country recently. I hear some
mails have even been broken into and burned on account
of it. I wonder if this question of slavery will ever be an
issue in our country. If it should be I can't help wondering
what the South will do. From what I've seen I feel sure
they will never stand to have their rights interfered with.

Now I have to confess that much as I rebelled against
giving up my work and coming down here, I feel it has
already benefitted me. I can take long walks without
weariness and can even talk and sing without becoming
hoarse. I don't believe my lungs have ever been affected,
and I feel I'm going to get well and come back to my
work. With that hope in my veins I can go through these
sunny days and feel new life creeping into me with every
breath of fresh air. We shall yet work shoulder to shoulder,
my friend—I feel it. God bless you and keep you and
show you the right way.

Yours faithfully,
Martin Van Rensselaer

Nathaniel folded the letter, placed it in his pocket with the
other letter, and leaned his head back to think.

Van Rensselaer had been his roommate for four years. They
had grown into one another's thoughts as two who are much
together and love each other often do. Nathaniel could not
quite tell why this letter troubled him. Yet he felt through the
whole epistle the stirring of a new principle that seemed to
antagonize his sympathy with Texas.

So through the long journey he debated the question back
and forth. His duty to his uncle demanded that he go to the
address given and investigate the matter of helping Texas.
And when he looked at it from his uncle's standpoint and
thought of his father, his sympathy was with Texas. On the

other hand, his love for his friend and his trust in him demanded that he investigate the other side also. He sensed intuitively that the two things could not go together.

Martin Van Rensselaer had been preparing for the ministry. His zeal and earnestness were great, too great for his strength, and before he finished his theological studies, he had broken down and been sent South, as it was feared he had serious lung trouble. The separation had been a great trial to both young men. Martin was three years older than Nathaniel and two years ahead of him in his studies, but in mind and spirit they were as one, so the words of his letter had great influence.

The day grew surly as the coach rumbled on. Sullen clouds lowered in the corners of the sky as if meditating mutiny. A hint of snow bit the air that whistled around the cracks of the coach windows. Nature seemed to have suddenly put on a bare, brown look.

Nathaniel shivered and drew his cloak close about him. He wished the journey were over or that he had someone to advise him. Once or twice he had broached the subject with Judge Bristol, but he'd hesitated to show him either of the letters. He felt that his uncle's letter might arouse antagonism in Judge Bristol on account of the claim it put upon him, as his father's son, to come and give himself. Judge Bristol was almost jealously fond of his sister's son and felt that he belonged to the North. Aside from that, his sympathies would probably have been with Texas. Keeping a few slaves himself as house servants and treating them as kindly as if they were his own children, he saw no reason to object to slavery and deemed it a man's right to do as he pleased with his own property.

The judge would likely have looked upon Martin Van Rensselaer's letter as the product of a sentimental fanatic whose judgment was unsound. Nathaniel was certain that if the judge should read those letters he would advise against having anything to do with either cause personally. Yet Nathaniel's conscience would not let him drop the matter so easily.

The coach thumped on over rough roads and smooth. The coachman called to his horses, snapped his whip, and wondered why Nathaniel, who was usually so sociable and liked to sit on the box and talk, stayed glumly inside without a word to him. He sat gloomily mile after mile, trying to think what girl of his acquaintance was good enough for Nathaniel.

But Nathaniel sat inside with closed eyes and tried to think, and ever and again there came a vision of a sweet-faced girl with brown hair and a golden dress sitting among the falling yellow leaves with bowed head. And somehow in his thoughts her trouble became tangled, and it seemed as if three instead of two needed setting free, and he must choose between them all.

Chapter 15

The cold weather had come suddenly, and Phoebe felt like a prisoner. Emmeline's tongue became a daily torture, and the little ways in which she contrived to make Phoebe's life a burden were too numerous to count.

Her paltry fortune in the bank was a source of continual trouble. Scarcely a morning passed without its being referred to in some unpleasant way. Every request was prefaced with some such phrase as "If you're not too grand to soil your hands," or "I don't like to ask a rich lady to do such a thing," till Phoebe felt sometimes that she could bear it no longer and longed to take the few dollars and fling them into the lap of her disagreeable sister-in-law, if by doing so she might gain peace. Like the continual dripping that wears away the stone, the unpleasant reference had worn upon a single nerve until the pain was acute.

But there was another source of discomfort still more trying to the girl than all that had gone before, and this was Hiram Green's new role. He had taken it upon himself to act the fine gentleman. It was somewhat surprising considering the fact that Hiram was known in the village as "near," and this new departure demanded an entirely new outfit of clothes. In his selection he aimed to emulate Nathaniel Graham. As he had neither Nathaniel's taste nor his New York tailor, the effect was far from perfect, except perhaps in the eyes of Hiram, who felt quite set up in his fine raiment.

On the first Sunday of his proud appearance in church thus arrayed, he waited boldly at the door until the Deanes came out and then took his place beside Phoebe and walked with her to the carryall as though he belonged there.

Phoebe's thoughts were on other things, and for a moment she hadn't noticed. But suddenly she became conscious of measured footsteps beside her own, looked up, and found the reconstructed Hiram strutting by her side like a peacock. In spite of her great annoyance her first impulse was to laugh, and that laugh probably did more than any other thing to turn the venom of Hiram Green's hate upon her innocent head. After all the effort he had made to appear well before her and the congregation assembled, she had laughed. She had dared to laugh aloud, and the hateful Miranda Griscom, who seemed to be always in the way whenever he tried to walk with Phoebe, had laughed back. A slow ugly red rolled into his sunburned face, and his eyes narrowed with resolve to pay back all and more than he had received of scorn.

Miranda was holding Rose by the hand and couldn't get much nearer to Phoebe that morning without attracting attention, so the girl could do nothing to get away from her unpleasant suitor except to hurry to the carryall.

And there before the open-eyed congregation Hiram Green helped her into the carryall with a rude imitation of Nathaniel Graham's gallantry. She should see that others besides the New York college dandy could play the fine gentleman. He finished the operation with an exaggerated flourish of his hat, and just because laughter is so near to tears, the tears sprang up in Phoebe's eyes. She could do nothing but drop her head and try as best she could to hide them.

The all-seeing Alma of course discovered them, and just as they were driving by Judge Bristol and his daughter she called out, "Aunt Phoebe's cryin'. What you cryin' 'bout, Aunt Phoebe? Is it 'cause you can't ride with Hiram Green?"

Thereafter Hiram Green was in attendance upon her at every possible public place. She couldn't go to church without finding him at her elbow the minute the service was over, ready to walk down the aisle beside her. She couldn't go to singing school without his stepping out from behind his gate as she passed and joining her, or if she evaded him he would sit beside her and manage to sing out of the same book. She couldn't go to the village on an errand without his appearing in the way and accompanying her. He seemed to have developed a strange intuition as to her every movement.

He was ever vigilant, and the girl began to feel like a hunted creature.

Even if she stayed at home he appeared at the door ten minutes after the family had gone, a triumphant, unpleasant smile on his face, and sauntered into the kitchen without waiting for her to bid him. There, tilted back in a chair in his favorite attitude, he would watch her every movement and drawl out an occasional remark. That happened only once, however; she never dared to stay again, lest it would be repeated.

She had been busy preparing something for dinner and turned suddenly and caught a look on his face that reminded her of a beast of prey. It flashed upon her that he was actually enjoying her annoyance. Without thinking she stepped into the woodshed and from there fled across the backyard and the meadows between and burst into Granny McVane's bright little room.

The dear old lady sat there rocking by the fire, with her open Bible on her knee. Phoebe was relieved to find her alone. In answer to the gentle "Why, dearie, what can be the matter?" she flung herself on the floor at the old lady's feet and, putting her head in her lap, burst into tears.

She lost her self-control only for a moment, but even that moment relieved the heavy strain on her nerves, and she was able to sit up and tell the old lady all about it. She hadn't intended to tell anything, when in her sudden panic she had beaten a hasty retreat from the enemy. But Granny McVane's face showed so much tender sympathy that all at once it seemed good to tell someone of her trouble.

Granny McVane listened, watched her sympathetically, smoothed back the damp tendrils of hair that had blown about her face, and then stooped over and kissed her.

"Don't you ever marry him, Phoebe. Don't you ever do it, if you don't love him, child!" she said solemnly, like a warning. "And just you run over here, dearie, whenever he bothers you. I'll take care of you."

Phoebe, with her natural reserve, hadn't drawn her family into the story except to say they favored the suit of the would-be lover. But it comforted her greatly to have someone on her side, even if it were only this quiet old lady who couldn't really help her much.

They watched out the back windows until they saw Hiram emerge from the Deane house and saunter off down the road. Even then Phoebe was afraid to go back until she saw the carryall far down the road. Then she flew across the fields and entered the back door before they had turned in at the great gate. When they got out and came into the house she was demurely paring potatoes, and Emmeline eyed her suspiciously.

"Seems to me you're pretty late with your potatoes," she remarked disagreeably. "I suppose you had a nice, easy time all morning."

But Phoebe did not explain. Only she didn't stay at home again when the family would all be away. She never knew whether Emmeline was aware of Hiram's Sunday visit or not.

Phoebe's state of mind after this occurrence was one of constant nervous alarm. She began to hate the thought of the man who seemed to haunt her at every turn.

Before this one of her greatest pleasures had been to walk to the village after the daily mail or for an errand to the store. Now such walks became a dread. One afternoon in early November she had hurried away and gone around by Granny

McVane's, hoping thus to escape Hiram Green's vigilance. She managed to get safely to the village and do her errands, but just as she emerged from the post office the long, lank figure of Hiram loomed before her and slouched into his dogged gait beside her.

"Did you get a letter?" he asked, looking suspiciously at the one she held in her hand. Then as she didn't answer he went on, "You must have a whole lot of folks writin' you quite constant. You seem to go to the post office so much."

Phoebe said nothing. She felt too indignant to speak. How could she get away from her tormentor unless she deliberately ran away from him? And how could she do that right here in the village where everyone was watching? She glanced up furtively. Hiram wore a look of triumph as he talked on, knowing he was annoying her.

"I s'pose you get letters from New York," he said, with a disagreeable insinuation in his tone.

Phoebe didn't know what he meant, but something in his tone made the color come into her cheeks. They were nearing the Spafford house. If only Miranda would come out and speak to her! She looked up at the great bully beside her and saw he was trying to calculate just how near the mark he had come. She stopped short on the pavement.

"I do not wish to walk with you," she said, struggling to keep her voice from trembling.

"Oh, you don't," he mocked. "How 'r' ye goin' to help yourself?"

She looked up into the pitiless cruelty of his eyes and shuddered involuntarily.

"I am going in to see Mrs. Spafford," she said with sudden inspiration, and her voice took on a girlish dignity. With that she put wings to her feet and flew to the Spafford front door, wondering if anyone would let her in before Hiram reached her.

Now Miranda was alone in the house that afternoon, and not much went on in the neighborhood that she didn't keep herself informed about. Therefore, when Phoebe, breathless, reached the front stoop the door swung open before her, and she stepped into her refuge with a gasp of relief and heard it close behind her as two strong freckled arms enclosed her.

"Ben waitin' quite a spell fer ye," she declared, as if it were the expected thing for Phoebe to fly into her arms unannounced in that way, "ever sence I see ye comin' down the street with that pleasant friend of yourn. Wonder you could tear yourself away. Take off yer bonnet and set a spell. Mis' Spafford's gone up t' th' aunts' fer tea and took Rose. I'm all alone. You set down, an' we'll have a real nice time, an' then I'll take you home by 'n' by."

"Oh, Miranda," gasped Phoebe, struggling hysterically between laughter and tears and trying to control the trembling that had taken possession of her body, "I'm such a miserable coward. I'm always running away when I get frightened!"

"Hm! I should hope yeh would!" said Miranda. "Such a snake in the grass as that! Le's see ef he's gone!" She crouched before the window and peered behind the curtain cautiously.

Hiram had watched Phoebe's sudden disappearance within the door with something like awe. It was almost uncanny having that door open and swallow her up. Besides, he hadn't expected Phoebe to dare run away from him. He stood a moment gazing after her and then sauntered on, calling himself a fool for having met her so near the Spafford house. Another time he would choose his meeting place away from her friends. He had lost this move, but he by no means meant to lose the game, and the hate in his heart grew with determination to have this tempting young life in his power and crush out its resistance.

It goaded him to madness for her to tell him she did not wish to walk with him. Why did she say that? Hadn't he always been respected and thought well of? His farm was as good a spot of land as could be found in the whole New York State, and his barn was talked about through the county. He was prosperous, everybody knew. Before he had married Annie, any girl in the vicinity would have thought him a great catch, and he knew well, by all the indescribable signs, that many girls as good as Phoebe would still be glad to accept his attentions. Why did this little nobody, who was after all merely a poor relation of his neighbor, presume to scorn him? He hated her for it, even while his heart was set upon having her. He wanted her at first because he admired her. Now he wanted to conquer and punish her for scorning him.

As he walked on alone his slow brain tried to form a new plan for revenge, and little by little an idea crept out of his thoughts and looked at him with its two snaky eyes until the poison of its fang had stolen into his heart. The post office! Ah! He would watch to see if she had a letter from that fellow, for surely only the knowledge that another man was at her feet could make her scorn his attentions. If that was so, he would crush the rival! He ground his teeth at the thought, and his eyes glittered with hate.

Meanwhile, Hiram Green's children and Alma Deane were playing together behind the big barn that had been one of the disappointments of Annie Green's married life, because it hadn't been a house instead of a barn. The children had dug houses in a haystack and chased the few venturesome hens that hadn't learned to be wary when they were around. Now, for the moment weary of their games, they mounted the fence to rest.

"There comes your pa," announced Alma from her perch on the top rail. The young Greens retired precipitately from the fence, and Alma was forced to follow them if she wished company. They hurried around the other side of the barn out of sight.

"Say," said Alma, after they had reached a spot of safety and ensconced themselves on the sunny exposure of a board across two logs, "my aunt Phoebe went to the village awhile ago. She'll be 'long pretty soon. Let's make up somethin' an' shout at her when she comes back. It'll make her mad as hops, an' I'd just like to pay her back fer the way she acts sometimes."

"Ain't she good to you?" inquired the youngest Green anxiously.

"Le's make up sumpin' 'bout her 'n' yer pa. There ain't nothin'll make her so mad. She's mad as mad can be when my ma says anythin' 'bout her gettin' married," went on Alma, ignoring the question.

"All right! What'll we make up?" agreed the three Greens.

They were not anxious to have a stepmother who might make life's restrictions more strenuous than they were already. They were prepared to do battle valiantly if they only had a general, and Alma was thoroughly competent in their eyes to fill that position.

"It'll have to be to a song, you know," went on Alma. "Le's sing the doxol'gy an' see how that goes." So they all stood in a row and droned out the doxology, piping shrilly where they knew words and filling in with homemade syllables where they didn't. Alma had practiced that art of rhyming before and was anxious to display her skill.

"Now listen!" she said and lined it out slowly, with many stops and corrections, until at last the doggerel was completed. And so they sang:

There-was-a-man-in-ow-wer-town
    His-name-was-Hi-rum-Gre-ee-een
And-he-did-ma-a-air-ree-a-wife
    Her-name-was-Phe-be-Dee-ee-eene.

Alma was no lax general. She drilled her little company

again and again until they could shout the words at the top of their voices, to say nothing of the way they murdered "Old Hundred." The young scapegraces looked at their leader with wide-eyed admiration and fairly palpitated for the moment when their victim would arrive. Between rehearsals they mounted the fence by the barn and kept a watchout down the road. At last it was announced that she was coming.

"But there's somebuddy with 'er," said a disappointed little Green.

"We won't dast, will we?"

Alma held up her undaunted chin and mounted the observation post to see who it was.

"Aw! That's all right," she presently announced. " 'Taint nobody but the redheaded girl down to Spaffords'. She can't do nothin'. Come on now—le's get ready."

She marshalled her forces behind the wide board fence next to the pigsty, and there they waited for the signal to begin. Alma thought it prudent to wait until Phoebe and Miranda had almost passed before they sang. Then she raised her hand, and they piped out shrilly, making the words more than plain.

Phoebe started at the first line and hurried her steps, but Miranda glanced back and said, "Hmm! I thought 'es much. Like father, like child!"

Maddened by such indifference the children ran along inside the fence and continued to yell at the top of their lungs, regardless of time or tune, until they reached the more open fields near the Deane house, where they dared go no farther. Then they retired in triumph to the shelter of the pigsty and the haystack to plume themselves on their success and recount the numerous faces they'd made and the times they'd stuck their tongues out. They didn't anticipate any trouble from the incident as they were too far away from the house for Hiram to hear, and they felt sure Phoebe would never tell on them, as it involved her too closely.

Suddenly, in the midst of the congratulations, without the slightest warning, a strong hand seized the sturdy Alma from the rear and pinioned her arms so she couldn't get away. She set up a yell that could have been heard for a half mile and began to kick and squirm. But Miranda's hands held her fast, while she took in the surroundings at a glance, moved her captive toward a convenient seat on a log, and, taking her calmly over her knee, administered in full measure the spanking that child deserved. Alma, meanwhile, was yelling like a loon, unable to believe the despised "red-haired girl from Spaffords' " had displayed so much ability and thoroughness in her methods of redress.

The valiant army of little Greens had retired with haste from the scene and were even then virtuously combing their hair and washing their hands and faces with a view to proving an alibi should the avenger seek further retribution. Alma was left to Miranda's mercy, and though she kicked and yelled right lustily, Miranda spanked on until she was tired.

"There!" she said, at last letting her go. "That ain't half yeh need, but I can't spend any more time on yeh today. Ef yeh ever do that er anythin' like it again I'll come in the night when everybody's asleep and give yeh the rest, an' I ken tell you now I won't let yeh off this easy next time. Mind you behave to yer aunt Phoebe, er I'll hant yeh! D'yeh understand? Wherever yeh go in the dark I'll be there to hant yeh. And when red-haired people hants yeh at night their hair's all on fire in the dark an' it burns yeh, so yeh better watch out!"

She shook her fist at the child, who, now thoroughly frightened, began to cry in earnest and ran home as fast as her fat legs could carry her, not daring to look back lest the supernatural creature with the fiery hair and the strong hand should be upon her again. It was the first time in her brief, impertinent life that Alma had ever been thoroughly frightened.

Her first act on reaching the house was to see how the land

lay. She found that her mother had gone out to get some eggs and Phoebe was up in her room with the door buttoned. No one else was about, so Alma stole noiselessly up to Phoebe's door, with righteous innocence on her tearstained face, her voice smoother than butter with deceit.

"Aunt Phoebe!" she called lovingly. "I hope you don't think I sung that mean song at you? I was real 'shamed of them Green children. I run after 'em an' tried to make 'em stop, but they jest wouldn't. I think their pa ought to be told, don't you? Say, Aunt Phoebe, you didn't think 'twas me, did you?"

No answer came from the other side of the door, for Phoebe was lying on her bed shaking with suppressed sobs and couldn't control her voice to reply even if she had known what to say. Her heart was filled with pain, too, that this child she had tended and been kind to should be so hateful.

Alma, rather nonplussed at receiving no answer, tried once or twice and then, calling out sweetly, "Well, I just thought I'd let you know 'twasn't me, Aunt Phoebe," stumped off downstairs to reflect upon the way of sinners. Her main fear was that Phoebe would "tell on her" to her father, and then she knew she would receive the other half of her spanking.

But Phoebe, with a face white with suffering and dark rings under her eyes, said not a word when she came downstairs. She went about her work not even seeming to see the naughty child, until Alma gradually grew more confident and resolved to put the "hanting" out of her mind entirely. This was easier said than done, however, for when night came she dreaded to go to bed and made several unsuccessful attempts to help Phoebe with the supper dishes. She thereby called upon herself much undeserved commendation from her gratified mother and father, which helped ease her conscience not a little.

Chapter 16

*H*iram Green put his new plan into practice the very next day. He took care to be on hand when the mail coach arrived, and as soon as the mail was distributed he presented himself at the post-office corner of the store.

"Any mail fer th' Deanes?" he inquired carelessly, after he was told there was nothing for him. "I'm goin' up there on business, an' I'll save 'em the trouble o' comin' down."

This question he put in varied forms, until it grew to be a habit with the postmaster to hand over the Deanes' mail to Hiram every day. This was rather expensive business, for Albert frequently received letters from people who didn't prepay the postage, and it went much against Hiram's grain to hand out eighteen cents or more for another man's letter, even though he was sure he'd receive it again. He made prompt collections from Albert, however, and by this means Phoebe became aware of Hiram's daily visits to the post office. Not that it made any difference to her, for she didn't expect a letter from anyone.

This went on for about two weeks, and during that time Hiram had seen very little of Phoebe, for she kept herself well out of his way. Then one day a letter bearing a New York postmark and closed with heavy seals arrived, addressed to Miss Phoebe Deane.

Hiram grasped it as if it were a long-sought fortune, put it hastily in his pocket, looking furtively around lest anyone had seen it, and slouched off toward home. When he reached there he went straight to his own room and fastened the door.

Then he took out the letter and read the address again, written in a fine large hand of a man accustomed to handling a pen. He frowned and turned it over. The seals were stamped with a crest on which was a rampant lion that seemed to defy him. He held the letter up to the light but couldn't make out any words.

Then without hesitation he took out his knife and inserted the sharpest blade under the seals one by one, prying them up carefully so they shouldn't be broken more than necessary. The letter lay open before him at last, and he read with rising fury.

New York, December 20, 1835

My dear Miss Deane,

Will you pardon my presumption in daring thus to address you without permission? My pleasant memory of our brief acquaintance has led me to wish a continuance of it, and I'm writing to ask you if you are free and willing to correspond with me occasionally. It will be a great source of pleasure to me if you can accede to my request, and I'm sure I shall be profited by it also.

Night before last our city was visited by a great calamity in the shape of a terrible fire which is still burning, although they hope they now have it under control. Its course has been along Wall Street, the line of the East River, and returning to William and Wall Streets. There must be nearly thirteen acres devastated, and I've heard it estimated there will be a loss of at least eighteen million dollars. I'm afraid it will be the cause of much suffering and distress. I was out last evening watching the conflagration for a time and helping fight the fire. It was a terrible and beautiful sight.

I've just had the honor and privilege of meeting a

*noble and brave gentleman. His name is William Lloyd
Garrison. I feel sure you would like to know about him
and the work he is doing. If I'm to have the pleasure of
writing you again I shall be glad to tell you more about
him, as I hope to meet him again and know him better.*

*Hoping that you are quite well and I shall soon have a
favorable reply from you, I am,*

*Yours with esteem,
Nathaniel Graham*

Hiram Green wasn't a rapid reader, and in spite of Nathaniel's clear chirography it took him some time to take in all the letter contained. His first thought was that his rival wasn't out of his way yet. He'd dared to write to her and ask if she was free. Ah! That showed he'd taken note of what Hiram had said about her belonging to him, and he was going to find out for himself. Well, he'd never find out by that letter, for Phoebe would never see it. That was easy enough.

Of course it was against the law to open another person's mail and was a state's prison offense, but who was to know he'd opened it? A letter could tell no tales when it was in ashes and the ashes well buried. How else could they prove it? They couldn't. He was perfectly safe and was getting more power over these two he was coming to hate and wished to crush. He congratulated himself on having been keen enough to have watched the mails. He'd outwitted them and was pleased with himself.

"Hm!" he exclaimed under his breath. "He's a-goin' to get up a correspondence with her, is he? Like to see him! I rather think by the time she answers this letter he'll uv give it up. When he gets around again to give her another try—supposin' he ain't stumped at not hearin' from her this time—I reckon she'll be nicely established in my kitchen doin' my work. Yes, she's worth fightin' for, I guess, fer she ken turn off the work faster'n anybody I've seen. Wal, I guess there ain't any cause to worry 'bout this."

Then he read it over again, jotting down on an old bit of paper the date, a few items about the New York fire, and William Lloyd Garrison's name. After that he sent the old woman who was keeping house for him to the attic in search of a coat he knew wasn't there, while he carefully burned the letter on the hearth, gathering every scrap of its ashes and pulverizing them, to make sure not a trace remained to tell the tale.

As he walked toward his barn he felt like a man of consequence, quite satisfied with himself. Hadn't he outwitted a college man? And no thought of the crime he'd just committed troubled his dull conscience.

That evening he went eagerly to Albert Deane's house and prepared to enjoy himself. The sunrise bed quilt was long since finished and rolled away in the chest of drawers in the spare bedroom. The spinning wheel had taken the place of the quilting frames. And on this particular night Emmeline had demanded that Phoebe stay downstairs and spin, declaring that the yarn should have been ready long ago for more winter stockings.

Hiram noted this fact with satisfaction and tilted his chair in anticipation.

"Heard anythin' 'bout the big fire in New York?" he began, watching Phoebe's back narrowly to see if she would start.

But Phoebe worked steadily on. She paid little heed to anything Hiram said, but as they talked of the fire she wondered whether Nathaniel Graham had been near it and hoped in a quiet way that he'd been kept safe from harm.

"Why, no," said Albert, sitting up with interest. "I haven't looked at the paper yet," he added, unfolding it with zest. "How'd you come to know, Hiram? You say you never read the papers."

"Oh, I have better ways o' knowin' than readin' it in the

papers," boasted Hiram. "I had a letter from New York straight, an' the fire's goin' on yet, an' mebbe by this time it's all burnt up."

Phoebe stood where he could see her face as he spoke about receiving a letter, but not a muscle moved to show she heard. Hiram was disappointed. He'd expected to catch some flitting expression that would show him she was interested in letters from New York. But Phoebe expected no letters from New York, so why should she start or look troubled?

"Yes," said Albert, bending over his paper, "an area of thirteen acres—693 houses burned!"

"Valued at eighteen million!" remarked Hiram. He was enjoying the unique position of knowing more than Albert about something.

"Nonsense!" said Emmeline sharply. "Thirteen acres! Why, that's not much bigger'n Hiram's ten-acre lot down by the old chestnut tree. Think of gettin' that many houses on that lot! It couldn't be done. That ain't possible. It's ridiculous! They must think we're all fools to put that in the paper."

"Oh, yes, it could, Emmeline," said Albert, looking up earnestly to convince her. "Why, even so long ago as when I stayed in New York for a month they built the houses real close without much dooryard. They could easy get that many into thirteen acres built close."

"I don't believe it!" said Emmeline, flipping her spinning wheel around skillfully. "And anyway, if 'twas so, I think it was real shiftless to let 'em all burn up. Why didn't they put it out? Those New York folks were born lazy."

"Why, Emmeline, the paper says it was so cold the water froze in the hose-pipes and they couldn't put it out."

"Serves 'em right then fer dependin' on such newfangled things as hose-pipes. It's jest some more of their laziness. Why didn't they form a line and hand buckets? A good fire line with the women an' all in it would beat all the new lazy ways invented to save folks from liftin' their fingers to even put out a fire. I'm surprised some of 'em didn't jest sit still and expect some kind of new machine to be made in time to wheel 'em away to safety 'stead of usin' their legs and runnin' out o' harm's way. Haven't they got a river in New York?"

" 'Course," said Hiram, as if he knew at all. "The fire burned the whole line of the East River." He was glad to be reminded of the rest of his newly acquired information.

"There, that just shows it!" exclaimed Emmeline. "That's just what I said. Shiftless lot, they are. Let their houses burn up right in front of a river! Well, I'm thankful to say I don't live in New York!"

The talk hummed on about her, but Phoebe heard no more. Somehow she kept her busy wheel whirring, but her thoughts had wandered off in a sunlit wood, and she was holding sweet converse with a golden day and a stranger hovering on the pleasant horizon. Near the close of the evening her thoughts came back to listen to what was going on. Hiram had brought the front legs of his chair down to the floor with a *thud*. Phoebe thought he was going home, and she was glad they'd soon be rid of his hated presence.

"Oh, by the way!" said Hiram, with a sway of conceit. "Albert, have you ever heard of a man named Garrison? William Lloyd Garrison, I believe it is."

He rolled the name out fluently, having practiced in the barn during the evening milking.

"Oh, yes," Albert said with interest. "You know who he is, Hiram. He's a smart fellow, though I'd hate to be in his boots!"

"Why?" Hiram's voice was sharp, and his eyes narrowed as they always did when he was reaching out for clues.

"Why, don't you know about Garrison? He's had a price on his head for some time back. He gets mobbed every time he turns around, too, but I guess he's pretty plucky, for he keeps right on."

"What doing?"

"Why, he's the great abolitionist. He publishes that paper, the *Liberator*, don't you know. You remember two years ago those antislavery meetings that were broken up and all the trouble they had? Well, he started it all. I don't know whether he's very wise or not, but he certainly has a lot of courage."

Hiram's eyes were narrowing to a slit now with knowledge and satisfaction.

"Oh, yes, I place him now," he drawled out. "He wouldn't be a very comfortable 'quaintance fer a man t' have, would he?"

"Well," considered Albert thoughtfully, "I wouldn't like to have any of my relations in his place. I'd be afraid of what might happen. I think likely 'twould take a bit of courage to be friend to a man like that. But they say he has friends, a few of them."

"Hm!" said Hiram. "I guess I better be goin'. 'Night." And he shuffled away at last, casting a curious smile at Phoebe as he left.

The next morning while they were working in the kitchen Emmeline remarked to Phoebe that Albert thought Hiram Green was changing for the better. He seemed to be growing real intellectual. Had Phoebe noticed how well he talked about that New York fire?

Phoebe hadn't noticed.

"What a strange girl you are!" exclaimed Emmeline, much vexed. "I should think you'd see he's takin' all this interest in things jest fer you. It ain't like him to care fer such things. He just thinks it will please you, and you're hard as nails not to 'preciate it."

"You're quite mistaken, Emmeline. Hiram Green never did anything to please anyone but himself, I'm sure," answered Phoebe, taking her apron off and going up to her room.

Phoebe was spending much more time in her room these days than pleased Emmeline. Not that her work suffered, for

Phoebe's swift fingers performed all the tasks required of her, but as soon as they were done she was off. The fact that the room was cold didn't affect her. Emmeline was in a state of chronic rage for this isolation from the rest of the family, though perhaps the only reason she liked to have her around was so she might make sarcastic remarks about her. Then, too, it seemed like an assumption of superiority on Phoebe's part. Emmeline couldn't bear superiority.

Phoebe hurried to the seclusion of her own room on every possible occasion because a new source of comfort and pleasure had been opened to her through Marcia Spafford's kindness.

Miranda had reported promptly Phoebe's two escapes from Hiram Green, and not only Marcia but also David was interested in the girl. Shortly after Alma's unexpected punishment Miranda was sent up to the Deanes to ask Phoebe down for the afternoon a little while, as "Mis' Spafford has a new book she thinks you'll enjoy readin' with her awhile." Much to Emmeline's disgust, for she'd planned a far different occupation for Phoebe, the girl accepted with alacrity and was soon seated in the pleasant library poring over one of Whittier's poems that opened up a new world to her. The poem was one David had just secured to publish in his paper, and they discussed its beauties for a few minutes. Then Marcia opened a delightful new book by Cooper.

Phoebe had a naturally bright mind, and during her school days she had studied all that came to her. Always she stood at the head of the classes, sometimes getting up at the first peep of dawn to study a lesson or work over a problem and sticking to her books until the very last minute. This had been a great source of trouble, because Emmeline objected to "taking her education so hard," as she expressed it.

"Some children have measles and whooping cough and chicken pox and mumps real hard," she'd say, "but most of 'em take learnin' easy. But Phoebe's got learnin' hard. She acts like there wasn't any use for anything else in the world but them books. Land! What good'll they do her? They won't make her spin a smoother thread er quilt a straighter row er sew a finer seam. She'll jest ferget everything she learnt when she's married. I'm sure I did." And no one ever disputed this convincing fact.

Nevertheless Phoebe had studied on, trying to please Emmeline by doing all the work required of her but still insisting on getting her lessons even if it deprived her of her rest or noon lunch. She devoured every bit of information that came her way, so that in spite of her environment she had a measure of true mental culture. It may have been this that so mystified and annoyed Emmeline.

So the afternoon was one of pure delight to Phoebe. When she insisted she must go home to help get supper, Miranda was sent with her, and the precious book went along to be read in odd moments. Since then Phoebe felt she had something to help her through the trying days.

The afternoons of reading with Marcia Spafford had become quite the settled thing every week or two, and always she had a book to carry home or a new poem or article to think about.

Emmeline had grown angry about this constant going out and asked questions until she had in a measure discovered what was going on. She held her temper in for a while, for when she spoke to Albert he didn't seem to sympathize with her irritation at Phoebe but only asked the girl to let him see the book she'd been reading. He became so delighted with it himself he forgot to bring in the armful of wood Emmeline asked for until she called him the second time.

After that Albert shared in the literary treasures Phoebe brought to the house, and it became his habit to ask when he came in to supper, "Been down to the village this afternoon, Phoebe? Didn't get anything new to read, did you?"

This made Emmeline furious, and she decided to express her mind once more to the girl.

She chose a morning when Phoebe was tied by a task she couldn't leave. "Now look here, Phoebe Deane, I must say you're goin' beyond all bounds. I think it's about time you stopped. I want you to understand I think the way you're actin' is a downright sin. It isn't enough you should scorn a good honest man that's eatin' his heart out fer yeh, an' you payin' no more 'tention to him 'n if he was the dust o' your feet, an' him able to keep you well, too. An' here you're willin' to set round an' live on relations that ain't real relations at all, an' you with money in the bank a-plenty an' never even offerin' to give so much as a little present to your little nephews and nieces that are all you've got in the world. It ain't enough you should do all that an' be a drug on our hands.

"But here you must get up a 'quaintance with a woman I don' like ner respect at all, an' let her send that poor, hard-workin', good-fer-nothin', red-headed girl after you every few days a-takin' you away from your home an' your good honest work that you ought to be willin' to do twice over fer all you've had.

"Phoebe Deane, d' you realize we let you go to school clear up to the top grade when other girls hed to stop an' go to work? It was all *his* doin's; I'd never hev allowed it. I think it jest spoils a girl to get so much knowledge. It's jest as I said 'twould be, too. Look at you! Spoiled. You want lily-white hands an' nothin' to do. You want to go to everlastin' tea parties an' bring home books to read the rest o' the time. Now I stopped school when I was in the fourth reader 'n' look at me. There ain't a woman round is better fixed 'n what I am. What do I need of more books? Answer that, Phoebe Deane! Answer me! Would it make me darn the children's stockin's er cook his meals er spin er weave better, er would it make me any better anyway? Answer me!"

Emmeline had two bright red spots on her cheeks and was very angry. When she was angry she always screamed her sentences at her opponent in a high key. Phoebe had the impulse to throw the wet dishcloth at her sister-in-law, and it was hard indeed to restrain her indignation at this speech. There was the lovely Mrs. Spafford lending her books and helping her and encouraging her in every way to improve her mind by reading and study, and even Mr. Spafford seemed anxious she should have all the books to read she desired. And here was this woman talking this way! It was beyond speech. She had nothing to say.

Emmeline stepped up close to the girl, grasped her arm, and shook it fiercely until the dishcloth came close to doing a rash deed of its own accord.

"Answer me!" she hissed in the girl's face.

"It might—" the exasperated girl began, then hesitated. What good would it do to say it?

"Well, go on," said the woman, gripping the arm painfully. "You've got some wicked word to say. Just speak it out to the one that hes been more than mother to ye, an' then I s'pose you'll feel better."

"I was only going to say, Emmeline, that more study might have made you understand others better."

"Understand! Understand!" screamed Emmeline, now thoroughly roused. "I'd like to know who I don't understand! Don't I understand my husband an' my children an' my neighbors? I s'pose you mean understand you, you good-fer-nothin' hussy! Well, that ain't necessary! You're so different from everybody else on earth that an angel from heaven er a perfesser from college couldn't understand you, an' learnin' won't make you any different, no matter how much you waste on it."

"Emmeline, listen!" said Phoebe, trying to stop this outburst. "I consider that I've worked for my board since I came here—"

"Consider! You consider! Well, really! Worked for your board, when you was scarcely more use 'n a baby when you come, an' think o' all the trouble o' raisin' ye! And you consider thet you've earned all you've got here! Well, I don't consider any such a thing, I ken tell you."

"Please let me finish, Emmeline. I was going to say I've tried to make Albert take the money I have in the bank as payment for any expense and trouble I've been to him. But he says he promised my mother he wouldn't touch a cent of it, and he won't take it."

"Oh, yes, Albert is softhearted. Well, I didn't promise yer ma, by a long sight, an' I ain't bound to no such fool notions."

"Emmeline, I don't feel the money belongs to you. You didn't bring me here or pay for whatever I've had. Albert did. I can't see why I should give you the money. You've done nothing for me but what you've had to do, and I'm sure I've worked for you enough to pay for that, but I'd much rather give the money to you than to have you talk this way—"

"Oh, I wasn't askin' fer yer money. I wouldn't take it es a gift. I was only showin' yeh up to yourself, what a selfish good-fer-nothin' you are, settin' up airs to read books when there's good honest work goin' on."

Albert happened to come in just then, and the discussion was dropped. But Phoebe with determination continued her visits to Mrs. Spafford whenever Miranda came for her— never alone, lest she encounter Hiram Green—and so the winter dragged slowly on its way.

Chapter 17

*M*eanwhile Hiram Green still kept up his attention to the post office, watching the Deanes so vigilantly that they couldn't receive mail without his knowing it. This never annoyed Albert, as he was too good-natured to suspect anyone of an ill turn, and he thought it exceedingly kind of Hiram to bring his mail up. As for Phoebe, it simply cut out all opportunity for her to go out, except when Miranda came for her.

"Why can't that Mirandy girl stay home an' mind her business an' let you come when you get ready?" asked Emmeline in a loud tone one day when Miranda was waiting in the sitting room for Phoebe to get ready to go with her. "She ac's if she was your nurse."

But Miranda continued her vigilance, and that without Phoebe's asking, and somehow Marcia always planned it that if Phoebe could stay to tea, then she and David would walk home with her. It was all delightful for Phoebe, but everything merely offended Emmeline more.

Miranda, in these days, was enjoying herself. She lost no opportunity to observe the detestable Hiram and rejoice that she'd foiled his attempts to bother Phoebe. One day, however, she happened to be in the post office when the mail was distributed. She was buying sugar and loitered a moment after the package was handed to her, watching Hiram Green who had slouched over to the counter and asked for his mail.

"Nothin' fer the Deanes?" she heard him ask in a low tone. "Nothin' fer Phoebe? She was 'spectin' somethin', I'm sure."

Miranda cast a sharp glance at him as she passed him. She was glad somehow that he received nothing. She wondered if Phoebe knew he was inquiring for her mail. Miranda tucked it in the back of her mind as something that might be of use in the future and left.

That very day the old woman who kept house for Hiram, in sweeping out his room, came across a bit of red sealing wax stamped with a part of a crest bearing a lion's head with the jaws apart. It was lying on a dark stripe in the rag carpet and hadn't been noticed before. She saw at once it was of no value and tossed it toward the open window, where it lodged on the sill next to the frame. When the window was closed it was shut in tight between sash and sill, with the lion's head, erect and fierce, caught in the crack, a tiny thing and hidden, but reminding one of "truth crushed to earth."

The next day Nathaniel Graham made a flying visit to his home to have a serious conference with his uncle the judge. His investigations concerning the two questions troubling him on his journey back to New York had involved him in matters that had now come to a crisis, and he found that some decision must be reached at once. He'd received several more letters from his uncle in Texas, urging him to come down at once and help their cause. It was becoming more dangerous to do, since Congress hadn't sanctioned any such help, and anyone who attempted it might be in serious difficulties. Yet it was being done every day. People who lived near Texas were gathering money and arms and sending men to help, and even as far away as New York many were quietly working. Public sentiment was strongly with Texas.

He'd been offered command of a company of men who were to sail soon, and he must say yes or no at once. The pressure was strong, and sometimes he almost thought he should go. The time had come to speak to Judge Bristol. Nothing could be decided without his final word, for Nathaniel felt too much honor and love for the one who had been his second father to do anything without his sanction.

As was to be expected, the judge was troubled at the thought of Nathaniel's going south to join the conflict. He argued for a long time against it, telling his nephew he had no right to consider such questions until he'd made a place for himself in the world. When Nathaniel admitted he'd been attending abolition meetings and was becoming intimate with some of the leaders, the judge was roused to hostility.

"Nathaniel, how could you?" he exclaimed in deep distress. "I thought your judgment was sound, but to be carried away by these fanatics shows anything but sound judgment. Can't you see this is a question you have no business with? If your uncle in Texas chooses to keep slaves, you have no more right to meddle with his choice than if he chose to keep horses or sheep. And as for this bosh about slavery being such a terrible evil, look at Pompey and Caesar and Dianthe and the rest. Do you think they want to be free? Why, what would the poor things do if I didn't care for them as if they were my own children? It's nonsense.

"Of course, there are a few bad masters and probably will be as long as sin is in the world. But to condemn the whole system of slavery because a few men who happen to own slaves mistreat them would be like condemning marriage because a few men abused their wives. It's nonsense for a few hotheaded fanatics to try to run the rest of the country into the molds they've made and call it righteousness. 'Let other men alone, and they'll let you go in peace' is a better motto. Let every man look out to cast the beam from his own eyes before he attempts to find a mote in his brother's."

When his uncle quoted scripture, Nathaniel was at a loss how to answer him.

"I wish you could hear Mr. Garrison talk, Uncle."

"I wouldn't listen to him for a moment," he answered hotly.

"He's a dangerous man! Keep away from all those gatherings. They only breed discontent and uprisings. You'll see that nothing but a lot of mobs will come from this agitation. Slavery can't be overthrown, and all these meetings are mere talk to let a few men get into prominence. No man in his senses would do the things Garrison has done unless he wanted to get notoriety. That's what makes him so foolhardy. Keep away from him, my boy. There's a price on his head, and you'll do yourself and your prospects no good if you have anything to do with him."

They talked far into the night, with Nathaniel trying to defend the man he'd met only once or twice but was compelled to admire. Janet pouted through the evening because Nathaniel didn't come out to talk with her, and she finally went to bed in a dark mood.

When at last Nathaniel pressed his uncle's hand at parting, they both knew he wouldn't go to Texas. Indeed, as the young man reflected during the night, he felt his purpose in going there was shaken before he came home to ask Judge Bristol's advice. He wasn't altogether sure, however, that his uncle had considered the matter from the correct viewpoint either, but the talk had somehow helped to crystallize his own views. So now he felt free, rather bound, to return and complete his law course. As for the other matter, that must be left to develop in its time. He was by no means sure he was finished with it yet, for his heart had been too deeply touched and his reason stirred.

As Nathaniel climbed into the coach at the big white gate, he felt he'd only put off these questions for a time, but he felt a certain relief that a decision had been reached at least for the present.

He had half a mind to ride on top with the driver, though it was a bitterly cold morning. But quite unexpectedly the driver suggested he better sit inside this time because of the weather.

Without giving it a passing thought he went inside, waving his hand and smiling at Janet, who stood at the front door with a fur-trimmed scarlet cloak about her shapely shoulders. The door closed, and he sat down.

There was one other passenger, a girl, who sat far back in the shadows of the coach, but her eyes shone out from the heavy wrappings of cloak and bonnet.

"Oh!" she said, catching her breath.

"And is it you?" he asked eagerly, reaching out to grasp her hand.

Then each remembered, the girl that she was alone in the coach with this man, the man that this girl might belong to another. But in spite of it they were glad to see one another.

The coach rolled out into the main street again, and as it lurched over the crossing Hiram Green, who was hurrying to his daily vigilance at the post office, caught a good view of Nathaniel's back through the coach window. The back gave the impression of an animated conversation being carried on in which the owner of the back was deeply interested.

Hiram almost paused in his walk over the crunching snow. "Oh!" he exclaimed in consternation. "Who knowed he was here!"

Then the thought that at least Nathaniel was about to depart calmed his perturbation, and he hurried on to the office.

Hiram didn't know Phoebe was in the coach. She'd managed to conceal it from him, for she felt sure that if he knew she was going that morning he'd have found it possible to have accompanied her, and she'd have found it impossible to get rid of his company. So the day before, when Emmeline suggested that somebody should go out to Miss Ann Jane Bloodgood's and get some dried saffron flowers she'd promised them last fall to dye the carpet rags, Phoebe said nothing until after Hiram had left that night. Then as she was going upstairs with her candle she turned to Emmeline.

"I've been thinking, Emmeline, that I could go over to Bloodgoods' by the morning coach if Albert could drive me down when he takes his corn to the mill. Then perhaps some of them would be coming over to the village, or I could catch a ride back, or if not I could come back by the evening coach."

Emmeline assented grimly. She wanted the dye and didn't relish the long, cold ride in the coach. Ann Jane Bloodgood was too condescending to please her, anyway. So, as Albert was going to mill early, Phoebe made her simple preparations that night and was ready bright and early. Moreover, she coaxed Albert to drive around by Granny McVane's that she might leave a bit of poetry for her which she'd told her about. The poem could have waited, but Albert didn't tell her that. And Phoebe didn't explain to Albert that if they went around by Granny's, Hiram wouldn't know she was gone and therefore wouldn't try to follow her. It was a pity Phoebe hadn't confided a little now and then in Albert, though he, poor soul, could do little against such odds as Emmeline and Hiram.

The ten-mile coach ride to Bloodgoods' wide farmhouse spun itself away into nothing in such company, and before Phoebe could believe it was half over she saw the distant roof, sagging low with overhanging snow, and the red barns glimmering warmly a little beyond. Nathaniel saw them, too, for she'd told him at once where she was going so he might not think she'd planned to go with him. He felt that the moments were precious.

"Do you remember what we talked of that night we walked to your home?" he asked.

"Oh, yes," she breathed softly. "You were talking of someone who needed setting free. I've been reading some wonderful poems lately that made me think a great deal of what you said."

He looked at her keenly. How could a girl who read poems and talked so well belong to Hiram Green?

"I've been thinking a great deal about it lately," he went on with just the breath of a sigh. "I may have to decide soon what I'll do. I wonder if I may ask you to pray for me?"

He watched her, this girl with the drooping eyes and rosy cheeks, the girl who had by her silence refused to answer his letter, and wondered if perhaps by his request he'd offended her. The coach lurched up to the wide piazza and stopped, and the driver jumped heavily into the snowy road. They could hear his steps plowing through the drift by the back wheel. His hand was on the coach door. Then quickly, as if she might be too late, her eyes were lifted to his, and he saw her heart would be in those prayers.

"Oh, I will."

Something like a flash of light went through them as they looked for that instant into one another's eyes, lifting them above earth's petty things. It was intangible. Nathaniel couldn't explain, as he sat back alone in the empty coach and went over the facts of the case, why his heart felt light and the day seemed brighter, just because a girl he knew so little had promised in that tone of voice to pray for him. It thrilled him as he thought it over, until he called himself a fool and told himself nothing was changed; Phoebe hadn't replied to his letter and had politely declined the correspondence, as she would certainly have been justified in doing even if she were the promised wife of Hiram Green. Yet his heart refused to be anything but buoyant.

He berated himself that he hadn't spoken frankly of his letter and heard what she had to say. Perhaps in some way it had never reached her, and yet after all, that was scarcely possible. Letters clearly addressed were seldom lost. It might only have embarrassed her if he had spoken.

At the next stop he accepted the coach driver's invitation to "come up top a spell. There's a fine sun comin' up now." He let old Michael babble on about the gossip of the town, until at last the sly old man asked him innocently enough, "And what did ye think av the other passenger, Mr. 'Than'el? An' ain't she a bonnie lassie?"

Then he was treated to a list of Phoebe's virtues sounded forth by one who knew very little of her except that as a child on the way home from school one day she had shyly handed him up a bunch of wayside posies as he drove by her on the road. That childish act had won his loyalty, and old Michael wasn't troubled with the truth. He was thoroughly capable of filling in virtues where he knew none. He went on the principle that what ought to be was. And so when Nathaniel arrived in New York his heart was strangely light, and he wondered often if Phoebe Deane would remember to pray for him. The momentous question seemed now to be in better hands than his own.

Meanwhile Hiram Green, finding in the post office a circular letter for Albert about a new kind of plow that was being put on the market, plodded up to the Deanes. He knew Albert had gone to mill that morning and wouldn't be home yet, but he thought the letter would be an excuse to see Phoebe. He wanted to judge whether Phoebe knew about Nathaniel's visit. He thought he could tell by her face whether she'd had a secret meeting with him or not. Yet it puzzled him to know when it could have been, for Phoebe had been quietly sewing carpet rags all evening before, and he was sure she hadn't gone by with Miranda in the afternoon to the Spaffords. Had she gone to the woods again in the winter, or didn't she know he was here? Perhaps his own skillful manipulating of the mail had nipped this miniature courtship in the bud, as it were, and there'd be no further need of his vigilance.

But when Hiram reached the Deanes and looked about for

Phoebe she wasn't there.

"Where's Phoebe?" he demanded, frowning.

"She's gone up to Ann Jane Bloodgood's t' get some saffron flowers," said Emmeline. "Won't you come in, Hiram? She'll be mighty sorry to know she missed you." Emmeline thought it was as well to keep up appearances for Phoebe.

"Yes, I'm sure," drawled Hiram. "How'd she go?" he asked her after an ominous silence in which Emmeline was thinking about what was best to say.

"She went on the coach, an' I reckon she'll come back that way by night ef there don't no one come over from Bloodgoods' this way. You might meet the coach ef you was goin' in to the village again. I don't know's Albert'll feel he hes time after losin' so much o' the day t' mill."

Hiram said nothing, but Emmeline saw he was angry.

"I'd 'a' sent you word she was goin' an' given you the chance to go 'long with her; only she didn't say a word till after you was gone home last night—" she began apologetically.

But Hiram didn't seem to heed her. He got up after a minute, his brows still lowering. He was thinking Phoebe had planned to go with Nathaniel Graham.

"I'll be over t' th' village," he said as he went out. "Albert needn't go."

Emmeline looked after him immediately.

"I shouldn't be a bit s'prised ef he give er up, the way she goes on. It's wonderful how he holds on to her. She's a fool, that's what she is, an' I've no pity fer her. I wish to goodness she was well married an' out o' the way. She does try me beyond all, with her books an' her visitin's an' her locked doors an' notions."

Meanwhile, Phoebe, unconscious of the plot growing around her, accepted an invitation to remain overnight and the next day with Ann Jane Bloodgood and drive in to town in the afternoon when she went to missionary meeting. Ann

Jane was interested in Christian missions and fascinated Phoebe with her tales of Eliot, Brainerd, Carey, Whiteman, and Robert Moffat. As she looked over Ann Jane's pile of missionary papers, Phoebe wondered how many people of one sort and another in the world needed setting free from something. It all seemed to be part of what she was praying for, the thing Nathaniel Graham was trying to decide, and he was another just like those wonderful men who were giving their lives to save others. Phoebe was glad she had come, though perhaps she might not have been if she could have seen the thought working in Hiram Green's heart.

After some reflection Hiram harnessed his horses and took the long ride over to Bloodgoods' that afternoon, arriving at the house just after Phoebe and Ann Jane were safely established in Ann Jane's second cousin's best room for a visit a mile away. Ann Jane's second cousin was an invalid and liked company, so the bright faces of the two girls cheered what would otherwise have been a lonely afternoon, and Phoebe escaped the unpleasant encounter with Hiram.

Hiram, his suspicions confirmed, met the evening coach, but no Phoebe appeared. He stepped up to Albert Deane's in the evening long enough to make sure she hadn't returned by any private conveyance. The next day he drove over again but again found the low farmhouse closed and deserted, for Ann Jane had driven with Phoebe by another road to the village missionary meeting.

His temper not much improved with his two fruitless rides, Hiram returned, watched every passenger from the evening coach alight and then drove to the Deanes' again, where he was surprised to find Phoebe had returned.

That evening when the saffron flowers were discussed he remarked that mighty nice saffron flowers were for sale in Albany and watched Phoebe narrowly. But the round cheek didn't flush or the long lashes flutter in any suspicious way.

Nevertheless, Hiram's mind never let go an evil thought once it lodged there. He felt he had a new power over Phoebe that he might use if occasion demanded. He could bide his time.

Chapter 18

Spring was coming at last, and Hiram Green, who'd been biding his time and letting his wrath smolder, thought it was time to do something. All winter Phoebe had kept comparatively free from him, except for his company with the family in the evening. He took every opportunity to make it apparent he was "keeping company" with Phoebe, through his nightly visit, and Phoebe made it plain on every occasion that she didn't consider his visit was for her. She got out of the way when she could, but Emmeline contrived to keep her unusually busy every evening, and her own room was so cold that escape was impossible.

Hiram had made several unsuccessful efforts to establish himself beside Phoebe in public, and he was getting desperate. Every Sunday when he tried to walk down the aisle with her he'd find Miranda and Rose on either side of her, or Mrs. Spafford herself, and sometimes all three, and all serenely unconscious of his presence. They accompanied her down to the carryall. She never went to the village anymore that he could discover, unless Miranda came for her or Albert took her back and forth. Once, though, he saw her flying across the fields from Granny McVane's house with a bundle that looked as if it came from the store.

He complained to Emmeline at last, and she agreed to help him. Albert wasn't taken into the scheme. For some reason it was deemed best not to tell Albert about it. He was apt to ask kind, searching questions, and he always took it for granted that one did everything with the best motives. Besides, he wasn't quick at evasion and might let the cat out of the bag.

A barn raising was to be held about ten miles on the other side of the village, and the whole country round about was invited. The Woodburys, whose barn was to be raised, were distant relatives of Emmeline, so of course the Deanes were going.

Emmeline had shown plainly she would be offended if Phoebe didn't go, though the girl would have much preferred remaining at home with the new book Mrs. Spafford had sent up the day before. It was a matter of selfishness with Emmeline. She wanted Phoebe to help with the big dinner and relieve her so she could visit with the other women.

Part of the scheme was for Albert to go in the chaise with Alma and start while Phoebe was still dressing. Emmeline had managed Albert very adroitly, telling him Hiram wanted a chance to "set in the front seat with Phoebe" in the carryall. Albert, always willing to do a good turn, acceded readily, though Alma was a somewhat reluctant passenger.

When Phoebe came downstairs she found Emmeline already seated in the back seat of the carryall with the other children. She gladly got into the front seat, as it was much pleasanter to be there than beside Emmeline, and she seldom had the opportunity of riding beside her brother, who was more congenial than the others. But in a moment Hiram Green appeared from around the corner of the house. He got quickly into the vacant seat beside Phoebe and whipped up the horses.

"Why, where is Albert?" asked Phoebe in dismay, wishing she could get out.

"He had to go on," explained Emmeline blandly. "Drive fast, Hiram. We'll be late." She added this last because she thought she saw a frightened sideways glance from Phoebe as if she might be going to get out.

Phoebe turned her head to the roadside and tried to watch

for the chance wildflowers and forget the talk of crops and gossip that was kept up between Emmeline and Hiram. But the whole pleasant day was clouded for her. Her annoyance was doubled when they passed through the village and Janet Bristol in dainty pink dimity stared at them with haughty sweetness from under her white shirred bonnet and pink-lined sunshade. Janet was evidently not going to the barn raising. She had many interests outside the village where she was born and didn't mingle freely with her fellow townspeople. Only a favored few were her friends and had the privileges of the beautiful old house.

Her passing called forth unfavorable comments from Emmeline and Hiram, and Phoebe writhed at her sister-in-law's tone, loud enough for Janet to hear easily, if she'd felt so inclined.

"The idea of wearing such fancy things in the mornin'!" she exclaimed. "I didn't think the judge was such a fool as to let his daughter come up like that, fixed up fit fer a party this early, an' a sunshade, too! What's she think it's for, I wonder! Her complexion's so dark, a little more of this weak sunshine couldn't make much difference. Mebbe she thinks she looks fine, but she's mistaken. A lazy girl all decked out never looks pretty to me."

"That's 'bout right," declared Hiram, as if he knew all about it. "Give me a good worker ev'ry time, I sez, in preference to one with ringlets an' a nosegay on her dress. But you couldn't expec' much of that one. She's goin' to marry that highfalutin Nate Graham, an' they'll have money 'nough betwixt 'em to keep her in prettys all the rest of her life. Say, did you hear Nate Graham'd turned abolitionist? Well, it's so; I heard it from a r'liable source. Hev a friend in Noo York writes me once in a while, an' I know what I'm talkin' 'bout. Hed it from headquarters like, you know. Er it's so he may git into trouble ennytime now. There's prices on them abolitionists' heads!"

Hiram turned to look straight into Phoebe's startled face, with an ugly leer of a laugh. The girl's cheeks grew pink, and she turned quickly away. Hiram felt he'd scored one against her. It made him good-natured all day.

But Phoebe found herself trembling with a single thought. Did it mean life or death, this that Nathaniel had asked her to pray about? And had her prayers perhaps helped put him in danger? Ah! But if it were true, how grand of him to be willing to brave danger for what he thought was right. Phoebe knew little about the real question at issue, though she'd read a number of Whittier's poems which had stirred her heart deeply. The great thought in her mind was that a man should be brave enough and good enough to stand against the whole world, if need be, to help a weak brother.

The day was full of noise and bustle and, for Phoebe, hard work. By instinct the women laid on her young shoulders the tasks they wished to shirk, knowing they'd be done well. They trusted Phoebe, and the fun and feasting went on, while she labored in the kitchen, gladly taking extra burdens upon herself, just to keep from being troubled by Hiram.

She was washing dishes and thinking about how she could manage not to sit next to Hiram on the return trip when a little Woodbury entered the kitchen.

"Say, Phoebe Deane," she called out, "your brother says you're to go in the chaise with him this time, an' when you get ready you come out to the barn an' get in. He says you needn't hurry, fer he's busy yet awhile."

The child was gone back to her play before Phoebe could thank her, and with lightened heart she went on washing the dishes. Perhaps Albert had surmised her dislike for riding with Hiram and planned this for her sake. She made up her mind to confide in Albert during this ride and see if he couldn't help her get rid of the obnoxious man once and for all. Albert was usually slow and undecided, but once in a great while, when he put his foot down about something, things would go as he said.

She wiped the last dish, washed her hands, and ran upstairs for her bonnet and mantilla. Everybody else was gone. The long, slanting rays of the setting sun were streaming in at the window and touching the great four-poster bed where only her wraps remained. She put them on quickly, glad everyone else was out of the way and she wouldn't have to wait for a lot of good-byes. The day had been wearying to her, and she was thankful it was over.

Mr. and Mrs. Woodbury stood together by the great stepping-stone in front of the house. They'd said good-bye to Albert and Emmeline an hour before and had just been seeing off the last wagon load of guests. They turned eagerly to thank Phoebe for her assistance. Indeed, the girl had many warm friends among older people who knew her kind heart and willing hands.

"What! Your folks all gone and left you, Phoebe?" exclaimed Mrs. Woodbury in dismay. "Why, they must 'a' forgot you."

"No, they're not all gone, Mrs. Woodbury. Our chaise is out in the barn waiting for me. Albert sent word to me by your Martha that I needn't hurry, so I finished the dishes."

"Oh! Now that's so good of you, Phoebe," said the tired farmer's wife, who expected to have plenty of cleaning to do after her guests departed. "You shouldn't ov done that. I could 'a' cleaned up. I'm 'fraid you're real tired. Wouldn't you like to stay overnight and get rested?"

But Phoebe shook hands happily with them and hurried down to the chaise. Now the Woodbury barn was out near the road, and the chaise stood facing the road. The horse wasn't tied but waited with turned head as if his master wasn't far away.

Phoebe jumped in, calling, "Come on, Albert. I'm here at

last. Did I keep you waiting long?"

Then before she had time to look around or know what was happening, Hiram Green stepped out from the barn door, sprang into the seat beside her, and with swiftness caught up the whip and gave the horse such a cut that it started off at a brisk trot down the road. He had sent the message by little Martha Woodbury, just as it had been given. Emmeline had managed the rest.

"Oh!" gasped Phoebe. "Why, Mr. Green, Albert is here waiting for me somewhere. Please stop the horse and let me find him. He sent word he'd wait for me."

"That's all right," said Hiram nonchalantly. "Albert decided to go in the carryall. Your sister-in-law was in a great stew to get back fer milkin' time an' made him come, so I offered to bring ye back home."

Phoebe's heart froze. She looked wildly about her and didn't know what to do. The horse was going too fast for her to jump. She had no idea if Hiram would stop and let her out if she asked him. His talk that last time they had an encounter had shown her she mustn't let him see he had her in his power. Besides, what excuse could she give for stopping except that she didn't wish to go with him? And how otherwise could she get home that night? How she wished she'd accepted Mrs. Woodbury's kind invitation. Couldn't she, perhaps, manage it yet?

"That's very kind of you," she faltered with white lips, as she tried to marshal her wits and contrive some way out. Then she pretended to look about her in the seat.

"I wonder if I remembered to bring my apron," she said faintly. "Would you mind, Mr. Green, just driving me back to see?"

"Oh, I reckon you'll find it," Hiram said easily. "Ef you don't, you got a few more, ain't you? Here, ain't this it?" He fished out a damp roll from under the seat.

Phoebe had hoped for one wild moment that she'd really dropped it when she got into the chaise, for it didn't seem to be about anywhere, but the sight of the damp blue roll dashed all her confidence. She could only accept the situation as bravely as possible and make the best of it. Her impulse was to turn angrily and tell Hiram Green he'd deceived her. But she knew that would do no good, and the safest thing was to act as if it were all right and try to keep the conversation on everyday topics. If he'd only keep on driving at this pace the journey wouldn't be so intolerably long after all, and they might hope to reach home a little before dark. She summoned all her courage and tried to talk pleasantly, although the countenance of the man beside her, as she glanced at his profile, frightened her. It had both triumph and revenge upon it.

"They had a pleasant day for the raising, Mr. Green," she began.

And then to her horror he slowed the horse to a walk and sat back close to her as if he intended to enjoy the tête-à-tête to its full.

It was an awful strain. Phoebe's cheeks blazed out in two red spots. They dragged their way through woods, and Phoebe sat up very straight, very much to her side of the chaise, and laughed and talked as if she were wound up.

Hiram didn't say much. He sat watching her, almost devouring her changing face, fully understanding her horror of him and this ride, yet determined to make her suffer every minute of the time. It made his anger all the greater as he saw her bravely try to keep up a semblance of respect toward him and knew she didn't feel it. Why couldn't she give it freely and not against her will? What was there about him she disliked? Never mind. She'd pay for her dislike. She would see she'd have to treat him as she would treat those she liked, whether she wished to or not.

She suggested they better drive faster, since it was getting

late and would be dark. He said that didn't matter, that
Emmeline had said they weren't to hurry. She told him she'd
be needed, but he told her it was right she should have a little
rest once in a while. And he smiled grimly as he said it,
knowing the present ride was anything but rest to the poor
tired soul beside him. He seemed to delight in torturing her.
The farther she edged away from him, the nearer he came to
her. Finally, when they emerged from the woods and met a
carryall with some people they both knew, he was sitting
quite over on her side, and she was almost out of her seat, her
face a picture of rage and helplessness.

Emboldened by the expression on the faces of their
acquaintances, Hiram threw his arm across the back of the
chaise, until it encircled Phoebe's back, or would have if she
hadn't sat upon the extreme front edge of the seat.

They'd reached a settlement of three houses, where a tollgate, stretching its white pole out across the way, and a little
store and schoolhouse went by the name of The Crossroads.
Hiram flung a bit of money out to the toll man and drove on
without stopping. Phoebe's heart was beating wildly. She
couldn't sit like that on the edge of her seat another instant.
Something must be done.

"Mr. Green, would you mind moving over just a little? I
haven't quite enough room," she gasped.

"Oh, that's all right," said Hiram, as heartily as if he didn't
understand the situation. "Just sit clos'ter. Don't be shy." His
arm came around her waist and by brute strength drew her up
to him, so that it looked from behind as if they were a pair of
lovers. The top of the chaise was thrown back so they could
easily be seen.

They'd just passed the last house. It was the home of old
Mrs. Duzenberry and her elderly daughter, Susanna. Living so
far from the village, they made it a point not to miss anything
that went by their door, and at this hour in the afternoon,

when their simple tea was brewing, they both sat by the front window, ready to bob to the door the minute anything of interest came by. Of course they both bobbed on this occasion, the daughter with folded arms and alert beak like some old bird of prey and the mother just behind with exclamatory interrogations written in every curve of her cap strings.

Phoebe, glancing back wildly, as she felt herself drawn beyond her power to stop it, saw them gaping at her in amazement, and her cheeks grew crimson with shame.

"Stop!" she cried, putting out her hands and pushing against him.

She might as well have tried to push off a mountain in her path. Hiram only laughed and drew her closer, till his ugly, grizzled face was near her own. She could feel his breath on her cheek, and the horse was going faster now. She didn't know just how it happened, whether Hiram had touched him with the whip or spoken a low word. They were down the road out of sight of the Duzenberrys' before she could wrench herself away from the scoundrel. Even then he let go of her for a moment only so that he might settle himself a little closer and more comfortably, and then the strong, cruel arm came back as if it had a right around her waist, and Hiram's face came cheek to cheek with her own.

She uttered one terrible scream and looked around, but no one was in sight. The sun, which had been slowly sinking like a ball of burning opal, suddenly dropped behind a hill and left the world dull and leaden with a heavy gray sky. Dark blue clouds seemed all around, which until now hadn't been noticed, and a quick uncertain wind was springing up. A low rumble behind them seemed to wrap them in a new dread. But the strong man's grasp held her fast, and her screams brought no help.

In the horror of the moment a thought of her mother came, and she wondered if that mother could see her child and whether it didn't give her deep anguish even in the bliss of heaven to know she was in such straits. Then as the sharp stubble of Hiram's upper lip brushed the softness of her cheek fear gave her strength, and with a sudden mighty effort she broke from his grasp.

Reaching out to the only member of the party who seemed at all likely to give any aid, Phoebe caught the reins and pulled back on them with all her might, while her heart was lifted in a swift prayer for help. Then quick, as if in instant answer, while the gray plow horse reared back upon his haunches and plunged wildly in the air, came a brilliant flash of jagged lightning, as if the sky were cloven in wrath and the light of heaven let through. This was followed instantly by a terrible crash of thunder.

With an oath of mingled rage and awe, Hiram pushed Phoebe from him and reached for the reins to try and soothe the frightened horse, who was plunging and snorting and trembling with fear.

The chaise was on the edge of a deep ditch half filled with muddy water. One wheel was almost over the edge. Hiram saw the danger and reached for his whip. He cut the horse a frantic lash which brought his forefeet to the ground again and caused him to start off down the road on a terrific gallop.

But in that instant, while the chaise poised on the edge of the ditch, Phoebe's resolve had crystallized into action. She gave a wild spring, just as the cut from the whip sent the horse tearing headlong down the road. Her dress caught in the arm of the chaise, and for one instant she poised over the ditch. Then the fabric gave way, and she fell heavily, striking her head against the fence, and lay huddled in the muddy depths. Down the hard road echoed the heavy hoofbeats of the horse in frenzied gallop with no abatement, and over all the majestic thunder rolled.

Chapter 19

*H*er senses swam off into the relief of unconsciousness, but the cold water creeping up through her clothing chilled her back to life again. In a moment more she opened her eyes in wonder that she was lying there alone, free from her tormentor. She imagined she could hear the echo of the horse's feet, or was it the thunder? Then came the awful thought: What would happen if he returned and found her lying here? He'd be terribly angry at her for having frightened the horse and jumped out of the chaise. He'd take it out on her in some way, she felt sure, and she'd be utterly defenseless against him.

Not a soul was in sight, and it was suddenly growing dark. She must be at least six or seven miles away from home. She didn't come that way often enough to be sure of distances. With near fear she sat up and crept out of the water. The mud was deep, and it was difficult to step, but she managed to get away from the oozy soil and into the road again. Then in a panic she sprang across the ditch and crept under the fence. She must fly from here. When Hiram succeeded in stopping the horse he'd undoubtedly come back for her, and she must get away before he found her.

Which way should she go? She looked back on the road but feared to go that way, lest he'd go to those houses and search for her. There was no telling what he'd say. She had no faith in him. He might say she'd given him the right to put his arm around her. She must get away from here at once where he couldn't find her. Out to the right, across the road, it was all open country. There was no place nearby where she could take refuge. But across this field and another was a growth of trees and bushes. Perhaps she could reach there and hide and make her way home after he'd gone.

She fled across the spring-sodden field as fast as her soaked shoes and trembling limbs could carry her, slipping now and then and almost falling, but going on, wildly, blindly, till she reached the fence. Once she thought she heard the distant bellowing of a bull, but she crept to the other side of the fence and kept on her way, breathless. And now the storm broke into wild splashes of rain, pelting on her face and hair, for her bonnet had fallen back and was hanging around her neck by its ribbons. The net had come off from her hair, and the long locks blew about her face and lashed her in the eyes as she ran. It was dark as night, and Phoebe could see only dimly where she was going. Yet this was a comfort to her rather than a source of fear. She felt it would cover her hiding better. Her worst dread was to come under Hiram Green's power again.

She worked her way through the fields, groping for the fences, and at last she reached an open road and stood almost afraid to try it, lest somewhere she'd see Hiram lurking. The lightning blazed and shivered all about her, trailing across the heavens in awful and wonderful display. The thunder shuddered above her until the earth itself seemed to answer, and she felt herself in a rocking abyss of horror. And yet the most awful thing in it all was Hiram Green.

She'd heard all her life that the most dangerous place in a thunderstorm was under tall trees, yet so little did she think of it that she made straight for the shelter of the wood. Though the shocks crashed about her and seemed to be cleaving the forest giants, there she stayed until the storm abated and the genuine darkness had succeeded.

She was wet to the skin and trembling like a leaf. Her

strongest impulse was to sink to the earth and weep herself into nothingness, but her common sense wouldn't let her even sit down to rest. She knew she must start at once if she hoped to reach home. Yet by this time she had very little idea of where she was or how to get home.

With another prayer for guidance she started out, keeping sharp lookout along the road so Hiram couldn't come upon her unaware. Twice she heard vehicles in the distance and crept into the shelter of some trees until they passed. She heard pleasant voices talking about the storm and longed to cry out to them for help, yet dared not. What would they think of her, a young girl out alone at that time of night and in such a condition? Besides, they were all strangers. She dared not speak.

She wouldn't have spoken to friends either, for they'd have been even more astonished to find her this way. She thought longingly of Mrs. Spafford and Miranda, but she dreaded lest even Mrs. Spafford might think she'd done wrong to ride even a couple of miles with Hiram Green after all the experience she'd had with him. Yet as she plodded along she wondered how she could have done differently, unless indeed she'd dared to pull up the horse and jump out at once. Very likely, though, she wouldn't have escaped from her tormentor as easily earlier in the afternoon as when she leaped into the ditch.

As she looked back upon the experience it seemed as if the storm had been sent by Providence to provide her a shield and a way of escape. If it hadn't been for the storm the horse wouldn't have been easily frightened into running, and Hiram would soon have found her and compelled her to get into the chaise again. What could she have done against his strength? She shuddered, partly with cold and partly with horror.

A slender thread of pale moon had come up, but it gave a sickly light and soon slipped out of sight again, leaving only the kind stars whose lights looked brilliant but so far away tonight. Everywhere was a soft dripping sound and the seething of the earth drinking in a good draught.

Once when it seemed as if she'd been going for hours, she sat down on the wet bank to rest, and a horse and rider galloped out of the blackness past her. She hid her white face in her lap so he may have thought her only a stump beside the fence. She was thankful he didn't stop to see. So far nothing had given her a clue to her whereabouts, and she was cold, so terribly cold.

At last she passed a house she didn't know, and then another, and another. Finally she figured out she was in a little settlement, about three miles from the Deanes' farm. She couldn't tell how she'd wandered or how she came to be so far away when she must have walked at least twenty miles. But the knowledge of where she was brought her new courage.

A road led from this settlement straight to Granny McVane's, so she wouldn't need to go back by the road where Hiram would search for her, if indeed he hadn't already given up the search and gone home. The lights were out everywhere in this village, except in one small house at the farthest end, and she stole past that as if she were a wraith. Then she breathed more freely as she came into the open country road again and knew only two or three houses stood between her and home.

It occurred to her to wonder dully if the horse had thrown Hiram out and maybe he was hurt, and whether she might not after all have to send a search party after him. She wondered what he'd do when he couldn't find her, supposing he wasn't hurt. Perhaps he'd been too angry to go back for her and her dread of him was unnecessary. But she thought she knew him well enough to know he wouldn't easily give her up.

She wondered if he'd tell Albert and whether Albert would be worried—she was sure he'd be good, kind Albert—and what would Emmeline say? Emmeline, who had been at the bottom of all this, she was sure—and then her thoughts would trail on ahead of her in the wet, and her feet would lag behind, and she'd feel she couldn't catch up. If only a kind coach would appear! Yet she kept on, holding up her heavy head and gripping her wet mantle close with her cold hands, shivering as she went.

Once she caught herself murmuring, "Oh, Mother, Mother!" and then wondered what it meant. So stumbling on, slower and slower, she came at last to Granny McVane's little house, all dark and quiet, but so kind-looking in the night. She longed to crawl to the doorstep and lie down to die, but duty kept her on. No one must know of this if she could help it. That seemed to be the main thought she could grasp with her weary brain.

The fields behind Granny McVane's were miry. Three times she fell and the last time almost lay still, but some stirring of brain and conscience helped her up and on again, across the last hillock, over the last fence, through the garden, and up to the back door of her home.

A light was burning inside, but she was too far gone to think about it now. She tried to open the door, but the latch was heavy and wouldn't lift. She fumbled and almost gave it up, but then it was opened sharply by Emmeline with her hair in a hard knot and old lines under her eyes. She wore a wrapper over her night robe and a blanket around her shoulders. Her feet were thrust into an old pair of Albert's carpet slippers. She held a candle high above her head and looked out shrewdly into the night. It was plain she was just awake and fretted at the unusual disturbance.

"Fer pity's sake, Phoebe! Is that you? Where on earth hev you ben? You've hed us all upside down huntin' fer yeh, an' Albert ain't got home yet. I tol' him 'twas no use. You'd mos' likely gone in somewheres out o' the storm, an' you'd be home all right in the mornin'. But it's just like your crazy ways to come home in the middle o' th' night. Fer goodness' sake, what a sight yeh are! You ain't comin' in the house like that! Why, there'll be mud to clean fer a week. Stop there till I get some water an' a broom."

But Phoebe, with deathly white face and unseeing eyes, stumbled past her without a word, the water and mud oozing out of her shoes at every step and dripping from her garments. Her soaked bonnet hung dejectedly on her shoulders, and her hair was one long drenched mantle of darkness. Emmeline, half awed by the sight, stood still in the doorway and watched her go upstairs, realizing the girl didn't know what she was doing. Then she shut the door sharply as she'd opened it and followed Phoebe upstairs.

Phoebe held out until she reached her own door and opened it. Then she sank without a sound upon the floor and lay there as if dead. All breath and consciousness had fluttered out, it seemed, with that last effort.

Emmeline set the candle down with a sudden, startled exclamation and went to her. She felt her hands cold, like ice, and her face like wet marble, and, hard as she was, she was frightened. Her conscience, so long on vacation, leaped into new life. What part had she borne in this that might yet be a tragedy?

She unlaced the clodded shoes, untied the soaked bonnet, pulled off the wet garments one by one, and wrapped the girl in thick warm blankets, dragging her light weight to the bed. But still no sign of consciousness had come. She felt her heart and listened for a breath, but she couldn't tell if she were alive or not. Then she went downstairs with hurried steps, flapping over the kitchen floor in the large carpet slippers, and stirred up the fire that had been banked down, putting the kettle over it to heat. In a little while she had plenty of hot water and various remedies applied, but life seemed scarcely yet to have crept back to her, with only a flutter of eyelids now and then or a fleeting breath like a sigh. The dawn was coming on, and Albert's voice in low strained tones could be heard outside.

"No, I'm not going to stop for anything to eat, Hiram. You may if you like, but I won't stop till I find her. It's been a real bad night, an' to think of that little girl out in it—I can't bear it!" There seemed to be something like a sob in Albert's last words.

"Well, suit yerself," answered Hiram gruffly. "I'm pretty well played out. I'll go home an' get a bite, an' then I'll come on an' meet yeh. You'll likely find her back at Woodburys', I reckon. She wanted to go back, I mind now. We'd ought to 'a' gone there in the first place."

The voices were under her window. Phoebe slowly opened her eyes and, shuddering, grasped Emmeline's hands so tightly that it hurt her.

"Oh, don't let him come—don't let him come!" she pleaded and sank away into unconsciousness again.

It was a long time before they could rouse her, and when she finally opened her eyes, she didn't know them. A fierce and terrible fever had flamed up in her veins till her face was brilliant with color, and her long dark hair was scorched dry again in its fires.

Granny McVane came quietly over the next day and offered to nurse her. Then the long blank days of fever stretched themselves out for the unconscious girl, and a fight between life and death began.

Now on that very afternoon of the barn raising Mistress Janet Bristol, in her pink and white frills and furbelows, with a bunch of pink moss roses at her breast and in her haughtiest air, drove over to the Deanes to call on Phoebe. It was a long-delayed response to her cousin Nathaniel's most cousinly letter requesting her to do so. She had parleyed long with herself whether she'd go or not. But, at last, curiosity to see what was in this country girl to attract her handsome, brilliant cousin led her to go.

One can scarcely conjecture what Emmeline would have said and thought if she'd seen the grand carriage drive up before her door, with its coachman and footman in livery. But no one was at home to tell the tale except the white lilacs on the great bush near the front gate, who waved a welcome rich with fragrance. Perhaps they sent the essence of the welcome Phoebe would have gladly given this girl she admired.

So half petulant at this reception when she had condescended to come, Janet scanned the house for some trace of the life of this unknown girl and drove away with the memory of lilac fragrance floating about a dull and commonplace house. She left half determined to tell her cousin she'd done her best and wouldn't go again. No sign was left behind to tell this other girl of the lost call. If she had been able to make her call on Phoebe that afternoon, it's doubtful whether either of the two could have found and understood the other at that time.

Janet drove back to her own world again, and the door between the two closed. That very evening's mail brought a brief letter from Nathaniel, saying his dear friend and chum Martin Van Rensselaer would be coming north in a few days, and he wanted Janet to invite him to spend a little time in the old home. He would try to get away from his work and run up for a few days, and they'd all have a good time together. So while this other girl, whose unsheltered life had been so full of sorrow, was plodding her way through the darkness and rain alone in the night with fear, Janet Bristol sat in her stately parlor, where a bright fire cast rosy lights over her white dress, and planned how to charm the young theologue.

Chapter 20

*M*iranda was out in the flower bed by the side gate. She had gathered a handful of spicy gray-green southern-wood and was standing by the fence looking wistfully down the street. The afternoon coach was in, and she was idly watching to see who came in, but not with her usual vim. The specter of the shadow of death was hovering too near Phoebe for Miranda to take much interest in things in general.

Three days after Phoebe's midnight walk Miranda had gone out to see her and bring her down to take tea with Mrs. Spafford. What was her dismay to find she was refused admittance and that too very shortly.

"Phoebe's sick abed!" snapped Emmeline. She'd been tried beyond measure over all the extra work thrown in her hands by Phoebe's illness, and she had no time for buttered words. "No, she can't see you today or next day. She's got a fever, an' she don't know anybody. The doctor says she mus' be kep' quiet. No, I can't tell yeh how she got it. The land only knows it! Ef she ever gits well mebbe she ken tell herself, but I doubt it. She'll uv forgot by that time. What she does know she fer-gets mostly. No, you can't go an' take care of her. She's got folks 'nough to do that now, more'n she needs. There ain't a livin' thing to do but let her alone till she comes out of it. You don't suppose *you* c'd take care o' her, do yeh? *Hm!* Wal, I ain't got time to talk." And the door was shut in her face.

Miranda, however, wasn't to be turned aside so easily. With real concern in her face she marched around the woodshed to the place under the little window of the kitchen chamber that she knew was Phoebe's room.

"Phoebe!" she called softly. "Phoe-bee!"

And the sick girl tossing on her bed of fever called wildly, "Don't you hear that Phoebe-bird calling, Mother! Oh, Mother! It's calling me from the top of the barn. It says, 'Phoebe, I'm here! Don't be afraid!' " And the voice trailed off into incoherence again.

Granny McVane hobbled to the window, perplexed, for she, too, had heard the soft sound.

"Oh, is that you, Granny?" whispered Miranda. "Say, what's the matter with Phoebe? Is she bad?"

"Yes, real bad," whispered back Granny. "She don't know a soul, poor little thing. She thinks her mother's here with her. I don't know much about how it happened. There was an accident, and the horse ran away. She was out in that awful storm the other night. She's calling, and I must go back to her."

In much dismay Miranda hurried back to the village. She besieged the doctor's house until he came home but could get only gravity and shakings of the head.

"She may pull through, she may—" the old doctor would say doubtfully. "She's young and strong, and it might be—but there's been a great shock to the system, and she doesn't respond to my medicines. I can't tell."

Every day the story was the same, though David and Marcia had gone themselves. And though Miranda traveled the mile and a half out to the Deane farm every afternoon after her work was done, there'd been no change. The fever raged on. Miranda's faithful heart was as near discouragement as it had ever come in its dauntless life.

And now this afternoon she had just returned from a particularly fruitless journey to the farm. She couldn't get sight or sound of anyone but Emmeline, who slammed the door in her face as usual after telling her she wished she'd mind her own business and let folks alone that weren't troubling her.

Miranda felt, as she trudged back to the village with tears in her eyes, as if she must cry out or do something. She had never come to a place before where her wits couldn't plan out some help for those she loved. Death was different. One could not outwit death.

Then, like a slowly dawning hope, she saw Nathaniel Graham coming up the street with his carpetbag in his hand.

Nathaniel had come up for a day to tell his uncle and cousin all about his dear friend he so much desired to have welcomed for a week or two. He'd been made junior partner in a law firm, the senior partner being an old friend of Judge Bristol, and his work would be strenuous. Otherwise he'd probably have planned to be at the old home all summer. As it was, he could hope for only a few days now and then when he could be spared.

Nathaniel came to a halt with his pleasant smile as he recognized Miranda.

"How do you do, Miss Miranda? Are all your folks well? Are Mr. and Mrs. Spafford at home? I must try to run over and see them before I go back. I'm only here on a brief visit and must return tomorrow. How's the place getting on? All the old friends just the same? Do you ever see Miss Deane? She's well, I hope."

Nathaniel was running through these sentences pleasantly, as one will who's been away from a town for a time. He didn't note the replies carefully, as he thought he knew pretty well what they'd be, having heard from home only a day or two before. He was just going on when something deep and different in Miranda's tone and clouded eyes made him pause and listen.

"No, she ain't well. Phoebe Deane ain't. She's way down sick, an' they don't nobody think she's goin' to get well, I'm sure o' that!"

Then the unexpected happened. Two big tears welled up

and rolled down the two dauntless, freckled cheeks. Nobody had ever seen Miranda Griscom cry before.

A sudden nameless fear gripped Nathaniel's heart. Phoebe Deane sick! Near to death! All at once the day clouded for him.

"Tell me, Miranda," he said gently. "She is my friend, too, I think. I didn't know—I hadn't heard. Has she been ill long? What was the cause?"

" 'Bout two weeks," said Miranda, mopping her face with the corner of her clean apron, "an' I can't find out what made her sick. But it's my 'pinion she's bein' tormented to death by that long-legged blatherskite of a Hiram Green. He ain't nothing' but a big bully, fer he's really a coward at heart, an' what's more, folks'll find it out someday ef I don't miss my guess. But he ken git up the low-downdest, pin-prickenist, soul-shakenest tormentin's that ever a saint hed to bear. An' ef Phoebe Deane ain't a saint I don't know who is, 'cept my Mis' Spafford. Them two's ez much alike's two peas—sweet peas, I mean, pink an' white ones in bloom."

Nathaniel warmed to Miranda's eloquence and felt that here was something that must be investigated.

"I believe that man is a scoundrel!" said Nathaniel earnestly. "Do you say he really dares to annoy Miss Deane?"

"Well, I rather guess you'd think so! She can't stir without he's at her side, 'tendin' like he b'longs there. She can't bar the sight o' him, an' he struts up to her at the church door like he owned her, an' ef 'twa'n't fer me an Rose an' Mis' Spafford, she couldn't get red of 'im. She can't go to the post office anymore 'thout he hants the very road, though she's told him up 'n' down she won't hev a thing to do 'ith him. I hev to go after her an' take her home when she comes to see us, fear he'll dog her steps, an' he's scared her most to death twice now, chasin' after her, once at night when she was comin' down to your house to bring some letter she'd found."

Nathaniel's face grew suddenly alert, and a glow of indignation rolled over it. He set down his carpetbag and came close to the fence to listen.

"Why, w'd you b'lieve it, that feller found she liked to go to th' post office fer a walk, and he jest follered her every time, an' when she quit goin', he hunted up other ways to trouble her. They tell a tale 'bout th' horse runnin' away an' her bein' out in a big storm the night she took sick, but I b'lieve in my soul he's 't th' bottom of it, an' I'd like to see him get his comeuppance right now."

"Miranda, do you happen to know—I don't suppose you ever heard Miss Deane speak of receiving a letter from me."

Miranda's keen eyes were on his face.

"Long 'bout when?" she demanded.

"Why, last December, I think it was. I wrote her a note and never received any reply. I wondered if it might have been lost, or whether she didn't like my writing it, as I'm almost a stranger."

"No, sirree, she never got that letter! I know fer sure, 'cause I happened to speak to her 'bout hearin' Hiram Green askin' pertick'ler fer her mail in the post office one day, an' I found out he gets the Deanes' mail quite often an' carries it out to 'em. I tole her I thought she wouldn't like him meddlin' with her mail, an' she jest laughed an' said he couldn't do her any harm thet way, 'cause she never got a letter in her life 'cept one her mother wrote her 'fore she died. Thet was only a little while back, 'bout a month er so, 'way after January, fer the snow was most gone the day I tol' her. She can't uv got your letter nohow. I'd be willin' to bet a good fat doughnut thet rascally Hiram Green knows what come o' thet letter. My, but I'd like to prove it on him!"

"Oh, Miranda, he would scarcely dare to tamper with another person's mail. He's a well-informed man and must know that's a crime. He could be put in prison for that. It must have been lost if you're sure she never received it."

"Could he?" said Miranda eagerly. "Could he be put in prison? My! But I'd like to help get him lodged there fer a spell 'til he learned a little bit o' politeness toward th' angels thet walks the airth in mortal form. Dast! Hiram Green dast? He's got cheek enough to dast ennythin'. You don't know him. He wouldn't think ennyone would find out! But, say, I'll tell you what you ken do. You jest write that letter over again, ef you ken rem'mber 'bout what you wanted to say b'fore, an' I'll agree to git to her firsthand this time."

Nathaniel's face was alight with the eagerness of a boy. Somehow Miranda's childish proposal was pleasant to him. Her honest face beamed at him expectantly.

"I'll do it, Miranda," he replied with earnestness. "I'll do it this very day and trust it to your kindness to get it to her safely. Thank you for suggesting it."

Then suddenly a cloud came over the freckled face, and the gray eyes filled with tears again.

"But I mightn't ever git it to 'er, after all, yeh know. They say she's jest hangin' 'tween life 'n' death today, an' t'night's the crisis."

A cloud seemed suddenly to have passed before the sun again; a chill almost imperceptible came in the air. What was that icy something gripping Nathaniel's heart? Why did all the forces of life and nature seem to hang upon the well-being of this young girl? He caught his breath.

"We must pray for her, Miranda, you and I," he said gravely. "She once promised to pray for me."

"Did she?" said Miranda, looking up with solemn awe through the tears. "I'm real glad you tole me that. I'll try, but I ain't much on things like that. I could wallup Hiram Green a grea' deal better'n I could pray. But I s'pose that wouldn't be no good, so I'll do my best at the prayin'. Ef it's kind of botched up, mebbe yours'll make up fer it. But, say, you better write that letter right off. I've heard tell there's things like thet'll help when crises comes. I'm goin' t' make it a pint t' git up there t'night, spite o' that ole Mis' Deane, an' ef I see chance I'll give it to her. I kind of think it might please her to have a letter t' git well fer."

"I'll do it, Miranda. I'll do it at once and bring it around to you before dark. But you must be careful not to trouble her with it till she's able. You know it might make her worse to be bothered with any excitement like a letter from a stranger."

"I'll use my bes' jedgment," said Miranda with happy pride. "I ain't runnin' no resks, so you needn't worry."

With a new interest in his face Nathaniel grasped his carpetbag and hurried to his uncle's house. He found Janet ready with a joyful welcome, but he showed more anxiety to get to his room than to talk to her.

"I suppose it was dusty on the road today," she conceded unwillingly, "but hurry back. I've a great deal to ask you and to tell, and I want you all to myself before your friend comes."

But once in his room he forgot dust and sat down immediately to the great mahogany desk where paper and pens were just as he'd left them when he went away. Janet had to call twice before he made his appearance, for he was deep in writing a letter.

My dear Miss Deane,

They tell me you are lying very ill, and I feel as if I must write a few words to tell you how anxious and sad I am about you. I want you to know I'm praying that you may get well.

I wrote you some time ago asking if you were willing to correspond with me, but I have reason now to think you never received my letter, so I have ventured to write again. I know it may be some time before you're able even to read this, but I'm sending it by a trusty messenger, and

I'm sure you will let me know my answer when you are better. It will be a great source of pleasure and profit to me if you will write to me sometimes.

Yours faithfully,
Nathaniel Graham

He folded and addressed it, sealing it with his crest, and then Janet called for the second time.

"Yes, Janet, I'm coming now, really. I had to write a letter. I'm sorry, but it couldn't wait."

"Oh, how poky! Always business, business!" exclaimed Janet. "It's a good thing your friend is coming tonight, for it's plain we'll have no good of you. How have you grown old and serious so soon, Nathaniel? I thought you'd stay a boy a long time."

"Just wait until I send my letter, Janet, and I'll be as young as you please for two whole days."

"Let Caesar take it for you then. There's no need for you to go."

"I'd rather take it myself, cousin," he said, and she knew by his look he would have his way.

"Well, then, I'll go with you," she pouted, and taking her sunshade from the hall table, unfurled its rosy whiteness.

He was dismayed at this but, making the best of it, smiled good-humoredly. Together they went out into the summer street and walked beneath the long arch of maples newly dressed in green.

"But this isn't the way to the post office," she said, when they had walked some distance.

"But this is the way for my letter," he said pleasantly. "Now, Janet, what have you to ask me so insistently?"

"About this Martin friend of yours. Is he nice? That is, will I like him? It isn't enough that you like him, for you like some very stupid people sometimes. I want to know if I'll like him."

"And how should I be able to tell that, Janet? Of one thing I'm sure—he'll have to like you," he said, surveying his handsome cousin with admiration. "That's a very pretty sunshade you have. May I carry it for you?"

"Well, after that pleasant speech perhaps you may," she said, surrendering it. "About this young man, is it really true, Nathaniel, that he's a minister and is to preach for Dr. MacFarlane while the doctor goes to visit his daughter? Father thought you had arranged for that. You see, it's very important that I like him, because if I don't I simply can't go to church and hear him preach. In fact I may stay away anyway. I'd be so afraid he'd break down if I liked him, and if I didn't I'd want to laugh. It'll be so funny to see a minister at home every day and know all his faults and peculiarities, and then see him get up and try to preach. I'm *sure* I'd laugh."

"I'm sure you would dare do nothing of the kind when Martin preaches."

"Oh, is he then so terribly solemn? I shan't like him in the least."

"Wait until he comes, Janet. The evening coach will soon be in."

They had reached the Spafford house now, and Nathaniel's anxiety about delivering his letter was relieved by seeing Miranda hurry out to the flower bed again. She was quite close to the fence as they came up, but she remained unconscious of their presence until Nathaniel spoke.

"Is that you, Miss Miranda?" he said, lifting his hat as though he hadn't seen her before that afternoon. "Will you kindly deliver this letter for me?"

He handed her the letter directly from his pocket, and Janet couldn't see the address. Miranda took it serenely.

"Yes, sir," she said, scrutinizing the address at a safe angle from Janet's vision. "I'll deliver it safe an' sure. Afternoon, Mis' Janet. Like a bunch o' pink columbine to stick in yer dress? Jes' matches them posies on the muslin delaine." And she snapped off a fine whirl of delicate pink columbine. Janet accepted it graciously, and the two turned back home again.

"Now I can't see why Caesar couldn't have done that," grumbled Janet. "He's just as trustworthy as that funny red-haired girl."

"You wouldn't have your columbine," smiled Nathaniel, "and I'm sure it was just what you needed to complete the picture."

"Now for that pretty speech I'll say no more about it," granted Janet, pleased.

And so they walked along the shaded street, where the sunlight was beginning to lie in long slanting rays on the pavement. Nathaniel talked as he knew his cousin liked for him to do, and all the time she never knew his heart had gone with the letter he'd given to Miranda. Perhaps her interest in the stranger who was coming kept her from missing something. Perhaps it was his light-hearted manner, so free from the perplexing problems that had filled his face with gravity on his recent visits. Perhaps it was just Janet's own gladness with life, the summer weather, and the holiday guests.

Yet underneath Nathaniel's cheerful manner two thoughts ran side by side—one, that Miranda had said Phoebe had repulsed Hiram Green; the other, that she was lying at death's door. And his strong heart was going out in a wild, hopeful pleading that her young life might yet be spared for joy. He felt that this mute pleading was her due, for hadn't she lifted her clear eyes and said, "Oh, I will," when he asked her to pray for him? He must return it in full measure.

The evening coach was late, but it rolled in at last, bringing the eagerly awaited guest, bronzed from his months in the South. The dinner was served around a joyous board, with the judge beaming his pleasure on the little company. The evening was prolonged far beyond the usual retiring hour, while laughter and talk floated on around him. And all the time Nathaniel was conscious of that other house only two miles away, where life and death were battling for a victim.

He went upstairs with Martin for another talk after the house was quiet, but at last they separated. Nathaniel was free to sit by the window in his dark room, looking out into the night now grown brilliant with the late rising moon, and kept tryst with one who was hovering on the brink of the other world.

Chapter 21

I've a notion to go up an' stay there t'night!" announced Miranda, as she cleared off the tea things. "This's the crisis, an' they might need me fer sumthin'. Anyhow I'm a goin' ef you don't mind."

"Will they let you in?" asked Marcia.

"I shan't ask 'em," said Miranda loftily. "There's more ways 'n one o' gettin' in, an' ef I make up my mind to git there you'll see I'll do it."

Marcia laughed.

"I suppose you will, Miranda. Well, go on. You may be needed. Poor Phoebe! I wish there was something I could do for her."

"Wal, thur is," said Miranda, with unexpected vim. "I've took a contrac' thet I don't seem to make much headway on. I'd like to hev you take a little try at it, an' see ef you can't do better. I 'greed t' pray fer Phoebe Deane, but t' save my life I can't think uv any more ways uv sayin' it thun jest to ast, an' after I've done it oncet it don't seem quite p'lite to keep at it, 'z if I didn't b'lieve 'twas heard. The minister preached awhile back 'bout the 'fectual prayer uv a righteous man 'vailin' much, but he didn't say nothin' 'bout a redheaded woman. I reckon I ain't much good at prayin', fer I'm all wore out with it. But ef you'd jest spell me awhile, an' lemme go see ef thur ain't sumpthin' to do, I think it would be a sight more 'vailin' then fer me to set still an' jest pray. 'Sides, ef you ain't better 'n most any righteous man I ever see, I'll miss my guess."

Thus the responsibility was divided, and Marcia with a

smile on her lips and a tear in her eye went away to pray, while Miranda tied on her bonnet, tucked the letter safely in her pocket after examining its seals and address most minutely, and went her way into the night.

She didn't go to the front door but stole around to the woodshed where, with the help of a milking stool standing there, she mounted to the low roof. With her strong limbs and courage, she found the climb nothing. She crept softly along the roof till she reached Phoebe's window and crouched to listen. The window was open a little way, though the night was warm and dry.

"Granny, Granny McVane," she called softly, and Granny, startled from her evening drowsiness, stole over to the window. A candle was burning behind the water pitcher and shed a weird, sickly light through the room. Granny looked old and tired as she came to the window, and it struck Miranda she'd been crying.

"Fer the land sake! Is that you, Miranda?" she exclaimed in horror. "Mercy! How'd you get there? Look out! You'll fall."

"Open the winder till I come in," whispered Miranda.

Granny opened the window cautiously.

"Be quick," she said. "I mustn't let the air get to the bed."

"I should think air was jes' what she'd want this night," whispered Miranda, as she emerged into the room and straightened her garments. "How's she seem? Any change?"

"I think she's failing, I surely do," moaned the old lady softly, the tears running down her cheeks in slow, uneven rivulets between the wrinkles. "I don't see how she can hold out till morning anyhow. She's jest burnt up with fever, and sometimes she seems to be gasping for breath. But how'd you get up there? Weren't you scairt?"

"I jes' couldn't keep away a minute longer. The doctor said this was the crisis, an' I had to come. My Mrs. Spafford's home prayin', an' I come to see ef I couldn't help answer them prayers. You might need help tonight, an' I'm goin' to stay. Will any of her folks be in again tonight?"

"No, I reckon not. Emmeline's worn out. The baby's teething and hasn't given her a minute's letup for two nights. She had his gums lanced today and hopes to get a wink of sleep, for there's likely to be plenty doing tomorrow."

Miranda set her lips hard at this and turned to the bed, where Phoebe lay under heavy blankets and comfortables, a low moan, almost a gasp, escaping her parched lips now and then.

The fever seemed to have burnt a place for itself in the white cheeks. Her beautiful hair had been cut short by Emmeline the second day because she couldn't be bothered combing it. It was as well, for it wouldn't have withstood the fever, but to Miranda it seemed like a ruthless tampering with the sacred. Her wrath burned hot within her, even while she was considering what was to be done.

"My goodness alive," was her first word. "I should think she would hev a fever. It's hotter'n mustard in here. Why don't you open them winders wide? I should think you'd roast alive yerself. And land sakes! Look at the covers she's got piled on! Poor little thing!"

Miranda reached out a swift hand and swept several layers off to the floor. A sigh of relief followed from Phoebe.

Miranda placed a firm, cool hand on the burning forehead, and the sufferer seemed to take note of the touch eagerly.

"Oh, mercy me! Miranda, you mustn't take the covers off. She must be kept warm to try and break the fever. The doctor's orders were very strict. I wouldn't like to disobey him. It might be her death."

"Does he think she's any better?" questioned Miranda fiercely.

"No." The old lady shook her head sadly. "He said this morning there wasn't a thread of hope, poor little thing. Her fever hasn't let up a mite."

"Well, ef he said that, then I'm goin' to hev my try. She can't do more 'n die, an' ef I was goin' to die I'd like to hev a cool comf'table place to do it in, wouldn't you, Granny, an' not a furnace. Let's give her a few minutes' peace 'fore she dies, anyway. Come, you open them winders. Ef anythin' happens I won't tell, an' ef she's goin' to die anyway, I think it's wicked to make her suffer any longer."

"I don't know what they'll say to me," murmured the old lady, yielding to the dominant Miranda. "I don't think mebbe I ought to do it."

"Well, never mind what you think now. It's my try. Ef you didn't open 'em I would, fer I b'lieve in my heart she wants fresh air, an' I'm goin' to give it to her ef I hev to fight every livin' soul in this house an' smash all the winder lights, so there! Now that's better. It'll be somethin' like in here pretty soon. Where's a towel? Is this fresh water? Say, Granny, couldn't you slip down to the spring without wakin' anyone an' bring us a good cold drink? I'm dyin' fer a dipper o' water. I come up here so fast, and it'll taste good to Phoebe, I know."

"Oh, she mustn't have a drop o' water!" exclaimed the old lady. "Fever patients don't get a mite of water."

"Fever fiddlesticks! You git that water, please, an' then you kin lay down on that couch over there an' take a nap while I set by her."

After much whispered persuasion and bullying, Miranda succeeded in getting the old lady to slip downstairs and go for the water, though the springhouse was almost as far as the barn and Granny wasn't used to prowling around alone at night. While she was gone Miranda boldly dipped a towel in the water pitcher and washed the fevered brow and face. The parched lips crept to the wetness eagerly, and Miranda began to feel assurance to her fingertips. She calmly bathed the girl's hot face and hands, until the low moans became sounds of relief and contentment. Then quite unconscious that she was anticipating science she prepared to give her patient a sponge bath. In the midst of the performance she looked up to see Granny standing over her in horror.

"What are you doing, Mirandy Griscom? You'll kill her. The doctor said she mustn't have a drop of water touch her."

"I'm takin' the fever out uv her. Jes' feel her an' see," said Miranda triumphantly. "Put yer lips on her forrid—thet's the way to tell. Ain't she coolin' off nice?"

"You're killing her, Miranda," said Granny in a terrified tone, "and I've cared fer her so carefully all these weeks, and now to have her go like this! It's death coming that makes her cold."

"Death fiddlesticks!" said Miranda wrathfully. "Well, ef 'tis, she'll die happy. Here, give me that water!"

She took the cup from Granny's trembling hand and held it to Phoebe's dry lips. Eagerly the lips opened and drank in the water as Miranda raised her head on her strong young arm. Then the sick girl lay back with a long sigh of contentment and fell asleep.

It was the first natural sleep she'd had since the awful beginning of the fever. She didn't toss or moan, and Granny hovered doubtfully above her, watching and listening to see if she still breathed, wondering at the fading crimson flames on the white cheeks, dismayed at the cooling brow, even troubled at the quiet sleep.

"I fear she'll slip away in this," she said at last, in a sepulchral whisper. "That was an awful daresome thing you did. I wouldn't like them to find it out on you. They might say you caused her death."

"But she ain't dead yet," said Miranda, "an' ef she slips away in this it's a sight pleasanter'n the way she was when I crep' in. Say now, Granny—don't you think so, honest?"

"Oh, I don't know," sighed Granny, turning away sadly.

"Mebbe I oughtn't to have let you."

"You couldn't 'a' he'ped yerself, fer I'd come to do it, an' anyway, ef you'd made a fuss I'd hed to put you out on the roof er somethin' till I got done. Now, Granny, you're all tired out. You jes' go over an' lie down on thet couch an' I'll set by an' watch her a spell."

The conversation was carried on close to Granny's ear, for both nurses were anxious lest some of the sleeping household should hear. Granny knew she would be blamed for Miranda's presence in the sickroom, and Miranda knew she would be ousted if discovered.

Granny settled down at last, with many protests, owned she was "jest the least mite tuckered out" and lay down for what she called a "catnap." Miranda, meanwhile, wide-eyed and sleepless, sat beside Phoebe and watched her every breath, for she felt more anxiety about what she'd done than she cared to admit to Granny. She'd never had much experience in nursing, except in waiting on Marcia, but her common sense told her people weren't likely to get well as long as they were uncomfortable. Therefore without much consideration she did for Phoebe what she'd like to have done for herself if she were ill. It seemed the right thing, and it seemed to be working, but supposing Granny were right, after all!

Then Miranda remembered the two who were praying.

"Hm," she said to herself as she sat watching the still face on the pillow. "I reckon that's their part. Mine's to do the best I know. Ef the prayers is good fer anything they ought to piece out whar' I fail. An' I guess they will, too, with them two at it."

After that she got the wet towel and went to work again, bathing the brow and hands whenever the heat seemed to be growing in them again. She was bound to bring that fever down. Now and then the sleeper would draw a long contented sigh, and Miranda felt she'd received her thanks. It was enough to know she'd given her friend a little comfort, if nothing else.

The hours throbbed on. The moon went down. The candle sputtered, and Miranda lighted another. Granny slept and actually snored, weary with her long vigil. Miranda had to touch her occasionally to stop the loud noise lest someone should hear and come to see what it was. But the others in the household were weary, too, for it was in the height of the summer's work now, and all slept soundly.

When the early dawn crept into the sky Miranda felt Phoebe's hands and head and found them cool and natural. She stooped and listened, and her breathing came regularly like a tired child's. For just one instant she touched her lips to the white forehead and rejoiced that the parched burning feeling was gone. The awful weakness yet remained to fight, but at least the fever was gone. What had done it she didn't care, but it was done.

She went gently to Granny and wakened her. The old lady started up with a frightened look, guilty that she'd slept so long, but Miranda reassured her. "It's all right. I'm glad you slep', fer you wa'n't needed, an' I guess you'll feel all the better fer it today. She's slep' real quiet all night long, ain't moaned once, an' jes' feel her. Ain't she feelin' all right? I b'lieve the fever's gone."

Granny went over and touched her face and hands wonderingly. "She does feel better," she admitted, "but I don't know. It mayn't last. I've seen 'em rally toward the end. She'll be so powerful weak now; it'll be all we can do to hold her to earth."

"What's she ben eatin'?" inquired Miranda.

"She hasn't eaten anything of any account for some time back."

"Well, she can't live on jest air an' water ferever. Say, Granny, I've got to be goin' soon, er I'll hev to hide in the closet all day fer sure, but 'spose you slip out to the barn now, while I wait, an' get a few drops o' new milk. Hank's out there milkin'. I heard him go down an' git his milk pails an' stool 'fore I woke you up. We'll give her a spoonful o' warm milk. Mebbe that'll hearten her up."

"It might," said Granny doubtfully. She took the cup and hurried away.

Miranda buttoned the door after her lest Emmeline should take a notion to look in.

When Granny got back, Miranda took the cup and, putting a few drops of the sweet warm fluid in a spoon, touched it to Phoebe's lips. A slow sigh followed, and then Phoebe's eyes opened. She looked straight at Miranda and seemed to know her, for a flicker of a smile shone in her face.

"There, Phoebe, take this spoonful. You've been sick, but it'll make you well," crooned Miranda.

Phoebe obediently swallowed the few drops, and Miranda dipped up a few more.

"It's all right, dear," she said. "I'll take care o' you. Jes' you drink this, an' get well, fer I've got somethin' real nice in my pocket fer you when ye take yer milk an' go to sleep."

Thus Miranda fed her two or three spoonfuls. Then the white lids closed over the trusting eyes, and in a moment more she was sleeping again.

Miranda watched her a few minutes and then cautiously stole away from the bed to the astonished Granny who had been watching with a new respect for the domineering young nurse that had usurped her place.

"I guess she'll sleep most o' the day," Miranda whispered. "Ef she wakes up you jes' give her a spoonful o' fresh milk, er a sup o' water, an' tell her I'll be back bime-by. She'll understan', an' that'll keep her quiet. Tell her I said she mus' lie still an' get well. Don't you dast keep them winders shet up all day again, an' don't pile on the clo'es. She may need a light blanket ef she feels cool, but don't fer mercy's sake get her all het up again, er we might not be able to stop it off so easy next time. I'll be back's soon es it's dark. Bye-bye. I mus' go. I may get ketched es 'tis."

Miranda slid out the window and down the sloping roof, dropping over the eaves just in time to escape being seen by Emmeline, who opened the back door with a sharp *click* and came out to get a broom she'd forgotten the night before. The morning was almost come now, and the long grass was dripping with dew as Miranda swept through it.

"Reckon they'll think there's ben a fox er somethin' prowlin' 'round the house ef they see my tracks," she said to herself as she hurried through the dewy fields and out to the road.

Victory was written upon her countenance as she sped along, victory tempered with hope. Perhaps she wasn't judge enough of illness, and it might be that her hopes were vain ones, and apparent signs deceitful, but come what might she would always be glad she'd done what she had. That look in Phoebe's eyes before she fell asleep again was reward enough. It made her heart swell with triumph to think of it.

Two hours later she brought a platter of delicately poached eggs on toast to the breakfast table just as Marcia entered the room.

"Good morning, Miranda. How did it go last night? You evidently got in and found something to do."

Miranda set down the platter and stood with hands on her hips and face shining with morning welcome.

"I tell you, Mrs. Marcia, them prayers was all right. They worked fine. When I got mixed and didn't know what was right to do I just remembered them an' cast off all 'sponsibility. Anyhow, she's sleepin', an' the fever's gone."

Marcia smiled.

"I shouldn't wonder if your part was really prayer, too," she said. "We aren't all heard for our much speaking."

It was a glorious day. The sun shown in a perfect heaven

without a cloud to blur it. A soft south breeze kept the air from being too warm. Miranda sang all the morning as she went about her belated work.

After dinner Marcia insisted she should go and take a nap. She obediently lay down for half an hour straight off and stiff on her bright neat patchwork quilt, scarcely relaxing a muscle lest she rumple the bed. She didn't close her eyes, however, but lay smiling at the white ceiling and resting herself by gently crackling the letter in her pocket. She smiled to think how Phoebe would look when she showed it to her.

In exactly half an hour she arose, combed her hair neatly, donned her afternoon dress and her little black silk apron that was her pride on ordinary occasions, and descended to her usual observation post with her knitting. Naps weren't in her line, and she was glad hers was over.

A little later the doctor's chaise drove up to the door, and Miranda went out to see what was wanted, a great fear clutching her heart. But she was reassured by the smile on his face and the goodwill in the expressions of his wife and her sister, who were riding with him.

"Say, Mirandy, I don't know but I'll take you into partnership. Where'd you learn nursing? You did what I wouldn't have dared do, but it seemed to hit the mark. I'd given her up. I've seen her slipping away for a week, but she's taken a turn for the better now, and I believe she's going to get well. If she does it'll be you that'll get the honor."

Miranda's eyes shone with happy tears.

"You don't say, doctor," she said. "Why, I was real scared when Granny told me you said she wasn't to hev a sup o' water, but it seemed like she must be so turrible hot—"

"Well, I wouldn't have dared try it myself, but I believe it did the business," said the doctor heartily.

"Yes, you deserve great credit, Miranda," said the doctor's wife.

"You do, indeed," echoed her sister pleasantly.

"Granny ain't tole Mis' Deane I was there, hes she?" asked Miranda, to cover her embarrassment. She wasn't used to praise except from her own household.

"No, she hasn't told her yet, but I think I'll tell her myself by tomorrow if all goes well. Can you find time to run over tonight again? Granny might not stay wide awake all the time. She's worn out, and I think it's a critical time."

"Oh, I'll be there!" said Miranda. "You couldn't keep me away."

"How'll you get in? Same way you did last night?" asked the doctor, laughing. "Say, that's a good joke! I've laughed and laughed ever since Granny told me, at the thought of you climbing in the window and the family all sleeping calmly. Good for you, Miranda. You're made of the right stuff. Well, good-bye. I'll fix it up with Mrs. Deane tomorrow so you can go in by the door."

The doctor drove on, laughing, and his wife and sister bowing and smiling.

Miranda, with her head high with pride and her heart full of joy, went in to get supper.

Supper was just cleared away when Nathaniel came over. He talked with David in the dusk of the front stoop a few minutes and then asked diffidently if Miranda was going up to see how Miss Deane was again soon.

Because of his love for Marcia, David half understood and, calling Miranda, left the two together for a moment while he went to call Marcia, who was putting Rose to bed.

"She's better," said Miranda, entering without preamble into the subject nearest their hearts. "The doctor told me so this afternoon. But don't you stop prayin' yet, fer we don't want no halfway job, an' she's powerful weak. I kinder rely on them prayers to do a lot. I got Mrs. Spafford to spell me at mine while I went up to help nurse. She opened her eyes oncet last night when I was givin' her some milk, an' I tole her I had somethin' nice fer her if she'd lie still an' go to sleep an' hurry up an' git well. She kinder seemed to understand, I most think. I've got the letter all safe, an' jes' ez soon ez she gits the least mite better, able to talk, I'll give it to her."

"Thank you, Miss Miranda," said Nathaniel, "and won't you take this to her? It will be better than letters for her for a while until she gets well. You needn't bother her telling anything about it now. Just give it to her. It may help her a little. Then later, if you think best, you may tell her I sent it."

He held out a single tea rose, half blown, with delicate petals of pale saffron.

Miranda took it with awe. It wasn't like anything that grew in the gardens she knew.

"It looks like her," she said reverently.

"It makes me think of her as I first saw her," he answered in a low voice. "She wore a dress like that."

"I know," said Miranda with understanding. "I'll give it to her and tell her all about it when she's better."

"Thank you," said Nathaniel.

Then Marcia and David entered, and Miranda went away to wonder over the rose and prepare for her night's vigil.

Chapter 22

Granny greeted Miranda with a smile as she crept in at the window that night. Phoebe, too, opened her eyes in welcome, though she made no other sign that she was awake. Her face was like sunken marble now that the fever was gone from it, and her two great eyes shone from it like lights of another world. It startled Miranda as she came and looked at her. Then at once she perceived that Phoebe's eyes had sought the rose, and a smile was hovering about her lips.

"It was sent to you," she answered the questioning eyes, putting the rose close down to the white cheek. Phoebe really smiled then faintly.

"She better have some milk now," said Granny anxiously. "She's been asleep so long, an' I didn't disturb her."

"Yes, take some milk," whispered Miranda, "an' I'll tell you all 'bout the rose when you're better."

The night crept on in quiet exultation of Miranda's part. While Phoebe slept, Miranda and the rose kept vigil, and Granny sank into the first restful sleep she'd had since she came to nurse Phoebe. The house was quiet. The watcher hadn't much to do but watch. Now and then she drew the coverlet up a little higher when a fresh breeze came through the window or gave another drink of water or spoonful of milk. The candle was shaded by the water pitcher, and the frail sweet rose looked spectral in the weird light. Miranda looked at the flower, and it looked back at her.

As the hours passed slowly, Miranda found her lips murmuring, "Thanks be! Thanks be!"

Suddenly she drew herself up with a new thought.

"Land sakes! That's sounds like prayin'. Wonder ef 'tis. Anyhow it's thanks-givin', an' that's what I feel. Guess it's my turn to give thanks."

The next day the doctor talked with Albert Deane. He told him how Miranda had crept in at the window and cared for Phoebe and how he believed it had been Phoebe's salvation. Albert was deeply affected. He readily agreed it would be a fine thing for Phoebe if Miranda could come and help Granny care for her, now that she seemed to be on the fair road to recovery.

It was all arranged in a few minutes, and Emmeline wasn't told until just before Miranda arrived.

"It's very strange," she said with her nose in the air, "that I wasn't consulted. I'm sure it's my business more'n yours to look after such things, Albert Deane. An' I wouldn't uv had that sassy creature in the house fer a good deal. Hank's sister would 'a' ben a sight better an' could 'a' helped me between times with Phoebe's extry work. I'm sure it's bad enough havin' sickness this way in the midst o' hayin' season, an' me with all them men to feed an' not havin' Phoebe to help. I could 'a' sent fer my own sister, when it comes to that, an' 'twould 'a' ben a sight pleasanter."

But before there was time for a protest or apology from Albert, a knock came at the door, and without waiting for ceremony, Miranda walked in.

"Ev'nin', Mis' Deane," she said. "Everything goin' well? I'll go right up, shall I?" Her smiling insolence struck Emmeline dumb for the moment.

"Well, I vow!" declared Emmeline. "Will yeh listen to the impedence. 'I'll go right up, shall I?' Es ef she was the Queen o' Sheby er the doctor himself."

But Miranda was marching serenely upstairs, and if she heard she paid no heed.

"She doesn't mean any harm, Emmeline!" pleaded Albert. "She's jest Phoebe's friend, so don't you mind. It'll relieve you a lot, and if you want Hank's sister to come over, too, I guess we can manage it."

Thus was Miranda domiciled in Phoebe's room for a short space, much to Phoebe's comfort and Miranda's satisfaction.

Emmeline was only half mollified when she came upstairs to look around and "give that Griscom girl a settin' down," as she expressed it. But she who attempted to "sit" on Miranda usually arose unexpectedly.

"Where'd that come from?" was Emmeline's first question, as she pointed at the unoffending rose.

"Mirandy brought it," said Granny, proud of her colleague.

"Hm!" said Emmeline with a sniff. "It ain't healthy to hev plants round in a bedroom, I've heard. D' you raise that kind down to Spaffords?"

"We ain't got just to say a-plenty yet," said Miranda cheerfully, "but we might hev sometime. Would yeh like a slip?"

"No, thank yeh," said Emmeline dryly. "I never had time to waste good daylight fussin' over weeds. I s'pose Mis' Spafford don't do much else."

"Oh, 'casionally!" answered Miranda, undisturbed. "This spring she put up a hundred glasses o' blueberry jelly, made peach preserves, spiced pears an' crabapple jam, crocheted a white bedspread fer the spare bed an' three antimacassars fer her aunt Hortense's best parlor chairs, did up the second-story curtains, tucked a muslin slip fer Rose, sewed carpet rags enough fer a whole strip in Shorty Briscutt's new rag carpet, made a set o' shirts fer Mr. Spafford, knit nine pair o' stockin's, spun the winter's yarn, cut out an' made Rose's flannel petticoats, an' went to missionary meetin'. But o' course that ain't much, nothin' to what you'd do."

(Oh, Miranda, Miranda! Of the short prayers and the long tongue! Telling all that off with a straight face to the sour-faced woman, Emmeline!)

"She must be a smart woman!" said Granny, much impressed.

"She is," said Miranda glibly. "But here all the time I was fergettin' we'd ought not to talk. We'll bring that fever up. Is there anything special yeh wanted me to look after t'night, Mis' Deane? 'Cause ef there is, jes' don' hesitate to say so. I'm here to work an' not to play."

And before she knew it, Emmeline found herself disarmed and walking meekly downstairs without having said any of the things she had meant to say.

From that time forth Phoebe grew steadily better, though she came near to having a serious setback the day Miranda went down to the village on an errand. Emmeline attempted to "clean up" in her absence, finishing the operation by pitching the tea rose out into the yard below the window.

"I never seen such a fuss," complained Emmeline to Miranda, who stood over Phoebe and felt her fluttering pulse, "all over a dead weed. I declare I can't understand folks gettin' 'tached to trash."

Emmeline was somewhat anxious at the upset state of the patient, who was yet too weak to talk much but roused herself to protest vigorously as the rose was hurled through the window and then couldn't keep back the disappointed tears.

But Miranda, mindful of her patient's weak state and wishing to mollify Emmeline as much as possible, tried to pour oil on the troubled waters.

"Never mind, Mis' Deane. No harm done. Phoebe jes' wanted to keep them leaves fer her han'kerchers; they smell real nice. I'll pick 'em up, Phoebe. They won't be hurt a mite. They're right on the green grass."

Miranda stole down and picked up the leaves tenderly, washing them at the spring, and brought them back to Phoebe. Emmeline had gone off sniffing with her chin in the air.

"I was silly to cry," murmured Phoebe, trying feebly to dry

her tears, "but I loved that sweet rose. I wanted to keep it just as it was in a box. You haven't told me about it yet, Miranda. How did she come to send it?"

"It ain't hurt a mite, Phoebe, only jest three leaves come off. I'll lay it together in a box fer yeh. Now lemme put my bonnet off, an' you lay quiet an' shet your eyes while I tell you 'bout that rose. First, though, you must take your milk.

"It wa'n't her at all that sent you that rose, Phoebe Deane. You s'picioned 'twas Mrs. Marcia, didn't you? But 'twa'nt 't all. It was a man—"

"Oh, Miranda!" The words came in a moan of pain from the bed. "Not—not—Miranda, you would never have brought it if Hiram Green—"

"Land sake, child, what's took yeh? 'Course not. Why, ef that nimshi'd undertake to send yeh so much ez a blade o' grass I'd fling it in his mean little face. Don't you worry, dearie. You jest listen. 'Twas Nathaniel Graham sent you that rose. He said I wa'n't to say nothin' 'bout it till you got better, an' then I could say 'twas from him ef I wanted to. I didn't say anythin' yet 'cause I hed more to tell, but I ain't sure you're strong 'nough to hear anymore now. Better take a nap first."

"No, Miranda, do tell me now."

"Wal, I reckon I better. I've most busted wantin' to tell yeh sev'ral times. Say, did you ever get a letter from Nathaniel Graham, Phoebe?"

"Why, no, of course not, Miranda. Why would I get a letter from him?"

"Wal, he said he wrote yeh one oncet, an' he ast me did I know ef you'd got it, and I said no, I was sure you didn't, 'cause you said oncet you hadn't ever got a letter 'cept from your mother, an' so he said he'd write it over again fer yeh, an' I've hed it in my pocket fer a long time waitin' till I dared give it to yeh. So here 'tis, but I won't give it to yeh 'thout you promise to go right to sleep 'fore you read it, fer you've hed more goin's on now than 's good fer yeh."

Phoebe protested that she must read the letter first, but Miranda was inexorable and wouldn't even show it to her until she promised. So meekly Phoebe promised and went to sleep with the precious missive clasped in her hands, the wonder of it helping her get quiet.

She slept a long time, for the excitement about the rose had taken her strength. When she awoke, before she opened her eyes she felt the letter, pressing the seals with her fingers, to make sure she hadn't been dreaming. She almost feared to open her eyes lest it shouldn't be true. A letter for her all her own! Somehow she almost dreaded to break the seal and have the first wonder of it over. She hadn't thought what it might contain.

Miranda had brought a little pail of chicken broth Marcia had made for Phoebe, and she had some steaming in a china bowl when Phoebe at last opened her eyes. She made her eat it before she opened the letter, and Phoebe smiled and acquiesced.

She lay smiling and quiet a long time after reading the letter, trying to get used to the thought that Nathaniel had remembered her, cared to write to her, and cared to have her write to him, too. It wasn't merely passing kindness toward a stranger. He wanted to be friends, real friends. It was good to feel that one had friends.

Phoebe looked over at Miranda's alert figure, sitting bolt upright and watching her charge with anxiety to see if the letter was all it should be. And then she laughed a soft little ripple that sounded like a shadow of her former self.

"Oh, you dear, good Miranda! You don't know how nice it is to have friends and a real letter."

"Is it a good letter?" asked Miranda wistfully.

"Read it," said Phoebe, handing it to her, smiling. "You certainly have a right to read it after all you've done to get it here."

Miranda took it shyly and went over by the window where

the setting sun made it a little less embarrassing. She read it slowly and carefully, and the look on her face when she returned it showed she was satisfied.

"I seen him the mornin' he went back to New York," she admitted after a minute. "He said he'd look fer that answer soon ez you got better. You're goin' to write, ain't you?" she asked anxiously. " 'Cause he seemed real set up about it."

"How soon may I answer it?" she answered.

"We'll see," said Miranda briskly. "The first business is to get strong."

Those two girls spent happy days together with nothing to worry them. As Phoebe began to get strong and could be propped up with pillows for a little while each day, Miranda at length allowed her to write a few lines in reply to her letter, and this was the message that in a few days thereafter traveled to New York.

> *My dear Mr. Graham,*
>
> *It was very pleasant to receive your letter and know you thought of me and prayed that I might get well. I think your prayers are being answered.*
>
> *It will be good to have a friend to write to me, and I shall be glad to correspond with you. I want to thank you for the beautiful rose. It helped me get well. Its leaves are sweet yet.*
>
> *I've been a long time in writing this, for I'm very weak and tired yet, and Miranda won't let me write any more now. But you will understand and excuse me, won't you?*
>
> *Your friend,*
> *Phoebe Deane*

Miranda had to go home soon after that, for it was plain Emmeline was wanting to get rid of her, and Marcia was to have guests for a couple of weeks. Squire Schuyler and his wife were coming to visit for the first time since little Rose's birth, for it was a long journey for an old man to take, and the squire didn't like to go away from home. Miranda felt she must go, much as she hated to leave Phoebe, and so she bid her good-bye, and Phoebe began to take care of herself.

She was able to walk around her room and soon to go downstairs. But somehow when she got down into the old atmosphere something seemed to choke her, and she felt weary and wanted to creep back to bed again. So, much to Emmeline's disgust, she didn't progress as rapidly as she should have.

"You need to git some ambition," said Emmeline, with loathing, the first morning Phoebe came down to breakfast and sat back after one or two mouthfuls. They had fried ham and eggs and fried potatoes. *Anybody ought to be glad to get that*, Emmeline thought.

But they didn't appeal to Phoebe, and she left her plate almost untasted.

"I think ef you'd get some work and do somethin' mebbe you'd get your strength again. I never see anybody hang back like you do. There ain't any sense in it. What's the matter with yeh, anyway?"

"I don't know," said Phoebe, with an effort at cheerfulness. "I try, but somehow I feel so heavy and tired all the time."

"She isn't strong yet, Emmeline," pleaded Albert kindly.

"Wal, don't I know that?" snapped Emmeline. "But how's she ever goin' to get strong ef she don't work it up?"

Such little pinpricks were hard to bear when Phoebe felt well, and now that her strength was only a breath, she seemed unable to bear them at all and after a short effort would creep back to her room and lie down.

Miranda discovered her all huddled in a little heap on her bed late one afternoon when she came up to bring Phoebe her second letter, for Nathaniel had arranged for the present to send his correspondence to Phoebe through Miranda. Neither of them said aloud that it was because Hiram Green brought up the Deanes' mail so often, but both understood.

Miranda and the letter succeeded in cheering up Phoebe, but the ex-nurse felt that things weren't going with her charge as prosperously as they should, and she took her trouble back to Marcia.

"Let's bring her down here, Miranda," proposed Marcia. "Father and Mother are going home on Monday, and it will be quiet and nice here. I think she might spend a month with us and get strong before she goes back and tries to work."

Miranda was delighted and took the first opportunity to convey the invitation to Phoebe, whose cheeks grew pink and eyes bright with anticipation. A whole month with Mrs. Spafford and Miranda! It was too good to be true.

Monday morning they came for her with the big old chaise. Emmeline and Hank's sister were out hanging up clothes. Emmeline's mouth was full of clothespins, and her brow was dark, for Hank's sister talked a great deal and worked slowly. Moreover, she made lumpy starch and couldn't be depended upon to keep the potatoes from burning if one went out to feed the chickens. It was hard to have trained up a good worker and then have her trail off in a thunderstorm and get sick and leave the work in someone else's hands without ambition enough to get well. Emmeline was very ungracious to Marcia. She told Albert she didn't see what business Mrs. Spafford had coming round to run their house. She thought Phoebe was better off at home, but Albert felt that Mrs. Spafford had been very kind.

So with little regret Phoebe was carried away from her childhood home into a sweet new world of loving-kindness and joy, where the round cheeks and happiness of health might be coaxed back. Yet to Phoebe it wasn't an undisturbed bliss, for always she carried with her the thought that by and by she must go back to the old life again. She shuddered at the very thought of it and couldn't bear to face it. It was like going to heaven for a little time and having to return to earth's trials again.

The spring had changed into the summer during Phoebe's illness, and it was almost the middle of July when she began her beautiful visit at the Spaffords'.

Chapter 23

Hiram Green had been exceedingly quiet since the night of the runaway.

The old plowhorse had kicked something loose about the chaise in his final lurch before he started to run, and it goaded his every step. He thought Hiram was striking him with a club. He thought the thunder was pursuing him and the lightning was reaching for him as it darted through the livid sky. Down the road he flew, mile after mile, not slowing up for curves or bumps in the road but taking a shortcut at the turns, rearing and shying at every flash of lightning. The chaise came lurching after, like one tied to a whirlwind, and Hiram, clinging, cursing, lashing out madly with his whip, was finally forced to spend his time in holding on, thinking every minute would be his last.

As the horse saw his own gate at last, however, he gave a final leap into the air and bounded across the ditch, regardless of what was behind him, perhaps hoping to rid himself of it. The chaise lurched into the air, and Hiram was tossed lightly over the fence and landed in the cow pasture. Something snapped, and the horse entered his own dooryard free at last from the thing which had been pursuing him.

The rain was coming down in driving sheets now and brought Hiram to his feet in spite of his dazed condition. He looked about him in the alternate dimness and vivid brightness and perceived that he was close to the Deanes'. A moment's reflection made it plain he must get up some kind of story, so he put on the best face he could and went in.

"We've hed an axident," he explained, limping into the kitchen, where Emmeline was trying to get supper and keep the fretful baby quiet. "The blamed horse got scared at th' lightnin'. I seen what was goin' to happen an' I held him on his haunches fer a second while Phoebe jumped. She's back there a piece now, I reck'n, fer that blamed critter never stopped till he landed to home, an' he placed me in a awkward persition in the cow pasture, with the chaise all broke up. I guess Phoebe's all right, fer I looked back an' thought I saw her tryin' to wave her hand to me, but I 'spect we better go hunt her up soon 's this here storm lets up. She'll likely go in somewheres. We'd just got past old Mis' Duzenberry's."

That was all the explanation the Deanes had ever had of the adventure. Phoebe had been too ill to speak of it at first, and after she got well enough to come downstairs, Albert questioned her at the table about it. She had shuddered and turned so white, saying, "Please, don't, Albert. I can't bear to think of it," that he'd never asked her again.

During her illness Hiram had been politely concerned about her welfare, taking the precaution to visit the post office every day and inquire solicitously for any mail for her in a voice loud enough to be heard all over the room and always being ready to tell just how she was when anyone inquired. It never entered Albert's head that Hiram wasn't as anxious as he was during those days and nights when the fever held sway over the sweet young life. As for Emmeline, she made up her mind that where ignorance was bliss 'twas folly to be wise, and she kept her lips sealed, accepting Hiram's explanation, though all the time secretly she thought there might be some deeper reason for Phoebe's terrible appearance than just a runaway. She was relieved Phoebe said nothing about it, if there had been trouble, and hoped it was forgotten.

The day after Phoebe went to visit at the Spaffords', Hiram came up to see Emmeline in the afternoon when he knew

Albert was out in the hayfield.

"Say, do you still favor livin' down to the village?" he asked, seating himself without waiting for an invitation.

Emmeline looked up keenly and wondered what was in the air. "I hev said so," she remarked tentatively, not willing to commit herself without further knowledge.

"Wal, you know that lot o' mine down there opposite the Seceder church? It has a big weepin' willer same 's in the churchyard and a couple o' plum trees in bearin'. How'd you like to live on thet lot?"

"Hm!" said Emmeline stolidly. "Much good 'twould do me to like it. Albert'll never buy that lot, Hiram Green. There ain't no use askin' him. You wasn't thinkin' of buildin' there yerself, was yeh?" Emmeline looked up sharply as this new thought entered her mind. Perhaps he wanted her to hold out the bait of a house in the village to Phoebe.

"Naw, I ain't goin' to build in no village at present, Mis' Deane," he remarked dryly. "Too fur from work fer me, thank you. But I was thinkin' I'd heard you say you wanted to live in the village, an' I thought I'd make a bargain with you. Say, Emmeline, 'taint no use mincin' matters. I'm a-goin' to marry Phoebe Deane, an' I want you should help me to it. I'll make you this offer. It's a real generous one, too. The day I marry Phoebe Deane, I'll give you a deed to that lot in the village. Now what d'yeh say? Is't a bargain?"

"What to do?" questioned Emmeline. She would be caught in no trap. "I've done all I know now. I'd like my sister Mandy to come here to live, an' there ain't room fer her while Phoebe stays. But I don't see what I kin do, more'n what I've done a'ready. Wouldn't she make up to yeh none the day you come home from the barn raisin'?"

"Wal, I was gettin' on pretty well 'til that blamed horse took an' run," said Hiram, shifting his eyes from her piercing ones.

"Wal, I can't compel her to marry you," snapped Emmeline.

"You don't hev to," said Hiram. "I've got my plans laid, an' all you got to do is stand by me when the time comes. I ain't tellin' my plans jest yet, but you'll see what they be, an' all is, you remember my offer. Ef you want that village lot jest remember to stand by me."

He unfolded his length from the kitchen chair and went out. Emmeline said nothing.

When he reached the door he turned back and said, "I broke ground this mornin' fer a new house on the knoll. Me an' Phoebe'll be livin' there by this time next year."

"Well, I hope to goodness yeh will," responded Emmeline heartily, "fer I've hed trouble 'nough a'ready with this business. I'll do what I ken, o' course, but do fer goodness' sake, hurry up!"

The house on the knoll steadily progressed. Hiram came little to the Deane house during Phoebe's absence but spent this time at the new building when his farmwork did not demand his presence. He also came often to the village and hung around the post office. He was determined for nothing to escape his vigilance in that direction.

Seeing him there one day when the mail was being distributed, Miranda took her place in the front ranks and asked in a clear cool voice: "Anythin' fer Phoebe Deane? She's stayin' t' our house fer a spell now, an' I'll take her mail to her."

Miranda knew the only mail Phoebe would likely receive came addressed to her, so she was more than surprised when the postmaster with his spectacles on the end of his nose held up a letter whose address he carefully studied and then handed it to her rather reluctantly. He would have liked a chance to study that letter more closely.

But nothing fazed Miranda. She took the letter as calmly as if there should be two or three more forthcoming and marched off. Hiram Green, however, got down scowling from his seat on the counter and stalked over to the postmaster.

"I sh'd think you'd hev to be keerful who you give letters to," he remarked in a low tone. "Phoebe Deane might not like that harum-scarum girl bringin' her letters. Did you take notice ef that letter was from New York? She was expectin' quite a important letter from there."

The postmaster looked over his spectacles at Hiram patronizingly.

"I sh'd hope I know who to trust," he remarked with dignity. "No, I didn't take notice. I hev too much to do to notice postmarks."

Hiram, however, was greatly shaken up by the sight of that letter in Miranda's hands and took himself to the hayloft to meditate. If he'd known the letter merely contained a clipping about the progress of missions in South Africa, which Ann Jane Bloodgood had sent thinking it might help Phoebe recover from her illness, as she heard she was feeling "poorly" yet and hoped she would soon hear she was better, he'd have rested easy.

But Hiram thought only that the letter was from Nathaniel; therefore his reflections were bitter.

Two days afterward Hiram was one of a group around a New York agent who had come down to sell goods. He was telling the story of a mob, and his swaggering air and flashy clothes attracted Hiram. He thought them far superior to any of Nathaniel Graham's and determined to model himself after this pattern in the future.

"Oh, we do things in great shape down in New York," he was saying. "When folks don't please, we *mob* 'em. If their opinions ain't what we like, we *mob* 'em. If they don't pay us what we ask, we *mob* 'em. Heard 'bout the mob down in Chatham Street last summer—er it might have been two years ago? A lot of black men met to hear a preacher in a little chapel down there. We got wind of it, an' we ordered 'em to leave, but they wouldn't budge 'cause they'd paid their rent, so we just *put* 'em out. There was a man named Tappan who lived down in Rose Street, an' he was there. He was an abolitionist, an' we didn't like him. He'd had somethin' to do with this meetin', so we follered him home with hoots and threats and give his house a good stoning. Did him good. Oh, we do things up in great shape in New York. Next night we went down to the Bowery Theatre. Manager there's English, you know, and he'd said some imperlite things about America, we thought, something about our right to own slaves, so we give him a dose. Oh, we're not afraid of anything down in New York."

Hiram was greatly fascinated by this representative New Yorker, and after the crowd had begun to disperse, he went to the stranger and buttonholed him.

"Say, look a' here!" he began, holding a five-dollar bill invitingly near the New Yorker's hand. "I know a feller you ought to mob. I could give yeh his name an' address real easy. He's prominent down there, an' I reckon 'twould be worth somethin' to you folks to know his name. Fact is, I've an interest in the matter myself, an' I'd like to see him come to justice, an' I'm willin' to subscribe this here bill to the cause ef you see your way clear to lookin' the matter up fer me."

"Why, certainly, certainly," said the stranger, grasping the bill affably, "I'll do anything I can for you. I'll hand this over to the treasurer of our side. In fact I'm the treasurer myself, and I thank you very much for your interest. Anything I can do I'm sure I'll be glad to. Can you tell me any more about this?"

Hiram took him to a quiet corner, and before the interview was ended, he had entered into a secret plot against Nathaniel Graham and had pledged himself to give the stranger not only one but four more five-dollar bills when the work should be complete and Nathaniel Graham stand revealed to the world as an abolitionist, a man who should be suppressed. It was all arranged before the stranger left on the evening stagecoach that he would write Hiram what day a move would be made in the matter and just how far he felt they could go.

Hiram went home chuckling and felt that revenge was sweet. He'd get the better of Nathaniel Graham now, and Nathaniel would never know who struck the blow.

A few days afterward a letter came from the stranger saying all things were prospering. But it would be impossible to get up a thoroughly organized mob and do the work without a little more money, for their funds were low. Would it be possible for Hiram to forward the twenty dollars now instead of waiting?

After a sleepless night Hiram doled out the twenty dollars. The stranger wrote that the time had been arranged, and he'd let him know all about it soon. They thought they had their man pinned down tight. The night Hiram received the letter he slept soundly.

Meanwhile the world had been moving in an orbit of beauty for Phoebe. She was tended and guarded like a little child. They made her feel that her presence was a joy to them all. Every member of the family down to Rose made it a point to brighten her stay with them. Rose brought her flowers from the garden, David brought the latest books and poems for her to read, Marcia was her constant loving companion, and Miranda cooked the daintiest dishes known to the culinary art for her tempting.

The letters went back and forth to New York every day or two, for as Phoebe was growing better she was able to write longer epistles, and Nathaniel seemed always to have something to say that needed an immediate answer. Phoebe was growing less shy of him and more and more opened her heart to his friendship like a flower turning to a newly risen sun.

Janet Bristol had been away on a visit during Phoebe's illness, but while she was still with the Spaffords, Janet returned and one afternoon came to return Mrs. Spafford's call.

Phoebe wore a thin white dress whose dainty frills modestly showed her white throat and arms which were now taking on something of their old roundness. She was sitting in the cool parlor with Marcia when the caller arrived. Her mother's locket was tied about her throat with a bit of velvet ribbon, and her hair, now coming out in soft curls, made a lovely fluffy halo of brown all about her face.

Janet watched her while she talked with Marcia and wondered at the sweet grace of form and feature. Somehow her former prejudice against this girl melted strangely as Phoebe raised her beautiful eyes and smiled at her. Janet felt drawn to her against her will, yet she couldn't tell why she held back, except that Nathaniel had been so strangely stubborn about that letter. To be sure that was long past, and her mind was fully occupied just now with Nathaniel's theological friend, Martin Van Rensselaer. She was attempting to teach him the ways of the world and draw him out of his gravity. He seemed to be a willing subject, if one might judge from the number of visits he made to the Bristol home during the summer.

Then one bright, beautiful day, just a week before Phoebe's visit was to close, Nathaniel came up from New York.

He reached the village on the afternoon coach, and as it happened Hiram Green stood across the road from the tavern where the coach usually stopped, lounging outside the post office and waiting for the mail to be brought. He didn't intend that any Miranda Griscom should stand in his way. Moreover, this night was the one set for Nathaniel Graham's undoing, and there might be a letter for him from his agent in New York. It filled Hiram with a kind of intoxication to be getting letters from New York.

He stood leaning against a post watching the coach as it rolled down the village street drawn by the four great horses, enveloped in a cloud of dust, and drew up at the tavern with a flourish. Then suddenly he noticed there were two passengers, and one was Nathaniel himself.

Hiram felt weak in the knees. If a ghost had suddenly descended from the coach he couldn't have been more dismayed. Here he had just put twenty-five good dollars into Nathaniel's discomfiture, only to have him appear in his own town smiling and serene as if nothing had been about to happen. It made Hiram sick. He watched him and the other young man who had been his fellow passenger, as they walked down the street toward the Bristol house.

He had sat down when the coach stopped, feeling inadequate to hold himself upright in the midst of his unusual emotions. Now he got up slowly and walked away heavily toward his home, as if he'd been stricken. With head bent down he studied the ground as he walked. He forgot the mail, forgot everything, except that he had put twenty-five dollars into the fruitless enterprise.

Midway between the post office and his home he stopped and wheeled around with an exclamation of dismay. Then after a pause he let forth a series of oaths. Hiram was stirred to the depths of his evil nature. He had just remembered that Phoebe was down in the village at the Spaffords and would likely see Nathaniel. His ugly face contracted in a spasm of anger that gradually died into a settled expression of vengeance. The time had come, and he would wait no longer. If he'd been more impulsive and less of a coward he would have shot his victim then and there, but such was not Hiram's way. Stealthily, with deadly surety he laid his plans, with the patience and fatality that could only come from the father of liars himself.

Three whole days Nathaniel stayed in the village, and much of that time he spent at the Spafford house, walking and talking and reading with Phoebe. Three whole days Hiram spied upon him at every turn, with evil countenance and indifferent mien, lounging by the house or happening in the way. He'd written an angry letter to the man in New York, who later excused himself for not having performed his mission because of Nathaniel's absence but, promising it should yet be done, demanded more money.

Janet and Martin Van Rensselaer came down to the Spafford house the last evening and made a merry party. Hiram hid himself among the lilac bushes at the side of the house, like the serpent of old, and watched the affair all evening, his heart filled with all the evil his nature could conceive.

Phoebe made a beautiful picture in her simple white dress, with her lovely head crowned with the short curling hair and her exquisite face gleaming with the light and mirth of youth, which she was tasting for almost the first time. Miranda saw this as she brought in the sugary seed cakes and a great frosted pitcher of cool drink, made from raspberry and currant jelly, mixed with water from the spring. If Miranda could have known of the watcher outside, the evening might have ended in comedy, for she would certainly have emptied a panful of dishwater from the upper window straight into the lilac bushes. But Miranda's time hadn't come yet, and neither had Hiram's.

So Nathaniel and Phoebe sat by the open window and said a few last pleasant words and looked a good-bye into one another's eyes, the depth and meaning of which neither had as yet fathomed. They didn't know that not two feet away was the evil face of the man who hated them both. He was so near that his viperous breath could almost have touched their cheeks, and his wicked heart, burning with the passionate fires of jealousy and hatred, gathered and devoured their glances as a raging fire will devour fuel. He watched them, and he gloated over them, as a monster will gloat over the victims he intends to destroy.

Chapter 24

$\mathcal{T}$he next morning on the early coach Nathaniel and Martin went away. Hiram was there to see that they were really gone and to send word at once to New York.

That afternoon Phoebe went back to her brother's house, with the light of health and happiness beginning to glow in her face. It was hard to go back, but Phoebe was happy in the thought that these friends were true and would continue even in the midst of daily trials.

Everybody had urged her to stay longer, but Phoebe felt she'd already stayed longer than she should have and insisted she must begin life again, that it wasn't right to lie idle.

The truth was, Phoebe had in mind a little plan she wanted to think about and talk over with Albert. This stay with the Spaffords had brought to a climax a great longing she'd had in her heart to go to school somewhere for a little while. She had a great thirst for knowledge and thought perhaps it might be possible to gratify it, for there was that money of hers lying idle in the bank. She might take some of it and go away for a year to a good school if Albert thought so, and she almost believed he would if only he could be persuaded before Emmeline heard of it.

Phoebe had felt her own deficiencies because of her delightful correspondence with Nathaniel Graham. She wished to make herself more his equal, that she might really be able to write letters worthy of his perusal. She little dreamed of the trouble that was swiftly descending.

In modern war we sow our harbors and coasts thick with

hidden mines ready to explode should the enemy venture within our borders. In much the same fashion that morning Hiram Green started out to lay his mines in readiness for the sweet young life that was unwarily drifting his way.

He had dressed himself soberly, as befitted the part he was to play. He harnessed his horse and chaise and, taking a wide berth of country in his circuit for the day, drove first to the home of an old aunt he'd never been bound to by many loving ties, yet who served his purpose, for she had a wagging tongue that reached far.

After the greetings were exchanged Hiram sat down with a funereal air in the big chair his relative had brought out of the parlor in honor of his coming and prepared to bring forth his errand.

"Aunt Keziah," he began, in a voice which indicated momentous things to come. "I'm in deep trouble!"

"You don't say, Hiram! What's up now? Any of the children dead or sick?"

"No, I ain't afflicted in that manner this time," said Hiram. "It's somethin' deeper than that, deeper than sickness er death. It's fear o' disgrace."

"What! Hiram! You ain't ben stealin' er forgin' anybody's name, surely?" The old lady sat up as if she'd been shot and fixed her eyes—little eyes like Hiram's with the glitter of steel beads—on her downcast nephew's face.

"No, Aunt, I'm thankful to say I've been kep' from pussonel disgrace," murmured Hiram piously, with a roll of his eyes indicating that his trust was in a power beyond his own.

"Well, you see it's this way, Aunt. You must uv heard I was takin' notice again."

"That was to be expected, Hiram, you so young an' with children to look after. I hope you picked out a good worker."

"Yes," admitted Hiram with satisfaction, "she's a right smart worker, an' I thought she was 'bout as near perfect all through as you could find 'em, an' I kinder got my heart sot on her. I've done everythin' she wanted that I knowed, even to buildin' a new house down on the knoll fer her, which wa'n't necessary 'tall, bein' as the old house is much better'n the one she's ben brung up in. Yet I done it fer her, an' I ben courtin' her fer quite a spell back now; ben to see her every night reg'lar, an' home from meetin' an' singin' school whenever she took notion she wanted to go."

Hiram drew a long sigh, got out a big red and white cotton handkerchief, and blew his nose resoundingly. The old lady eyed him suspiciously to gauge his emotion with exactness.

"Long 'bout six or eight weeks ago"—Hiram's voice grew husky now—"she took sick. 'Twas this 'ere way. We was comin' home from a barn raisin' over to Woodburys', an' it was gettin' near dark, an' she took a notion she wanted to pick some vi'lets 'long the road. I seen a storm was comin' up, an' I argued with her agin it, but she would hev her way, an' so I let her out an' tole her to hurry up.

"She got out an' run back o' the kerridge a piece an' begun pickin', an' in a minute all on a sudden somethin' hit the horse's hind leg. I can't tell what it was, mebbe a stone er it might 'a' ben a stick, but I never took no thought at the time. I grabbed fer them reins, an' jest as the horse started to run there come a big clap o' thunder that scared the horse worse'n ever. I hung on to them reins, an' lookin' back I seen her standin' kind o' scared-like an' white in the road a-lookin' after me, an' I hollered back, 'You go to the Widder Duzenberry's till I come back fer yeh. It's goin' to rain.' Then I hed to tend to that horse, fer he was runnin' like the very old scratch. Well, 'course I got him stopped and turned him round an' went back, but there wasn't a sign of her anywhere to be seen.

"The Widder Duzenberry said she hedn't seen her sence we druv by fust. I went back fer her brother, an' we searched everywhere but couldn't find her no place, an' will you b'lieve it, we couldn't find a sign of her all night. But the next mornin' she come sailin' in lookin' white an' scared and fainted away an' went right to bed real sick. We couldn't make it all out, an' I never said much 'bout it, 'cause I didn't 'spicion nothin' at the time, but it all looked kinder odd afterward. An' what I'd like to know is, who threw that ar stone thet hit the horse?

"You see, it's all come out now thet she's been cuttin' round the country with a strange young man from New York. She's met him off in the woods an' round. They say they used ter meet not far from here—right down on the timber lot back o' your barn was one place they used to meet. There's a holler tree where they'd hide their letters. You 'member that big tree taller than the rest, a big white oak, 't is, that has a squirrel harbor in it? Well, that's the one. They used to meet there. And once she started off on some errand fer her sister-in-law in the coach, an' he es bold es life went 'long. Nobody knows whar they went—some sez Albany, some sez Schenectady— but anyhow she never come back till late the next day, an' no countin' fer where she'd been.

"Her sister-in-law is a nice respectable woman, and they all come of a good family. They'll feel turrible 'bout this, fer they've never 'spicioned her anymore'n I done. She's got a sweet purty face like she was a saint—"

"Them is always the very kind that goes to the dogs," said Aunt Keziah, shaking her head and laying down her knitting.

"Well, Aunt Keziah," said Hiram, getting out his handkerchief again, "I come to ask your advice in this matter. What be I to do?"

"Do?" snapped Aunt Keziah. "Do, Hiram Green? Why be thankful you found out 'fore you got married. It's hard on you, 'course, but 'tain't near so hard es 'twould 'a' ben ef you'd 'a' found out after you was tied to 'er. An' you just havin' had such a hard time an' all with a sickly wife dyin'. I declare,

Hiram Green, you suttin'ly hev been preserved!"

"But don't you think, mebbe, Aunt Keziah, I ought to stick to her? She's such a purty little thing, an' everybody's down on her now, an' she's begged me so hard not to give her up when she's in disgrace. She's promised she'll never hev nothin' more to do with these other fellers—"

Some hypocritical tears were actually being squeezed out of Hiram's little pig eyes and rolling down in stinted quantities upon the ample kerchief. It wouldn't do to wipe them away when they were so hard to manufacture, so Hiram waited till they were almost evaporated and then mopped his eyes vigorously.

"Well, Hiram Green, are you that softhearted? I declare to goodness, but you do need advice! Don't you trust in no sech promises. They ain't wuth the breath they're spoken in. Jest you hev nothin' more to do with the hussy. Thank goodness there's plenty more good workers in the world—healthy ones, too, that won't up 'n' die on ye jest in harves'!"

"Well, Aunt Keziah!" Hiram arose and cleared his throat as if a funeral ceremony had just been concluded. "I thank yeh fer yer good advice. I may see my way clear to foller it. Jest now I'm in doubt. I wanted to know what you thought, an' then I'll consider the matter. It ain't as though I hedn't been goin' with her pretty steady fer a year back. Yeh see what I'll do'll likely tell on how it goes with her from now on."

"Well, don't you go to be sentimental-like, Hiram. That wouldn't set on you at your time o' life. Jest you stand by your rights an' be rid of her. It's what your ma would 'a' said ef she was alive. Now you remember what I say. Don't you be softhearted."

"I'll remember, Aunt," said Hiram dutifully and went out to his chaise.

He took his slow and doleful way winding up the road, and as soon as he was out of sight beyond the turn, the alert old lady put on her sunbonnet and slipped up to her cousin's house half a mile away. She was out of breath with the tremendous news she had to tell and marvelling all the way that Hiram had forgotten to tell her not to speak of it. Of course he intended to do so, but then of course he wouldn't object to having Lucy Drake know. Lucy was his own cousin once removed, and it was a family affair in a way.

Hiram's next visit was at the Widow Duzenberry's.

Now the Widow Duzenberry had often thought her good daughter would make a wise choice for Hiram Green and could rule well over the wild little Greens and be an ornament to the Green house and farm. Therefore it seemed a special dispensation of Providence that Susanna had that afternoon donned her best sprigged chintz and done her hair up with her grandmother's high-backed comb. She looked proudly over at her daughter as Hiram sat down in the chair Susanna had primly placed for him near her mother.

When the few preliminary remarks were concluded, and the atmosphere had become somewhat breathless with the excitement of wondering why he'd come, Hiram cleared his throat ominously and began.

"Mrs. Duzenberry," he said, and his countenance took on a deep sadness, "I called today on a very sad errand." The audience was attentive in the extreme. "I want to ask, did you take notice of me an' Phoebe Deane a-ridin' by, the day of Woodburys' barn raisin'?"

"Wal, yes," admitted old Mrs. Duzenberry reluctantly. "Now 't you mention it, I b'lieve I did see you drivin' by, fer there was black clouds comin' up, an' I says to Susanna, says I, 'Susanna, we mebbe ought to bring in that web o' cloth that's out to bleach. It mebbe might blow away.'"

"Well, I thought p'raps you did, Mis' Duzenberry, an' I want to ask, did you take notice of how we was sittin' clost to one 'nother, she with her head restin' on my shoulder like? I hate to speak of it, but, Mis' Duzenberry, wouldn't you 'a' thought Phoebe Deane was real fond o' me!"

Mrs. Duzenberry's face darkened. What had the man come for?

"I certain should," she answered severely. "I don't approve of sech doin's on an open road."

"Well, Mis' Duzenberry, mebbe 'twas a little too sightly a place, but what I wanted to know from you, Mis' Duzenberry, was this. You saw what you saw. Now won't you tell me when a man has gone that fur, in your 'pinion is there anything that would justify him in turnin' back?"

"There might be," said the old lady, somewhat mollified.

"Well, what, fur instance?"

"Wal, he might 'a' found he thought more o' someone else." Her eyes wandered toward her daughter, who was modestly looking out the window.

"Anything else?" Hiram's voice had the husky note now as if he were deeply affected.

"Wal, I might think of somethin' else. Gimme time."

"What ef he found out she wa'n't all he thought she was?"

Mrs. Duzenberry's face brightened.

" 'Course that might 'fect him some," she admitted.

"I see you don't understand me," sighed Hiram. "I take it you ain't heard the bad news 'bout Phoebe Deane."

"She ain't dead, is she? I heard she was better," said Susanna, turning her sharp thin profile toward Hiram.

"No, my good friend," sighed Hiram, "it's worse'n death. It certainly is fer that poor girl. She's to be greatly pitied, however much she may have aired."

The two women were leaning forward now, eager for the news.

"I came to you in my trouble," said Hiram, mopping his face vigorously, "hopin' you would sympathize with me in my extremity an' help me to jedge what to do. I wouldn't like to do the girl no wrong, but still, considerin' all that's come out the last two days—say, Mis' Duzenberry, you didn't see no man hangin' round here that day a little before we druv by, did you? No stranger, ner nuthin'.'"

"Why, yes, Ma," said Susanna excitedly. "There was a wagon come by a-goin' toward the village, and there was two men, an' one of 'em jumped out an' took somethin' from the other, looked like a bundle er sumthin', an' he walked off toward the woods. He had butternut-colored trousers."

"That's him," said Hiram, frowning. "They say he always wore them trousers when anybody's seen him with her. You know the day they went off in the stage to Albany he was dressed thata way!"

"Did they go off in the stage together in broad daylight? That's scandalous!" exclaimed the mother.

"You know, most o' their goin's on happened over near Fundy Road. Aunt Keziah knows all 'bout it. Poor ole lady. She's all broke up. She always set a good store by me, her only livin' nephew. She'll be wantin' me to give up havin' anythin' more to do with Phoebe now, since all this is come out 'bout her goin's on, but I can't rightly make up my mind whether it's right fer me to desert her er not in her time o' trouble."

"I should think you was fully justified," said Mrs. Duzenberry heartily. "There's other deservin' girls, an' it's puttin' a premium on badness to 'ncourage it that way."

"Good afternoon, Mis' Duzenberry." Hiram rose sadly. "I'm much 'bliged to yeh fer yer advice. I ain't sure what I shall do. 'Course I'll be 'bliged to yeh ef you'll jest keep people from talkin' much as yeh ken. I knowed you knowed the fac's, an' I thought 'twould be best to come straight to you. Good afternoon, Miss Susanna. Perhaps we may meet again under pleasanter circumstances."

"Land alive!" exclaimed Susanna, as they watched him drive sadly away. "Don't he look broke up! Poor feller!"

"Serves him right fer makin' up to a little pink-cheeked critter like that," said the mother. "Say, Susanna, I ain't sure but you better put on yer bonnet an' run up to Keziah Dart's house an' find out 'bout this. We've got to be real keerful not to get mixed up in it, nohow, but I'd like to know jest what she's done. Ef Keziah ain't home, run on to Page's. They'll mebbe know. He said they'd ben seen round there. But speak real cautious. It won't do to tell everything you know. I'll mebbe jest step over to the tollgate. They'll be wantin' to know what Hiram Green was here for. It won't do no harm to mention he was callin' on you. It might take their 'tention off'n him, so's they wouldn't speak 'bout him goin' so much with Phoebe. My! Ain't it a pity! But that's what comes o' havin' good looks. You know I allus told you so, Susanna."

Susanna tossed her head, drew her sunbonnet down over her plain face, and went off, while her mother fastened the door and went up to the tollgate.

Hiram's method, as he pursued his course the rest of the afternoon, was to call ostensibly for some other reason and then speak of the gossip as a matter of which everyone knew and refer to those he'd called on before as being able to give more information concerning the facts than he could. He didn't ask any more advice, but in one case where he was asked what he was going to do about it he shook his head dubiously and went away without replying.

Most of his calls were in the country, but before he went home he stopped at the village dressmaker's home. His excuse for going there was that his oldest girl needed a dress for Sunday, and he thought the old woman who kept house for him had enough to do without making it. He asked when she could come and said he'd let her know if that day would be convenient. Just as he was leaving he told her that, since she was going everywhere to other people's houses, he supposed she'd soon hear the terrible stories going around about

Phoebe Deane. But he wished that if she heard anything about his breaking off with Phoebe she'd just say he intended not to do anything rashly but would think it over and do what was right.

The keen-eyed newsmonger asked enough questions to have the facts in hand and looked after Hiram's tall, lanky form with admiration. "I tell you," she said to herself, "it ain't every man would hev the courage to say that! He's a good man! Poor little Phoebe Deane. What a pity! Now her life's ruined, fer of course he'll never marry her."

Then Hiram Green, having wisely scattered his calumnies against the innocent, took himself virtuously to his home and left his thistle seed to take root and spring up.

Phoebe Deane, meanwhile, settled down in her own little chamber beside her candle and prepared to write a letter to Nathaniel Graham, as she had promised him she'd do that very night, and in it she told him her plans of going away to school.

Chapter 25

The tongues Hiram had set wagging were all experts, and before many days had passed, the fields of gossip were green with springing slander and disgrace for the fair name of Phoebe Deane. All unconsciously she moved above it, making happy plans and singing her sweet song of hope. She didn't mind work, for it was pleasant to feel strong again. She even hummed a sweet tune she heard Marcia play. Emmeline was puzzled to understand it all.

But the thing that puzzled Emmeline most was that Hiram Green hadn't been near the house since the day he had the talk with her about the village lot and boasted he was going to marry Phoebe before another year.

Steadily every day Hiram's new house was growing. Emmeline could see it from her window and wondered if perhaps he was preparing to break his promise and court another girl instead of Phoebe, or was this part of his plan to stay away until the house was done? It troubled Emmeline every day. Neither could she understand how Phoebe could be happy and settle down so cheerfully, having driven her one suitable lover away.

Phoebe had ventured to discuss the plan of her going away with Albert, who seemed rather disappointed for her to go but was nevertheless willing and said he thought such a plan would have pleased her mother. He broached the subject to Emmeline and thereupon brought down on the family a storm of rage.

Emmeline scoffed at the idea. She said Phoebe was already

spoiled for anything in life, and if she used up her money getting more spoiling, she couldn't see how in the world she expected to support herself. *She* wouldn't be a party to Phoebe's living any longer on them if she spent her money on more schooling. Then Emmeline put on her bonnet and ran across the field to Hiram's farm, where she found him at the knoll superintending the putting up of a great stone chimney.

"Say, look-a-here, Hiram Green," she began excitedly, getting him off a little way from the workmen. "What do you mean by sech actions? Hev you give up Phoebe Deane, er haven't yeh? 'Cause ef yeh ain't yeh better be tendin' to business. She's got it int' her fool head now to go off to school, an' she'll do it, too. I ken see Albert's jest soft enough to let 'er."

Hiram smiled a peculiar smile.

"Don't you worry, Emmeline. I know what I'm 'bout, an' you'll git your corner lot yit. Phoebe Deane won't go off to no boardin' school, not yet a while, er I'll miss my guess. Jest you leave it to me!"

"Oh, very well!" said Emmeline, going off in a huff. She returned by a roundabout route to her home, where she proceeded to make life miserable for Phoebe and Albert in spite of all they could do.

Then one morning, lo, the little town was agog with the gossip about Phoebe Deane. It had grown into enormous proportions, for as it traveled from the circle of country round about into the town it condensed into more tangible form, and the number of people who had seen Phoebe Deane with strange young men at the edge of dark or in lonely places grew with each repetition. Everybody seemed to know it and be talking about it except Phoebe herself and her family and friends. Somehow no one had quite dared to mention it before any of them yet; it was too new and startling.

Sunday morning the Deanes went to church, and the people turned strangely away from them, with much whispering, nodding, and nudging as they passed. They hadn't expected Phoebe to appear in church. It was considered brazen in her to do so. It was evidently all and more true.

Hiram Green came to church, but he didn't look toward the Deanes' pew. He sat at the back with pious manner and drooping countenance and after church made his melancholy way out without stopping to talk or attempting to get near Phoebe. This was observed significantly, as well as the fact that Mrs. Spafford walked down the aisle in friendly conversation with Phoebe Deane as if nothing had happened. Evidently she hadn't heard yet. Somebody should tell her. They discussed the matter in groups on the way home.

Old Mrs. Baldwin and her daughter Belinda were quite worried about it. They went so far as to call to the doctor and his wife who were passing their house that afternoon on the way to see a sick patient.

"Doctor," said Mrs. Baldwin, coming out to the sidewalk as the doctor drew up to speak to her, "I ain't a going to bother you a minute, but I just wanted to ask if you knew much about this story that's been going round about Phoebe Deane. It seems as though someone ought to tell Mrs. Spafford. She's been real kind to the girl, and she don't seem to have heard it. I don't know her so well, or I would, but somebody ought to do it. I didn't know but you or your wife would undertake to do it. They walked down the aisle together after church this morning, and it seemed too bad. David Spafford wouldn't like to have his wife so conspicuous, I know. Belinda says he was out of town yesterday, so I s'pose he hasn't heard about it yet, but I think something ought to be done."

"Yes, it's a very sad story," chirped the doctor's wife. "I just heard it myself this morning. The doctor didn't want to believe it, but I tell him it comes very straight."

"Oh, yes, it's straight," said Mrs. Baldwin, with an ominous shake of her head and a righteous roll of her eyes. "It's all too straight. I had it from a friend who had it from Hiram Green's aunt's cousin. She said Hiram was just bowed with grief over it, and they were going to have a real hard time to keep him from marrying her in spite of it."

The doctor frowned. He was fond of Phoebe. He felt that they all had better mind their own business and let Phoebe alone.

"I'd be quite willing to speak to Miss Hortense or Miss Amelia Spafford," said the doctor's wife. "I'm intimate with them, you know, and they could do as they thought best about telling their niece."

"That's a good idea," said Mrs. Baldwin. "That quite relieves my mind. I was real worried over that sweet little Mrs. Spafford, and she with that pretty little Rose to bring up. They wouldn't of course want a scandal to come anywhere near them. They better look out for that Griscom girl. She comes from poor stock. I said long ago she'd never be any good, and she's been with that Phoebe Deane off an' on a good bit."

"Oh, I think that was all kindness," said the doctor's wife. "Mrs. Spafford was very kind during Phoebe Deane's illness. The doctor knew all about that."

"Yes, I s'pose the doctor knows all 'bout things. That's the reason I called you and on Sunday, too. But I thought it was a work of necessity and mercy. Well, good afternoon, doctor. I won't keep you any longer."

"There's that pretty Miss Bristol ought to be told, too, Ma," said Belinda.

"That's so, Belinda," said the doctor's wife. "I'll take it upon myself to warn her, too. So sad, isn't it? Well, good-bye." And the doctor's chaise drove on.

The doctor was inclined to prevent his wife from taking part in the scandal business, but his wife had her own plans which she didn't reveal. She shut her thin lips and generally did as she pleased.

The very next day she took her way down the shaded street and called on the Spafford aunts, and before she left she had drooped her eyes and told in sepulchral whispers of the disgrace that had befallen the young protégée of their niece, Mrs. David Spafford.

Aunt Amelia and Aunt Hortense lifted their hands in righteous horror and thanked the doctor's wife for the information, saying they were sure Marcia knew nothing of it, and of course they would tell her at once and she would have nothing further to do with the Deanes.

Then the doctor's wife went on her mission to Janet Bristol.

Janet Bristol was properly scandalized and charmingly grateful to the doctor's wife. She said of course Phoebe was nothing to her, but she'd thought her rather pretty and interesting. She was obviously bored with the rest of the good woman's call, and when it was over she went to her writing desk where she scribbled off a letter to her cousin Nathaniel concerning a party she wished to give and for which she wanted him and his friend Martin Van Rensselaer to come up. At the close she added a hasty postscript.

The doctor's wife has just called. She tells me I must beware of your paragon, Miss Deane, as there is a terribly scandalous story going around about her and a young man. I didn't pay much attention to the horrid details of it. I never like to get my mind filled with such things. But it's bad enough, and of course I shall have nothing further to do with her. I wonder Mrs. Spafford didn't have the discernment to see she wasn't all right. I suspected it from the first, you know, and you see I was right. My intuitions are usually right. I'm glad I didn't have much to do with her.

Now it happened that Rose wasn't well that Sunday and

Miranda had stayed at home with her; otherwise, she would surely have discovered the state of things and revealed it to Marcia. It happened also that Marcia started off with David on a long ride early Monday morning. Therefore when Aunt Hortense came down on her direful errand Marcia wasn't there, and Miranda, seeing her coming, escaped with Rose through the back door for a walk in the woods. So another day passed without the scandal reaching either Miranda or Marcia.

On Monday morning the storm broke upon poor Phoebe's defenseless head.

A neighbor had come over from the next farm a quarter of a mile away to borrow a cup of hop yeast. It was an odd time to borrow yeast, at an hour in the week when every well-regulated family was doing its washing, but that was the neighbor's professed errand. She lingered a moment by the door with the yeast cup in her hand and talked to Emmeline.

Phoebe was in the yard hanging up clothes and singing. The little bird was sitting on the weather vane, calling merrily, "Phoe-bee! Phoe-bee!"

"Are yeh goin' to let her stay here now?" the visitor asked in a whisper fraught with meaning and nodded her head toward the girl in the yard.

"Stay?" said Emmeline, looking up aggressively. "Why shouldn't she? Ain't she been here ever since her mother died? I s'pose she'll stay till she gets married."

Emmeline wasn't fond of this neighbor and therefore didn't care to reveal her family secrets to her. She lived in a red house with windows both ways and knew all that went on for miles about.

"Guess she won't run much chance of that now," said the neighbor with a disagreeable laugh. She was prepared to be sociable if Emmeline opened her heart, but she knew how to scratch back when she was slapped.

"Well, I sh'd like to know what you mean, Mis' Prinn. I'm sure I don't know why our Phoebe shouldn't marry es likely as any other girl, an' more so'n some what ain't got good looks."

(Mrs. Prinn's daughter wasn't spoken of generally as a beauty.)

"Good looks don't count fer much when they ain't got good morals."

"Indeed, Mis' Prinn! You do talk kind of mysterious. Did you mean to insinuate that our Phoebe didn't have good morals?"

"I didn't mean to insinuate anything, Mis' Deane. It's all over town the way she's been goin' on, an' I don't see how you can pertend to hide it any longer. Everybody knows it an' b'lieves it."

"I'd certainly like to know what you mean," demanded Emmeline, facing the woman angrily. "I brung that girl up, an' I guess I know what good morals is. Phoebe may have her weak points, but she's all right morally."

"Fac's is fac's, Mis' Deane," said the neighbor with a relish.

"I deny there is any fac's to the contrary," screamed Emmeline, now thoroughly excited into championing the girl she hated. The family honor was at stake. The Deanes had never done anything dishonorable or disgraceful.

"I s'pose you don't deny she spent the night out all night the time o' the storm, do yeh? How d' ye explain that?"

"I should like to know what that hes to do with morals."

The neighbor proceeded to explain with a story so plausible that Emmeline grew livid with rage.

"Well, 'pon my word, you've got a lot to do runnin' round with sech lies as them. Wher'd you get all that, I'd like to know?"

"It all come straight enough, an' everybody knows it, ef you are stone blind. Folks has seen her round in lonely places with a strange feller. They do say he kissed her right in plain sight of the road near the woods one day. An' you know yerself she went off and stayed all night. She was seen in the stagecoach 'long with a strange man. There's witnesses! You can't deny it. What I want to know is, what are you goin' to do 'bout it? 'Cause ef you keep her here after that, I can't let my dotter come here anymore. When girls is talked about like that, decent girls can't hev nothin' to do with 'em. You think you know a hull lot 'bout that girl out there, singin' songs in this brazen way with the hull town talkin' 'bout her, but she's deceived you, that's what she's done. An' I thought I'd be a good enough neighbor to tell you, ef you didn't know a'ready. But es you don't seem to take it as 'twas meant, in kindness, I'd best be goin'."

"You'd best had," screamed Emmeline, "an' be sure you keep your precious dotter to hum. Hum's the place fer delikit little creatures like that. You might find *she* was deceivin' you ef *you* looked sharp enough."

Then Emmeline turned and faced the wondering Phoebe, who had heard the loud voices and slipped in through the woodshed to escape being drawn into the altercation. She had no idea what it all was about. She had been engaged with her own happy thoughts.

"I'd like to know what all this scandal's about, Phoebe Deane. Jest set down there and explain. What kind of goin's on hev you hed, that all the town's talkin' 'bout you? Mis' Prinn comes an' says she can't let her dotter come over here anymore ef you stay here. I don't know that it's much loss, fer she never come to 'mount to much, but I can't hev folks talkin' that way. No decent girl ought to have her name kicked around in that style. I may not hev hed a great ejjacation like you think you've got to have, but I knowed enough to keep my name off folks' tongues, an' it seems you don't. Now I'd like to know what young man or men you've been kitin' round with. Answer me that? They say you've been seen in the woods alone, walkin' at night with a strange man, an' goin' off in the stagecoach. Now what in the world does it all mean?"

Phoebe, turning deathly white, with a sudden return of her recent weakness, sank upon a kitchen chair, her arms full of dried clothes, and tried to understand the angry woman who stormed back and forth across her kitchen, livid with rage, pouring out a perfect torrent of wrath and incriminations.

When a moment's interval came, Phoebe would try to answer her, but Emmeline, roused beyond control, wouldn't listen. She stormed and raged at Phoebe, calling her names and telling her what a trial she'd always been, until suddenly Phoebe's newfound strength gave way entirely, and she dropped back in a faint against the wall. She would have fallen if Albert hadn't come in just then unnoticed and caught her. He carried her upstairs tenderly and laid her on her bed. In a moment she opened her sad eyes again and looked up at him.

"What's the matter, Phoebe?" he asked tenderly. "Been working too hard?"

But Phoebe could only answer by a rush of tears.

Albert, troubled as a man always is by a woman's tears, stumbled downstairs to Emmeline to find out and was met by an overwhelming story.

"Who says all that 'bout my sister?" he demanded in a cool voice, rising with a dignity that sat strangely upon his kind figure.

"She ain't your sister," hissed Emmeline. "She ain't any but a half relation to you, an' it's time you told her so an' turned her out of the house. She'll be a disgrace to you an' your decent wife an' children. I can't have my Alma brought up in a house with a girl that's disgraced herself like that."

"You keep still, Emmeline," said Albert gravely. "You don't rightly know what you're saying. You've got excited. I'll attend to this matter. What I want to know is, who said this about my sister? I'll go get Hiram Green to help me, and we'll face the scoundrel, whoever it is, and make him take it back before the whole town."

"What ef it's true!" mocked Emmeline.

"It isn't true. It couldn't be true. You know it couldn't, Emmeline."

"I'm not so sure o' that," raged his wife. "Wait till you hear all." And she proceeded to recount what Mrs. Prinn had told her.

"I'm ashamed of you, Emmeline, that you'll think of such a thing for a minute, no matter who told you. Don't say another word about it. I'm going out to find Hiram."

"Ain't you noticed that Hiram ain't ben comin' here lately?" Emmeline's voice was anything but pleasant.

Albert looked at her in astonishment.

"Well, what o' that? He's a good man, and he's fond o' Phoebe. He'll be sure to go with me and defend her."

Albert went out, and she saw him hurrying down the road toward Hiram's.

Hiram, like an old spider, was waiting for him in the barn. He'd been expecting him for two days, not thinking it would take so long for the news to spread into the victim's home. He looked gloomy and noncommittal as Albert came up, and he greeted him with half-averted eyes.

"I've come to get your help," said Albert with expectant goodwill. "Hiram, have you heard all this fool talk about Phoebe? I can't really believe folks would say that about her, but Emmeline's got it in her head everybody knows it."

"Yes, I heard it," admitted Hiram, reaching out for a straw to chew. "I spent one hull day last week goin' round tryin' to stop it, but 'twa'n't no use. I couldn't even find out who started it. You never ken, them things. But the wust of it is, it's all true."

"What!"

"Yes," said Hiram dismally, " 'tis. I'm sorry t' say it to you, what's ben my friend, 'bout her I hoped to marry someday, but I seen some things myself. I seen thet day they talk 'bout in the edge o' the woods, an' I seen her cut an' run when she heard my wagon comin', an' when she looked up an' seen it was me she was deadly pale. That was the fust I knowed she wa'n't true to me."

Hiram closed his lying lips and looked off sorrowfully at the hills in the distance.

"Hiram, you must be mistaken. There is some explanation."

"All right, Albert, glad you ken think so. Wish't I could. It mos' breaks my heart thinkin' 'bout her. I'm all bound up in havin' her. I'd take her now with all her disgrace an' run the resk o' keepin' her straight ef she'd promise to behave herself. She's mighty young, an' it does seem too bad. But, yeh see, Albert, I seen her myself with my own eyes in the stagecoach along with the same man what kissed her in the woods, an' yeh know yerself she didn't come back till next night."

With a groan Albert sank down on a box nearby and covered his face with his hands. He had been well brought up, and disgrace like this was something he'd never dreamed of. His agony amazed the ice-hearted Hiram, and he almost quailed before the sight of such sorrow in a man, sorrow he himself had made. It embarrassed him. He turned away to hide his contempt.

"It comes mighty hard on me to see you suffer thet way, Albert, an' not be able to help you," he whined after a minute. "I'll tell you what I'll do. I'll marry her anyway. I'll marry her an' save her reputation. Nobody'll dast say anythin' 'bout my wife, an' ef I marry her that'll be es much es to say all this ain't so, an' mebbe it'll die down."

Albert looked up with manly tears in his eyes.

"That's real good of you, Hiram. I'll take it as mighty kind of you if you think there isn't any other way to stop it. It seems hard on you, though."

"I ain't thinkin' o' myself," swelled Hiram. "I'm thinkin' o' the girl, an' I don't see no other way. When things is true, you know, there ain't no way o' denyin' them, 'specially when folks hes seen so many things. But just oncet get her good an' respectably married, an' it'll all blow over an' be forgot."

They talked a long time, and Hiram embellished the stories that had been told by many a new incident out of fertile brain, until Albert was thoroughly convinced the only way to save Phoebe's reputation was for her to be married at once to Hiram.

Albert went home at last and entered the kitchen with a chastened air. Emmeline eyed him keenly. Phoebe hadn't come downstairs, and his wife had all the work to do again. She wasn't enjoying the state of things.

Albert sat down and looked at the floor.

"Hiram has been very kind," he said slowly, "most kind. He has offered to marry Phoebe at once and stop all this talk."

A light of understanding began to dawn in Emmeline's eyes.

"Hm!" she said. Then, after a thoughtful pause, she added, "But I guess Miss Phoebe Deane'll hev a word to say 'bout that. She don't like him a bit."

"Poor child!" moaned Albert. "She'll have to take him, whether she likes him or not. Poor little girl. I blame myself I didn't look after her better. Her mother was a real lady and so good to me when I was home. I promised her I'd keep Phoebe safe. She was such a good woman. It would break her heart to have Phoebe go like this."

"Hm! I don't reckon she was no better than other folks. Only she set up to be!" sniffed Emmeline. "Anyhow, this is just what might 'a' ben expected from the headstrong way that girl went on. I see now why she was set on goin' off to school. She knowed this was a-comin' an' wanted to slip an' run 'fore it got out. But she got caught. Sinners generally does."

Emmeline wrung out her dishcloth with satisfaction.

"I'll go up now and talk with Phoebe," said Albert, rising sadly as if he hadn't heard his wife.

"I'm sure I wish you joy on your errand. Ef she ac's to you es she does to me you'll come flyin' down faster'n you went up."

But Albert was tapping at Phoebe's door before Emmeline had finished her sentence.

Chapter 26

*P*hoebe," said Albert, gently sitting down beside the bed where she lay wide-eyed, in white-faced misery, trying to comprehend what this new calamity might mean, "I'm mighty sorry for you, little girl. I wish you had come to me with things more. I might 'a' helped you better if I hadn't been so stupid. But I've found a way out of it all for you. I've found a good man that's willing to marry you and give you the protection of his name and home, and we'll just have you married right away quietly here at home, and that'll stop all the talk."

Phoebe turned a look of mingled horror and helplessness on her brother. He didn't comprehend it and thought she was grasping for a thread of hope.

"Yes, Phoebe, Hiram Green is willing to marry you right off in spite of everything, and we've fixed it up to have the wedding right away, tomorrow. That'll give you time to straighten out your things, and Hiram to get the minister—"

But Albert stopped suddenly as Phoebe uttered a piercing scream of fear and started up as if she would fly from the room.

Albert caught her and tried to soothe her.

"What's the matter now, little girl? Don't look like that. It'll all come out right. Is it because you don't like Hiram enough? But, child, you'll get to like him more as you know him better. Then you'll be so grateful to think what he saved you from. And besides, Phoebe, there isn't any other way. We couldn't stand the disgrace. What would your mother think? She was always so particular about how you should be brought up. And to have you turn out disgraced would break her heart. Phoebe, don't you see there isn't any other way?"

"Albert, I would rather die than marry that wicked man. He is a bad man. I *know* he is bad. He has been trying to make me marry him for a long time, and now he's just taking advantage of this terrible story. Albert, you know these stories are not true. You don't believe them, Albert, do you?"

She looked at him with piteous pleading in her beautiful eyes, and he had to turn his own eyes away to hide their wavering. He couldn't see how this sweet girl could have gone wrong, and yet—there was the evidence!

"You do," said Phoebe. "Albert, you do! You believe all this awful story about me! I never thought you would believe it. But, Albert, listen! I will never marry Hiram Green! You may kill me or send me away, or anything you like, but you cannot make me marry him!"

Albert turned his eyes away from the pitiful figure of the pleading girl and set his lips firmly.

"I'm sorry, Phoebe, but it's got to be done," he said sorrowfully. "I can't have this talk go on. I'll give you a little more time to get used to it, but you can't have much, for this story has to be stopped. We'll say a week. One week from today you'll have to marry Hiram Green, or I'll be forced to turn you out of my house. And you know what that means. I couldn't allow any respectable person to harbor you. You've disgraced us all. But if you marry Hiram it'll be all right presently. Marriage covers up gossip. Why, Phoebe, think of my little Alma. If this goes on, everybody'll point their fingers at her and say her auntie was a bad girl and brought dishonor on the family, and Alma'll grow up without any friends. I've got to look out for my little girl as well as you, Phoebe, and you must believe me; I'm doing the very best for you I know."

Phoebe sat down weakly on the edge of her bed and stared

wildly at him. She couldn't believe Albert would talk to her so. She couldn't think of anything to say in answer. She could only stare blankly at him as if he were a terrible apparition.

Albert thought she was quieting down and going to be reasonable, and with a few kind words he backed out of the room. Phoebe dropped back upon her pillow in a frenzy of horror and grief. Wild plans of running away rushed through her brain, which was after all futile, because her limbs seemed suddenly to have grown too feeble to carry her. Her brain refused to think or take in any facts except the great horror of scandal that had risen about her and was threatening to overwhelm her.

Emmeline declined to take any dinner up to her. She said if Phoebe wanted anything to eat she might come down and get it; she wasn't going to wait on a girl like that any longer. Albert fixed a nice plate of dinner and carried it up, but Phoebe lay motionless with open eyes turned toward the wall and refused to speak. He put the plate on a chair beside her and went sadly down again. Phoebe wondered how long it would take someone to die and why God hadn't let her die when she had the fever. What had there been to live for anyway? One short bright month of happiness!

The memory of it gripped her heart anew with shame and horror. What would they say, all those kind friends? Mrs. Spafford and her husband, Miranda, and Nathaniel Graham? Would they believe it, too? Of course they would, if her own household turned against her. She was defenseless in a desolate world. She would never again have friends and smiles and comfort. She couldn't go away to school now, for what good would an education be to her with such a disgrace clinging to her name and following her wherever she went? It would be of no use to run away. She might better stay here and die. They couldn't marry her to Hiram Green if she was dead. Could someone die in a week by just lying still?

So the horror in her brain raged over and over, each time

bringing some new phase of grief. Now it was a question of whether her friends would desert her; and now it was the haughty expression on Janet Bristol's face that day she carried the letter to Nathaniel; and now it was the leer on Hiram's face as he put his arm about her on that terrible drive; and now it was the thought that she would have no more of Nathaniel's long, delightful letters.

All day long she lay in this state, and when the darkness fell, a half-delirious sleep came upon her, which carried the fears and thoughts of the day into its unresting slumber. The morning broke into the sorrow of yesterday, and Phoebe, weak and sick, arose with one thought in her mind, that she must write at once to Nathaniel Graham and tell him all. She mustn't be a disgrace to him.

With trembling hands and eyes filled with tears, she wrote:

Dear Mr. Graham,

I am writing to you for the last time. A terrible thing has happened. Someone has been telling awful stories about me, and I am in disgrace. I want you to know that these things are not true. I don't even know how they started, for there has never been any foundation for them. But everybody believes them, and I won't disgrace you by writing to you anymore. You will probably be told the worst that is said, and perhaps you will believe them as others do. I shall not blame you if you do, for it seems as if even God believed them. I don't know how to prove my innocence or what the end of this is to be. I only know it isn't right to keep you in ignorance of my shame and to let you write any longer to one whose name is held in dishonor. I thank you for all the beautiful times you have put into my life, and I must say good-bye forever.

Gratefully,
Phoebe Deane

The letter was blistered with tears before it was finished. She addressed it and hid it in her dress, for she began to wonder how it would get to the mail. Probably Miranda would never come near her again, and she couldn't be seen in the village. She dared not ask anyone else to mail the letter lest it would never reach its destination.

She spent the rest of the day in quietly putting to rights her little belongings, unpacking and gathering things she would like to have destroyed if anything happened to her. She felt weak and dizzy, and the food Albert continued to bring to her seemed nauseous. She couldn't bring herself to taste a mouthful. It was so useless to eat. One only ate to live, and living had been finished for her, it appeared. It wasn't that she had resolved to make away with herself by starvation. She was too right-minded for that. She was simply stunned by the calamity that had befallen her and was waiting for the outcome.

Sometimes as she stood at the window looking out across the fields that had been familiar to her since her childhood, she had a feeling she was going away from them all soon. She wondered if her mother felt so before she died. Then she wondered why she didn't run away. But always when she thought that, something seemed to hold her back, for how could she run far when she couldn't keep up about her room more than a few minutes at a time for dizziness and faintness! And how could she run fast enough to run away from shame? It couldn't be done. Whenever in her dreams she started to run away she always stumbled and fell and then seemed suddenly struck blind and unable to move farther. And the whole village came crowding about her and mocking her like a great company of cawing crows met around a poor dead thing.

Late Tuesday afternoon Miranda came out to see her. Emmeline opened the door, and her countenance darkened when she recognized the visitor.

"Now you ken just turn right around and march home," she

commanded. "We don't want no folks around. Phoebe Deane's in turrible disgrace, an' you've hed your part in it ef I don't miss my guess. No, you ain't goin' to see her. She's up in her room and ben shut up there ever since she heard how folks hes found out 'bout her capers. You an' yer Mis' Spafford can keep yer pryin' meddlin' fingers out o' this an' let Phoebe Deane alone from now on. We don't want to see yeh anymore. Yer spoilin' an pettin' has only hastened the disgrace."

The door slammed in Miranda's indignant face, and Emmeline went back to her work.

"She needs a good shakin'," remarked Miranda indignantly to herself, "but it might tire me, an' besides, I've got other fish to fry."

Undaunted, she marched to the back shed and mounted to Phoebe's window, entering as if it had always been the common mode of ingress.

"Wal, fer the land, Phoebe Deane, what's ben happenin' now?" she asked mildly, surveying Phoebe, who lay white and weak upon her bed, with her untasted dinner beside her.

"Oh, don't you know all about it, Miranda?" Phoebe began to sob.

"No, I don't know a thing. I ben shut up in the house cookin' for two men Mr. David brung home last night, an' they et an' et till I thought there wouldn't be nothin' left fer the family. They was railroad men er somethin'. No, I guess 'twas bankin' men. I fergit what. But they could eat if they did wear their best clothes every day. But, say, ef I was you, I wouldn't talk very loud fer the lady downstairs wasn't real glad to see me this time, an' she might invite me to leave rather suddint ef she 'spicioned I was up here."

But Phoebe didn't laugh as Miranda had hoped. She only looked at her guest with hungry, hopeless eyes, and it was a long time before Miranda could find out the whole miserable story.

"And, Miranda, I've written Mr. Graham a note telling him about it. Of course I couldn't disgrace him by continuing to write any longer, so I've said good-bye to him. Will you do me one last kindness? Will you mail it for me?"

Phoebe's whisper was tragic. It brought tears to Miranda's well-fortified eyes.

" 'Course I'll mail it fer yeh, child, ef yeh want me to. But 'tain't the last kindness I'll do fer yeh by a long run. Shucks! D'you think I'm goin' to give in this easy an' see you sucked under? Not by a jugful. Now look-a-here, child. Ef the hull fool world goes against yeh, I ain't a-goin', ner my Mrs. Marcia ain't, neither, I'm plumb sure o' that. Bet *ef* she did I'd stick *anyhow*, so there! Cross my heart ef I don't! *Now*. D'yeh b'lieve me? An' I'll find a way out o' this, somehow. I ain't thought it out yet, but don't you worry. You set up 'n' eat fer me. I can't do nothin' ef yeh don't keep yer strength up. Now you do your part, an' we'll get out o' this pickle es good es we did out o' the other one. I ain't goin' to hev all my nursin' wasted. Will yeh be good?"

Phoebe promised meekly. She couldn't smile. She could only press Miranda's hand, while great tears welled through the long lashes on her cheeks.

"So that old serpent thinks he's got you fast, does he? Well, he'll find himself mistaken yet, ef I don't miss my guess. The game ain't all played out by a long shot. Marry you next week, will he? Well, we'll see! I may dance at your weddin' yet, but there won't be no Hiram Green as bridegroom. I'd marry him myself 'fore I'd let him hev you, you poor little white dove." And Miranda pressed Phoebe's trembling hand between her strong ones and stole out of the window.

As she hurried along down the road, the waving grain in the fields on either side reminded her of whispered gossip. She seemed to see a harvest of scandal ripening all about the poor stricken girl she loved, and in her ignorant and original phraseology she murmured to herself the thought of the words of old, "Lo, an enemy hath done this." Miranda felt she knew pretty well who the enemy was.

Chapter 27

"I hev a notion I'd like to go to New York," said Miranda, bouncing in on Marcia.

"Well," said Marcia, "I think you'd enjoy the trip sometime. We might keep a lookout for somebody going who would be company. Or perhaps Mr. Spafford will be going again soon and he'd have time to look after you."

" 'Fraid I can't wait that long," said Miranda. "I've took a great notion I'd like to have a balzarine dress, an' ef I'm goin' to hev it I'd best get it straight off an' git more good out of it. I look at it this way: I ain't goin' to be young but once, an' time's gettin' on. Ef you don't get balzarine dresses when you're young you most likely won't git 'em 't all, 'cause you'll think 'taint wuthwhile. I've got a good bit of money laid by, an' ef you've no 'bjections, an' think you ken spare me fer a couple o' days, I think I'd like to go down to New York an' git it. I don't need no lookin' after, so you needn't worry 'bout that. Nobody steals me, an' es long es I got a tongue I ken ast my way round New York es well es I can round Fundy er any other place."

"Why, of course I can spare you, Miranda, and I suppose you'd be perfectly safe. Only I thought you'd enjoy it more if you had good company. When did you think you'd like to go?"

"Well, I've been plannin' it all out comin' up the street. I've baked an' washed, an' the sweepin' ain't much to do. Ef you don't mind I think I'll go tomorrer mornin'."

"What in the world makes you want to go in such a hurry?"

"Oh, I've just took the notion," said Miranda, smiling.

"Mebbe I'll tell yeh when I get back. I shan't be gone too long."

Marcia was a little worried at this sudden turn of affairs. It wasn't like Miranda to hide things from her. Yet she had such confidence in her that she finally settled down to the thought that it was only a whim and perhaps a good night's sleep would overcome it. But the next morning she found the table fully set for breakfast and the meal prepared and keeping warm. Beside her plate a scrawled note lay.

> *Mrs. Marcia, deer.*
>
> *I'll liklie be bak tomorrer nite er next, but donte wor-rie. I got biznes to tend to an I'll tel you bout it wen i get home.*
>
>

yours til deth, respectfuly,
Miranda Griscom

> *P.S. you mite pray ef your a mind. Tak keer uf Feby ef I dont git buk.*

Before Marcia could get time to run up and see Phoebe, for she somehow felt that Miranda's sudden departure to New York had to do with her visit to Phoebe the day before, Miss Hortense arrived with her most commanding air.

"Marcia, I came on a very special errand," she began primly. "I was down on Monday, but you were away." There was reproach in the tone.

"Yes, I went with David," responded Marcia brightly, but Miss Hortense would brook no interruption.

"It's of no consequence now. I would have come yesterday, but we had company all day, the Pattersons from above Schenectady. I couldn't leave. But I hurried down this morn-ing. It's about the Deane girl, Marcia. I suppose you haven't heard the dreadful reports that are going around. It really is disgraceful in a decent town. I'm only glad she got out of your house before it became town talk. It all shows what ingratitude there is in human nature, to think she should repay your kindness by allowing herself to be talked about in this shameful way."

Marcia exclaimed in dismay, but Miss Hortense went straight on to the precise and bitter end, giving every detail in the scandal that had come to her ears, details at which even Hiram Green would have opened his eyes wide in surprise and would never have believed they grew out of his own story.

Marcia listened in rising indignation.

"I'm sorry such a dreadful story is going around, Aunt Hortense," she answered earnestly. "But really, if you knew the girl, you'd understand how impossible it is for this to be true. She's as sweet and pure and innocent as my little Rose."

"I should be sorry to have David's child compared to that miserable girl, Marcia," said Miss Hortense severely, rising as she spoke. "And I'm sure that after my warning if you don't shut that wretched creature forever out of your acquaintance I shall feel it my duty to appeal to David and tell him the whole story, though I should dislike to have to mention anything so indelicate before him. David is very particular about the character of women. He was brought up to be, and Amelia and I both agree he must be told."

"I shall tell him myself, of course, and he'll see if anything can be done to stop this ridiculous gossip," said Marcia indignantly. "David is as fond of Phoebe as I am."

"You'll find David will look on it in a very different way, my dear. You're young and a woman. You don't know the evil world. David is a man. Men know. Good-bye, my dear. I've warned you!" And Aunt Hortense went pensively down the street, having done her duty.

Marcia put her bonnet on, took little Rose, and walked straight out to Albert Deane's house, but when she reached there she was denied admission.

Alma opened the door but didn't ask the caller in. In a moment she came back from consulting her mother and said, "Ma says Aunt Phoebe's up in her room an' don't wish to see no one."

The door was shut unceremoniously by the stolid little girl, who was embarrassed before the beautiful, smiling Rose in her dainty attire. Marcia turned away, dismayed and hurt at the reception she had received, and walked slowly homeward.

"Wasn't that a funny little girl?" said Rose. "She wasn't very polite, was she, Mother?"

Then Marcia went home to wait until she could consult with David.

When Nathaniel Graham received his cousin Janet's letter, his anger rose to white heat. Every throb of his heart told him the stories about Phoebe were false. Like Miranda, he felt at once that an enemy had done this, and he felt like searching out the enemy at once and throttling him into repentance. He read the postscript through twice and then sat for a few minutes in deep thought, his face shaded by his hand. The office work went on about him, but his thoughts were far away in a sunlit autumn wood. After a little while he got up suddenly and, going into the inner office where he could be alone, sat down quickly and wrote:

> *My dear Phoebe* (he had never called her that before; it was always "Miss Deane"),
> *I have loved you for a long time, ever since that afternoon I found you among the autumn leaves in the woods. I have been trying to wait to tell you until I could be sure you loved me, but now I can wait no longer. I am lonely without you. I want you to be here with me. I love you, darling, and will love you forever and guard you tenderly, if you will give me the right. Will you forgive*

this abrupt letter and write immediately, giving me the
right to come up and tell you all the rest?
                                    Yours in faithful love,
                                    Nathaniel Graham

After he had sent it off enclosed to Miranda, he scribbled
another, to Janet.

Dear Janet,
    Wherever did you get those ridiculous stories about
Phoebe Deane? They are as false as they are foolish.
Everybody who knows her at all knows they could not be
true. I insist that you deny them whenever you have the
opportunity and for my sake that you go and call upon
her. I may as well tell you I am going to marry her if she
will have me, and I want you, Janet, to be like a sister to
her, as you have always been to me. Any breath against
her name I shall consider as against mine also, so please,
Janet, stand up for her for my sake.
                                    Your loving cousin,
                                    Nathaniel

After these two letters had been dispatched Nathaniel put
in the best day's work he had ever done.

Miranda had reached Albany in time to catch the evening
boat down the Hudson. She was more tired than she'd ever
been in all the years of her hardworking life. The bouncing of
the stagecoach, the constant change of scenery and fellow
passengers, and the breathlessness of going into a strange
region had worn on her nerves. She hadn't let a single thing
pass unnoticed, and the result was that even her iron nerves
had reached their limit at last. Besides, she was more worried
about Phoebe Deane than she had ever been about anything
in her life. The girl's ethereal look as she bid her good-bye the

night before had gone to her heart. She half feared Phoebe might fall asleep and never awaken while she was gone on her desperate errand of mercy.

"Land sake alive," she murmured to herself as she crept into her bunk in the tiny stateroom and lay down without putting off any of her garments except her bonnet and cape. "Land sake alive! I feel as ef I'd ben threshin'. No, I feel as ef I'd ben *threshed*!" she corrected. "I didn't know I hed so many bones."

Nevertheless she slept little, having too much to attend to. She awakened at every stop in the night, and she heard all the bells and calls of the crew. Half the time she thought the boat was sinking and wondered if she could swim when she struck the water. Anyhow she meant to try. She had heard it "came natural" to some people.

When morning broke over the heights above the river, she watched them grow into splendor and majesty, and long before the city was in sight she was on deck sniffing the air like a veteran warhorse. Her eyes were dilated with excitement, and she made a curious and noticeable figure as she gripped her small bag of modest belongings and sat strained up and ready for her first experience of city life. She felt a passing regret that she couldn't pause to take in more of this wonderful trip, but she promised herself to come that way again someday and hurried over the gangplank with the others when the boat finally landed.

Tucked safely away in her pocket was Phoebe's letter to Nathaniel and safe in her memory was its address. Every passenger she had talked with on the voyage—and she had entered into conversation with all except a man who reminded her of Hiram Green—had given her detailed directions on how to get to that address, and the directions had all been different. Some had told her to walk one way and take a cab, some another way. Some had suggested she take a cab at the wharf.

She did none of these things. She gripped her bag firmly and marched past all the officials, through the buildings, out onto the street. There she stood a moment bewildered by the noise and confusion, a marked figure even in that hurrying throng of busy people. Small boys and drivers immediately beset her. She looked each over carefully and then calmly walked straight ahead. So far New York didn't look very promising to her, but she meant to get into a quieter place before she made any inquiries.

At last after she had walked several blocks and was beginning to feel there was no quiet place and no end to the confusion, she met a benevolent old gentleman walking with a sweet-faced girl who looked as she imagined little Rose would look in a few years. These she hailed and demanded directions and ended by being put into a Broadway coach under the care of the driver, who was to put her out at her destination.

Nathaniel was in the inner office attending to some special business when the office boy tapped at the door.

"There's a strange client out here," he whispered. "We told her you were busy and couldn't be bothered, but she says she's come a long distance and must see you at once. Shall I tell her to come again?"

Nathaniel glanced through the door, and there, close behind the careful office boy, stood the wily Miranda. She had run no risks of not seeing Nathaniel. She had followed the boy, strictly against orders.

Her homely face was aglow with the light of her mission, but in spite of freckles and red hair and her dishevelled appearance, Nathaniel put out an eager hand to welcome her. His first thought was that she had brought an answer to his letter to Phoebe, and his heart leaped up in sudden eagerness. Then at once he knew it was too soon for that, for he had only sent his own letter in the evening mail.

"Come right in, Miranda," he said eagerly. "I'm glad to see you. Are you all alone?" Then something in her face caused a twinge of apprehension.

"Is everyone all well?"

Miranda sat down and waited until the door was shut. Then she broke forth.

"No, everythin' ain't all well. Everythin' 's all wrong. Phoebe Deane's in turrible trouble, an' she's wrote a letter sayin' good-bye to you an' ast me to mail it. I said I would, an' I brung it along. I reckon it didn't make no diff'rence whether it traveled in my pocket er in the mailbag, so it got here."

She held out the letter, and Nathaniel's hand shook as he took it. Miranda noticed what he feared.

"Oh, it's that ole snake-in-th'-grass," said Miranda. "I'd be willin' to stake my life on that. No knowin' how he done it, but it's done. There's plenty to help in a business like gossip, when it comes to that. There's ben awful lies told about her, and she's bein' crushed by it. Wal, I hed to come down to New York to get me a new balzarine dress, an' I jest thought I'd drop in an' tell yeh the news. Yeh don't know of a good store where I won't get cheated, do yeh?" she asked, making a pretense of rising.

"Sit down, Miranda," commanded Nathaniel. "You're not going away to leave me like this. You must tell me about it. Miranda, you know, don't you, that Phoebe is my dear friend. You know I must hear all about it."

"Well, ain't she told you in the letter? I reckon you'll go back on her like her own folks hev done, won't you? An' let that scoundrel git her next week like he's planned."

"What do you mean, Miranda? Tell me at once all about it. You know Phoebe Deane is very dear to me."

Miranda's eyes shone, but she meant to have things in black and white.

"How dear?" she asked, looking up in a businesslike way.

"Be you goin' to b'lieve what they all say 'bout her an' let them folks go on talkin', 'til she's all wilted down an' dead? 'Cause ef you be, you don't git a single word out o' me. No, sir!"

"Listen, Miranda. Yesterday I wrote to Phoebe asking her to marry me!"

Satisfaction began to dawn upon the face of the self-appointed envoy.

"Well, that ain't no sign you'd do it again today," said Miranda dryly. "You didn't know nothin' 'bout her bein' in trouble then."

"Yesterday morning, Miranda, I received a letter from my cousin telling me about it, and I sat down at once and asked Phoebe to marry me."

"You sure you didn't do it out o' pity?" asked Miranda, lifting sharp eyes to search his face. "I shouldn't want to hev nobody marry her out o' pity, the way Hiram Green's going to do, the old nimshi!"

"Miranda, I love her with all my heart, and I will never believe a word against her. I shall make it the object of my life to protect her and make her happy if she will give me the precious treasure of her love in return. Now are you satisfied, you cruel girl, and will you tell me the whole story? For the little I heard from my cousin has only filled me with apprehension."

Then the freckles beamed out and were lost in smiles as Miranda reached a strong hand and grasped Nathaniel's firm one with a hearty shake.

"You're the right stuff. I knowed you was. That's why I come. I didn't darst tell Mis' Spafford what was up, 'cause she wouldn't 'a' let me come, an' she'd 'a' tried to work it out in some other way. But I hed it all figgered out, an' there wasn't time for any fiddlin' business. It hed to be done 'twoncet ef 'twas to be done 't all, so I told her I wanted a pleasure trip an' a new balzarine, an' I come. Now I'm goin' to tell you all 'bout it, an' then ef there's time fer the balzarine 'fore the evenin' boat starts I'll get it; otherwise it'll hev to git the go-by this time, fer I've got to git right back to Phoebe Deane. She looked jest awful 'fore I left, an' there's no tellin' what they'll do to her while I'm gone."

Nathaniel, with loving apprehension in his eyes, listened to the story, told in Miranda's inimitable style, his face darkening with anger over the mention of Hiram's part.

"The scoundrel!" he murmured, clenching his fingers as if he could hardly refrain from going after him and giving him what he deserved.

"He's all that," said Miranda, "an' a heap more. He's made that poor stupid Albert Deane think all these things is true, an' he's come whinin' round with his 'sorry this' an' 'sorry that,' an' offered to marry Phoebe Deane to save her reputation. Es ef he was fit fer that angel to wipe her feet on! Oh, I'd like to see him strung up, I would. There's only one man I ever heard tell of that was so mean, and he lived here in New York. His name was Temple, Harry Temple. Ef you ever come acrost him jest give him a dig fer my sake. He an' Hiram Green ought to be tied up in a bag together an' sent off the earth to stay. One o' them big, hot-lookin' stars would be a fine place, I often think at night. Albert, he's awful taken back by disgrace, an' he's told Phoebe she hez to git married in jest a week, er he'll hev to turn her out o' the house. Monday mornin' 's the time set fer the marriage, an' Albert 'lows he won't wait 'nother day. He's promised his wife he'll keep to that."

Nathaniel's face grew stern as he listened and then asked questions. At last he said, "Miranda, do you think Phoebe Deane cares for me? Will she be willing to marry me?"

"Wal, I sh'd think, ef I know anythin' 't all 'bout Phoebe Deane, she'd give her two eyes to, but she'll be turrible set 'gainst marryin' you with her in disgrace. She'll think it'll bring shame on you."

"Bless her dear heart," murmured Nathaniel. "I suppose she

will." And he touched her letter tenderly as if it had been a living thing.

Miranda's eyes glistened with jubilation, but she said nothing.

"But we'll persuade her out of that," added Nathaniel with a light of joy in his eyes.

"If you're quite sure it will make her happy," he added, looking at Miranda keenly. "I wouldn't want to have her marry me just to get out of trouble. There might be other ways of helping her, though this way is best."

"Well, I guess you needn't worry 'bout love. She'll love you all right, er my name ain't M'randy!"

"Well, then, we'll just have a substitute bridegroom. I wonder if we'll have trouble with Hiram. I suppose very likely we will, but I guess we can manage that. Let me see. This is Thursday. I can arrange my business by tomorrow night so I can leave it for a few days. If you can stay over till then, I'll take you to my landlady, who is very kind and will make your stay pleasant. Then we can go back together and plan the arrangements. You'll have to help me, you know, for you're the only means of communication."

"No, I can't stay a minute longer 'n t'night," said Miranda, rising in a panic and glancing out the window at the sun as if she feared it were already too late to catch the boat. "I've got to get back to Phoebe Deane. She won't eat, an' she's just fadin' away. There might not be any bride by the time you got there. 'Sides, she can't git your letter till I get back nohow. I'll hev to go home on the boat tonight, an' you come tomorrow. You see, ef there's goin' to be a weddin' I'd like real well to git my balzarine made 'n time to wear it. That'll give me plenty time, with Mis' Spafford to he'p cut 't out. Do you s'pose there's time fer me to go to the store? It took a long time to git up here from the river."

Nathaniel stood up.

"You have plenty of time, and if you'll wait ten minutes I'll go with you. We can get some dinner and go to the store, and we can arrange things on the way."

Miranda settled down in the great office chair and watched Nathaniel's fingers as they wrote on the legal paper. When it was finished and folded he took another piece of paper and wrote:

> *My darling,*
>
> *I've just received your letter, and I'm coming to you as quickly as I can arrange my business to get away. Miranda will bring you this and will tell you all I've said. I will be there in time for the wedding morning, and if you will have me instead of Hiram Green, I shall face the whole world by your side and tell them they are liars. Then I'll bring you back with me to stay with me always. My heart is longing to see you and comfort you, but I mustn't write any more for I have a great deal to do before I go. Only this I must say, if you don't feel you love me and don't want to marry me, I will help you some other way to get free from this trouble and to have it all explained before the world. I am resolved upon one thing, and that is that you shall be guarded and loved by me, whether you will marry me or not. You are too precious to suffer.*
>
> *Yours with more love than you can fathom,*
> *Nathaniel*

He sealed and addressed it and handed it to Miranda, who took it with a gleam of satisfaction in her honest eyes. She was almost willing to run home without her balzarine now that she had that letter. She didn't know what he had written, of course, but she knew it was the right thing and would bring the light of hope again to Phoebe's eyes.

Then they went out into the bustling, strange streets of the city.

Miranda was too excited to eat much, though Nathaniel took her to his own boarding place and tried to make her feel at home. She kept asking if it wasn't almost time for the boat to leave, until he had to explain to her just how much time there was and how quickly they could get to the wharf.

They went to a store, and Miranda didn't take long to pick out her dress. It seemed as if the very one she had always longed for lay draped on the counter, and with quick decision she bought it. It had great stripes of soft colors in a palm-leaf pattern, blended into harmony in an oriental manner in the exquisite fabric. It seemed to her almost too fine to go with red hair, but she bought it with joyous abandon. The touch of rich blue and orange and crimson with the darker greens and browns stood out against the delicate whiteness of the background and delighted her. She bought a dainty ruffled muslin shoulder cape to wear with it, and a great shovel bonnet with a white veil tossed hilariously back from its cumbersome shirred depths.

Then Nathaniel added a parasol with a pearl handle that would unhinge and fold up, and Miranda climbed into the coach and rode off to the evening boat feeling she'd had the greatest day of her life. She looked about her on the interesting sights of the city with a kind of pity they had to stay there and not go with her to the wedding.

Chapter 28

*M*iranda reached home on the afternoon coach and bounced into the house with a face full of importance.

"Wal, I'm glad to git back. Did you find the blueberry pies? I put 'em out the pantry winder to cool an' fergot 'em. I thought of 'em when I was on the boat, but 'twas mos' too late to come back then, so I kep' on.

"Here's my balzarine. Do yeh like it?" And she tossed the bundle into Marcia's lap. "I'm going right at it when I git the work done in the mornin' fer I want to hev it t' wear at Phoebe Deane's weddin'. Did yeh know she was goin' to marry Nathaniel Graham? Say, where's that Rose? I'm most starved for a sight o' her little sweet face. Yer lookin' real good yerself. All's well?"

Marcia listened smilingly to Miranda's torrent of words and gradually drew the whole story from the girl, laughing heartily over the various episodes of Miranda's journey and gravely tender over what Nathaniel had said. Then Miranda heard about Marcia's call on Phoebe and how she'd written Phoebe a letter asking what she could do to help her, inviting her to come at once to them, but had received no answer.

"An' yeh won't, neither," said Miranda decidedly. "She'll never git no letter, I'm sure o' that. Ef that ol' skunk of a Hiram Green don't git it fust, Mis' Deane'll ferret it out an' keep it from her. She's the meanest thing in the shape of a woman I've seen yit, an' I've hed some experience."

Then Miranda rapidly sketched out her plan, and Marcia added some suggestions. Together they prepared the supper, with the single object of getting Miranda off to Phoebe as soon as darkness should come.

It was quite dark, and Phoebe was lying in a still white heap on her bed when Miranda stole softly in. By her side lay a long white package she had taken from her little trunk in the closet, and on it was pinned a note: *"Dear Miranda, if I die, please take this, from Phoebe."*

She hadn't lighted her candle nor eaten a mouthful all day. The terrible faintness and weakness were becoming constant now. She could only lie on her bed and wait. She couldn't even think anymore. The enemies all about her with their terrible darts had pierced her soul, and her life seemed ebbing away. She felt it going and had no desire to stop it. It was good to be at rest.

Miranda stole in softly and began to move quietly about the room, finding the candle and softly striking the flint and tinder. Phoebe became gradually conscious of her presence, as out of the midst of a misty dream. Then Miranda came and looked down tenderly into her face.

"Raise yer head up, you poor little thing, an' drink this," whispered Miranda, putting a spoonful of strong broth to her lips, that she had taken the precaution to bring with her. "I've got two o' the nicest letters fer yeh that ever was writ, an' another one from my Mrs. Marcia, an' ef yeh don't git some color into them cheeks an' some brightness into them eyes now, my name ain't Mirandy."

Miranda handed out the letters one at a time in their order.

She brought the candle, and Phoebe with her trembling hands opened the first, recognizing the handwriting, and then sat up and read with bated breath.

"Oh, Miranda," she said, looking up with a faint color in her cheeks, "he's asked me to marry him. Wouldn't it be beautiful! But he didn't know when he wrote it—" And the brown head went down as if it were stricken like a lily before a fierce blast.

"Shucks!" said Miranda, dabbing away the mistiness from her eyes. "Yes, he did know, too. His cousin wrote him. Here, you read the other one."

Again Phoebe sat up and read, while Miranda held her candle and tried not to seem to look over her shoulder at the words she could feel in her soul if she couldn't see with her eyes.

"Oh, it can't be true!" said Phoebe, with face aglow with something that almost seemed to be the light of another world. "And I mustn't let him, of course. It wouldn't be right for him to have a wife like this—"

"Shucks!" said Miranda again. "Yes, 'tis true, too, and right an' all the rest, an' you've got to set up and get spry, fer there's a sight to do, an' I can't stay much longer. That weddin' 's comin' off on Monday mornin—time set fer it. 'Taint good luck to put off weddin's, an' this one 's goin' to go through all right.

"Mr. Nathaniel, he's goin' to bring his cousin an' the jedge, an' my Mr. David an' Mrs. Marcia's comin' wether they're ast er not, 'cause they knew 'twa'n't no use fer um to wait fer an invite from that sister-in-law of yourn, so they're comin' anyway. Mr. Nathaniel said as how you weren't to worry. He'll git here Saturday night sure, en' ef there was any other 'rangement you'd like to make he was ready, an' you could send your word by me. But he 'greed with me 'twould make less talk ef the weddin' come off at your home where 'twas to be in the fust place, an' then you could go right away from here an' never come back no more. Say, hev ye got anythin' thet's fit to wear? 'Cause ef yeh ain't I'll let yeh have my new balzarine to wear. I'll hev it all done by Sat'day night. Mrs. Marcia's goin' to help me."

Between tears and smiles Phoebe came to herself. Miranda fed her with more of the strong broth she had brought along. Then together in the dim candlelight the two girls opened the great white box that lay on the floor beside the bed.

"It's my wedding dress, Miranda. Mother made it for me long ago, before she died, and put it in my trunk to keep for me. It was marked, *'For my little girl when she is going to be married.'*

"I opened it and found the letter on top, for I thought I was going to die, and I wanted to read Mother's last letter, but I didn't take the dress out because I thought I would never wear it, and it made me feel so bad that I left it in its wrappings. I thought if I died I'd like you to have it, because it's the most precious thing I have and you've done more for me than anybody else ever did, but Mother."

Miranda gulped a sudden unexpected sob at this tribute, and it was some time before she could recover her equanimity, though she said "Shucks!" several times.

They took the white bridal garment out of its wrappings, and Phoebe tried it on, there in the dimness of the room. It was thin white book muslin, all daintily embroidered about the neck and sleeves by the dead mother's hand. It fell in soft sheer folds about the white-faced girl and made her look as if she were just going to take her flight to another world.

In another paper was the veil of fine thread lace, simple and beautiful, and a pair of white gloves that had been the mother's, both yellow with age and breathing a perfume of lavender. A pair of dainty little white slippers lay in the bottom of the box, wrapped in tissue paper also. Miranda's eyes shone.

"Now you look like the right kind of bride," she said, standing back and surveying her charge. "That's better 'n all the balzarines in New York."

"You shall wear the balzarine and stand up with me, Miranda," whispered Phoebe, smiling.

"No, sir! We ain't goin't hev this here weddin' spoiled by no red hair an' freckles, even if 't has got a balzarine. Janet Bristol's got to stan' up. She'll make a picter fer folks to talk 'bout. Mr. Nathaniel said he'd manage his cousin all right an' 'twould quiet the talk down ef his folks took sides along of you. No, sir, I ain't goin' to do no standin' in this show. I'm goin' to set an' take it all in. Come now, you get into bed, an' I'll blow out the light an' go home. I reckon I'll be back tomorrer night to take any messages you want took. Ther'll be plenty o' chance fer you to rest 'fore Monday. Don't say nothin' to yer folks. Let 'em go on with their plans, an' then kinder s'prise 'em."

The next morning Phoebe arose and feeling much refreshed dressed herself carefully and went downstairs. She had a quiet, grave look upon her face, but in her eyes there was a strange light she couldn't keep back. Emmeline looked up in surprise when Phoebe came and took hold with the work. She began to say something slighting, but the look in Phoebe's face somehow stopped her. It was a look of joyful exaltation. And Emmeline, firmly believing the girl was justly talked about, couldn't understand and thought it hypocrisy.

Albert came in in a few minutes and looked relieved.

"Well, Phoebe, I'm glad you've made up your mind to act sensibly and come downstairs. It wasn't right to fight against what had to be and every one of us knew was for the best," he said.

Phoebe didn't answer. In spite of the help that was coming to her, it hurt her that Albert believed the slander against her, and the tears came into her eyes as he spoke.

Emmeline saw them and spoke up in a sermonizing tone. "It's right she should feel her shame and repent, Albert. Don't go an' soft-soap it over es ef she hadn't done nothin' to feel sorry fer."

Then Phoebe spoke.

"I have done nothing to feel sorry for, Emmeline. I have not sinned. I'm only sorry you have been willing to believe all this against me."

Then she went quietly on with her work and said no more,

though Emmeline's speech was unsealed, and she gave Phoebe much good advice during the course of the day.

The next morning near church time Emmeline told Phoebe that Hiram was coming over to see her that morning, and she might open the front parlor to receive him.

"I don't wish to see Hiram, Emmeline," she answered calmly. "I have nothing whatever to say to him."

"Well, upon my word, Phoebe Deane," said Emmeline, getting red in the face with indignation toward the girl. "Goin' to get married tomorrow mornin' an' not wantin' to see Hiram Green! I should think you'd want to talk over 'rangements."

"Yes, I'm going to be married tomorrow morning," said Phoebe with a triumphant ring to her voice, "but I do not want to see Hiram Green. I have no arrangements to talk over with him. My arrangements are all made."

Phoebe went away to her room and remained there for the rest of the day.

Nathaniel had arrived. She knew that by special messenger coming and going over the woodshed roof. He had sent sweet messages of cheer and promised to come for her in the morning. Everything was arranged. She could possess her soul in peace and quietness and wait. Her enemies would soon be put to flight. Nathaniel had promised her that, and although she could not in the least see how, she trusted him perfectly.

She had sent her love to him and the locket with her mother's picture. It was all she had to give him, and he understood. It was the one she had worn the first time he ever saw her.

The balzarine dress was finished. The last hook was set in place before supper Saturday night, and Marcia had pronounced it very becoming. It was finished in spite of the fact that Miranda had made several secret excursions into the region of Hiram Green's house and farm. She had made discoveries she told no one, but over which she chuckled when quite alone in the kitchen working.

On her first trip she had seen him go out to his milking and had passed close to the house, where his window was open. She had glanced in, and there on the sill her sharp eyes discovered the bit of red seal with the lion's head on it. She'd carried too many letters with that seal not to know it at once, and she gleefully seized it and carried it to Nathaniel. She had evidence at last that would give her power over the enemy.

She also discovered that Hiram Green attended to his milking himself and had a habit—if one might judge from two mornings as samples—of going to the springhouse with the milk and placing the pans on the great stone shelf. This she had seen by judicious hiding behind shrubbery and trees and the springhouse itself and spying on him. Birds and squirrels tell no tales, and the dewy grass soon dried off and left no trace of her footsteps. During one of these excursions she had examined the fastening of the springhouse carefully and knew the possibilities of button, hasp, staple, and peg.

The Spaffords and Miranda went to church as usual, and so did the Bristols. The advent of Nathaniel and his friend Mr. Van Rensselaer in the Bristol pew diverted attention from the empty seat behind them, for this morning the Deanes were conspicuous by their absence.

The day passed quietly. Miranda made her usual visit in the early evening. Phoebe had asked her to stay with her, but Miranda said she had some things to do and departed sooner than usual. The night settled into stillness, and Phoebe slept in joyous assurance that it was her last night in the room where she had seen so much sorrow.

In the morning she went down to breakfast as usual. She didn't eat much but drank some milk and then washed the breakfast dishes as calmly as if she expected to keep on washing them all the rest of her life in this same kitchen.

"Hiram'll be over 'bout half past nine, I reckon," said Albert.

He had been instructed by Emmeline to say this. "The minister won't come till ten. If you need to talk to Hiram you'll have plenty of time between. You better be all ready."

"I shall not need to talk to Hiram," said Phoebe as she hung up the dish towels.

Something in her voice as she said it made Albert look at her wonderingly.

"She's the oddest girl I ever seen!" grumbled Emmeline. "One would think by her looks that she expected a chariot of fire to come down an' take her straight up to heaven like 'Lijah. It's kind of dreadful the way she ac's! 'F I was Hiram I'd be 'fraid to marry her."

Miranda arrived over the shed roof soon after Phoebe went upstairs. She wore her old calico, and if those who knew had observed closely, they would have said it was a calico Miranda never used anymore, for it was very old. Her hair was combed with precision, and on her head was an elaborate New York bonnet with a white barege veil, but her balzarine was in a bundle under her arm. It wasn't calculated for roof travel. It worked well for their plans that the shed roof was back and hidden from the kitchen door; otherwise Miranda might have been discovered.

"There! Emmeline can hev that fer a floor cloth," said Miranda as she flung her old calico in the corner. "I don't mean to return fer it."

She fastened her balzarine with satisfaction, adjusted her muslin shoulder cape, her bonnet, and mantilla, the latter a gift from Mrs. Spafford, laid her new sunshade on a chair, and pronounced herself ready.

"Has Hiram Green come yet?" asked Phoebe anxiously. She was dreading a scene with Hiram.

"Wal, no, not 'zactly," said Miranda. "An what's more, I don't think he will. Fact is, I've got him fixed fer a spell, but I ain't goin' to say nothin' more 'bout it at present, 'cept that he's detained by bus'ness elsewhar. It's best you shouldn't know nothin' 'bout it ef there's questions ast, but you don't need to worry. 'Less sompin' quite unusual happens he ain't likely to turn up till after the ceremony. Now what's to do to you yet? Them hooks all fastened? My, but you do look han'some!"

"Oh, Miranda, you haven't done anything dreadful, have you?"

"No, I ain't," laughed Miranda. "You'd jest split your sides laughin' ef you could see him 'bout now. But there! Don't say 'nother word. I hear voices. The Bristols hev come an' the minister, too. I reckon your sister-in-law'll hev her hands full slammin' the door in all them faces."

Phoebe, aghast, pulled the curtain aside and peered out.

There in the yard were several carriages and more driving in the gate. She could hear a great many voices all at once. She saw Mrs. Duzenberry and Susanna getting out of their chaise, and Lemuel Skinner and his wife, Hannah. And she thought she heard the village dressmaker's voice high above all, sharp and rasping, the way it always was when she said, "That seam needs pressin'. It does hike up a mite, but it'll be all right when it's pressed."

Phoebe retreated in dismay from the window.

"Oh, Miranda! How did all those people get down there! Emmeline will be so angry. She's still in her room dressing. It doesn't seem as if I dared go down."

"Fer the land sake, how should I know? I s'pose Providence sent 'em, fer they can't say a single word after the ceremony's over. Their mouths'll be all nicely stopped. Don't you worry."

Miranda answered innocently, but for one instant as she looked at Phoebe's frightened face her guilty heart misgave her. Perhaps she had gone a step too far. For it was Miranda who had slipped here and there after church on Sunday and whispered a brief invitation to those who had gossiped the hardest, wording it in such a way that they all thought it was a personal invitation from Phoebe. In every case she added, "Don't say nothin' till after it's over."

Each thinking himself especially favored had arrived in conscious pride, and as they passed Hiram Green's new house they had remarked to themselves what a fine man he was for sticking to Phoebe in spite of all the talk.

But Miranda never told her part in this, and Emmeline never got over wondering who invited all those people.

Miranda's momentary confusion was covered by a gentle tap on the door, and Phoebe in a flutter rushed to hide her friend.

"I'm afraid it's Emmeline," she whispered. "She may not let you go down."

"Like to see her keep me up," said Miranda boldly. "My folks hes come. I ain't 'fraid now." She boldly swept the trembling bride out of the way and threw the door open.

Janet Bristol in a silken gown of palest pink entered and walked straight up to Phoebe.

"You dear little thing!" she exclaimed. "How sweet you look. That dress is beautiful, and the veil makes you perfect. Nathaniel asked me to bring you this and make you wear it. It was his mother's."

She fastened a rope of pearls around Phoebe's neck and kissed her as a sister might have done.

Miranda stood back and gazed with satisfaction on the scene. All was set as it should be. She saw nothing further to be desired. Her compunctions were gone.

"Nathaniel is waiting for you at the foot of the stairs," whispered Janet. "He has his mother's ring for you. He wanted me to tell you. Come, they're ready. You must go ahead."

Down the stairs went the trembling bride, followed by her bridesmaid. Miranda grasped her precious parasol and tiptoed down behind.

Nathaniel stood at the foot of the stairs, waiting for her.

Emmeline, with a red and angry face, was waiting on her most unexpected guests and hadn't time to notice what was going on about her. The original wedding guests, consisting of a row of little Greens and the old housekeeper, were submerged in the Sunday gowns of the new arrivals.

"Where's Hiram?" whispered Albert in Emmeline's ear, just as she was giving Hiram's aunt Keziah Dart a seat at the best end of the room.

"Goodness! Ain't he come yet? I s'posed he was upstairs talkin' to Phoebe. I heard voices."

She wheeled around, and there stood the wedding party.

Nathaniel, tall and handsome, with his shy, pale bride on his arm; Janet, sparkling in her pink gown and enjoying the discomfiture of guests and hostess alike and smiling over at Martin Van Rensselaer, who stood supporting the bridegroom on the other side—it all bewildered Emmeline.

The little assemblage reached out into the front dooryard and peeped curiously in at the doors and windows as if loathe to lose the choice scene that was passing. The old minister was talking now, and a hush fell over the company.

Anger and amazement held Emmeline still as the ceremony progressed.

"Dearly beloved, we are gathered together—" said the minister, and Emmeline looked around for Hiram. Surely the ceremony wasn't beginning without him! And who was that girl in white under the veil! Not Phoebe! It couldn't be Phoebe Deane, who only a few short minutes before had been hanging up her dish towels. Where did she get the veil and dress? What had happened? How did all these people get here? Had Phoebe invited them? And why didn't somebody stop it?

"Let him speak now or forever after hold his peace," came the words, and Emmeline gave a great gasp and thought of the corner lot opposite the Seceder church.

Then Emmeline became conscious of Miranda in her

balzarine and New York bonnet, the very impersonation of mischief, standing in the doorway just behind the bride and watching the scene with a face of triumph.

An impulse came to her to charge across the room at the offending girl and put her out. Here surely was one who had no right in her house and knew it, too. Then all at once she caught the eye of Judge Bristol fixed sternly on her face, and she became aware of her own countenance and restrained her feelings. For after all it was no mean thing to be allied to the house of Bristol and know the cloud of dishonor that had threatened them was lifted forever. She looked at Judge Bristol's fine face and heavy white hair and began to swell with conscious pride.

The last "I will" was spoken, the benediction was pronounced, and the hush that followed was broken by Nathaniel's voice.

"I want to say a few words," he said, "about a terrible mistake that has been made by the people of this village regarding my wife's character. I have made a thorough investigation of the matter during the last two days, and I find that the whole thing originated in an infamous lie told with intention to harm one who is entirely innocent. I simply wish to say that whoever has spoken against my wife will have to answer to me for his words in a court of justice. And if any of you who are my friends wish to question any of her past actions, be kind enough to come directly to me and they will be fully explained, for there is not a thing in her past that will not bear the searching light of purity and truth."

As soon as he stopped speaking, David and Marcia stepped up with congratulations.

There was a little stir among the guests. The guilty ones melted away faster than they had gathered, each one anxious to get out without being noticed.

The Bristol coach, drawn by two white horses, with

coachman and footman in livery, drew up before the door. Nathaniel handed Phoebe in, and they were driven away in triumph, with the guests they passed shrinking out of sight into their vehicles as far as possible.

Albert and Emmeline looked into each other's dazed faces, then turned to the old housekeeper and the row of little Greens, their faces abnormally shining from unusual contact with soap and water, and asked in concert, "But where is Hiram?"

Miranda, as she rode guilelessly in the carryall with Mrs. Spafford, answered the same question from that lady, with "Whar d' you s'pose? I shet him in the springhouse airly this mornin'!"

Then David Spafford laid down the reins of the old gray horse on his knee and laughed, loud and long. He couldn't stop laughing, and all day long it kept breaking out, as he remembered Miranda's innocent look and thought of Hiram Green, wrathful and helpless, shut in his own springhouse while his wedding went on without him.

An elaborate and merry wedding breakfast was given at Judge Bristol's, presided over by Janet, who seemed as happy as though she'd planned the match herself and whose smiling wishes were carried out immediately by Martin Van Rensselaer.

Nathaniel had one more duty to perform before he took his bride away to a happier home. He must find and face Hiram Green.

So, leaving Phoebe in the care of Mrs. Spafford and his cousin Janet, and accompanied by his uncle, Martin Van Rensselaer, and Lemuel Skinner in the capacity of village constable, he got into the family carryall and drove out to Hiram's farm.

Now Nathaniel hadn't been idle during the Sabbath which intervened between his coming back to the village and his marriage. Aside from the time he spent at the morning church service, he had been doing a Sabbath day's work which he felt would stand well to his account.

He had carefully questioned several of the best-known gossips in the village regarding the story about Phoebe. He had asked keen questions that gave him a plain clue to the whole diabolical plot.

His first act had been to mount his horse and ride out to Ann Jane Bloodgood's, where he had a full account of Phoebe's visit together with a number of missionary items which would have met with more of his attention at another time. With several valuable facts he went pretty straight to most of the houses Hiram visited on the first afternoon when he scattered the seed of scandal. Facing the embarrassed scandalmongers, Nathaniel made them tell just who the first was to speak to them of this. In every case after a careful sifting down, each owned that Hiram himself had told them the first word. If Nathaniel hadn't been a lawyer and keen at his calling, he might not have followed the story to its source as well or as quickly as he did. Possibly his former encounter with Hiram Green and his knowledge of many of his deeds helped unravel the mystery.

The old housekeeper and the little Greens hadn't been at home long when the carryall drew up in front of the door and the four men got out.

"I ben everywhar but to the springhouse," said the housekeeper, shaking her head dolefully, "an' I can't find trace of him nowhar. 'Taint likely he'd be in the springhouse, fer the door is shet an' fastened. I ken see the button from the buttery winder. It's the way I allus tell when he's comin' in to breakfast. It's my 'pinion he's cleared out 'cause he don't want to marry that gal, that's what I think."

"When did you last see Mr. Green?" questioned the judge sternly.

"Why, I seen him take the milk pails an' go down toward

the barn to milk, an' I ain't seen him sence. I thought 'twar odd he didn't come eat his breakfast, but he's kinder oncertain thet way, so I hurried up an' got off to he'p Mis' Deane."

"Have the cows been milked?" The judge ignored the old woman's elaborate explanations.

"The hired man, he says so. I ain't ben down to look for myself."

"Where are the milk pails?"

"Well, now, I ain't thought to look."

"What does he usually do with the milk? He surely hasn't taken that with him. Did he bring it in? That ought to give us a clue."

"He most gen'rally takes it straight to the springhouse—" began the old woman.

"Let's go to the springhouse," said Nathaniel.

"I don't see what business 'tis o' yourn," complained the old woman, but they were already on the way. So after a moment's hesitation she threw her apron around her shoulders and went after them.

The row of little Greens followed, a curious and perplexed little procession, ready for any scene of interest that might be about to open before them, even though it involved their unloving father.

It was Lemuel Skinner, with his cherry lips pursed importantly, who stepped forward by virtue of his office, turned the wooden button, drew out the peg, pulled off the hasp, and threw the heavy door open.

Out stumbled Hiram Green, half blinded by the light and rubbing his eyes.

"Mr. Green, we have called to see you on a matter of importance," began Lemuel apologetically, quite as if it were the custom to meet householders on the threshold of their springhouse.

"Sorry I can't wait to hear it," swaggered Hiram, blinking

and trying to make out who these men were. "I got 'n engagement. Fact is, I'm goin' to be married, an' I'm late a'ready. I'll hev to be excused, Lem!"

"It's quite unnecessary, Mr. Green," said Lemuel, putting out a detaining hand excitedly. "Quite unnecessary, I assure you. The wedding is all over. You're not expected anymore."

Hiram stood back and surveyed Lemuel with contempt.

"How could that be when I wa'n't thar?" he sneered. "I guess you didn't know I was goin' to marry Phoebe Deane. I'm right sure no one else'd marry her."

Nathaniel stepped forward, his face white with indignation.

"You are speaking of my wife, Mr. Green," he said, and his voice was enough to arrest the attention of even the self-complacency of a Hiram Green. "Let me never hear you speak of her in that way again. She did not at any moment in her life intend to marry you. You know that well, though you've tried to weave a web of falsehood about her that would put her in your power. The whole thing is known to me from beginning to end, and I do not intend to let it pass lightly. My wife's good name is everything to me—though it seems you were willing to marry one whom you had yourself defamed.

"I've come here this morning, Mr. Green, to give you your choice between going to jail or going with me at once and taking back all the falsehoods you have told about my wife."

Hiram, in sudden comprehension and fear, glanced around the group. He took in Judge Bristol's presence, remembered Nathaniel's threat of the year before about bringing him up before his uncle, remembered that Lemuel Skinner was constable, and was filled with consternation.

With the instinct of a coward and a bully he made a sudden lunge forward toward Nathaniel, his fists clenched and his whole face expressing the fury of a wild animal brought to bay.

"You lie!" he hissed.

But the next instant he lay sprawling at Nathaniel's feet, with Lemuel bustling over him like an excited old hen.

It was Martin Van Rensselaer who had tripped him up just in time.

"Now, gentlemen, gentlemen, don't let's get excited," cackled Lemuel, laying an ineffective hand on the prostrate Hiram.

"Step aside, Mr. Skinner," said Nathaniel, towering over Hiram. "Let me settle this matter first. Now, sir, you may take your choice. Will you go to jail and await your trial for slander, or will you come with us to the people you scattered this outrageous scandal to and take it all back?"

"You've made a big mistake," blustered Hiram. "I never told no stories 'bout Phoebe Deane. It's somebody else 's done it ef 'tain't true—I was goin' to marry her to save her reputation."

"How did you think that would save her reputation?" questioned Judge Bristol, and somehow his voice made cold chills creep down Hiram's spine.

"Why, I—I was goin' to deny everythin' after we was married."

"Your stories don't hang together very well," remarked the judge dryly.

"You will be obliged to deny them now," said Nathaniel wrathfully. "Take your choice at once. I'm not sure after all but the best way would be to house you in jail without further delay. It's almost a crime to let such a low-lived scoundrel as you walk at large. No one's reputation will be safe in the hands of a villain like you. Take your choice at once. I will give you two minutes to decide."

Nathaniel took out his watch.

Silence hung over the meadow behind the springhouse, but a little bird from the tree up the road called, "Phoe-bee! Phoe-bee!" insistently, and a strange, tender light came into Nathaniel's eyes.

"The time is up," said Nathaniel.

"What do you want me to do?" asked the captive sullenly.

"I want you to go with me to every house you visited the day you started this mischief and take it all back. Tell them it was untrue and that you got it up out of whole cloth for your own evil purposes."

"But I can't tell a lie," said Hiram piously.

"Can't you? Well, it won't be necessary. Come, which will you choose? Do you prefer to go to jail?"

"Gentlemen, I'm in your hands," whined the coward. "Remember I have little children."

"You should have remembered that yourself and not brought shame upon them and other innocent beings." It was the judge who spoke these words, like a sentence in court.

"Where hev I got to go?"

Nathaniel named the places.

Hiram looked dark and swallowed his mortification.

"Well, I s'pose I've got to go. I'm sure I don't want to lose my good name by goin' to jail."

They set him upon his feet, and the little posse moved slowly up the slope to the house and then to the carryall.

After they were seated in the carryall, with Hiram in the backseat with Lemuel and Martin on either side of him, Nathaniel turned to Hiram.

"Now, Mr. Green, we are going first to your aunt's house and then around to the other places in order. You are to make the following statement and nothing else. You are to say: 'I have come to take back the lies I told about Miss Phoebe Deane and to tell you that they are not true, not one of them. I originated them for my own purposes.' "

Hiram's face darkened. He looked as if he would like to kill Nathaniel. He reached out a long arm again as if to strike him, but Lemuel clutched him convulsively, while Martin threw his weight on the other side, and he subsided.

"You can have from now until we reach the jail to think about it, Mr. Green. If you prefer to go to jail instead, you will not be hindered. Mr. Skinner is here to arrest you on my charge if you will not comply with these conditions."

Sullen and silent sat Hiram. He didn't raise his eyes to see the curious passersby as he rode through town.

They looked at Nathaniel and the judge, driving with solemn mien as if on some portentous errand. They noted the stranger and the constable on either side of the lowering Hiram. And they drew their own conclusions, for the news of the wedding had spread like wildfire through the village. Then they stood and watched the carryall out of sight and even followed it to see if it stopped at the jail.

As they drew near the jail Nathaniel turned around once more to Hiram.

"Shall we stop and let you out here, or are you willing to comply with the conditions?"

Hiram raised his eyelashes and gave a sideways glance at the locality, then lowered them quickly as he encountered the impudent gaze of a small boy and muttered, "Drive on."

Hiram went through the distasteful ordeal sullenly. He repeated the words Nathaniel insisted upon, after one or two vain attempts to modify them in his own favor, which only made it worse for him in the eyes of his listeners.

" 'Pon my word," said Aunt Keziah Dart in a mortified tone. " 'F I'd uv told fibs like that I'd 'a' stuck to 'em an' never give in, no matter what. I'm 'shamed to own I'm kin to sech a sneak, Hiram Green. Wan't there gals 'nough 'round the country 'thout all that to do?"

At the Duzenberrys' Susanna rendered Hiram the sympathy of silently weeping in the background, while the Widow Duzenberry stood coldly in the foreground acting as if the whole performance were a personal affront. She closed the interview by calling after Hiram from her front door.

"I'm sorry to see yeh in trouble, Mr. Green. Remember you'll always find a friend here."

Hiram brightened up some. Nevertheless, very little of his old conceit remained when he had gone over the whole ground and was finally set free to go his way to his own home.

Then Nathaniel and Phoebe hastened away in the family coach toward Albany to begin their long life journey together.

Late that afternoon Hank Williams coming up from the village brought with him a letter for Hiram Green which he stopped to leave, hoping to find out from Hiram what had happened during the afternoon. The old housekeeper took the letter saying, "Hiram wa'n't well," and Hank went onward crestfallen.

A few minutes later Hiram tore open his letter. It read:

> *Mistur Grene,*
> *You hev ben fond out. We want no mor lyres an crimnles in our toun. We hev fond the seels off 'n Phebe Denes leter in yor poseshun an we hev uther good evedens thet you open unitd stats male we will giv yo 1 wek to sel ot an lev toun. Ef yo ever sho yer hed agin hear or in Noo York yo wil be tard an fethured an punisht cordin to law.*
>
> *Yors fer reveng,*
> *A Feller Tounsman*

That night while his household slept Hiram Green went forth from his home to parts unknown, leaving his little children to the tender mercies of Aunt Keziah Dart or whoever might be touched with a feeling of pity for them.

And Miranda, who, without the counsel or knowledge of anyone, had written the remarkable epistle which sent him out, lay down serenely and slept the sleep of the just.

And that same night the moon shone brightly over the

Hudson River, like a path of silver for the two who sat long on deck, talking of how they loved Miranda, with laughter that was nigh to tears.

Also available from
BARBOUR PUBLISHING, INC.

Lo, Michael

A newsboy saves the life of an heiress—
opening doors of opportunity for himself.
ISBN 1-59310-675-0

Miranda

Miranda longs for the day
she'll see the man she loves.
ISBN 1-59310-678-5

Lone Point

Loss of fortune forces Maria to
reconsider her perspective on life.
ISBN 1-59310-676-9

Marcia Schuyler

Marcia is married to David,
but her sister claims his love.
ISBN 1-59310-677-7

The Witness

Paul Courtland is tormented by
the consequences of his choices.
ISBN 1-59310-680-7

Available wherever books are sold.